UNEXPECTED VENTURES

BELLES OF BROAD STREET BOOK 3

AK LANDOW

DEDICATION

For Thorunn K. and Lakshmi P. Thank you for your friendship, guidance, selflessness, being perverts, availability for bitch duty, and for being all around good girls.

"Happiness and confidence are the prettiest things you can wear." Taylor Swift

Knight & Lawrence
FAMILY TREE

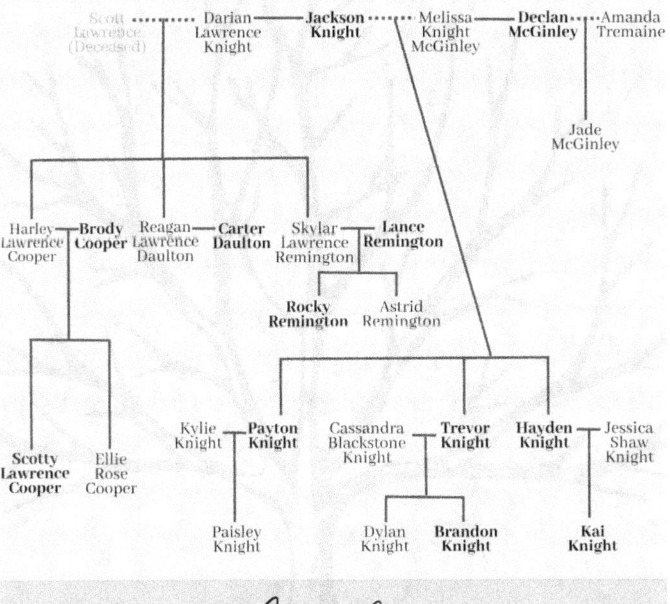

PROLOGUE

FOUR YEARS AGO

REAGAN'S TWENTY-EIGHTH BIRTHDAY PARTY

BETH

"Joseph isn't coming tonight?"

"Oh, um, no. He's working." I hate lying to my sister, but I don't feel like talking about my breakup with Joseph just yet. It's not that I cared very much about Joseph, it's that Cassandra Blackstone Knight is a force of nature, and when she finds out the reasoning behind our breakup, she'll never let me live it down.

What exactly am I supposed to tell her? *Cassandra, Joseph has a foot fetish. I was cool with it at first, enjoying the extra attention showered on my feet. The care, the massages, the nail painting. It was nice to feel pampered like that. I never minded wearing sexy heels when we had sex. But finding out that he hires hookers so he can jerk off on their feet was my tipping point.*

My sister will be relentless when she learns the truth. I'm looking at years of jokes at my expense. I mean, we were only together for a few months. It's not like we were serious.

"I guess that's the life of a surgeon."

I nod as if she can see me through the phone.

"Beth, are you there?"

"Sorry. I'm here. Yes, surgery. That's it. He has a surgery tonight."

"Do you want Trevor and me to pick you up on our way to the party?"

"You don't have to. I can Uber. It's not far from me."

"You're on our way. It's no big deal. This way you don't have to walk in by yourself."

I'm used to walking in places by myself at this point, but I suppose it would be nice to go with them. "Okay. Thanks. That would be great. My sitter will be here at seven. She's new, so Luke will likely cry for a good fifteen minutes. Don't come in. That will only make it worse."

Luke is obsessed with Cassandra's husband, Trevor. It will only make him more upset if he knows I'm with Trevor for the evening.

"Sounds like a plan. We'll see you at a little after seven."

"Okay. Bye."

A few minutes before seven, I'm in my bathroom putting the final touches on my makeup. Luke watches on with rapt fascination. For some reason, my three-year-old son loves watching me put on makeup.

"Mama, you're so pretty."

I turn and smile at my mini-me, with his dark hair and light blue eyes. "Thank you, baby. Are you excited to meet

Rose? I heard from Colton and Hazel's mommy that she's a lot of fun. She'll be here in a few minutes."

His little lip comes out. Luke does great when I drop him at daycare in the mornings, but he struggles with babysitters. It's always a bit of a nightmare, especially when they're new. When it first started, I would immediately cancel my plans, afraid to leave him while he was upset, but now I know the tears eventually go away. It used to completely break my heart, but I'm trying to be a bit tougher. I just feel guilty leaving him when he's sad.

Rose was recommended by my close friend, Giselle. She babysits for Giselle's kids. I've never met Rose. I only know that she's a fourteen-year-old from the local junior high who Giselle claims is responsible and great with her kids.

At precisely seven, the doorbell rings. Her being on time is a good sign. I take a deep breath. Here we go. I hate seeing my baby cry, but I know it's coming. I warned Rose about it when we spoke.

I see worry hit his handsome little face and tears start to fill his eyes. I quickly open the door and smile at the adorable, young redhead before me. I hold out my hand. "You must be Rose."

She smiles back and shakes my hand in return. "Yes, Ms. O'Connell. It's nice to meet you."

I open the door wider to introduce her to Luke. As soon as his eyes find Rose, they widen. "Are you Ariel?"

She bends so they're eye to eye. "No, my name is Rose."

"You look like Princess Ariel."

"From *The Little Mermaid*?"

He nods.

"I get that a lot. I think it's the hair."

"You're so pretty. You look like a princess."

Rose smiles again. "Aren't you a little charmer?" She

tickles his belly button, and he giggles. "You're cute too, Luke."

Luke breaks into a huge grin. And just like that, my son, who has cried every single time a babysitter has walked through the door, takes Rose's hand and pulls her into the house without a single tear in sight.

I have to hide my smile. My son has his first crush. How adorable. Rose is officially a keeper.

A few minutes later, I see Trevor and Cassandra's car pull into my driveway. I poke my head into the living room. Luke and Rose are engrossed in a board game.

"Bye, baby. Be good."

He doesn't even lift his head. "Bye, Mama."

I'm not sure what's more heartbreaking, leaving him in tears screaming for me or the fact that he doesn't appear to care that I'm leaving.

I walk outside and get into the back seat of their car. Cassandra turns back toward me. "How bad was he?"

I shake my head. "Not a single tear. The babysitter is very pretty, and Luke was immediately taken with her. He didn't even notice me leaving."

Trevor and Cassandra both start laughing. Trevor asks, "Did he compliment her and then find a way to touch her?"

"Yes. Why do you know that?"

I see his smirk in the rearview mirror. "I may have taught him a few things about how to handle the ladies. He's a handsome boy. The girls are already drawn to him. He asked me for a little guidance."

I'm in shock. "Trevor, he's three."

Trevor simply continues smirking. "It's never too early to learn how to treat a lady."

Cassandra looks me up and down. "You look hot. Are

you hoping to get laid tonight? Poor Joseph doesn't know what he's missing."

My sister has zero filter and will say anything to anyone. Her husband might be twenty-four years her junior, but he's the exact same way. The two of them together bring nuclear levels of crazy.

"Just keeping my options open."

She looks me up and down again. "You don't look like you've been fucked properly in a while. I guess Joseph isn't getting the job done. You should find someone else."

My sister also has an amazing gift for knowing when I am and am not getting laid. Unfortunately for me, it's usually the latter.

I roll my eyes and say nothing as we make the short drive to the hotel. The party is for one of the daughters of Cassandra's longtime best friend, Darian Lawrence Knight. They were college roommates. Darian's three adult daughters consider Cassandra family, calling her Aunt Cass.

Cassandra is twenty years older than me. We share a father, who we both resemble with our dark hair and blue eyes. She had no relationship with him, and he passed when I was quite young.

Cassandra and I had nothing to do with each other until two years ago when my mother was dying. Cassandra is my only sibling, I was freshly divorced, a new mother, and I desperately wanted to reconnect with her. I secured a job at her law firm to try to get to know her. It took her a few months to figure out who I was, but once she did, she immediately welcomed me into her life. Being in her life also meant that I was in Darian's life with her enormous, blended family.

A few years after Darian's husband passed, she remarried Jackson Knight, a well-known, successful

Philadelphia developer. He has three adult sons. Trevor is one of those sons. Despite the substantial age difference, he and Cassandra began secretly dating. At the same time I came into the picture, their relationship had just become public. It was a bit of a mess for a while, but they're happily married now and have twin babies, carried via gestational host.

We arrive at the hotel, and Trevor exits the car and opens my door for me. I take in his entire appearance: he's wearing a dark suit, dark shirt, and red tie that matches Cassandra's dress. Good god, he's a handsome man. I can't blame my sister for being unable to resist him. He must be six feet, three inches, with wavy dark hair, green eyes, and a perfect body. He looks exactly like his father, who's equally attractive.

Trevor is just as handsome on the inside. I'm so thankful to him. My ex-husband has less and less involvement in Luke's life every month that goes by. Trevor has stepped into a fatherly role with him. He even mentioned coaching his little league team next year. Luke adores Trevor and hangs on every word he says.

He smiles at me. "You look beautiful. That shade of blue matches your eyes."

"Thank you." I can't deny that I did try my best to look good tonight. Even though they don't know it, I'm single again. I know this party will be crawling with people my age. Darian's daughter, Reagan, is turning twenty-eight. Her husband, Carter Daulton, is thirty-five. They only recently got married. She's very outgoing and is the CEO of one of the biggest companies in the world. Carter is the president. They're a bit of a power couple and know everyone. I imagine there will be hundreds of people here tonight.

Trevor walks around and helps Cassandra out of the car. He kisses her hand as he does so. "You're breathtaking."

He unashamedly dotes on her. I'm so happy that she found him. She had a long road to happiness, one filled with many ugly bumps.

We walk into the hotel. It's one of the oldest in Philly. The chandelier in the lobby is bigger than most houses. It's gorgeous. No matter how many times I've been here, I'm always taken aback by its beauty.

We make our way to the ballroom. As expected, Carter spared no expense in throwing this party for Reagan. There are at least three-hundred people here. The décor is over the top, with a club vibe. There's a band, a huge dance floor, and several bars. Things seem to be in full swing.

We immediately spot Reagan and Carter, who are talking to a man. His back is to us, so I can't see him. We head that way. Trevor scoops up Reagan and twirls her around. "Happy birthday, *sis*."

She laughs. "Thanks, *bro*."

Trevor and Reagan have only been stepsiblings for a few years, but the two of them are the best of friends, both being the extreme extroverts of their respective families.

Cassandra hugs her. "Happy birthday, gorgeous girl. I can't believe you age and I don't."

Reagan winks at her. "Trevor keeps you young, Aunt Cass."

"Yes, he does." Trevor pulls Cassandra close and whispers in her ear. She smiles at whatever he said. He never shies away from giving her affection. It's sweet. "And he fucked my brains out before we got here."

I think I already mentioned her filter issue.

Reagan and Carter start laughing hysterically. Trevor proudly nods in agreement.

Reagan turns to me and kisses my cheek. "Thanks for coming, Beth."

"Thanks for having me. Happy birthday."

"Thank you." She moves her hand to the man she was speaking with. I suck in a breath when I turn my head to see him for the first time.

He may be the most attractive man I've ever seen. He's Latino, with olive skin, dark, curly hair, and piercing brown eyes. Eyes that practically ooze *come fuck me*.

Reagan grabs his arm. "Cassandra, Trevor, Beth, this is Dominic Mazzello. He's our Vice President of Strategy and Operations."

He smiles. "Please, call me Dom. Most people do."

Cassandra and Trevor both shake his hand. I'm frozen in shock at the gorgeous man before me. Cassandra elbows me.

As if on autopilot, I immediately hold out my hand. "I'm sorry. It's nice to meet you, Dominic."

He takes it in his big, soft, warm hand and brings it to his lips, bowing his head. "You as well, *princesa*." His lips then meet my hand. Shivers work their way down my spine.

We stare at each other until Trevor interrupts my daze. "Beth, I'm going to grab drinks. I assume you want wine?"

I nod. "Yes, any cabernet will do." Dominic and I have yet to break eye contact, though he releases my hand. I would have preferred he kept holding it.

Reagan loops her arm through Dominic's. "I need to introduce you to a few people." She looks at Cassandra and me. "We'll see you guys in a bit."

We nod as the three of them walk away. Cassandra stares at me. "I don't think I've ever seen you eye-fuck someone like that."

"I didn't eye-fuck him."

"Yes, you did. I don't blame you. He's hot as hell. Sexy as sin. Italian men are very good lovers. Trust me, I know."

"He's not Italian. He's Latino."

"His name is Dominic Mazzello. Of course he's Italian."

"You're wrong. I don't know about his name, but he's absolutely Latino." And the most ridiculously handsome man I've ever seen.

We drink and make small talk with a few people, including Trevor's mother, Melissa, her new husband, Declan, her teenage stepdaughter, Jade, and her new-in-town nephew, Lance.

As we're finishing our first round of drinks, everyone starts to make their way to the dance floor. Cassandra turns to me. "Come dance with us."

"I'll join you in a minute. Let me finish my wine."

She nods as they leave to dance. I admittedly scan the room looking for Dominic. I was watching him for a bit but lost track of him a few minutes ago. I don't see him now. Damn.

He was smiling and laughing with several people. He's clearly charming and outgoing. I want to talk to him again. I keep looking but don't see him. Where the hell is he?

Before I realize what's happening, I feel an arm around my waist and hot breath on my neck. "You've been watching me, princesa. Here I am. I'm all yours."

My whole body is covered in goosebumps at his voice, his touch, his smell, his proximity.

"I...I don't know what you're talking about."

His lips still hover by my ear. "It's okay. I've been watching you too. It's hard not to. You're the most beautiful woman in this room."

He brushes his lips over my neck. I have to close my eyes to keep myself from moaning in pleasure.

His hand is on my stomach, pulling me tight to his body. He starts moving our hips to the beat of the music. My hips instinctually sway in sync with his.

He whispers again, "Let's take this to the dance floor. I want to see your body move. I want to feel you in my arms."

I nod my head as he takes my hand, leading me to the dance floor. I set my wine glass down on a nearby table along the way.

As soon as we reach the dance floor, he pulls me into his big, strong arms. It's not a fast song, but not exactly a slow song either. He doesn't seem to care.

With his body pressed tight to mine, he begins to sway his hips again, urging me to follow suit. I do.

He rubs the backs of his fingers down my face. "Tell me more about you, princesa. What do you do?"

I'm finding it hard to speak while in his arms, but I somehow find my voice. "I'm a lawyer at Cooper and Kronfeld." It's a well-known, big Philadelphia law firm.

"And what's your relationship to Reagan? How do you know her and Carter?"

"Reagan's mother, Darian, and my sister, who you met, are longtime best friends."

He looks confused for a moment. "I assume your sister is much older than you?"

I nod. "She is. We had different mothers." Words are not coming easily to me right now. I need to get him to speak. "What does the Vice President of Strategy and Operations do?"

"I work on acquiring new businesses for the Daulton Holding's umbrella."

"Do you work with Skylar?" Skylar is Darian's youngest

daughter who I know has a similar role at Daulton Holdings.

He nods. "Yes. We have the same title, but I focus on acquiring existing businesses, and she focuses on building new ones. We help each other though. Do you know Skylar well?"

"Of course. I spend time with the whole family."

"We work well together. She's highly intelligent and very good at her job."

He expertly twirls me around and then brings me back to him, all while continuing to move those sexy hips of his. "Tell me more, princesa. I want to know everything."

I take a breath, trying to gather myself enough to behave like a normal adult. "I'm divorced, with a three-year-old son. He's the light of my life. My ex isn't in the picture at all, so most of my free time is spent with my son."

Dominic smiles. It's a soft, loving smile. "I have a three-year-old daughter. She's my everything."

"What's her name?"

"Valentina." His entire face lights up at the mention of her name. It's sweet.

"Tell me, Dominic Mazzello, why do you have an Italian name if you're Latino?"

He smiles again. "Everyone assumes I'm Italian because of my name. I'm impressed that you knew otherwise."

"I knew as soon as I saw you. Even if I didn't, you've been calling me princesa."

He tucks my hair behind my ear. "You are a princesa." His eyes bore into mine. "You have the most penetrating blue eyes I've ever seen."

Admittedly, most men do mention my eyes, they're an unusually light shade of blue, but there's something so sincere and sexual in the way he says it. His use of the word *penetrating* has my mind spinning.

He licks his lower lip. "My paternal grandfather was Italian. My grandmother was Cuban, and my entire mother's side of the family is Cuban. I was raised in a Spanish-speaking house, not Italian."

"Do you still speak much Spanish?"

His sexy eyes meet mine. "Solo cuando estoy enojado o encendido." He licks his lower lip again as I look at him in question. He smiles. "Only when I'm angry or turned on."

He pulls me as close as possible, so I can feel just how impressively turned on he is. "Me gusta la forma en que tu cuerpo se siente en el mío." *I like the way your body feels on mine.*

I swallow hard. I don't know what he said, but it sounded good, and I know he's turned on. He's the most effortlessly sexual man I've ever been around. It practically oozes out of him. His gaze alone is soaking my panties.

We continue to sway. I'm not sure if it's to the beat of the music. I can't hear or see anything else right now except Dominic.

We're silent, staring at each other. There's something happening here. Something I've never before experienced with a man. I'm not sure I've ever met someone and wanted him the way I want Dominic right now. I can feel my heart beat between my legs.

His hands run up and down the sides of my body. I can't help but trace my fingertips along his soft face and over his lips. I'm losing control of my own actions. I'm not a forward woman, but I'm feeling a bit uninhibited around him.

He begins to bring his lips toward mine, but before they meet, someone crashes into us. Their foot comes down onto my ankle, rolling it awkwardly. Dominic catches me so I don't fall, but it hurts.

I wince in pain as the man apologizes.

Cassandra and Trevor come running over. She grabs my arm. "Are you okay?"

"I'm fine." Though when I try to put weight on it, I nearly collapse. Again, Dominic catches me.

He lifts me and cradles me into his arms. "I'll take her for some ice."

Oh my god. I'm so embarrassed. "Dominic, you don't need to carry me. I can walk."

He shakes his head. "Let's get you ice and take a look at your ankle before you put any pressure on it."

Cassandra smirks at our interaction and closeness. "You two kids have fun. Don't do anything I would do. Let me know if you need me."

At that, Dominic moves us toward the bar and asks the bartender for a bag of ice. Once he brings it to us, we exit the ballroom.

"Let's find somewhere quiet to ice your ankle."

He opens one door, but we hear moans of ecstasy. "Yes, Jackson. Like that."

Dominic and I smile at each other. That was definitely Darian and Jackson. I suppose I'm not surprised. His hands are never far from her body, and they're well known for disappearing at parties.

We move on to another door, but it's locked. We can hear moans through that door too.

We move to a third door with the same result. Is this a fancy hotel or a brothel?

Finally, when we get to a fourth door, an attractive, familiar man that I can't quite place walks out and looks around a bit frantically. "Did you see a brunette woman walk out of here? Did you see which way she went?"

We both shake our heads. We didn't see anyone.

He nods and motions his hand toward the room. "It's all yours."

Dominic walks us inside and closes the door. It appears to be some sort of dressing room. There's a sitting area with a sofa.

He gently places me on the cushions. He then removes his jacket, lays it on the back of the sofa, and sits, bringing my foot onto his lap.

He's extremely broad. The buttons on his shirt look like they might pop off with the slightest movement. His arms are practically bulging through his shirt. Who is he, Superman?

"You don't need to fuss over me. I'm sure I'm fine."

He ignores me and carefully examines my ankle. My body's reaction to his touch is not lost on me. "I think it's a little swollen, but not too bad. Let's keep the ice on it for a bit."

He gently places the bag on it. "Is it too cold?"

"I'm fine, Dominic, really. This was all very unnecessary."

He gives me a sexy smile. "Maybe I just wanted an excuse to be alone with you."

The air between us is like nothing I've experienced with a man. It's thick, sexual, and more than obvious to both of us.

My breathing begins to pick up. I sit up a little straighter, bringing myself closer to him. I look at his juicy lips. I desperately want to know what those lips would feel like on mine. What those big hands would feel like on more than just my ankle.

He pulls me closer to him so that it's no longer my feet resting on his legs, but my thighs. Our faces are now mere inches apart.

I lick my lips in anticipation. His eyes don't miss it as he runs his tongue across his lower lip again. Do all men do that? I've never noticed it until tonight. He's done it several times.

He slowly runs his hand up my outer thigh until it's under my dress. With that hand, he squeezes the outside of my hip. With the other, he threads his fingers through my hair and pulls my face toward his until our lips meet.

He murmurs into my mouth, "Eres tan hermosa." *You're so beautiful.* His lips fully suck in mine. His tongue immediately makes its way into my mouth. It tastes like bourbon and cigars. It's sexy as hell. And it's thick. He has a thick tongue. I immediately imagine what else it could do to my body.

I grab onto his shirt, pulling him as close to me as I can. My tongue meets his and he moans. I feel his moan everywhere. My need for him is overwhelming.

His kiss, his smell, his taste, all have my body reacting in a way I haven't felt before. I've never been kissed like this. It's slow and sensual, yet somehow also needy and passionate.

I can feel his dick pushing on my leg. I bet it's thick like his tongue. His hand on my hip squeezes hard, as if he's trying to control himself. I spread my legs a bit so he knows he can do more to me. I want more from him.

He immediately takes the cue and slides his fingers over to my center. I'm wet and desperate for his touch.

He runs his fingers over my panty-covered pussy a few times. I thrust my hips, wanting more friction.

I feel him smile into my mouth as he unexpectedly rips

my panties straight off my body. I gasp in shock, though it causes a shot of liquid lust to drip out of me.

He runs his fingers through me. Now it's my turn to moan into his mouth.

Breaking the kiss, he pushes my body down until my back meets the sofa and maneuvers his own body until it's situated between my legs. He lifts the bottom of my dress to my waist and bends to bring his lips to my inner thighs.

He open-mouth kisses and bites his way up my thighs. He gets to my pussy and runs his nose through it. "Huelos increíble. Quiero follarte." *You smell incredible. I want to fuck you.*

I don't know what he said, but whatever it was, it was hot as hell. I'm confident it was dirty.

He runs that wide tongue through me. Oh. My. God. That feels good.

He moves his tongue through me several more times before slipping it into my opening. He pushes it all the way in. I swear I've had dicks in me smaller than his giant tongue.

He basically tongue-fucks me. I've never experienced anything like it. Every time he pulls his tongue out, he slurps my juices. I can only imagine how wet I am. I'm confident I haven't ever been this turned on in my life.

Pulling his tongue out, he says, "Dame tus jugos." *Give me your juices.*

He swirls that magical tongue through me until he reaches my now severely sensitive and swollen bundle of nerves. He works me over in no time at all, with fast, hard circles causing heat to spread throughout my body.

At times, I've struggled to come from this. Clearly I've had the wrong partners. My orgasm is seconds away.

As if hearing my thoughts, he sucks on my clit and

simultaneously slips two fingers inside me. It's not gentle or slow. It's rough, hard, and fast. As soon as they reach deep, my body takes on a life of its own. I start to shake uncontrollably. I grab his hair and thrust my hips as I open and explode, coming in a way I never have before.

Where has this guy been my whole life?

He licks and relentlessly pushes his fingers in and out through it all. He's speaking Spanish into me, but I'm too incoherent to hear a word of what he says, not that I would understand it anyway.

When my orgasm subsides and I regain my senses, I immediately reach for his belt, desperate for more of him. As soon as I do, his phone rings. I can see it lighting up in the pocket of his jacket draped over the sofa next to us.

He sighs. "My daughter is with a new sitter. Let me check to see if it's her."

I nod and breathe, "Of course. I understand."

He pulls out the phone. It's clearly not his daughter because he rejects the call.

He places the phone down and smiles at me. "Where were we?"

I grab for his belt buckle once more but his phone rings again.

He shouts. "Coño!" *Cunt!* "I better take it. She'll keep calling."

"Who will keep calling?"

He stands. Just before he accepts the call he says, "My wife."

He accepts and starts yelling in Spanish, but I don't hear a word through the buzzing in my head. Did he just say *wife*? He's married? Oh my god. I just made out with a married man. I'm feeling sick to my stomach.

He's in obvious distress. He's pulling on his hair with his free hand.

I hear, "Cómo pasó esto?" *How did this happen?*

He looks at me. His sexy smile is completely gone. His earlier expressive eyes look completely void of life. I think I see them fill with tears.

Before I can process anything, he grabs his jacket off the back of the sofa and pulls the phone away from his head. "I'm sorry, I have to go."

He brings the phone back to his head and is talking on his way out the door.

I'm in shock. I look down. My dress is around my waist. I'm naked from there down. My legs are still spread wide.

I immediately close them and pull down my dress. I look around for my panties, but they're nowhere to be found. I suppose it doesn't matter since he ripped them off me.

I sit with my head in my hands. I'm in a state of complete and total shock. He said *wife*, right? I didn't imagine that.

What the hell just happened?

CHAPTER ONE

FOUR YEARS LATER

BETH

I wake to the sound of my front door opening. I instinctively look next to me in my bed. It's empty, as it has been every morning since my divorce just over six years ago.

I've been with a few men since the divorce, but none have slept in my bed. I usually use Luke as an excuse, but the truth is, it's a sacred place to me. I don't want any random guy in my space. It took me long enough to erase my dickhead ex-husband, Gary, from my memory bank. The handful of men I've been with since were hardly worthy of sleeping in my bed or meeting my son.

Every morning I look over and am reminded that I'm alone. In most ways, I always have been, considering the shitty marriage I endured. I don't see that changing anytime soon. Maybe I should start sleeping in the middle of the bed. It would be less depressing, but I feel as though it's like throwing in the towel.

I do see my little furball at the bottom of the bed. He makes me smile. "Trex, you're supposed to sleep in Luke's room, not mine. Did you miss him last night?"

Meow.

I shake my head. "You're not exactly the kind of man I want in my bed."

Meow.

"Don't worry, Luke will be home later."

I hear a loud voice, "Beth! Where are you?"

I don't answer.

Cassandra walks into my bedroom and sighs. "There you are. Why are you still in bed? Why is your cat the only male in your bed? That's step one to becoming a cat lady."

"Ugh. Leave me alone to wallow in my old age misery."

"You're turning thirty-five, not ninety-five. Do I have to remind you how old I am?"

"Yeah, but you get to fuck a hot thirty-two-year-old every night, so it's different."

"It's not every *night.*"

I lift my eyebrows. "Really? I thought it was. The honeymoon phase is finally over?"

She gives me her mischievous smile. The one where I know something absurd is about to come out of her mouth. "It's morning *and* night. And if we have time for office visits, sometimes during the day too. He's extremely virile."

I scowl at her. "I hate you."

"No, you don't." She throws a box on my bed. "Here, I figured yours is about to die from overuse. Happy birthday."

I look and see that it's a new vibrator.

I shake my head. "You're the worst sister ever."

She lets out a laugh. "Or the best. You're welcome."

I inspect it carefully as Trex paws at the box. "That looks very elaborate. I'd need a master's degree just to be able to understand how to work that thing. I prefer simple."

She walks over to my night table and opens the drawer, pulling out my vibrator.

I stare at her in shock. "I think touching another woman's vibrator is a severe boundary line that should not be crossed."

She examines it. "This model is at least five years old. You need an upgrade." She tosses it in the trash can. "I got you the latest and greatest. It practically fucks you by itself. You don't even need to do anything but lay there. And if you prefer it on top, there's an attachment that holds it up for you."

I narrow my eyes at her. "There is something truly wrong with you."

"I know, but my husband totally digs it."

I mumble, "You're both nuts."

"Maybe. Come on. We have the whole day. Let's get going." She pulls my blankets off me and audibly gasps. "No wonder you can't get laid. What fucking thirty-five-year-old owns a granny nightgown? Burn that thing. Immediately."

"It's comfortable."

"Naked is comfortable. Granny gowns are ugly, and they repel men."

"You sleep naked every night?"

"Of course. We both do."

"What about the kids? What if they come in?" Cassandra and Trevor have fraternal twins who are almost five, a boy and girl named Brandon and Dylan.

"They know we sleep naked. They don't even notice it anymore. They sleep naked too. They said they want to be like us."

"What about when Luke sleeps over? They don't sleep naked then, do they?"

"They wear pajamas for sleepovers. Pajamas that are much cuter than your Queen Elizabeth raided sleep wardrobe."

I roll my eyes. "Was Luke okay last night?" He slept there. Trevor coaches his little league baseball team. He and Luke said they needed time to mentally prepare for the big game this afternoon.

Trevor is a godsend to me and Luke. Not only does he spend time with my son to give me a little break, but he's the only father figure in Luke's life. My piece of shit ex has gradually disappeared throughout the years to the point where I can't tell you the last time we saw him. It's understandably a sensitive topic for Luke, but fortunately, Trevor gives him a lot of time and attention that would normally be reserved for a father.

I make way more money than Gary. I've never asked for a dime of child support. I happily pay for all of Luke's needs. All I want is for Luke to have his father in his life. Gary can't even give of himself. I don't know what I ever saw in him, but Luke came from my short-lived marriage, so I can't regret it.

"Casanova O'Connell was fine."

I scowl at her. "You know I hate when you call him that."

She smirks. Luke has earned that nickname at school. He's into girls. *Very* into girls. He always has been. I think our babysitter Rose was his first crush, and he's never looked back. Trevor feeds the beast with lines and reassurances. I've been called by the school countless times about him smooth-talking and kissing girls. They all chase after him. He's handsome, has an outgoing personality, which I think he got from Trevor, and is extremely confident. He may have also gotten his confidence from Trevor. I can't imagine what it's going to look like in a few years when he hits puberty.

"He was perfect. As always. Brandon worships him. Luke played with him until they both passed out."

"Did they exclude Dylan? I hate when they do that."

"Dylan doesn't give a crap. She marches to her own beat. She happily does her own thing."

"She's a chip off the old block."

"She is. All three were asleep early. It wasn't a big deal."

"Well, thank you. It was nice to have a relaxing, quiet evening to myself at home."

"You're welcome, though I'd rather have sleepovers so *you* can have sleepovers. And Trex doesn't count."

I mumble, "Me too."

"Now get dressed. We have a celebratory brunch with all the girls."

"It's not for over an hour."

"We need to stop at a lingerie shop. I can't have you wearing this kind of shit to bed. If you won't sleep naked, we'll find something sexier. Like a trash bag."

"Fine. We can go." Maybe if I feel sexy, it will get me out of the rut I've been in lately.

"By the way, there were two women standing by your front door when I got here. They looked like they were waiting for you."

"Ugh. A brunette and blonde around my age? Both attractive?"

She nods. "Yep. Who are they?"

"They're my crazy neighbors, Brittany and Mindy. They have it in their minds that we need a mom's neighborhood watch."

"Neighborhood watch? You live in the safest neighborhood around. What are they watching?"

"Not for crime. For teens making out. They think our kids are young and impressionable. They don't want them seeing the teens in this neighborhood getting it on."

"What are you supposed to do about it?"

"They want me to patrol the neighborhood with them at night. I think Brittany even made us personalized patrol T-shirts. She's relentless. I've been avoiding them both."

She lets out a laugh. "They're going to hate Luke in a few years. He's totally going to be one of those teens making out in the bushes."

I narrow my eyes at her. "Stop it. He's seven."

"You know I'm right."

Shit. I do know she's right.

I slide out of bed, stand up, and stretch.

She shakes her head. "That thing is even worse when you're standing. Are you Amish? Did a bonnet and chastity belt come with that outfit? Do you ride to work in a little horse-drawn buggy?"

I can't help but laugh as I look down at myself. Maybe my nighttime wardrobe needs an adjustment.

Ninety minutes later, we arrive at brunch with a sea of shopping bags. I have enough lingerie to wear something different every day for a month. And it's not classy silk nighties. It's stripper-approved sleepwear. My sister is nuts.

I still can't help but smile at the notion of having a sister. I spent my first twenty-nine years knowing I had one, but not knowing her in the slightest. I met her a few times when I was a baby and toddler, but I never truly met her until the day I walked into her office.

SIX YEARS AGO

I bring Mom a bowl of soup while she lays in bed looking frailer each and every day. I gave her nurse two hours off so I could enjoy some precious alone time with my mother.

The end is almost here. It's likely a matter of months. I've never felt more alone. Thank god for Luke.

My father was slightly older than Mom and died suddenly when I was a small child. I barely remember him. In fact, my most vivid memories of him are when he told me what a superstar my sister was. She was in law school at the time and wasn't in our lives.

I do remember his funeral though. I was five years old. My mom and I sat in the front row crying our eyes out. I looked in the back and saw her. Cassandra Blackstone. I knew who she was from her pictures. I remember thinking how pretty she was and that I hoped to look like her when I grew up. She was standing with a shorter, pretty brunette. Both of their faces were stoic, but neither was crying like us.

When the funeral was over, the brunette dragged her to Mom and me. Cassandra kissed Mom's cheek. "I'm sorry for your loss, Barbara."

Mom took her hand and squeezed it. "Yours too. Can we talk sometime? There are things you should know about your father."

Cassandra shrugged. "I don't know. Give me some time."

"Okay, sweetie. Just let me know when you're ready."

Mom wrapped her arm around me. "Lizzie, do you remember Cassandra?" My full first name is Elizabeth. I went by Lizzie for my first ten years, but then decided to go by Beth, which I much preferred.

I shook my head. I didn't remember her at all.

"She's your sister. Perhaps you guys can spend some time together in the future. Get to know one another."

Cassandra warned, "Barbara, don't overpromise. I'm not sure what I want."

Mom nodded. "Okay. You know where to find us. Our door is always open to you."

And that was it. We never heard from her again.

When I was in high school, I began to follow Cassandra's budding legal career online. She became a partner in one of the biggest law firms in Philadelphia. The first female in firm history to make partner. My sister was a trailblazer.

I was determined to be a lawyer, just like she was. I felt like I wanted some commonality with her. I worked my ass off and did just that. I even trained to become a mergers and acquisitions attorney, just like Cassandra.

I've worked for a few years since law school making a name for myself and learning the specialized form of law. I've been patient. Now it's time to make my move. In a few months, Cassandra will be the only family I have left. I want to get to know her. I assume she's cold and nasty based on her complete rejection of me my entire life, but I don't care. Besides Luke, she's all I'll have. I'll take what I can get.

Mom grabs my hand. "Elizabeth, will you bring Luke by this weekend? I know I won't get to see him grow up, but I'd like to spend as much time with him as I can now."

I hate that it's the truth. She won't see him grow up.

That pains me. She'd be such a great grandmother. FU cancer!

"Of course, Mom."

"Thank you." She takes a few labored breaths. "Distract me. Tell me what's going on with you. Are you seeing anyone?"

"I'm a little busy for that right now." And I'm less than a year removed from walking into my house and finding my husband, the only man I had ever been with, in bed with another woman. It doesn't exactly inspire confidence.

"Make time. I know I didn't have long enough with your father, but I cherish every minute I had with the love of my life. When you find true love, it's so special. You feel it in your bones. Gary was never good enough for you. One day you'll find the right man and you'll realize what I'm saying is truc."

"I hope you're right, Mom."

"I am. Now tell me about work."

"It's fine, but I have an interview at a new firm, Cooper and Kronfeld, tomorrow. I'm thinking of making a move."

"I thought things were going well."

"They are, but it's a bit of an old boy's network. I want to be in a more female-friendly firm. The mergers and acquisitions department at Cooper and Kronfeld is chaired by a woman. I want to work for her."

My mother has no clue that it's Cassandra. I don't think she's ever really understood what type of law Cassandra and I practice and certainly doesn't know where she works. She'd probably be encouraging about me reaching out to my estranged sister, but I don't want to add any stress to her plate. If we reconcile, I'll tell her.

The next day, I interview with the managing partner. The next week I'm offered the job. On my first day, that partner tells me we're going to meet Cassandra Blackstone, the best in the business, and that she's agreed to be my direct supervisor and mentor.

I can't believe this day is finally here. Will she recognize me? She hasn't seen me since I was five. We do look alike though. And maybe she's followed me like I've followed her. I hope she has. Then I'll know she cares.

Steven, the managing partner, walks me to Cassandra's open office door and knocks. She looks up and smiles. I see no recognition from her. I have a pang of disappointment. Part of me wanted her to care enough to check in on me to know what I look like now.

"Cassandra, this is Beth O'Connell. I mentioned her to you earlier." Again, no recognition at the name. I kept my married name for Luke's sake. She only knows me as Lizzie Blackstone, not Beth O'Connell.

Cassandra stands to shake my hand. I'm sweating. The closer she gets, the more obvious it is that we're related. I'm shorter than her, and her hair is shorter than mine, but the resemblance is unmistakable. Yet I see nothing from her.

She gives me a warm smile. "Hi, Beth. It's so nice to meet you. I'm Cassandra Blackstone. Welcome to Cooper and Kronfeld."

I compliment her and talk about how excited I am to work for her. She cracks a few jokes before Steven leaves. When he does, we sit and engage in a bit of get to know you chit-chat.

I can't believe I'm sitting here with my sister. This is surreal. I want to reach across her desk and hug her, but I don't. I want to beg her to be in my life, but I don't.

She asks about my personal life. I tell her about my new divorce and my one-year-old son. She doesn't ask me his name. It's the same as our father.

She does mention that she has a godson around the same age. I didn't know that.

We spend the rest of the day getting me caught up on her files. At the end of the day, her phone rings with an emergency. She mentions that her niece is in premature labor.

Niece? I'm so confused.

I later find out that it's Darian's girls who she considers her nieces. I want to tell her that she has a nephew too, but I don't. I ask her if she has any siblings, and she says no. I can feel my heart breaking. She doesn't think of me at all. She never has. Maybe this was a mistake.

But as the weeks and months go on, we strike up a friendship. She's not at all what I expected. She's not cold. She's not nasty. She's amazing. She's smart, warm, and maybe the funniest person I've ever met. I want her in my life as my sister, not just my co-worker.

PRESENT

I look around the table and smile. If Cassandra wasn't in my life, this would be a table for two. Giselle and me. Instead, it's a table for eleven. Darian, Darian's three daughters, Harley, Reagan, and Skylar, Melissa, her stepdaughter, Jade, and Melissa's three daughters-in-law, Kylie, Jessica, and of course, Cassandra.

They beg me to open my gifts. I do and it's all sex toys. One after another. I turn and look suspiciously at Cassandra. She smirks as she shrugs. "I may have told them there was a theme."

I can't help but smile at my sister. *My* sister.

CHAPTER TWO

DOMINIC

"Valentina! We need to get moving. Bring Matteo downstairs with you."

"Okay, Papa."

My gorgeous brown-haired, brown-eyed daughter walks into the kitchen with her little brother. I kiss her cheek. "You look pretty." She's in a white dress. "Are you excited for your first day at your new school?"

She smiles. The smile that lights up my universe. "Yes. I can't wait."

I turn to Matteo. "You're going to be a good boy, right? Now you get to go to big boy school like your sister."

He simply nods. He's not at all verbal and is extremely shy. It's frustrating at times. I was spoiled by Valentina being incredibly verbal and social so early. His doctors say it's normal for boys, especially one that, so far, has only spent less than half of his time with me, but I'm fearful that it's something more. He'll be spending so much more time with me now, so perhaps he'll come out of his shell. I'm hopeful.

I hand them each a plate of scrambled eggs. Hers with cheese, his without. He can be a bit particular at times.

I turn back to Valentina. "You'll check on Matteo today?"

She nods. "If I'm allowed."

"I told the school that your brother is very dependent on you. They understand you may be needed from time to time."

My angel daughter is such a good big sister, though there's one part of her that is not so angelic. "You'll control your temper, won't you?" My daughter inherited my temper. When she gets going, it can turn ugly.

She nods as she bats her eyelashes and looks at me innocently. "Yes, Papa, I'll try."

I can't help but smirk at her. She smirks right back at me as we exchange a silent understanding that we're both a bit hot-headed.

Even though we're already well into the school year, Valentina is switching schools. She went to a school near her mother's house, about thirty minutes away. I live between there and my office.

My ex-wife stayed home with Matteo. Her mother in Cuba has grown ill, and she needs to spend time there. Though she promised to come back for visits now and then, I wouldn't agree to let her take the children out of the country for that amount of time. It was ugly for a bit as we came to terms.

Once we agreed that the children would stay with me and she'd visit, I signed Valentina up for a local private school that also has a daycare for younger kids, and an after-school care program because I can't get there by dismissal time.

We make our way to The Primary Academy and get Matteo situated in the daycare. After a few tears, he seemed happy playing with the Legos. I hope he makes friends. My ex-wife rarely has him around other kids. I think it's stunted his social growth. It's always been a bone of contention between her and I.

Clad in my normal business suit attire, I grab Valentina's hand and walk her into the second-grade classroom. Her teacher introduces herself. "Welcome, Valentina. We're so happy to have you. I'm *Ms.* Longfellow." She emphasized Ms. That was for my benefit, to let me know she's single. I roll my eyes. As if I'd ever start something with my daughter's teacher. As if Ms. American Pie can handle me.

Valentina holds out her hand. "It's nice to meet you, Mrs. Longfellow."

"It's Ms. Longfellow."

Valentina gives me a little side-eye. She's messing with the teacher. I love this kid.

"I'm so sorry. It's nice to meet you, Ms. Longfellow."

"Aren't you polite." She shakes her hand in return. Ms. Longfellow turns her head and motions to a boy in the class. "Luke, can you come here for a moment?"

A little boy walks over. He's got dark hair and insanely light blue eyes. They remind me of a woman I once met. The one that stars in my dreams. I've never seen eyes as blue as hers until now. It's almost the exact same shade.

"Luke, this is Valentina. Today is her first day. Can you show her around and introduce her to everyone?"

Luke's face lights up. "I love showing pretty ladies around." He grabs Valentina's hand and pulls her away. "Come on, I'll help you make new friends."

My face drops. Did he just hold her hand? Did he just compliment her? Is that little shit hitting on my seven-year-old daughter? What is happening right now?

Ms. Longfellow touches my arm. "Don't worry. She's in good hands. Luke is very popular."

I bet he is.

Valentina looks back. Her eyes move to Ms. Longfellow's hand on my arm. "Papa, you can leave now. I know you have a breakfast date with your *girlfriend*."

I bite my lip to hide my smile. I don't have a date, and I don't have a girlfriend. She doesn't like her teacher's hand on me. Unfortunately, she's seen this type of behavior too many times. Having a woman hit on me in front of my kids is a nonstarter.

I smile. "Yes, I must get going. Valentina will be fine. My son, Matteo, is in the daycare. He may need to see Valentina at some point today if he becomes upset. She soothes him."

Ms. Longfellow nods. "Yes, I've been told. Don't worry about a thing."

"Thank you."

I leave and make my way to the office. I have a morning meeting with Reagan Lawrence, the CEO of our company, and her husband, Carter Daulton, the President of our company.

When I arrive, I drop my computer bag in my office and walk down the hallway toward Reagan's office.

As I walk by her sister Skylar's office, I see the door is open and decide to pop my head in. Jade is sitting with her. Jade is Reagan and Skylar's cousin. She's only twenty-two but is second in command of our design department. She started here as an intern four years ago, but quickly and impressively proved herself to be a valuable commodity. If you can imagine it, Jade can make it come to life in virtual modeling. She's very good at her job, though highly inappropriate. Sexual innuendo is her second language. Sometimes it's funny, and sometimes it makes me uncomfortable being that I'm over twenty years older than her.

"Good morning, ladies." I smile at them both.

Skylar lifts her head toward me and smiles in return. "Good morning, Dom. I left a file on your desk this morning. It's a bid I have coming up. Would you mind taking a quick look? I'd like your input."

"It would be my pleasure." I like that Skylar feels comfortable asking for my help from time to time. Even though I always offered it, she never used to. I think she was more insecure about her job when she first started. Now that she's flourished in her role, we're better able to bounce ideas off each other.

"Thank you. No rush."

Jade runs her eyes up and down my body, as she often does. "I like your suit, Dom. It hugs your body nicely." She gives me her unique smile that spells trouble.

"Thank you. I need to chat with Reagan first, but will you stop by my office later? I may have something I need you to work on."

"I would *love* to."

"Great." I motion my head out the door. "I have a meeting with her now. I'll catch you two later."

I make my way to Reagan's office area and approach her longtime assistant. "Good morning, Sheila."

She looks up from her computer with her always fashionable, outfit-matching glasses. "Good morning, Dominic. How are you today?"

"I'm great, thank you. I have a meeting with her."

"She's expecting you. Go ahead."

I hesitate for a moment. "Is it safe to go in?"

Sheila shrugs. "You never know with the two of them, but I haven't heard any noises suggesting otherwise."

It's common knowledge and mostly accepted at this point that Reagan and Carter are often intimate in one of their offices. It's nearly a daily occurrence. I certainly don't care, but I also have no need to see it.

I knock loudly and hear her shout, "Come in."

I walk into the office. Fortunately, they're clothed. They're sitting on the couch in the small sitting area she maintains. Her bare feet are on his lap and he's rubbing them as they talk. He doesn't stop when I walk in. He's madly in love with her and is never afraid to show it.

She turns her head and smiles at me. "Hey, Dom. Have a seat."

I do.

"How did things go with your kids?" I never talk about my family in the office, having my reasons. I imagine most people know nothing about my personal life. Due to my altering family situation, I did have to talk to Reagan and Carter last week. I'm not going to be able to work long nights for the foreseeable future, and I wanted to give them the heads up. As I expected, given the type of people they are, they were more than accommodating. Reagan may be young at only thirty-two, but she's a good boss. She values quality over quantity. My work needs to get done. She doesn't care how or where. She knows my work product well enough at this point that she can be certain things will get handled properly.

I started here well before Reagan's time, when Carter's father was the CEO. He was a miserable prick of a human being. I was in the process of interviewing at other companies when Carter effectively had his father tossed out by the Board. Carter was next in line for the job, being both the president of the company and the next generation of Daulton men, but he recommended Reagan to the Board instead. I have a lot of respect for him for that.

When I first met Reagan, I was immediately impressed by her. She's very smart and extremely forward-thinking. A bit out of the box at times, and she's got a dirty sense of humor, but I think that makes her more relatable and genuine with the employees. She's both respected and loved by all. Our stock values have quadrupled since she took over nearly four-and-a-half years ago.

She and I hit it off immediately. I was promoted to

my current position as soon as she took over, and she promised me autonomy in deciding which businesses to acquire. She has lived up to her word. She assists me when I need it and is a sounding board when I need that, but otherwise, she allows me to do my job. I know she thinks I do it well.

"It went smoothly, thanks for asking."

"How's life as a full-time dad?"

"It only just began, but I'll manage. My daughter is very helpful with my son."

"That's great. Do what you need to do, Dom. We know your work won't suffer. We trust you."

I smile. "Thanks for the vote of confidence and for being so understanding."

"Of course. You should talk to Skylar. She somehow manages to balance work and family life well." Skylar has two young kids with her husband, Lance, both under three.

"That's not a bad idea. Maybe I will."

"I never knew you had kids."

"I prefer to keep my work and personal lives separate. I think it's best that way."

We all laugh as we look at Carter rubbing her feet. He smirks as he nods. "We're not as good at that."

She looks at him with all the love in the world. "We'll have to figure it out soon."

It hits me. "You guys are expecting?"

They both grin and nod enthusiastically.

"Congratulations. I'll have to place a bet in the company pool." There's a company pool over when Carter and Reagan will announce a pregnancy. They've been married for over four years. People have been relentlessly gossiping about it since day one.

They laugh. She says, "We'll announce it soon. No need until I'm showing. Let them all speculate a little longer. I may have a few dollars in the pool under a pseudonym."

I chuckle. "Well, get ready for the ride of a lifetime."

"We are. Anyway, I called you in here to talk about the Wallingford acquisition. You mentioned issues."

Wallingford is a popular, trendy brand of sneakers. They're growing faster than they can manage it. They need our help to become the internationally best-selling brand they're projected to become.

I nod. "Yes. There's employee and stockholder resistance. They can't manage to get out of their own way on this one."

"I don't want to mess around with it. Time is of the essence. I don't care what it costs to move this along. Call my aunt. Hire her to deal with everything. Our in-house counsel can't handle it. This is too complicated for them."

I've worked with Cassandra on a few other occasions. She's a barracuda. She's phenomenal at what she does.

"I did. She's a bit tied up right now. She said she'll make some calls as soon as she can, but it doesn't sound like it will be anytime soon."

Reagan sighs. "I don't think we can sit around holding our dicks on this one. What about her sister, Beth? She's great too."

Fuck. I've been avoiding dealing with Beth O'Connell for over four years. I completely mistreated her at Reagan's birthday party. I should explain myself, but so much time has passed. At this point, it's insulting to her.

When we've needed to use their legal services throughout the years, I've made it seem like we'd only use Cassandra because she's the chair of the department and known to be the best in the business. I've learned that Beth is just as well respected, but I couldn't bear to see her gorgeous face after what I did to her.

I give a quick nod. "I'll see what they can swing." Meaning: I'll beg for Cassandra.

CHAPTER THREE

BETH

"To good friends and good orgasms."

I giggle as I clink my glass with Giselle's at our monthly dinner. Giselle is my best friend and has been since we met on the first day of law school. She's about my height, with gorgeous, thick auburn hair and green eyes. She was already married at the time and had her daughter, Hazel, between our first and second years of law school.

After graduation, she decided to work at the District Attorney's office, prosecuting criminals. It's a noble profession. It may be significantly lower paying than mine, but she works government hours and is home early to be there for her kids.

A few years later, we were both pregnant at the same time, and she had her son, Colton, a month before I had Luke. Unfortunately, we also both went through our divorces at the same time. We leaned on each other for support. Her divorce was a bit more amicable than mine, as no infidelity was involved. They have joint custody.

Her ex-husband is very involved in the lives of her children. She's lucky for that. Her kids are *really* lucky for that.

We try to have dinner and drinks at least once a month. I cherish this time with her.

I ask, "Have you been on any dates lately?"

She shakes her head. "Unfortunately, no. I'm sick of the whole scene. Honestly, a glass of wine and my vibrator are much easier, though I miss having a man's hands on my body." She sighs. "At least I don't have to wash my hair or put on makeup for my vibrator. As we get older, the pool of decent men gets smaller and smaller. I don't want a man who's never been married because I don't want any more kids. But then the divorced men all want twenty-two-year-olds with perfect bodies who give them all the anal they can handle. It's such bullshit. Divorced men have it so much easier."

I let out a laugh. Giselle is always good for a truth bomb. It's probably why she and Cassandra get along so well. "Is Tom dating anyone?" Her ex-husband, Tom, is attractive. I imagine he hasn't had any trouble in the dating department.

She shrugs. "I don't know. We agreed to let the other know if anything progresses to the point of meeting the kids. That's it. I'm sure he's out there riding the twenty-two-year-old anal train like the rest of the divorced men." She smiles. "Lucky for their asses his dick is small."

I laugh as I shake my head. "That's so wrong."

She smirks. "But so true."

She sighs. "I'm so hard up for dick right now. I swear, if a man that smelled good walked by this table, I might have an orgasm. If he accidentally brushed up against me, I know I would."

We both giggle as I nod in agreement. "Dating at thirty-five sucks."

She scrunches her nose. "No one for you either?"

I shake my head. "No, not for a very long time."

"Do you even remember that last great non-self-induced orgasm you had? I don't remember mine. I'm not sure it was this decade."

I look down and she notices.

"Shit. Sorry, I forgot."

Giselle is the only person that knows about that night with Dominic Mazzello. I never told anyone else, including my sister. I know he works with Reagan and Skylar. They hire our firm from time to time too. It seemed easier to keep it quiet. Cassandra saw him carry me off the dance floor. She suspects we fooled around, but I've never confirmed it or mentioned anything about it to her. As far as she knows, I was dating someone else at the time and nothing happened.

"It's fine. It's just embarrassing. Considering my history, being the other woman is something that's hard for me to move past."

She takes my hand. "You didn't know. Stop beating yourself up about it. We both know that intent matters. He's the one in the wrong, not you."

I nod. "You're right. I just find myself thinking of his wife sometimes. Does she know? Does she hate me? Are they still married? Did they end it because of me?"

What I won't admit to her is that I've tried to stalk him on social media to get answers to these questions, but he doesn't have any accounts. Other than the work website, I can't find substantive information on him anywhere.

"Stop. You're not the asshole. He is. We need to talk about something else. Tell me about this new vibrator

Cassandra got for you. She said it's very advanced technology."

I bite my lip. "I hate to admit it, but she's right. It does everything. *Everything.*"

"Interesting. Maybe it's time for me to give up my old, trusty Magic Wand and try something different."

"Magic Wands have been around for over fifty years for a reason."

She bats her eyelashes. "I don't mean to brag, but I now have the Magic Wand Plus."

We both laugh.

She raises her eyebrow. "Do you still watch Spanish porn?"

I scrunch my nose. "I didn't realize I had told you about that."

"You were four martinis in one night and you started speaking Spanish. Fluently. I asked you when the hell you learned the language. I know you didn't speak it in law school. You said you've watched so much Spanish porn in the past four years that you think you've picked up the language."

I smile. "I'm pretty sure I have. I understand it shockingly well. I know the dirty words even better."

"I'm not surprised considering the way your mind works. You pick up things quickly. There's a reason you were the number one student in our law school class."

I do have a bit of a photographic memory. I need to only see or hear something once for it to stick. I know I'm lucky for that. It certainly made law school easier for me.

I give her a self-satisfied smile. "All these people waste years in school studying languages. All they really need to do is watch a little foreign language porn."

She nods. "You might be on to something. You're a

pioneer in this methodology. You could bring porn to schools everywhere. I bet teenage boys would learn languages a lot faster if it was through dirty movies."

Now we're in a fit of giggles. It's nice to be out with Giselle. She's easy to be with and makes me laugh.

———

THE NEXT DAY, I'm in Cassandra's office chatting about a file when my cell phone rings. I take a quick peek at it, as does every parent when their phone rings. I must have a look of panic on my face.

Cassandra asks, "Is everything okay? Who is it?"

"Luke's school. Sorry. I need to take it."

"Of course. Go ahead." She smirks. "Maybe Cassanova O'Connell was caught making out with a girl again?"

I give her the finger as I answer. "Hello?"

"Is this Ms. O'Connell?"

"It is."

"This is Amy Roberts, principal at The Primary Academy. Luke is fine." I breathe a sigh of relief.

"Why the call? What's wrong?"

"Luke has had an altercation with another student. We'd like for you to come down here. He's quite upset about it."

"He got into a fight? That doesn't sound like Luke. He's gentle."

"Not a physical fight."

"Tell me what it was then."

"Can you come down here? The girl's father is on his way as well."

A girl? Luke fought with a girl? This makes no sense. "I'm on my way."

I end the call and Cassandra looks at me in question.

"Luke had some sort of altercation. I need to get to the school."

"That doesn't sound like Luke at all. He's a lover, not a fighter. Call me and let me know what happened."

"I will."

I rush to the school, quickly park, and head inside. When I approach the principal's office, there's an older woman there that appears to be an administrative assistant.

"Hi, I'm Beth O'Connell, here to see Principal Roberts."

She nods. "Yes, Ms. O'Connell, they're waiting for you. You can head right in."

I walk into an open office door and see a middle-aged woman with salt and pepper hair in a tight bun and glasses, sitting behind the desk. There's a man with dark hair in an expensive suit sitting with his back to me.

I smile at the woman as I hold out my hand. "You must be Principal Roberts. I don't think we've ever met. I'm Beth O'Connell."

As she shakes my hand, the man turns his head toward me wide-eyed. The air is almost knocked out of my lungs.

Dominic Mazzello.

The man who left me over four years ago with my dress around my waist. The man I was never able to erase from my memory. The man who left me barely able to be intimate with other men since that night. The married man who I currently can't look at without pangs of guilt washing over me for being the other woman in an adulterous relationship.

I was once the married woman who was cheated on. I know how it feels to have a philandering husband. The fact that I was on the other side of it still pains me all these years later. I hope his wife isn't coming. I couldn't possibly look at her.

The shock at seeing me is written all over his face. That face. Those eyes. *Oh, those eyes.*

He mostly looks the same, though now he has a short beard. It suits him. I suppose nothing would look bad on him. He's still the most perfect-looking man I've ever seen.

He breathes, "Beth."

I force a smile, trying to mask my emotions. "Hello, Dominic. It's nice to see you."

We stare at each other for a moment. Likely a moment too long.

Principal Roberts interrupts us. "Oh, I see you two know each other. That's wonderful. I hope we can keep this civilized."

The obvious and only place for me to sit is in a chair next to Dominic, so I do. I can smell him. He smells the same. Memories come flooding through my mind. Flashes of his face between my legs, covered in my juices. His tongue. That thick, naughty tongue. Him speaking to me in Spanish. I didn't know at the time what he was saying, but I knew it was dirty and I've needed it to get off ever since.

"Ms. O'Connell? Did you hear me?"

"Sorry, can you repeat that?" My mind was in the gutter.

The principal intertwines her own fingers in front of her on the desk. "As I was saying, it appears that Luke has a bit of a crush on Valentina. Normal stuff, especially for Luke."

Dominic asks, "What does that mean? Why *especially for Luke*?"

She smiles. "Luke is...well...he's..."

I interrupt. "Social. He's very social."

Principal Roberts nods. "Yes, that's a good way to put it. Luke is highly social for his age, particularly when it comes to the girls."

Dominic mumbles, "I knew it."

She continues, "He has a crush on Valentina, but she's been spending much of the past week making new friends. She's already quite popular."

I notice Dominic smile with pride.

"In particular, she's been spending time with Scotty Cooper."

I sigh. Dominic notices and looks at me in question. "Scotty is Reagan and Skylar's nephew. He and Luke aren't technically related, but the families are obviously extremely close. I hope it doesn't cause any issues."

He nods in understanding, though we're now staring at each other again. Wow, those eyes...

Principal Roberts clears her throat and we both snap our heads toward her. "Luke told Scotty to stay away from Valentina. Scotty is a laid-back boy, so he simply turned and walked away. Valentina then..."

Dominic interrupts, "What? What did she do?"

"She yelled at Luke. Loudly. They were screaming and arguing until the teachers broke them apart."

With his pointer finger and thumb, Dominic pinches the space between his eyebrows. "They're seven. Are we really having this conversation?"

She slowly nods. "It's the screaming and yelling we can't have. Both were taken to separate rooms to calm down. They were both quite upset. As I'm sure you can imagine, it's highly disruptive to the class, which is why we called you to come down here. We suggest you take them home for the day. Perhaps chat about not carrying on like that at school."

I feel like we're missing something. What set them off? I don't know Valentina, but Luke doesn't have a temper. He's not a yeller and screamer, especially with girls. It can't just be about her preferring Scotty to him.

"Do you know exactly what was said?"

She swallows, clearly uncomfortable. "Umm, well, there was apparently some mention by Valentina that Luke doesn't have a father. He grew quite agitated over it."

Tears form in my eyes. My poor baby. It's bad enough that his father is absent, but now kids at school are throwing it in his face.

Dominic places his head in his hands for a moment before turning it to me. "If it's true, I'm sorry she said that to him."

I nod. "Thank you. Why don't we just gather our kids and take them home? It sounds like it's been a long day for them."

Principal Roberts nods. "Why don't you two wait here? We'll get the kids and bring them to you. Perhaps they can resolve things before they leave so that they can start with a clean slate in the morning."

Before we can answer, she stands and leaves. I'm suddenly aware that I'm in a room alone with Dominic.

"Beth…"

I hold up my hand. "Don't. We have nothing to say to each other."

"Please just let me apologize for that night."

"We're a bit beyond that, and I think it's your wife you should be apologizing to, not me."

"Beth, I'm not married. I've been divorced for some time."

"Well I suppose I can understand why."

"It's not what you think. If you'll just let me explain."

"I'm not interested. It's ancient history. It doesn't matter anymore."

I hate that tears are welling in my eyes. God I'm weak.

He stands and walks over to me. I can feel my heart thumping in my chest. He rubs the backs of his fingers down my cheek. I close my eyes, despising that I like it. Despising how much his touch affects me.

We hear commotion in the hallway, and he pulls away from me. As soon as Luke sees me, tears start streaming down his cheeks and he runs to me. I scoop him up in my arms.

"I'm sorry, Mommy."

I hold him tight. "It's okay, baby. Why don't we go home and talk about it?"

I start walking to the door when I hear Dominic's voice. "Valentina, do you have something to say to Luke?"

"But Papa…"

In a stern voice, he says, "Valentina, tienes que disculparte!" *You have to apologize!*

Valentina looks down and mumbles, "I'm sorry for what I said, Luke."

Luke sniffles. "It's okay."

We walk out without another word to anyone. I just want to get Luke out of here.

When we get into the car, I turn back to him. "What happened?"

"I wanted her to be my girlfriend and she wanted Scotty."

"Luke, she's entitled to be interested in someone else."

"But she's pretty. All the pretty girls like me."

I sigh, knowing there's much more to the story. "Luke, tell me exactly what happened."

"I told her that she was going to be my girlfriend. She

said she likes Scotty more and went over to sit with him. I walked over and told him that she's mine, so he got up and left. She got upset and started yelling at me. Then I told her about how lucky she should feel because all the girls like me and I'm choosing her. She got mad. *Really* mad. First, she started yelling at me Spanish. I have no idea what she was saying. Then she said that I didn't know how to treat girls because I don't have a father."

I reach back and squeeze his hand. "I'm sorry for that last comment. It wasn't very nice. But you were wrong too. You have no right to demand that anyone be your girlfriend. You owe her an apology just like she gave you."

"No."

"Yes. It's the right thing to do."

He crosses his arms in defiance. "I'm not apologizing."

"Well then, no baseball until it happens." I turn my head and see Dominic clearly scolding Valentina in the parking lot. I turn back to Luke. "They're walking out now. Let's do the right thing."

Luke is mad, but baseball means everything to him. Baseball and spending that time with Trevor.

We get out of the car and walk across the parking lot to Dominic and Valentina. I crouch down to Valentina's height. "Valentina, thank you for apologizing to Luke. He told me the whole story. It sounds like he owes you an apology as well."

She narrows her eyes at Dominic, giving him an *I told you so* look.

I nod at Luke. "Go ahead."

He mumbles, "I'm sorry. I guess you can date Scotty if you want."

Dominic interrupts, "She won't be dating anyone until she's thirty."

I can't help but smile subtly at that.

I stand. "Good. Now you've both apologized. You can both accept it and move on. Why don't you go back to being friends?"

Dominic looks at me. "Yes, when someone apologizes, you should accept it and move on as friends. In fact, it's lunchtime. Why don't we all go out for pizza and celebrate our friendship?"

The kids both shout, "Yeah!"

I narrow my eyes at him, and he smirks. I suppose I cornered myself into that.

Luke looks up at me, "Can we?"

I know it's the right thing to do for the kids, so I reluctantly nod. Luke and Valentina cheer again.

Dominic smiles. "Let's go to the pizza restaurant right down the street. I have to be back later to pick up my son."

"You have a son too? How old is he?"

Valentina answers, "Matteo is three and a half."

Oh my god. He and his wife had another child after we were together. Was she home pregnant while he and I were making out in a hotel bathroom?

He whispers, "I know you're doing the math. I'll explain."

I don't know if I can do this. I turn to Luke, "Wouldn't you rather get lunch with Aunt Cassandra at my office? You can push all the buttons in the elevator."

He shakes his head and pouts. "You just said we could have pizza with Valentina. They have arcade games at that restaurant. I want to go there."

I blow out a breath. "Okay. We'll go for a quick lunch."

We agree to meet and make our way to our cars. I give myself a mental pep talk while driving the short distance.

Thirty minutes. I can handle being around him for thirty minutes.

We walk in. Dominic has already managed to order a pie for us as everyone slides into the booth.

Luke looks up at me. "Do you have quarters for the games?"

I reach into my purse and hand him a ten-dollar bill. "Get quarters for both of you. Split it evenly."

"Thanks, Mom." He turns to Valentina. "Come on. Let's go."

She breaks into a big smile as they both run to the arcade machines. I wish adults had the short memories that kids are able to have when it comes to contentious situations.

I turn to the man across from me. "She's beautiful, Dominic. Truly stunning." She is. She looks just like the feminine version of him.

He smiles. "Thank you. So is Luke. I met him the other day, Valentina's first day. I saw his eyes and immediately thought of you. They're the exact same unique shade of blue. I'm not surprised he's yours."

He places his hand over mine, but I pull it away. "Don't do that."

"I want to explain."

"There's nothing to explain. That night was very out of character for me, Dominic." I wave my fingers around. "I got swept up in you and your attractiveness."

He smiles. "You think I'm attractive?"

I give him an incredulous look. "I just…"

"Give me a minute to at least explain. Then you can go right back to hating me. I had a terrible marriage. We weren't compatible, we never were. I asked for a divorce. We were proceeding. I had moved out. We had already told

Valentina. She was a little young to understand, but she knew I lived somewhere else. She was spending nights in my new place. My ex-wife was drinking heavily at the time. One night she called me hysterical. I was worried for both her and Valentina's safety. I went over to help. One thing led to another, and things happened. It certainly didn't change anything for me. For us. Two months later was the night you and I met. You were so beautiful. You still are. I was completely taken with you. I couldn't help myself." He pauses, as if remembering the night. "The call that night was from her telling me she was pregnant with Matteo from that one and only night I spent with her in the previous year. I was in shock. I'm ashamed of how I left you. My mind was reeling. It's almost like I blacked out. I hate how I treated you. It still eats at me."

I'm silent. I have no words for this story.

"I was lost at the time. I should have immediately come to you and explained, but I was dealing with the fallout of everything."

"You didn't owe me an explanation."

"I did, and I still do. I also owe you an apology. The months that followed were terrible. I moved back in, thinking I needed to do it for my family. But in the end, I couldn't stay with her. I didn't love her. While I know growing up in a divorced home isn't ideal, I think growing up in a loveless home is even worse. I left for good before Matteo was even born."

I blow out a long breath. I'm not sure what for. Maybe sadness for what he's been through. Maybe relief in knowing I'm not a homewrecker. Maybe a little bit of both.

"Thank you for telling me. I'm sorry for what you dealt with. It sounds painful."

"It was a tough time, but things are better now. We've found a happy place for everyone."

"Why is Valentina switching schools mid-year, if you don't mind my asking?"

"My ex-wife's mother has fallen ill. Her mother is in Cuba, and she had to go and take care of her. I wouldn't allow her to take the children out of the country. She needs my agreement for that, and she wasn't getting it. I feel horrible that her mother is dying, but I'm not going to lose out on seeing my kids for months or even a full year until she returns. Once it was decided that they would be living with me, I realized that I needed them in a school closer to my home, one that has a daycare for Matteo, and one with an after-school care program."

"That makes sense. Well, good luck. Being a single parent without a present co-parent is no walk in the park."

"I take it your ex-husband isn't involved with Luke?"

I shake my head. "No. Not at all. We haven't seen him in months."

"What about financially?"

I shake my head, and he scowls.

"What kind of man doesn't take care of his family?"

"A shitty one. Honestly, I don't care about the money. I make way more money than he does anyway. The only thing I want from him is time for Luke, and he can't seem to even manage that. It's a struggle for Luke at times."

"And then my daughter rubbed salt in the wound."

"It's not ideal, but they're kids. They don't quite understand exactly what they're saying." I turn and look at them laughing and playing together. "They seem to have moved on."

He tilts his head to the side. "Can we move on?"

"Does it matter? We're not in each other's lives."

He briefly pauses, as if thinking. "I've been putting this off, given our history, but I need your legal expertise."

"Call Cassandra. You've worked with her before."

"I have. She can't get to it in our timeframe. Time is of the essence. Reagan told me to hire you specifically."

I close my eyes for a brief moment. "Send everything to my office in the morning. I'll take a look."

He smiles. It's breathtakingly beautiful. "Thank you."

Before anything else can be said, they bring our pizza, and the kids return.

I do my best to make it through lunch sitting across from the man I've never been able to get out of my mind, knowing that I'm about to work with him and still desperately attracted to him.

CHAPTER FOUR

DOMINIC

I look at Gabriela's face on the computer screen. "How's your mother doing?"

She shakes her head. "She's not well. When I came down here, I wasn't sure of the timeframe. It's going to be slowly drawn out. She's dying but it won't happen this month or next. She's so frail. I hate seeing her suffer this way."

"I'm sorry. I know firsthand how hard it is to watch your mother slowly die."

"I know you do. Thank you. The two of them will be reunited soon enough." My mother and Gabriela's were childhood best friends which carried through until the day my mother died.

"How's your father?"

She lets out a laugh. "You know how he is. He's barking out orders, yelling at everyone within a ten-mile radius, throwing his money and power around at the doctors and hospital as if it will cure her.

Always the puppet master, needing to pull all the strings." She rolls her dark brown eyes. "He's pissed as hell that the kids aren't with me. He's been ranting about it since I got here. How are they managing?"

I smile. "They're doing well. Valentina seems to have made many friends at her new school. Matteo is quiet, as always, but I think being around other children all day is best for him."

She shakes her head. "I still disagree. It makes him uncomfortable. You should have hired a nanny to stay home with him all day."

"It's uncomfortable because staying home is all he's ever known, with you refusing to properly socialize him."

"Dom, it's embarrassing to have the one kid in a playgroup who doesn't want to play with the others. It was hard for me."

"It's not really about what's best for you. It's about what's best for him. Kids need to socialize with other kids. It's an important part of their development. You can't lock him away forever."

She sighs. "I didn't call to fight, especially about this never-ending topic. I don't have it in me. Have the kids Facetime me when they wake up in the morning."

"I'm sorry. You're right. I will."

TEN YEARS AGO

I hold my mother's hand, knowing she's about to take her last few breaths. Tears are streaming down my face.

"Te quiero, Mama." *I love you, Mom.*

She's barely able to speak, but wheezes out, "Hacer una cosa por mi??" *Do one thing for me?*

"Lo que sea." Anything.

"Cásate con Gabriela Navarro. Es una buena mujer y será una buena esposa. Su madre es mi amiga antigua. La union de nuestras dos familias significa algo, Dominic. Es todo lo que siempre hemos querido. Es mi ultimo deseo." *Marry Gabriela Navarro. She's a good woman and will make a good wife. Her mother is my oldest friend. The joining of our two families means something, Dominic. It's all we've ever wanted. It's my dying wish.*

I close my eyes. This isn't what I want. I don't even like Gabriela as a person, let alone a wife. But how can I deny my mother right now? How do I tell her that I'm not the marrying type? I don't think I ever will be. It would break her heart. Regular women can't handle the way I am. My needs.

She cups my face. "Harás esto por mí?" *You'll do this for me?*

I do the only thing a son can do at this moment. "Sí, Mama." *Yes, Mom.*

PRESENT

I walk into Beth's office for our scheduled appointment. I sent her over the information on the Wallingford acquisition last week. She had her assistant call mine to set up this meeting.

Her assistant shows me into her office and informs me that Beth will return in a few minutes.

I walk around and look at her pictures. I inwardly laugh at the difference between us. She has dozens of family photos. I keep none in my office. I don't like my co-workers knowing anything about my life. I have photos of Valentina and Matteo on my phone when I need to see their faces.

Almost all her photos are of Luke, though there arc a few of Reagan and her whole big family. I know that Reagan has two sisters. Obviously, Skylar. I think the other is named Harley. I know they each have two kids. I also know that her mother married Jackson Knight a few years ago, who's a very well-known Philadelphia developer. I've had drinks with him a few times in the past. He's a good man. He has three adult sons, one of whom I met and is married to Cassandra.

I look at the big family picture. It's on a beach. It looks like Jackson's two other sons are married too, both with one child. At least when this picture was taken. There's another blonde woman and blond man. Jade is standing with them. That must be her father and stepmother.

I pick up the frame. They're all laughing hysterically in the photo. It's nice. They seem close. Beth has a huge grin. I run my finger over her face. She's so beautiful.

"Snooping in my office?"

I turn and smile. Beth is in a conservative blue skirt suit, though it still hugs her sexy figure. She's the epitome of elegance and class.

I hold up the photo. "This is a nice picture. Everyone looks so happy."

Her face lights up. "It's a happy family. I'm lucky to have them all in my life."

"Remind me how Jade is related? I know she's a cousin, but I'm not sure how."

"Her father, Declan, and Darian's deceased first husband were brothers. So Jade is first cousins with Reagan and her sisters. Ironically, Declan's also married to Jackson's ex-wife, Melissa. Jade didn't grow up with her cousins though. Apparently, Declan and his brother didn't speak for many years leading up to his death. They only found out about Jade a little over four years ago. Just before you and I met."

"That's about when Jade started working at Daulton."

She nods. "Yes, they offered her a job the day they met her."

"She's excellent at what she does in our design department."

"That's nice to hear. She's a bit of a wild child, but it's good to know she gets it done in the office."

I laugh. "She most definitely is wild, but when it comes to work, she's just about the best around."

Beth smiles. "Good for her. I know she had a tough childhood. I'm happy things are working out for her."

I didn't know that, but I don't prod. It's not my business. Frankly, I'd rather not know.

She motions for me to sit on her couch, and I do.

She grabs a file from her desk and then sits next to me, opening the file as she does. I can smell her perfume. It's the same as she was wearing the night we met. I'd recognize it anywhere. It's uniquely her and so sexy.

She looks at me with the prettiest blue eyes in the world. "I've reviewed everything."

"And?"

"Stock prices are going to increase dramatically if this deal goes through."

I nod. "I agree."

"From what I can tell, the employee resistance probably comes from fear of job loss. If the company moves international, they can hire cheaper laborers. That's what's driving your first problem."

I shake my head. "No, the president is adamant that production remains here."

"Has she reassured the employees?"

"I don't know. I doubt it. It's a big company. It's not like they can all meet in the conference room."

"I suggest doing that. She could always sweeten the pot with stock options for them. As for shareholders, there's an upcoming meeting. As the liaison, you should be the one to talk at the meeting. The owner will be seen as wanting a sweetheart buyout deal. That's why you need to talk about the practicalities of the acquisition. Appeal to their greedy side. Lay it all out. This is a smart acquisition. They stand to earn a huge return on their investments. Make them see it."

I think for a moment. I hadn't considered talking myself. An idea occurs to me. "Will you come with me? You can tell them everything you just told me."

She's so close to me. Her scent is wreaking havoc

on my body. The need to touch her is overwhelming. I can't help but reach over and rub her face with the backs of my fingers. Her breathing picks up and she closes her eyes and whispers, "It's not a good idea."

I remove my hand. What was I thinking? "You're right. We shouldn't be together."

"I meant that it's not a good idea for me to go to the meeting. No one likes lawyers. They don't trust them."

I let out a laugh. "That's true."

She bites her lip. I'm jealous. I want to bite that lip. Hard. "What did you mean when you said we *shouldn't* be together?"

"Nothing. We're getting off course. I'm going to have the president arrange an employee tele-call. She can explain the job security to them. I'll let her know of your suggestion to offer stock options."

"If you do a tele-call with the stockholders, I'll dial in and listen if you want. I can have one of my guys put together charts with some numbers for them. The shareholders really do stand to gain from this deal."

She strategizes for another five minutes, but I don't hear a word. She's so beautiful and so smart. And sexy, in a natural way. She doesn't try to be sexy, she just is. I'm completely taken with her. Attracted to her. I would give anything to bend her over that desk and have my way with her. I bet she has the best ass. My cock starts to harden at the thought, and I have to shift my papers to cover it.

"Does that work?"

I have no idea what she just said, but I nod in agreement.

WHEN I LEAVE HER OFFICE, I dial the number I've called so many times that I have it memorized.

A familiar, smooth voice answers. "Hush Hush. How may I help you?"

"Crystal?"

"Mr. Mazzello. It's sublime to hear from you."

"I'm coming in. Is there someone around with dark hair and blue eyes?"

"Of course, Mr. Mazzello. It's been the same for four years. We're well-versed on how to keep our favorite customer happy."

"Good. I'll be there in fifteen minutes. I want something a little different today. I'll explain when I get there. Just make sure you have what I want."

"Of course. Whatever you need."

CHAPTER FIVE

BETH

Sunday night family dinners at Darian and Jackson's house have become a staple in our life. This family is big and keeps growing. Poor Darian is on her third or fourth dining room table since Luke and I started coming.

I'm always invited. When my mother died, I thought it was going to be just me and Luke moving forward. And then Cassandra accepted us into her life, and I gained this family, which has grown into nearly thirty people, seemingly growing more every few months.

Jackson and Darian have an enormous playroom for all the kids. They usually eat before the adults and then head to the playroom. Luke is in there. It's nice for him to have this time with all of them.

The conversation topics with this family often turn inappropriate for children, so it's best that the kids are out of earshot.

I'm at the table with all the adults. It's Jackson and Darian, her three daughters and their spouses, Cassandra and Trevor, his two brothers and their spouses, Jade, Declan, and Melissa.

Reagan and Skylar are both pregnant. Most of the discussion tonight is centered around that, as well as a big fishing trip Jackson has planned for him, his sons, and his sons-in-law.

Darian smiles at me. "Beth, are you seeing anyone? You know they'd always be welcome here for dinner."

"Thank you. I appreciate it. I'm not seeing anyone right now and it would probably take someone pretty special for me to introduce him to Luke. I've never introduced a man I've dated to Luke. I haven't come close to finding anyone special. Dating at my age is just brutal."

Melissa scoffs. "Try doing it at fifty. One hundred and eighteen first dates, Beth. I went on one hundred and eighteen first dates after my divorce before I found my forever man."

Declan growls. "Can we not discuss that? I'm not comfortable thinking about you with that many other men."

Declan is alpha male personified. He's possessive over Melissa, sometimes to the point of making things uncomfortable, but she seems to enjoy it and teases him about it constantly.

She simply smiles and winks at me.

I let out a laugh. "I definitely haven't been on that many dates since my divorce. Not even close. Good men are hard to find."

Cassandra shakes her head. "That's because you wear granny nightgowns to bed. You can't attract good men wearing that crap."

"I'd have to want someone in my bed first before they'd get to the point that they'd see the *granny nightgowns.*

Regardless, you threw away all my nightgowns and replaced them with lingerie that would make most strippers blush. By the way, my housekeeper does not care for any of our new purchases. She refuses to put them away. She leaves them on top of my dresser. It's her passive-aggressive way of showing me that she disapproves."

Cassandra laughs. "You have a judgmental laundress?"

I nod. "Apparently."

"You could just sleep naked."

"That feels weird to me." I look around. "What do you all wear to bed?"

They all smile at each other.

I shake my head. "You *all* sleep naked, don't you?"

They universally nod.

"Maybe it's because you have someone with you."

Jade interrupts, "Nope. I only have someone in my bed half the time, and I always sleep naked."

Declan sighs. "That better not be true. No one should be in your bed. Ever."

Jade is twenty-two but Declan treats her like she's eleven. He hates the thought of her dating, which only eggs her on to push his buttons that much more. If there's one thing I'm certain of, it's that Jade doesn't spend many nights alone. Declan is in denial.

She shrugs. "It could be worse. My friend Pandora injured her wrist from masturbating too much. She's legit in physical therapy for it."

There are a bunch of laughs throughout the table. I look at her in shock. "Can that really happen?" Shit. I engage in more than a healthy amount of self-pleasure.

She nods. "A hundred percent. She felt something pop in her wrist when she was softening the peach a few weeks ago. I almost peed my pants when she told me. Can you imagine the PT prescription?" In a deep, authoritative voice, she says, "Due to excessive self-stimulation, Pandora Jones requires two months of wrist strengthening physical therapy." She shakes her head. "It's epic. I'll never let her live this one down."

Trevor nods. "Masturbation injuries are real. I have a friend who injured his elbow. He had to go lefty for, like, two months until it healed."

Cassandra looks at me. "Careful, Beth, that could be you."

I give her a giant, fake smile. "Thanks for the warning, sis. If I get injured, it will be due to the ridiculous vibrator you bought me."

Jade's eyes light up. "Which one did you get her?"

Cassandra answers, "The Lelo Soraya. It's big and has a four-hour battery. I figured she'd need the longevity."

I narrow my eyes at her.

Reagan chimes in. "Have you tried the Lelo Ora? It mimics oral. I like that one."

Jackson stands. "Gentlemen, we've clearly reached the inevitable part of the evening where the ladies smash all normal societal boundaries. Why don't we clear the table while they continue this scintillating conversation."

Declan whispers something in Melissa's ear while all the guys clear the plates and make their way out of earshot.

Harley says, "I'm still a fan of the ole trusty Bullet. I guess I'm old school."

Skylar smiles. "I have one that's heated. It's more real that way."

Cassandra turns to Melissa. "What did Declan whisper to you on the way out?"

Melissa smiles and then looks at Jade for permission.

Jade rolls her eyes. "I don't care. Tell them whatever craziness my father said."

"He said something about me being the only woman here who doesn't need a vibrator."

Cassandra laughs. "He's jealous of your vibrator?"

Melissa nods. "You know Declan. He's jealous of everyone and every*thing*. I have to hide it from him. He's already thrown out two."

The conversation comes to an abrupt end when Luke runs into the room. "Mommy, can Valentina and Scotty come over for a playdate tomorrow?"

I guess their love triangle is a thing of the past.

"Sure, sweetie. I'll text Valentina's dad to make sure." Luke smiles and runs back out of the room.

I turn to Harley. "Can Scotty come over as well?"

Harley nods. "That would be great. Thank you. Is Valentina the new girl I've been hearing about?"

"Yes." I look at Reagan. "She's Dominic's daughter. She seems to have gained instant popularity, especially with the boys."

Reagan lets out a laugh. "Does she look like Dominic?"

I nod. "She does. She's a beautiful little girl. Luke is quite enamored with her."

Cassandra smiles. "Is he heeding Trevor's advice and playing it cool? Drawing her in?"

"Nope. Just the opposite. He's got a crush on her, and she has a crush on Scotty."

Harley sighs, "Oh boy."

I smile. "They're seven. I think they're all friends. I'm glad they all want to spend time together tomorrow. That's how it should be."

DOMINIC

My father is over for dinner tonight. He's aged so much since my mother passed. His once dark hair is now mostly gray. She was the love of his life. The light in his world. He's a bit of a lost soul without her.

He's a wonderful grandfather, doting on Valentina, but he struggles with Matteo's lack of communication and lack of warmth. After dinner, the kids watch a movie so my father and I can have a drink together.

We sit in my study, each with a glass of bourbon and a cigar. It's a bit of a Sunday night tradition for him and me.

He takes a slow puff of the Cuban cigars I keep on hand for both of us. After he exhales, he says, "Valentina seems to like her new school. I think it was a good change for her."

I nod. "I agree. It's a much better school. She's very smart. The curriculum is more advanced. I think it will be good for Matteo too."

"Why won't he talk? I don't understand it. You were chatty at that age. And he's so cold. I can barely get him to hug me. That's not the way this family is."

I run my fingers through my beard. Dealing with Matteo is hard for my father. He lacks patience. "I don't know, Papa. I think Gabriela made a mistake keeping him home with her and away from other kids. I'm hoping his new daycare will help in that regard. I'm hoping spending more time with me will do the same. You know Gabriela isn't the warmest person. Perhaps he's just a bit more like her."

"Gabriela was never the right woman for you."

I sigh. "I can't disagree." We've had this conversation a million times throughout the years.

"She's a cold bitch."

I let out a laugh. "Don't hold back. Tell me how you really feel."

He smiles. "You were being a good son to your mother, honoring her dying wish. But I told you at the time you didn't have to marry her. I knew she wasn't right for you."

"I know, but I don't regret it. I have Valentina and Matteo. They mean everything to me."

He nods in approval. "You're an amazing father and a great man. I'm very proud of you." He reaches over and squeezes my hand.

My hearts swells as I squeeze his in return. "Thank you. I learned from the best."

He leans back and takes another puff of his cigar before asking, "Are you dating anyone?"

I hate this question. How am I supposed to answer it? No, I don't date because the type of woman you'd bring home and the type of woman that satisfies my needs can never be one and the same. And I'm a little obsessed with a woman I met over four years ago, who's way too good for me. I would never drag her into my world.

"I don't have time for that right now. I'm focused on the kids."

He lets out a small laugh. "Dominic, I'm your father. I may not be young, but I'm no fool. You can't bullshit me. You're a man with needs. You're no saint. You never were."

I smile. He may be getting older, but he's still sharp. "Satisfying my needs and dating are two separate things."

"Not if you find the right person. The woman that satisfies your needs in and out of the bedroom. I found that."

I scrunch my face in disgust. "Ugh. Please don't talk about Mama that way."

"Why not? That's an important part of a marriage. It's perfectly healthy."

"I don't need to think of you two like that."

He rolls his eyes. "There's no one that strikes your fancy?"

I'm quiet. Too quiet. He smiles. "Is it someone new or the woman you've been pining after for years?"

I take another sip of my bourbon. "I saw *her*. Coincidentally, her son and Valentina are in the same class."

"Tell me more about this mystery woman that captivated you four years ago."

"There's nothing to tell. She's too good for me. She's sweet and wholesome. I won't go there."

"Hmm."

"What does that mean?"

"It means that you can't control the heart. It wants what it wants. You're a good man. No one is too good for you. Everyone sees that but you."

My phone buzzes in my pocket and I pull it out. I can't help but smile when I see who it's from.

> Beth: Sorry to bother you on a Sunday. Luke was hoping Valentina could come over for a playdate tomorrow. I can pick her up from school when I get Luke.

I immediately reply.

Me: I'm sure she'd love that. Thank you. What are you up to?

Beth: I'm at Darian's house. Reagan's mother. Another crazy dinner here.

Me: Why is it crazy?

Beth: You've seen how Reagan and Carter are. Now multiply it by ten, and you know what goes on here. Among tonight's many wholesome dinner table topics were self-pleasure and whether the women here sleep naked or not.

My dick twitches at the thought of Beth naked in bed touching herself. I know what I'll be imagining in bed later tonight.

Me: And where did you land on your sleep attire, Ms. O'Connell?

Beth: Undecided at this time.

Me: Well, I highly recommend naked sleeping. There are studies that suggest it's better for your overall health.

Beth: Is that really true?

Me: I'll send you a link to the studies. You can't argue with science.

Beth: LOL. Maybe I'll give it a go.

Me: Your sheets will thank me.

"I assume that's her?"
I look up. "Huh?"

"You've been smiling for five straight minutes while texting with someone."

"Oh. Sorry. She's just inviting Valentina over for a playdate."

He nods in understanding and smiles because he knows he busted me. "You're allowed to be happy, son. Don't forget that."

Later that night I'm in bed scrolling through my texts with Beth. She's so adorable. I find myself wondering how different my life would have been if I met her when I was younger, before I became hardened to women and relationships. Before the monster in me was born.

I see my door open slowly and Valentina walks in. She's wearing pajamas and her hair is messy. I look up at her. "Are you okay?"

She frowns. "My mind won't turn off. Can I sleep with you?"

I lift up my blankets and she crawls into bed with me. She nestles into my chest, and I put my arm around her. I pull the stray strands of her hair away from her face. "Do you want to talk about it?"

"It's a boy issue."

Oh shit. Where's Gabriela when I need her?

"Do you want to call Mama? She's probably awake."

"No. I'd rather talk to you."

I swallow and attempt to brace myself. "Go ahead."

"Luke said he wants to kiss me, but I want to kiss Scotty."

You've got to be fucking kidding me. Remain calm. Remain calm.

I take a few breaths before answering. "Sweetie, you're seven. There's no kissing boys at seven."

"How old do you have to be?"

"Well, you can't kiss unless you're officially boyfriend and girlfriend, and you can't be boyfriend and girlfriend until you're an adult. So when you're eighteen, you can have your first kiss."

She pinches her eyebrows together. "Oh, I didn't know that."

I mentally pat myself on the back. Parenting win.

I continue, "But you always only kiss the boys you want. No one else tells you who to kiss. Is that clear?"

I see her little mind processing. "Okay. I'll tell them what you said."

I kiss her head. "Good girl."

"Papa, do you have a girlfriend?"

I shake my head. "No, baby. I don't." And I never will.

"Don't you want to kiss someone?"

I smile as I squeeze her. I pepper her head with kisses. "I save my special kisses for you because you're the most special girl in the world."

She giggles.

We chat a little longer until she eventually falls asleep in my arms. I lay awake thinking about her question about me wanting to kiss someone. I would love to live in a world where Beth could be my girlfriend, but that's not the world I live in anymore. It hasn't been for a long time.

CHAPTER SIX

TWENTY-FOUR YEARS AGO

DOMINIC

"Where are you going, cariño?" *Honey*. I pull her back into bed with me and cuddle her naked body to mine.

She shifts onto her back and looks up at me with the smile that makes my world spin. She runs her fingers through my hair. "I have to get to the studio. Professor Whittaker already despises me. I don't need to give him another reason to hate me. And you have a game today. You need to get going too."

She lifts her head and kisses my jaw. It's a fleeting moment of tenderness from her. At least in the past few weeks. Before that, she was always so loving. She's the sweetest woman I've ever met. That's what I fell for. Well, that and the fact she's beautiful.

She's become a bit distant, at times seeming like

she's not present. I think she's falling in with the wrong people at school and they're a bad influence on her.

I use my strength advantage to pull her under the blankets, cocooning her inside. "Two more minutes. I need to get my fix."

"Fine. Two minutes—and I'm counting—but then I really have to go, and so do you."

I smile as I sink my face into her neck and take in her fruity scent. I can't help but get aroused. She does it to me all the time. Her smell, her gorgeous face, her perfect body, it all does it to me.

She shakes her head and giggles, wiggling her hip. "I feel that. It's not happening this morning, love."

"Just a quickie?"

Her honey-brown eyes give me an incredulous look. "You don't do quick." She pretends to look at her watch. "Ninety more seconds left before I get up."

I begin kissing her neck, and after a few seconds she turns her body to mine and moans. Her fingers start roaming my body. I know I've got her right where I want her.

The door to my dorm room flies open with a loud thud, and Sebastian walks in wearing last night's clothes, with his dark hair looking like it hasn't been brushed in a week. He looks at us. "Shit. Sorry. You're supposed to put a cowboy hat on the door when she's here."

I roll my eyes. "That's so cliché. I'm not doing that."

"I do it all the time."

"I know. Trust me, I know."

He gives me a self-satisfied smirk. Cocky fucker.

"We have to be in the locker room in fifteen minutes. We need to get going."

I plop back down and sigh. There goes my morning happiness. I have no chance now.

She sits up with the blankets tucked under her armpits. "Seb, can you give me like two minutes to get dressed? I'll be quick. I promise."

He narrows his eyes and points at us. "No funny business. I'm coming back in exactly two minutes no matter what. I've been his roommate all year. I know loverboy can't finish in two minutes."

She laughs. "Marathon man promises to keep his hands off me."

Sebastian nods, grabs a change of clothes, and walks out.

I pull her to me one last time, but she pulls away and stands in my dorm room completely naked. Fuck, she's hot. She's tiny but has full breasts and a full ass I love to grab. Her silky, long brown hair with blue streaks hangs all the way to her ass. Her skin is golden and smooth. She's like a doll. A perfect doll.

"You're so beautiful, cariño." I reach over and run my hand up her leg.

She smacks my hand. "And you're trying to get me back in bed, sweet talker."

I smile. "Is it working?"

She narrows her eyes at me. "No. I'm leaving."

"Are you coming to my game today?"

She slides into her jeans and a T-shirt. "I'll try. I'm behind on this project. A certain sexy man keeps me in bed for hours."

She leans over and kisses my lips one last time. "I'll see you later, love. Have a good game."

I nod and she heads out. Sebastian makes his way back in while I'm getting dressed.

I can't help the smile on my face. He shakes his head. "Cool it, man. You're obsessed with her. You're too young for that. You're almost as good-looking as me. You could be scoring with a new chick every night like I do. Why dip in the same well twice?"

I shrug. "Because I'm in love with her. I don't want anyone else."

"You're nineteen. She's hot and is a good lay. Relax with the love talk." He mumbles, "She's gonna fuck with your head."

"Why do you say that?"

"She's weird. I saw her hanging with the hippies on campus getting loaded the other day. You're an athlete. You can't be around that kind of shit. Dom, you might get drafted. You could actually play professional baseball one day. You can't get mixed up with someone like her. She's sexy and has a banging body, but she's bad news."

I'm getting angry. "Stop it. She's not bad news. She's the best thing that ever happened to me."

He places his hand on my shoulder. "I'm your best friend. I want to shoot straight with you. She's not the best thing that ever happened to you. She could be your undoing though. Focus on baseball. There might be professional scouts at the game today. They're here to watch you pitch. Your dreams are about to come true. Don't let a tight, wet pussy derail you."

I hit his hand off me. "Don't talk about her like that. I love her. She'll be my wife one day."

He runs his hands through his hair. "What? You're fucking nuts. Take a breath. You're young. Enjoy the good sex and then let it go when it's time." He shakes his head. "Come on, let's head down to the field and warm up. I told Kevin to get breakfast for us since we don't have time."

I spend the whole game looking in the stands, but she never comes. Gabriela Navarro was there, as she always is, but not my girl. Gabriela was smiling and waving every time I looked that way. I think she thought I was looking at her. I wasn't.

Her mother and mine are best friends. They live in hope that we'll end up together. That will never happen. They think she's sweet and innocent, but I know for a fact she's not. It's all a facade with her.

I also notice a lot of Major League Baseball scouts at the game. I'm proud that they're here to see me.

I speak with two of them after the game. They tell me that they're thinking about drafting me this year. I can't believe my lifelong dream of playing professional baseball is about to come true.

I can't wait to tell my girl. I head straight to her house after the game. She's a year older than me so she doesn't live in the dorms. She lives in off-campus housing with six other girls.

I arrive at the house, and it looks like there's already a party going on. The music is blasting, and people are coming in and out of the front door.

I walk in the house to the now louder beat of music and smoke-filled air. The scent of pot is overwhelming.

I head into the kitchen where I see her best friend, Regina. She's trashed, sitting with a group of people sharing a bong. She smiles at me with glassy eyes. "Hey, loverboy. She's in her room."

I nod. "Thanks, Reggie."

I make my way upstairs to her bedroom. I hear her laugh before I see her. I love her laugh. It's so genuine and carefree.

I open her door and am shocked by what I see. She's sitting on the floor with her back against her bed. There's one guy next to her smoking something, and a different guy sitting on the other side of her, kissing her neck.

She looks up at me when I walk in. Her eyes are completely bloodshot. With a big smile, she reaches for me and says, "Dom, my Latin lover, I *need* you."

I pull her up, as she can barely stand on her own. I grab her face, so our eyes meet. She's totally out of it. "What's going on here? Who are these guys? What did you take?"

She leans into me and grabs my cock. "Just a little Ecstasy. It makes sex amazing. With you, it will be next level amazing." She thinks she's whispering, but she's not, when she says, "I want to suck that big dick of yours and then feel it inside me all night."

The two guys in the room start laughing.

I shake my head. "I'm not having sex with you while you're like this."

She reaches into her pocket and grabs a few pills, placing them in my hand. "Take them, love. You haven't experienced sex until you've done it on Ecstasy."

I'm steaming mad at her, but I don't want to leave her here in this condition with these two guys.

I put the pills in my pocket and throw her over my shoulder. She screeches but then starts laughing and smacks my ass over and over.

"Dom, you have the best ass. I stare at it when you're not looking." She giggles again.

I walk down the stairs and toward the front door with her still over my shoulder. I need to get her out of here.

As soon as I walk out the front door, there's a bright light in my face. "Freeze. Don't move. Put the woman down and get your hands in the air where I can see them."

He lowers the flashlight enough for me to see that it's a police officer.

CHAPTER SEVEN

PRESENT

DOMINIC

I was slammed at work today. I needed to stay late to deal with a few things. I hated to ask, but I did text Beth about taking Matteo too when she picked up Luke and Valentina. She happily acquiesced. I told her to call me if he made a fuss, but she wasn't worried, and I never heard from her.

I texted that I was on my way. She said they're all working on a puzzle, and she gave me the code to her front door so I can simply go inside.

I walk into her house and it's what I expected, warm and cozy, just like her. It's shockingly quiet at first until I hear a bunch of chatter coming from another room toward the back of the house. I walk in the opening to the room and nearly suck in a breath at what I see.

Valentina, Luke, and Scotty are on the floor happily contemplating a huge puzzle. Beth is sitting on the sofa with Matteo cuddled in her lap, reading him a book.

He's melting into Beth, holding her free arm that's around him with one hand, and stroking a cat with the other. He's hanging on every word she says. I've never seen him like this with anyone, let alone a stranger. Not even Gabriela or me.

This is the first time I've seen Beth dressed casually. Her hair is up in a messy bun, and she's removed her makeup. She is legitimately the most effortlessly stunning woman I've ever seen in my life.

She smiles at Matteo, and he smiles back. I think my heart skips a beat.

She eventually notices me. "Oh, Dominic. I didn't hear you come in."

"I didn't want to disturb you all. It looks like you're having fun."

She wraps both arms around Matteo and squeezes him tight. I hold my breath, waiting for him to freak out, but it doesn't come. He smiles and nuzzles into her.

She kisses his cheek. "This little lovebug is so cuddly. I forgot what it was like to have one this age where they want so much affection. I've missed it."

I swallow hard, unable to answer. Lovebug, cuddly, and affectionate are words that have *never* been used to describe Matteo, but he seems extremely content. In fairness to him, if I were wrapped in her arms, I'd be happy too.

She looks up at me. "There's an open bottle of wine in the kitchen if you want a glass."

"Thank you, but I should take them and get them dinner."

She smiles. "I already fed them. I left a plate for you in the kitchen. Help yourself."

Before I can answer, I hear the front door open and close. A woman walks in. A woman that looks exactly like a slightly younger version of Darian Knight. A woman I immediately recognize from the photo in Beth's office. She turns to me. "You must be Dominic, Valentina's father. I don't think we've officially met." She holds out her hand. "I'm Harley, Scotty's mom. You work with my sisters."

I nod as I shake her hand. "I do. It's nice to finally meet you."

"You too. Scotty adores Valentina."

"The kids have all been so welcoming to her."

She smiles and then looks at Scotty. "We should get going. Daddy and Ellie are in the car." She turns to Beth. "Thank you for having him. I hope he was well-behaved."

Beth lets out a laugh. "Always. He's an angel."

Scotty thanks Beth too, and he and Harley leave.

Beth looks down at Matteo. "I'm going to go get your dad's dinner. Do you want to help your sister with the puzzle?"

He nods.

"Can you hold onto Trex for me? He seems to like you."

Matteo smiles and nods again as he moves to sit next to Valentina, never letting go of the cat.

Beth rises and walks toward the kitchen. I follow her in. "Thank you for this."

She shrugs. "It's not a big deal. Us single parents

need to stick together and help each other."

"I'm new to it being full-time, so thank you."

"My pleasure." She pours two glasses of wine and hands me a plate of food.

"This is great. I haven't had a home-cooked meal in months."

"I'm not superwoman. It's takeout."

I laugh as we both sit. "It looks perfect." I pause for a moment as I sip my wine. "You're very good with him."

"Matteo?"

"Yes."

"He's such a sweetheart. He makes it easy."

"Actually, he doesn't. I've never seen him that warm to anyone, my ex-wife and me included."

Her face drops. "I didn't mean to overstep."

"You didn't. Thank you. It was wonderful to see him that way. It's good to know he has it in him. If you get him to speak, you officially *will* be superwoman."

"I didn't realize it. I thought he was just being shy because he didn't know me."

I shake my head. "It's a little deeper than that. His doctors don't seem to think it's anything more than social anxiety. Despite my protests, my ex-wife wouldn't socialize him. I think that's part of it. She's also a bit cold."

"How were you married to a cold woman? When I met you, you were anything but cold. You were incredibly warm."

She places her hand over her mouth in embarrassment. "I'm sorry. That slipped. It's not my business."

I shake my head. "It's okay. Yes, I consider myself warm. We weren't a match. Let's just say that she's nothing like you."

She pinches her eyebrows together, as if in thought. "He's great with Trex, our cat. Valentina said you don't have any pets. Have you ever considered getting one?"

"No. It's hard with the kids normally splitting time between our houses. Why?"

"I think they're supposed to help kids with anxiety. There is a lot of science on it. It's soothing. Perhaps that's why he was comfortable here. He definitely latched on to Trex right away. I originally got the cat when my ex-husband stopped spending time with Luke. I think he helped Luke cope."

"I never considered it. Perhaps I'll look into a pet. That might be a good idea."

She smiles. It warms my heart.

I can't help but take her hand in mine. It's soft and feminine. I see her cheeks flush and her breathing picks up. She's as affected by my touch as much as I am by hers. I get a thrill from that. She's staring at my lips. She wants me to kiss her. I desperately want to.

But then I look at her trusting, sweet face and pull my hand away. "I'm sorry. I shouldn't have done that."

"I wasn't complaining, Dominic." She visibly swallows. "I'm...I'm still very attracted to you." She moves her eyes down, as if she's embarrassed by it.

I tilt her chin back up so our eyes meet and give her a small smile. "I'm attracted to you too, princesa, but I'm not the right man for you. You're a kind, amazing woman. You should find a nice guy who will commit to you and treat you well. I'm not him."

"You seem nice to me."

She's so beautiful and innocent when she says that. She has no idea.

"I'm not. I have issues. You deserve better."

She's quiet for a moment. "Maybe you're right. I don't know that I've ever been with a nice guy who treats me well." She smiles in a way that doesn't quite reach those beautiful eyes of hers and sarcastically adds, "Maybe I should find one and give it a go."

"Your ex wasn't nice?"

"Nope. Even at our best, we were never great, and he was *never* nice to me. I was just a kid when we started dating. I didn't know any better. It was doomed from the start, but I was too young and naïve to see it."

She motions toward the room where the kids are doing the puzzle. "He doesn't make time for Luke. He's in and out of his life. I'm sure it's confusing for Luke. You know what pisses me off? He'll be gone from our lives for months at a time, and then he'll just walk in the front door like he owns the place. No call ahead. No knocking. He'll simply walk in and plop down on the couch as if he owns the place."

"Maybe it's time to change the locks."

"As you know, it's a code, which happens to be Luke's birthday. Part of me feels bad changing it because he should have access to Luke, but the disrespect drives me nuts."

"If I were you, I'd change the code."

"Maybe I should, but I still hold out hope for a relationship between him and Luke."

I let out a small laugh. "Like I said, you're too sweet for me."

CHAPTER EIGHT

BETH

Dominic is coming to my office for another meeting today. The other night was confusing. He mentioned being attracted to me but said he's no good for me. I don't understand why. I want to find out. There's a chemistry between us. I feel it when I'm around him. He must feel it too.

An attractive lawyer named Shawn was in my office yesterday. He was charming and asked me to have dinner tonight. I accepted because I had no reason not to, but it was halfhearted. He's got dark hair and chocolate-brown eyes like Dominic, but it's just not the same. The undeniable attraction isn't the same.

It's hard to explain. When I'm around Dominic, something happens to my body that doesn't happen around other men. All my senses are on high alert in his presence. I feel my temperature rising. I simply look at him and know I would give anything at that moment to have him kiss me, to feel his body on mine.

My assistant buzzes me that Dominic is here. I look down at myself. I'm in a classy, white pantsuit, and it's flattering, but not sexy. Damn. I should have worn something different, but I'm not sure I own anything that fits the bill. Somehow Cassandra dresses business sexy every single day. I need to enlist her to help me.

He walks in and I stare openmouthed. The suit company should pay him to wear their clothes. He's just so handsome.

He gives me a sexy smile, undoubtedly knowing what I'm thinking. He then looks me up and down. "You look beautiful."

"Thank you." I point toward my sofa. "Have a seat so we can get started." We could definitely do this sitting across from each other at my desk, but I'd rather sit next to him. I want to be close to him again.

For the next hour, we review strategies for his acquisition. He manages to touch my leg, my arm, and my back. I'm not sure if it's intentional or not, but it's driving me crazy. I wonder if he's like this with everyone or if it's just me. I want to believe it's the latter.

I can't help but shift my body toward his. The pull toward him is magnetic.

He grabs my hand. "Princesa, I feel so drawn to you. I want you to know that I'm holding back for your own good. It's not easy for me."

"I don't understand. If we both feel something, don't you want to explore it?"

He blows out a long breath. "I'm too much for a normal woman like you to handle." He rubs his thumb along my knee sending chills to scatter all over my body. Doesn't he notice how much his touch affects me?

He takes a few long breaths as if carefully

contemplating whatever it is he's about to say. "I'm not *normal* boyfriend material. I don't date or do relationships at all. To be perfectly honest, I like it rough. *Very* rough. I need it often. *Very* often. Along with a few other kinks, I'm just not right for someone like you. You're perfect and sweet. I'm anything but. You're the kind of girl you take home to your family. I'm the kind of man who should be kept a dirty secret."

I'm not sure what to say to all of that. I feel insulted, though I don't think he means it that way. "Did your ex-wife like all of that too?"

He shakes his head. "No, not even close. Not that I ever really wanted anything with her. We had a marriage of convenience, not love. Regular women don't like what I do. That's why I can't get involved with you. I can't have a normal relationship. I never have."

"You've *never* been in a real relationship?"

He looks pained. "Once, but it was a long time ago and I swore to myself never again."

He's been hurt before. I certainly understand the feeling.

"You said you need it often. Who are the women you date?"

"Like I said, I don't date. I go somewhere that has women who know how to cater to my particular needs. It's best that way for me."

I pull away from him. "You have sex with hookers?"

"It's not exactly what you're thinking. They're not hookers. They're people like me who have particular needs and don't want anything more than a physical encounter. It's a place for people like us to be satisfied. There's no need to get into details, but it's high-end and clean. I just want you to see that I'm no good for you. We want different things. We have different needs."

I'm in shock and confused. He doesn't date. He goes somewhere for sex only. It sounds like hookers to me. Why would he do that? I have no doubt that women would line up to be with Dominic.

Maybe he's right. I'm in over my head with him.

I'm not sure I have anything left to say at this point. After a few tense moments, he leans over and kisses my cheek. He keeps his face close to mine for an extra few seconds and whispers, "I wish I was different. I wish I was worthy of you, princesa."

He kisses my cheek again, stands, and leaves.

I sit there in complete and total confusion. I'm not sure what I was expecting, but it wasn't that.

At some point, Cassandra walks into my office. She looks at me still sitting on the couch in obvious shock. "Are you okay?"

I sink my head back into the soft cushion of the couch. "Honestly, I don't know."

She closes my door and sits next to me. "What's going on?"

"Dominic."

She nods. "Are you finally going to tell me what happened with you two? I know something went down."

I can't help but smile. "*He* went down."

She returns my smile. "At Reagan's party, right?"

I nod. "Yes"

"Trevor owes me a hundred bucks and OOD. I knew something happened between you two that night.

"What's OOD?"

"Oral On Demand. I can ask for it anytime, anywhere, and he has to do it. We always use it for our bets, and we both go out of our way to cash it in at the most inconvenient time for the other. It's a little game we play."

I shake my head. "You two are deranged."

She smirks. "Yet perfect for each other."

"True. Anyway, Dominic and I had this amazing instant connection. We went into a private room. Things were starting to happen." I close my eyes for a moment, remembering how perfect it was until his phone rang. "Shit, Cassandra, it was the best orgasm I've ever had in my life."

"What happened? Why didn't you see him again?"

"When things were about to progress further, his phone rang." I pause dramatically. "It was his wife."

Her eyes pop open. "Dominic is married?"

"He was. Not anymore. At that time, they were separated, which I didn't find out until recently. She told him on the phone that she was pregnant. He freaked out and left me sitting there with my dress around my waist. Literally, it was around my waist. That was the last time I saw him until a few weeks ago at Luke's school, and now, obviously, he's a client."

She blows out a breath. "Wow. What a mess."

"That's not even the messy part. We have a clear mutual attraction. I'm so drawn to him, and I honestly believe he's drawn to me."

"He's hot as hell. Of course you're drawn to him. Every woman with eyes is drawn to him."

"It's more than that. There's something there. I'm sure of it. He says he feels it too, but he keeps telling me that I need a nice guy, not him. That he's not good enough for me."

She looks confused. "What does that mean?"

"He just told me that he needs a lot of sex. A lot of rough sex. He said normal women like me can't give him that, so he gets it from some kind of sex club. I'm not exactly clear on what it is."

Her eyes widen. "Holy fuck. It's hard to imagine a guy that looks like Dominic needs prostitutes."

"I know. He said they're not prostitutes, but it sounds like it to me."

"So what are you going to do?"

I shake my head. "I don't know. Honestly, part of me is terrified and part of me is...curious."

She smiles again. "I see. Have you ever had rough sex?"

"No, not really. Have you?"

"All the time. That's how I like it. I always have."

"How rough?"

"Really rough, Beth. I like to be tossed around and smacked around."

"Does Trevor hurt you?" I have a hard time believing Trevor could hurt anyone.

"Not once. There's a fine line between pain and pleasure. Everyone has their happy medium. You need to find yours."

CHAPTER NINE

DOMINIC

Gabriela is in town and took the kids for a few days. I miss them already. I've gotten used to having them around all the time.

The nice thing is that I can go out with a few friends tonight, something I haven't done much of since the kids have been with me full time.

I'm out with my longtime friends, Sebastian and Kevin. The three of us have been close since college. Kevin is happily married with two kids. He started dating his wife, Claudia, our senior year. She's kind and thoughtful, like him. They're a true all-American family.

Sebastian is divorced and has sex with everything that walks. He always has. He never should have gotten married. I was shocked when he said he was. I was even more shocked when I met Lindsay, and she was a compassionate, beautiful, wonderful woman who was completely in love with him. He's my best friend, but even I know he didn't deserve her.

In fairness to him, he tried hard at first to be a good husband, but it's not in his grain. He likes to party too much. He enjoys having a variety of women. I do respect that he divorced her before he was with anyone else but watching him break her heart was terrible.

Neither of their wives ever cared for Gabriela. They tolerated her, much like I did.

We sit with our cigars in one of the only restaurants that still allows them. I ask Kevin, "What's Claudia up to tonight?"

He scrunches his nose. "She said she was taking Lindsay out for margaritas with a bunch of their friends to try to cheer her up."

Sebastian's face drops. "I thought she was doing okay. She said as much when I spoke to her last week. It's been over a year."

Kevin shrugs. "I guess not. Claudia said she's still hurting. For some unknown reason, she loves your unlovable, self-centered ass."

Sebastian rubs his face in obvious distress. He still cares about her. Maybe once he gets this shit out of his system, he'll find his way back to her.

I would never tell him, but I check in on Lindsay every month or so. I know she puts on a brave face for me, but she's still struggling.

Kevin recognizes that we need a topic change and turns to me. "How are things going having the kids full time?"

I smile. "Honestly, I love it. It's been good for my relationship with Matteo. I've seen him come out of his shell at times. I think we're making progress. And Valentina es mi amor. She's so smart. I can't wait to see what she becomes."

It has truly been great having so much time with them. Matteo is finally starting to warm up to me a little. He's still quiet, but we're making progress. Seeing him with Beth the other day gives me hope. I looked into having a pet as therapy, like Beth mentioned. She's right. It's supposed to be helpful for kids like Matteo. I'm seriously considering it.

He nods in understanding. "Gabriela is home now?"

"Yes, for a few days. I'm sure the separation isn't easy for her. I don't envy her situation."

They both roll their eyes. Neither of them understood why I married Gabriela, knowing I didn't love her. They knew the real reason. What they never understood was why Gabriela agreed to it. I told her beforehand that I didn't love her. I told her beforehand that I was not capable of being faithful to her. She's very attractive, but I was never attracted to her. She was fine with all of it, just wanting to marry me.

I shake my head. "Have some compassion. Her mother is dying, and she barely gets to see her kids."

Fortunately, the conversation turns back to Sebastian's sexcapades. He's telling us about how women in their twenties are now very into anal. He drones on and on about it.

Kevin hangs on every word he says, but I find myself disinterested. There's only one person, one woman, on my mind right now, and she's not a twenty-something bimbo. Just the opposite. She's refined, classy, beautiful, kind, smart, and just plain perfect.

The look of shock on her face today was unbearable. I know it was the right thing to say and do, but I hated every second of it. Being close to her, smelling her, knowing she wants me nearly as much as I want her made it all the more difficult, but I'm protecting her from the animal that lives inside me. The hurt I know I would inevitably cause her. I can never be the kind of man deserving of her.

Sebastian turns to me. "Dom, why don't we hit the club scene later tonight? The girls are all in their twenties and purely looking for sex. Nothing else. It's like fishing with dynamite."

Kevin pouts. "Hey! What about me? I thought we were hanging tonight. I can't go to a place like that without my wife."

Sebastian shrugs. "Sorry, man, but there are perks to being single again."

Kevin narrows his eyes. "One day you'll truly fall. It's not a bad place to be. I love Claudia. I don't remotely want anyone else."

I envy Kevin because I know he means that. Since the second he met Claudia, he's only had eyes for her.

Sebastian looks back at me. "Dom?"

I wave my hand in a dismissive fashion. "Not interested. I prefer real women. I don't want a woman half my age. It's beneath us at this point."

"Get off your high horse. You bang prostitutes."

"They're not prostitutes. Nobody gets paid. And I don't bang all of them. I do it because they know what they're getting into and it's what they want. Regular women don't like it that way, and even if they do, they want a relationship. I don't. It's not worth the headache. My way is better."

Kevin mumbles, "If you want to spend your life alone and miserable."

My jaw ticks. "Back off, Kev."

"Fine, but it's not like you're happy. At some point, you should consider something more substantive."

I don't reply, simply sipping my drink and taking a puff of my cigar.

Sebastian goes back to yapping about younger women and their lack of inhibitions.

I'm staring off into space, annoyed with this whole conversation, when I hear a familiar laugh in the distance. I turn and see Beth walking in with a man. He said something that made her laugh.

She's so fucking beautiful in such an effortless way. She's in a tight, sexy, black wrap dress that shows every sultry curve of her body. She's got round hips and a tiny waist. Her breasts are a perfect handful. Her skin is peaches and cream. My hands twitch at the thought of touching her. All of her.

Her date's hand is on the small of her back as he leads her to a table across the restaurant from us. He's smiling down at her, clearly very enamored with the brunette bombshell on his arm. I have no read on whether she returns those feelings. I'm nauseous at the thought that she could.

Sebastian follows my line of sight. "Ooh. She's hot and was actually alive in the nineties. Maybe I should see if I can steal her away from that douche."

I snap my head at him. "Stay away from her. She's too good for you."

He lets out a laugh. "How would you know, Dom?"

"Let's just say that I know her. Hands off. She's out of your league. She's out of all our leagues."

He and Kevin look at each other, no doubt in shock. I haven't felt any possessiveness over a woman in a very long time. Not since *her*, and certainly not over my ex-wife.

I can feel my blood pressure rising. I'm going out of my mind seeing Beth with another man. She's smiling at him, but I want it to be me she smiles at.

She takes a sip of her wine and then licks her lips clean. I'm mesmerized watching her tongue sweep across her red, luscious lips. I want them wrapped around...Stop it. I can't go there.

The minutes tick by in slow motion. I hear nothing my friends are saying. I'm watching Beth. They're clearly engaged in a pleasant conversation. Both are smiling and laughing. I guess that's what dating looks like. I wouldn't know.

My forehead is covered in sweat. All of a sudden, my necktie feels tight. I loosen it. I can't take this anymore.

I pull out my phone, needing a reason to text her. I think for a moment and then scroll to a photo I took of Valentina and Matteo in the park the other day. They're on a tire swing laughing. I send it to her via text.

I see the moment she hears her text tone. No parent can avoid their phone when it chimes. It's the unwritten rule of parenthood.

She lifts it and swipes to open the text. She has a

big smile looking at the picture. Bigger than that asshole gave her. Take that, motherfucker.

But she doesn't respond. She places her phone back on the table. I need to text her again.

> Me: What are you doing tonight?

She lifts her phone again and stares at it, pinching her eyebrows together in confusion. She places it down, again without answering.

She goes back to chatting with that loser. I can feel my heart racing. My anger is about to boil over.

I contemplate what will happen after the date. Will he go back to her place? Will she go to his? Now I'm imagining his hands on her body. Her soft, beautiful body.

My sanity finally snaps. I grab for my phone again and start typing.

> Me: You look fuckable in that tight, black dress.

She picks her phone up. Her eyes widen and her cheeks flush. She looks around the restaurant until our eyes meet.

Her lips part when she sees me. I can see her breathing pick up. Her eyes haven't left mine. Those bright blue eyes that I dream about. I want them staring up at me while I pound into that perfect, luscious body.

I type on my phone again.

> Me: He's not good enough for you.

She looks down at her phone, thinks for a brief moment, and then places the phone on the table.

My teeth clench. She's got some nerve not responding to me.

Her date reaches for her hand and brings it to his mouth for a soft kiss. Something awakens in me. Something I don't recognize.

Me: If he touches you again, I can't be held responsible for my actions.

She peeks down at her phone when it pings. I see her swallow hard and look up at me again.

She stands, says something to her date, and then makes her way toward the bathroom area.

I practically jump out of my chair, leaving my burning cigar behind. Sebastian smiles at me. "Go get your girl, loverboy."

I don't bother with a response as I quickly make my way to the bathroom area. When I reach the hallway, I see her leaning with her back and head against the wall. Her chest is heaving, looking like she's trying to gather herself.

She turns when she hears me nearby. "Dominic, what are you doing? I don't understand."

I say nothing as I approach her. I don't know what to do with myself, I just know that the need to touch her is overwhelming.

I bring my body flush to hers, pinning her to the wall. She gasps at the unexpected contact but her eyes flutter telling me she likes it.

I run my lips and nose up and down her neck, taking in her intoxicating scent.

"Me encanta la forma en que hueles. Lo quiere por todos los partes de mi cuerpo." *I love the way you smell. I want it all over my body.*

Her breathing becomes labored.

She whispers, "You said you didn't want me."

I grab her face so our eyes meet. "I never said that I don't want you. I do want you. Desperately. I said I shouldn't have you. You deserve better."

Her eyes pierce mine. "What if I don't want better? What if you're what I want? What I need."

I bring my forehead to hers. "I don't want to hurt you, but I can't watch another man touch you."

"Then *you* touch me."

My hands twitch to do just that. Her breasts are pushed up against my body. I want to run my hands under her dress to touch the soft skin of her thighs. I know she's aroused right now. I can smell it. I ache to run my fingers through her so I can feel it. Taste it.

I stare at her sweet, innocent face, looking up at me with so much trust. The future flashes before me. One in which I hurt her, both physically and emotionally. One where those big blue eyes are filled with tears. All because of me.

I think of poor Lindsay and everything Sebastian has put her through. I don't want to cause Beth that same type of pain.

I pull back, grab her hand, and kiss it. "Go back to your date, princesa. He seems nice, like you."

Without bothering to say goodbye to Sebastian or Kevin, I turn and leave the restaurant. I should go to the only place that gives me satisfaction, but I know that tonight it won't. There's only one woman who can give me what I need, and I can't have her.

CHAPTER TEN

BETH

Cassandra and I are walking through the park toward Luke's baseball game. It's about to start. The twins are on the playground next to the field. Giselle's twelve-year-old daughter, Hazel, offered to stay with them so we can watch the game.

I spot Luke, number eight, looking adorable in his blue Lightning jersey, hat, and cute little baseball pants that he barely fills out. Trevor is hitting groundballs to them. He's got on a matching blue Lightning shirt and hat with black athletic shorts that he more than fills out.

Cassandra's arm is looped through mine. I nod toward the stands. "Look at all the moms drooling over Trevor."

She lifts her head. Every single mother is legitimately watching him with drool practically falling out of their mouths.

She lets out a laugh. "He's such a stud, isn't he?"

I nod. "He is. But they don't know that he's even better

on the inside. I can't tell you what him coaching the team means to Luke."

As if sensing her approaching, Trevor turns his head our way and blows a kiss to Cassandra.

Because my over-fifty sister is so mature, she brings her fist up to her mouth and gives him the universal sign for a blow job.

I can only shake my head at her while he smiles and winks in return.

She lets out a laugh before turning back to me. "He enjoys the time with Luke, and he loves baseball. Speaking of sports with balls, you really squeezed Molosky's balls on that deal. I saw the final paperwork before I left the office."

I roll my eyes. "You have a way with words. And thank you, I did sort of kick ass on this case. The client was very happy with the outcome. It looks like everything will go through." I hit a grand slam for our client on this one. I was definitely on my A game.

"I want to push for you to be made a partner. You've earned it. I'm bringing it up at the next partners' meeting. I don't anticipate any resistance. Everyone sees your value at the firm."

I can't help my huge grin. "Really? That would be incredible. Thank you." I wouldn't mind a big salary bump.

"It's my pleasure."

We approach the stands and Giselle waves for us to sit with her. She holds up two discreet water bottles that I have no doubt are filled with vodka.

We sit and she hands them to us. I take a sip as I sit and scrunch my face. "Did you put any mixer in this or is it just straight vodka?"

She shrugs. "Mixers are a waste of space and calories."

Cassandra clinks her bottle with Giselle's. "Truth."

Giselle leans over and whispers, "Did you see all the moms on both teams salivating over Trevor?"

I nod. "We did. He's a hottie. I can't blame them."

She rubs her shoulder against mine. "Speaking of hot, how was your date last night?"

Cassandra quickly snaps her head toward us. "You had a date?"

"Yes." I give Giselle a dirty look. I hate Cassandra knowing when I have dates. She gets all crazy. "A cute attorney asked me out and I accepted. Let's not make a big deal of it."

Her eyes widen. "And?"

I sigh. "It was an eventful night. Shawn, my date, was fine. He was very charming and attentive. But Dominic was at the restaurant and got all crazy jealous. He's fucking with my head."

Giselle and Cassandra give each other knowing looks. Clearly, they've discussed my love life when I wasn't around.

Giselle asks, "What happened? Tell us."

"He started texting me how fuckable I looked in my dress and how he didn't want my date touching me."

She fans herself. "That's hot. Please tell me you fucked him."

"Here's the crazy part. He had me pinned to the wall by the bathroom. I swear I would have let him do anything to me in that moment. He's just so sexy. I lose my mind around him."

"And?"

"And, per usual, he went from scorching hot to ice cold in seconds. He was back to the whole *you're too sweet for me, find a nice guy* bit. He's giving me whiplash. Part of me thinks he's right. Maybe I need someone more stable. But then part of me is dying to be with him. To know what it's like to have the kind of passion I know we'd have."

I choose not to tell them that I abruptly ended my date, went home, turned on the Spanish porn I've been watching for over four years, and made myself come. Twice.

Cassandra gives me a knowing smile. "Did you go home and get yourself off?"

I narrow my eyes at her. "Why do you know that?"

She snickers. "I just know you. Did you watch dirty-talking Latino men to get off?"

I gasp. "How do you know about that?"

She toggles her eyes between me and Giselle. "Giselle may have let it slip a few weeks ago."

I turn and give Giselle another dirty look. I didn't want Cassandra to know. She's going to have a field day with this information.

Just then, my crazy neighbors Mindy and Brittany walk over to us. Their sons are on the opposing team. I mumble, "Oh shit, what do these crazy bitches want?"

Brittany asks, "Who is the sex god coaching your team? Why do you get the eye candy and we get an eye sore?"

Mindy nods. "Our coach hasn't even been able to see his dick since the nineties."

The three of us laugh as we look over to their coach waddling around the dugout area with his huge belly hanging well over his belt.

"Brittany, Mindy, this is my sister, Cassandra. Our coach, Trevor, is her husband."

They both stand there, wide-eyed. While Cassandra is stunning and looks younger than her years, it's obvious that Trevor is much younger than her.

Cassandra simply smirks. "For what it's worth, Trevor could be as heavy as your coach, and he'd still be able to see his dick."

Giselle bursts out laughing. "My ex could have a flat six-pack and still not see his dick."

They both cackle. How did these two lunatics become my two closest friends?

All our eyes move to Giselle's ex, Tom, who has two divorced moms hanging on his every word.

Giselle shakes her head. "One of those poor women will soon be asking, *is it in yet?*"

All five of us giggle. Poor Tom.

She looks around. "I suppose it could be worse. At least George isn't here today. We can enjoy the peace and quiet."

Giselle's former father-in-law, George, is eccentric. He's very loud and opinionated about his grandson's playing time. His antics, which I find hysterical, are often the source of embarrassment for Tom, Giselle, and the kids.

Brittany interrupts my thoughts. "We're going to go out on patrol next week, Beth. Will you join us?" They never ask Giselle even though she lives in our neighborhood. She has *fuck off* written on her forehead. I need to learn to be more like her.

"Umm...I have a lot going on. I'll see if I can make the time." Hell, no.

They nod and head back to the other side of the field.

Giselle shakes her head. "Why don't you just tell them you don't have interest in the pussy party-pooper patrol squad?"

I hear Cassandra snicker, but I just shrug. "They're nice women and well-intended. I feel bad being mean to them."

As I'm looking at the other side of the field, I notice Luke wave to a little girl in the stands. She smiles like she just won an entire ice cream truck. Trevor fist bumps Luke. What the hell are the two of them up to?

Cassandra interrupts my thoughts. "Beth, can I ask you a question?"

I look at her. "I've never known you to hold back from asking anyone anything, ever."

She lets out a laugh. "True. You're very good at what we do at work. That's not bullshit just because we share a sperm donor."

I give her a disapproving look. I hate when she bashes our father.

"Sorry. We share a biological father. That's the most I'll give you."

The father Cassandra and I knew were completely different men. She remembers him as the distant man who abandoned her. A man who was cold to her and her mother. Though short-lived, I remember him as warm, loving, and involved, with both me and my mother. I remember a man who sung Cassandra's praises. I remember him as a man my mother kept on a pedestal. Sometimes it's hard to reconcile our different experiences.

"Go on. What are you getting at?"

"At work, you're aggressive, demanding, and, at times, relentless. Look what you did with Molosky. You were an animal in that case. But in your personal life, I see none of those qualities."

Giselle nods in agreement. "You're definitely super passive in your personal life."

I toggle my head between the two of them. "Should I be aggressive and relentless with my son?"

Cassandra purses her lips. "You know that's not what I meant. I mean with men. I've known you, *really* known you, for six years. I've never seen you pursue someone. You just sort of stand back and let things happen. I can count on one hand how many lovers you've had in that time. All nothing special. All very vanilla. None of them seemed to be...the multi-orgasm type."

I mumble, "You're not wrong about that."

Giselle nods. "That's true. You were confident and assertive in law school, and I know you're good at your job, but when it comes to men, you're more of a pushover. Gary walked all over you. You settle for what you're given. You're smart and fucking beautiful with a crazy good body. Own it. Use it to your advantage."

Cassandra asks, "Why? Why are you so strong and aggressive at work but not in your personal life? At work, you demand things from people. You push and push until you get exactly what you want and deserve. You play games and strategize. But in your personal life, you're none of those things. You're almost indifferent at times. You don't bring out the tiger I see at work. You could use some of that ball squeezing with men." She elbows me. "With a particular man that I know does it for you. He thinks you're too sweet for him? Maybe show him a less-than-sweet side to Beth. If he thinks you're too nice for him, maybe show him the less-than-nice side of Beth. I know you have it in you. I see it every day."

Wow. I've never looked at it that way. They're right. I'm a completely different person when it comes to my personal life. I'm a wimp. I take what I'm given, not what I want.

I tilt my head. "What was your sex life like before Trevor? I know you have an amazing sex life with him. I definitely don't need more details on that. But before him. I've only known you with Trevor. It's hard for me to imagine you with anyone else."

"I always had an active, good sex life. Things are

different with Trevor in part because he's a freak of nature stallion, and in part because of the feelings involved, but it's not like I didn't have great sex before him. I've had lots of great sex and experiences. Have *you* ever had great sex, Beth?"

"Define great sex?"

She sighs. "I think I have my answer."

I blow out a breath. "Maybe it's me. Maybe I'm vanilla in bed."

Cassandra shakes her head. "You're related to me. That can't be true. Plus, I've seen things from you at work that suggest to me there's an inner tigress in there. Do you really think it's that you're vanilla or do you think that maybe you've been with the wrong men? Maybe personal Beth is too apathetic, when she needs to be assertive, like work Beth. Flip the switch. Turn it on. I have a feeling that under the right circumstances, there's a different side of you lying underneath your well-tailored, conservative suits. Either you need the right man to draw it out, or..."

"Or?"

"Or perhaps you need to go after what you want and need. Bring your *take no prisoners, never take no for an answer*, work persona into your personal life."

I have to admit, she does make good points.

"Tell me about your ex-husband. I've never met him, and you rarely speak of him."

"Gary?"

"Yes."

"There's not much to tell. He was my high school sweetheart. We were comfortable. He was all my firsts. We probably should have broken up when I went to college, but we didn't. He went to community college while I obviously went to a four-year college. He was on and off employed while I went to law school. We got married because I didn't think I would ever want anyone but him. But as my career began to blossom, so did his resentment. It got ugly. Luke was unplanned. I tried to stick it out for Luke's sake, but even before the infidelity, it was obvious we were over. We were headed down two completely different paths in life."

"And the sex?"

"Nothing spectacular. I didn't know any different at the time. He was the only man I had been with."

Giselle seems to agree. "I knew Gary. Trust me, he wasn't giving her great sex."

Cassandra takes a slow sip of her drink. "Have I ever told you about my second husband, Roman?"

I shake my head. "No." I know she was married three times before Trevor. I know the first was a drunken night gone wrong and was over before it started. I know the third was a pregnancy scare that was also over before it started. Her second marriage was to a man named Roman and it lasted a few years. I know nothing beyond that.

"Like Gary, he resented my success. It got ugly. It got physical."

I grab her hand. "Oh Cassandra, I didn't know that. I'm so sorry."

She brushes it off. "I'm fine. He also cleared out all my bank accounts. I lived with Darian, Scott, and the girls for months until I got my finances sorted out and back on track. Thank god I had them."

"You could have come to us. We would have welcomed you."

"Honestly, I never even considered it. Scott immediately insisted I move in and that's what I did."

"He sounds like a good guy."

"He was the best man I ever met. Everyone should be so lucky to have a Scott Lawrence in their life."

I smile. "Darian hit the jackpot twice, didn't she?"

She nods. "She did. Scott and Jackson both are among the most incredible men I've ever been around. They both love her so wholly. I never thought I'd have it. It took me fifty years, but I do. I have it."

I smile. "I know you do. Trevor is wonderful. I love the way he loves you."

"I still find it hard to believe at times. I had given up. I thought I was happy sleeping around but waking up alone in an empty bed. I wasn't. Don't wait fifty years like I did, Beth. If there's something or someone you want, go for it. Don't be shy. Take what you want. Do what feels good. Be aggressive, relentless Beth. We know she's in there."

I nod. "You're right. I never thought about it this way, but you're right."

She gives me her mischievous smile. "He's been messing with you for weeks with the hot and cold nonsense. It's time to turn the tables on him. Isn't that what you'd do at work?"

Giselle grins at Cassandra. "You're a fucking genius."

Cassandra lets out an over-exaggerated laugh. "I prefer evil fucking genius."

I think for a moment. I'm sick of playing by his rules in his court. If this was work, I'd change courts and make him play by *my* rules.

An idea occurs to me. "Will you go shopping with me during lunch tomorrow?"

Her face lights up. "Tell me what you have in mind, temptress."

I smile. "It's time for Mr. Mazzello to see a different side of me. He's been messing with my head and my libido, constantly leaving me panting and wanting more. It's time for him to get a dose of his own medicine."

CHAPTER ELEVEN

BETH

I walk into my parent-teacher conference evening with a new sense of confidence. I'm in my new form-fitting Dolce and Gabanna black and blue business dress that fits my body like a glove and shows my assets in the most flattering, yet sophisticated, way possible. I've never worn anything quite like this in my life, especially in the realm of *business attire*.

My hair and makeup are perfect. I added red lipstick to give it a little something extra. I may have waxed and bleached too, just for the mental game of it all.

I look good. I feel good too. I'm business sexy personified, and I'm loving it.

I needed that pep talk from my sister and Giselle. It was a wake-up call.

I know Dominic has the appointment before me. I wait just outside the classroom door. When his conference is over, he opens the door, looking like sex on a stick in his expensive suit. His eyes find me standing there and immediately widen. *Jackpot.*

I give a small, unaffected smile. "Dominic. Lovely to see you."

His eyes unashamedly move up and down my body, taking in my uncharacteristic wardrobe. Those eyes are practically oozing sex right now. I've never met a person with a gaze like his. He could melt endless panties with one look, mine included. But I'm playing it cool, at least on the outside. On the inside, I'd like to take him into a classroom and give him a dirty detention.

If he's going to toy with my emotions, I'll toy with his right back. I'm not taking his hot and cold crap anymore. I'm taking control of this situation, just as I would if this were a business deal.

He licks his lower lip, not having moved from the doorway.

"Are you going to move so I can get into the classroom?"

He grits his teeth. "No."

I inwardly smile, knowing I've got him right where I want him. I shrug. "Suit yourself."

I make my way into the classroom, unnecessarily rubbing the front of my body over his along the way. He feels so good, but I'm doing my best to outwardly appear unaffected.

As I pass, he whispers, "I can smell your arousal."

I look down at his pants and whisper back, "I can see yours."

I manage to move past him, though I do let my fingertips lightly brush across his body, just above his belt. He's solid and warm. *Just keep moving, Beth. Play it cool.*

He lets out a low growl.

Holy shit, this is actually working.

It takes all my willpower to calmly walk into the classroom, but I do it and add a little sway to my hips for added effect.

I make my way into the meeting with the teacher, smile at her, and sit. I turn to the door and, with a coy grin on my face, say, "Dominic, would you be a peach and close the door for us?"

The intensity with which he's staring at me would make a lesser woman crumble. I'm not her. Not today. His face twitches for a moment, but I simply continue innocently smiling, and he eventually closes the door.

I have my meeting and then walk out feeling quite proud of myself for how I handled Dominic. It was very unlike me, and I loved it. Maybe this will be the new me. Sexy and confident.

I'm not completely paying attention as I exit the schoolhouse, when two large hands grab me and pull me around to the side of the brick building. It's dark and secluded.

My front is pushed against the cold brick with a big body pressing against me from behind. I close my eyes and inhale deeply. "I can smell you, Dominic."

He presses his erection to my ass and whispers into my ear, "You think you can mess with me?"

I wiggle my ass over his cock.

He spanks me. Hard. "Te voy a follar el culo si sigues moviéndolo así." *I'm going to fuck your ass if you keep moving it like that.*

I immediately respond, "Eres todo hablar y nada de acción." *You're all talk and no action.*

He turns me around until my back is against the wall, looking wide-eyed. He places his palms on the brick wall on either side of my head, effectively trapping me. I take in his breath. It's minty and manly, with a hint of cigar. I want it mingled with mine. Those big, red lips of his taunt me. I want them all over my body.

His eyes bore into mine. "You learned Spanish?"

I give him a small smile. "I'm a quick study." I reach down and run my hand up his long, hard length. "For example, I know you want to fuck me. You can pretend like you don't, but I know you do." I innocently shrug. "Maybe I'm not quite as nice as you seem to think."

He licks his lower lip. It's so sexy and, for some reason, empowers me further.

I whisper, "I can be bad, just like you." I give his cock a squeeze for emphasis at the end of my words.

I don't know who I am right now, but I like the reaction I'm getting from him.

He thrusts his hips and pushes it further into my hand, trapping it between his body and mine. With his lips close to my face, he growls, "You can't handle me."

I smile back, "Try me. I promise I won't break."

My breathing is becoming labored. His closeness to me has my head spinning. My arousal is at an all-time high. He's the most innately sexual man I've ever met. There's nothing I won't do in this moment to make it happen. I won't have a repeat of the other day. Days.

He moves his hand down the front of my dress until it meets my bare inner thigh. My dress is unforgiving, so it rides up with his hand as he makes his way to my center. I suppose someone could see us, but neither of us cares.

His fingers continue to slowly travel up my upper thigh, almost making me whimper, but I'm trying to be strong. He cups my pussy. "You'll never be the same again."

I look back at him with all the bravado I'm currently feeling. "Neither will you."

In one seemingly quick motion, he grabs onto my panties, tears them off, and sinks his fingers into me. I have no idea how many fingers, but it feels like a lot, and he's pushing them deep.

This time I can't help but let out a moan.

"Once I'm in here, princesa, I'll own it."

I nod. "Take it." I don't care about anything right now other than the fact that I want him inside me. I need him inside me.

I breathe, "Fuck me. However you need it."

His eyes turn darker than normal. I see him battling with his self-control. He licks his bottom lip again. I'm learning he does that when he gets turned on, and it only serves to ramp up my arousal.

I can't help but open my mouth and sink my teeth into that lower lip of his, pulling it out. I can feel him tense. I just need him to finally snap.

There's a noise in the parking lot behind us. We're out of sight, but unfortunately it brings us back to reality.

I release his lip, and he pulls his fingers out of me and straightens my dress. "Not here."

"What? Why not here? No one can see us." I can't wait a minute longer.

"Because when I finally have you, you're going to scream so loud that people will think I'm murdering you, not fucking you."

God yes.

He takes the fingers that were inside me and rubs them all over my lips, coating them in my juices. He snakes out his thick, long tongue, the one that stars in my dreams, and runs it across my lips. I nearly collapse.

I grab fistfuls of his hair and open my mouth around his tongue, sucking it into my mouth. He pulls my ass so I'm achingly tight to his erection and begins to kiss me back.

I'm quickly transported to our first kiss over four years ago. The need. The want. The passion. The way he kisses is like nothing I've ever experienced. His tongue is everywhere, yet the suction is perfect.

He picks me up and starts walking, all without breaking the kiss. My dress is too tight to wrap my legs around him, but he nonetheless carries me effortlessly. His big, strong hands are pulling my body tight to his.

When we get to his car, he breaks the kiss. He opens the door and I attempt to get my feet back on the ground, but he squeezes me tight. "You're not going anywhere. You started this, and now you'll see it through."

In the darkness of the empty parking lot, he lifts the bottom of my dress to my waist, pulls my legs around him, and sits down in the driver's seat. He closes the door and turns the car on before beginning to unbutton and unzip his pants.

"Sácame la verga, princesa." *Pull my cock out, princess.*

I reach into his pants and grab hold of him. I close my eyes. I knew this was coming. I knew what kind of man I was dealing with. He's thick. Insanely thick. My fingers don't come close to meeting when I wrap my hand around him. He's going to ruin me.

I pull him out and look down. I almost gasp. It's the longest, thickest, angriest penis I've ever remotely imagined. It's engorged with veins popping out. He's rock hard and already oozing from the tip.

He smiles. "I told you that you'll never be the same again. Rub that wet pussy of yours against me while I drive and make yourself come. Trust me, you'll want at least one orgasm to loosen you up before I destroy you."

He slams the car into gear and peels out of the parking lot. I shift my hips so that my pussy sits on top of his long length.

I don't know who I am right now. I've never been this woman. I've always been cautious. Reserved. I've never even had sex outside of a bed. I've never been so overcome by desire that I threw caution to the wind. My night with Dominic at Reagan's party was the craziest thing I've ever done, at least until tonight.

But in this moment, I just don't care. I'm physically aching for this man. I've been aching for him since the first time I saw him all those years ago. Is it a bad decision? Probably. Have I earned the right to make a few bad decisions for something that feels good? Fuck yes, I have. For once, I want to take something just for me. Consequences be damned.

I begin to rock my hips over his massive length as I move my lips to his neck. His smell is entirely consuming me. It drives me wild. It's so uniquely him and triggers my body in the best way possible.

"Mueve ese coño mojado sobre mi, princesa. Hazte correrte. Si, eso es. Puedo sentir tu goteras sobre mí." *Rock that wet pussy over me, princess. Get yourself off. Yes, that's it. I can feel you dripping onto me.*

I've never been so thankful to have learned Spanish. His Spanish dirty talk is a direct line to my clit, which is throbbing right now.

I'm biting, sucking, and nibbling on his neck. My fingers are gripping his hair. I'm sliding back and forth over his massive length. When he flexes his dick, my eyes roll to the back of my head.

I'm dying for him to be inside me. Each time his tip passes my entrance, I'm so tempted to impale myself on him.

I can feel every ridge and vein run through my slickness. I can't wait to feel all of it inside me.

I mumble into his neck. "Dominic, it feels so good. I want you inside me."

I haven't stopped moving my hips, riding him back and forth. I'm grinding down too, taking what I need.

"Haz que ese coño explote sobre mí. Córrete para mí, princesa." *Make that pussy explode onto me. Come for me, princess.*

I push down, increasing the pressure on my clit. He flexes his dick again and that's my final undoing. My vision goes dark. I dig my nails into his neck and yell out as my body detonates onto his.

He grabs both of my hips and rubs me harder, back and forth, drawing it out. His lips find mine and swallow my moans. His tongue moves through my mouth. I want it everywhere on my body. I want him everywhere.

The pace begins to slow as my orgasm subsides. It all of a sudden occurs to me that both of his hands were on my hips, and he was kissing me. How did he drive?

I look around. We're parked in the garage of a house. I was so lost in my own universe that I have no recollection of pulling in. In fact, I don't remember anything of the ride here except what was happening to my body.

He threads his fingers into my hair and begins to kiss me again. He's very kissy. I'm not complaining though.

I mumble, "Are your kids here?"

"No, their mother is in town. They're with her."

He moves his lips to my neck as his hands roam my body.

"Estas lista para ser jodida? Tengo que estar adentro de tu cuerpecito apretado. He esperado lo suficiente." *Are you ready to be fucked? I need to be inside your tight little body. I've waited long enough.*

I nod, knowing I've never wanted anything as much as I want him right now. He's just so...masculine. Everything he says and does seduces me that much further.

He brings his hands to the hem of my dress, which currently sits at my waist. There's a small slit and he grabs each side of it.

I shake my head. "Don't you dare."

He gives me that unique Dominic stare as he tears my dress in half. All the way up.

I should be mad. It was a new, expensive dress, but it was worth every penny just to watch his face when he ripped it off me. It doesn't get sexier than this man.

He unclasps and removes my bra as he slowly runs his eyes appreciatively up my body. His eyes unashamedly drink me in. Every single inch. "Qué bonita." *How beautiful.*

A warmth like I've never known spreads across me. A feeling of being so utterly adored and wanted. I've never felt more desired or sexy.

He reaches down to his pants and pulls out a condom from his wallet. Do they make condoms that wide? There's no way that a normal condom fits on him. I find myself wondering if it's a special order.

I watch as he opens it and rolls it on.

"A mi princesa le gusta mirarme." *My princess likes looking at me.*

Without moving my eyes from his impressive length, I nod in agreement. You bet I do. Any sane woman would.

He trickles a hand up my thigh and runs his fingers

through my center. "Tan mojada. Tan necesitada." *So wet. So needy.*

I squirm, begging for it, until he finally sinks two fingers into me. At the same time, he grabs my hair and smashes my mouth to his again. Like every single kiss with him, it turns feverish quickly.

He pushes his fingers deep into me as I run my nails down his shirt-covered chest. I wish he was naked. I want to touch him everywhere. I want to feel his bare chest on mine.

My walls are already trembling around his fingers. I'm officially mad with desire. I reach into his shirt and rip it open, the buttons flying all over the car.

He growls as he pulls his fingers out. "Abre ese coño ancho." *Spread that pussy wide.*

My legs are spread as far as they can go. I can't get any wider, especially in the car.

He lifts my hips and brings his tip to my entrance. I squeeze my eyes shut. I know this is going to be intense.

"Abre los ojos." *Open your eyes.*

I open them and look down as he feeds his monster cock into me. We both watch it gradually disappear. It's insanely erotic.

He's moving slowly, but as he travels further in, my whole body starts to convulse. I can't control it. He's all-encompassing.

"Relájate." *Relax.*

Relax? How can I relax when a giant whale dick is working its way into me? I've never had anything remotely this size inside me, and my damn sister got me the biggest vibrator on the market.

He bends his head to my breasts. I feel his warm breath skirt across my nipples until he sucks one into his mouth.

As he applies more pressure on my nipple, he sinks deeper into me.

I feel every part of him inside me, each vein and ridge rubbing me along the way. I throw my head back and moan, "Dominic."

I finally feel his body flush to mine. He's so deep. I don't think I have another inch in me left to give him. He's stretching me to the max.

Without otherwise moving, he pulls my face to his and begins kissing me again. His tongue sweeps through my mouth. I can feel my body begin to loosen, taking him. Absorbing what he's giving me.

He pulls his face away. "Estás lista?" *Are you ready?*

"Dámelo." *Give it to me.*

I assumed we were going to have sex right there in the car. I was wrong.

Without exiting my body, he opens the car door, steps out, closes the door, and pins me to it. He throws my legs over his forearms. I'm open and extremely vulnerable in this position. I'm totally at his mercy right now.

He licks across my lips as he pulls his body nearly all the way out before slamming back into me.

I gasp in complete and total shock. Holy. Shit.

And then he does it again. And again. And again.

My body trembles as it forms around him. The deepest parts of my body are being reached. It's being stretched and pulled, giving me levels of pleasure I didn't know existed.

I can do nothing but grab onto the tattered remains of his shirt as he moves in and out of me at a perfect pace. The slow, deep, hard strokes are ecstasy. I feel him on every nerve-ending.

He pounds my body into the car over and over. I will

definitely have bruises on my back, but I don't care. The pleasure far outweighs the pain.

I'm clawing at him for dear life. "Oh god, Dominic, keep going."

I feel him swell inside me. Is he getting bigger? Is that possible?

He slows his strokes, perhaps to give me a break. But then says, "Now you're ready."

Huh? Ready for what? Wasn't that it?

I stare at him. He's got a layer of sweat coating his gorgeous face, his hair is messy, and he's got on a suit with the shirt ripped open. I have a god inside my body right now. I might be able to come just from looking at him like this.

He releases my legs, slowly placing them on the ground. He pulls out, moves us over to the hood of the car, turns me around, and bends me over. My front is flush with the warm hood of the car. I didn't bother to notice what kind of car we were in. It's fancy and sporty. Looking up, it appears there are quite a few cars in this garage.

"Abre tus piernas." *Spread your legs.* My brain isn't totally functioning, so I don't comply right away.

Smack.

He spanks my ass hard.

I suck in a breath both in shock that he did it, and in shock at how much I enjoyed it. My pussy clenches in appreciation. This is the first time my bare ass has been smacked and, fuck, it's making me wet. More wet. I can feel my juices dripping down my legs.

I need him back inside me.

His hands grab my inner thighs and spread my legs apart until they're where he wants them. The feeling of his big, warm hands sends shivers up and down my spine. His touch is so sensual.

He smacks me again, squeezes my ass cheek hard, and then slams his cock back into me. I scratch and claw at the car as he pushes himself deep into my body over and over again.

It's still deep and hard, but it's no longer slow. It's fast and angry. I'm orbited into a different universe as I feel him move inside me. I can feel his heavy balls smacking me each time he slams into me.

He spanks and grips me hard through it all. My hips, ass, and legs will be covered in red marks and bruises. I can't help but smile at the thought of his marks on me, memorializing what he's doing to my body right now.

He pulls my hair hard enough that my body lifts off the car a few inches as he bites my neck, undoubtedly breaking skin. Damn, it turns me on. Knowing that I'm driving him as crazy as he's driving me amplifies every sensation. My body is oozing fluids right now.

He leans over my back and grabs onto my breasts as the onslaught continues. "No sé lo que quiero más-estas tetas o este culo. Voy a follar los dos." *I don't know what I love more, these tits or this ass. I'm going to fuck both of them.*

My legs start shaking. I'm glad his weight is on me, or I might collapse to the ground.

He lifts and bends one of my legs, placing it on the car, which spreads me even wider. My knee is practically at my ear. Somehow, he's now deeper inside my body. I didn't think he could get deeper, but he manages to do so.

"Llévame profundamente en ese hermosa coño tuyo." *Take me deep in that beautiful cunt of yours.*

My orgasm comes out of nowhere. I think his dirty words in Spanish make me lose all semblance of control.

I scream out, "Oh fuck, Dominic. I'm coming. Yes. Oh god yes."

I reach back and grab for him. My nails scrape the side of his ass. My body takes on a life of its own as my orgasm barrels through me.

"Fuck yes. Your pussy is milking me, princesa."

I can feel his cock swell and jerk inside me as he comes on a loud grunt. His strokes slow as he empties himself and my drawn-out orgasm finally ends, though aftershocks work their way through my body for several more minutes.

My pussy is throbbing. My entire body is throbbing. I've never felt so sated in my life. If this is how he fucks, sign me up for more.

We both lay lifeless, completely spent, completely out of breath.

I may never be able to walk again. Hell, I may never be able to move again. But it was worth it.

He kisses my back. "Are you okay, princesa?"

"Hmm." That's about all I can muster.

He peels himself off me. I hate it. I immediately feel cold without his body on top of mine. I remain unmoving, lifeless, bent over the hood of his car in nothing but my heels. He gently rubs and massages all the places he smacked and clawed in the heat of passion. It feels so nice and relaxing.

He lifts me up and cradles me into his warm embrace. I grab his face and bring my lips to his for a soft kiss. "Thank you. That was incredible."

He smiles into my mouth. "We're only just getting started, princesa."

He must be joking.

He peppers kisses up my neck as we enter the house, and he gently lays me on the kitchen island. The cold marble feels good on my heated back and raw, sensitive backside.

He bends and brings his mouth to my center, licking all around.

"The taste of your come is so sweet. Voy a disfrutarlo toda la noche." *I'm going to enjoy it all night long.*

And just like that, my arousal is ramped up again, as if I didn't have an earth-shattering orgasm moments ago. As if I wasn't fucked senseless into the hood of a car.

He stands to his full, powerful height. His monster cock is hanging heavy and pointing at me. Taunting me. Ready to go again.

He undresses for me, never breaking eye contact. The intensity of his gaze is something that will never leave me. I could stare into his eyes all day long. All night long.

He removes his jacket and tie, and then the remnants of his shirt, sliding it off his shoulders.

I take him in. His chest is broad, with the same dark hair that sits on his head. His arms are big, way bigger than I had imagined, and I imagine his body a lot.

He continues undressing until he stands before me completely naked. He's so thick. Everything on his body is thick. His legs are massive. No wonder he was able to rut into me the way he did. He is the most perfect male specimen ever created.

I run my fingertips down his chest and abs. I look up at him. "You're a beautiful man."

"Y tienes un coño bonita que quiero disfrutar de nuevo." *And you have a beautiful pussy that I want to enjoy again.*

He takes me hard on the kitchen island. I've never had sex that feels like this. It's perfect. He's perfect.

We then move to his shower, where he takes me softly against the tile wall. Well, not softly, but softer.

When it's over, we lay in his bed, both completely out of energy. His arms are around me and my head is on his chest.

"Did I hurt you, princesa?"

I smile into his chest. "I had six orgasms tonight. I would say hurting me is the last thing you did. I may not walk straight for a week, but it was worth the price of admission."

He lets out a laugh and then sighs as if he's about to fall asleep.

"Dominic, we can't fall asleep. I have a sitter. I need to get home."

Between our second and third times, I had texted Rose that I'd be very late. She said she'd just sleep in our guestroom for the evening. I can't sleep here though.

I look up and see his eyes flutter. I sit up. "You sleep. I'm going to call an Uber."

He shakes his head awake and sits up with me. "No. I'll drive you back to your car."

I stand to stretch, and he gasps. He gently runs his fingers over my ass, hips, and thighs. He turns me around, checking every inch of my body. "Beth, you have bruises and marks all over your body from me." He tugs on his hair. "I'm such a monster. What's wrong with me? This is why I told you we can't be together."

I sit down, grab his hands, and look into his eyes. "Dominic, tonight was the best sexual encounter of my life. I've never experienced anything remotely like it. Please don't ruin it for me."

He gently rubs my face. It's such a contrast to the way

he fucked me all night. "I hate seeing you hurt. You deserve better."

"You didn't hurt me. I wear these with pride. I'll be reminded all week of how amazing tonight was. It was an eye-opening experience for me. You gave me something I never knew I wanted or needed. I wouldn't change a thing about it."

He nods, but I can tell I didn't appease him. I attempt to lighten the mood. "You tore off my panties and dress. All I have is a bra. I can't walk out of here in just that. I think I might need some clothes."

He smiles. Damn, he's handsome.

"I'll grab you something."

He unashamedly walks into his closet naked and returns with one of his work shirts for me. I slide into it and can't help but bury my nose and take in his scent. My eyes flutter.

He lifts my chin. "I like the way you look in my shirt." I grab the T-shirt he's now wearing and pull him to me so our lips meet. I want him again. I can't get enough of him.

He eventually pulls away. "If we don't stop, I'll end up taking you again."

I smile into his mouth. "That wouldn't be so bad."

"No. I can't touch you. I won't hurt you again. Let's go."

I'm afraid to ask what he means by that, so I don't.

He's silent as we drive back to the school, and distant when I say goodbye to get back into my car.

CHAPTER TWELVE

BETH

I wake after a limited amount of sleep. I walk into my bathroom with a smile that won't go away. Maybe not quite walk. It's a bit of a limp. My body is battered and bruised, but I wouldn't have it any other way. I love the things he made me feel.

Looking in the mirror, I can't stop smiling while examining all the marks on my body. I run my fingertips over them as I replay our evening over and over in my head. The way he touched me. The way he took control. The way he spoke to me with those dirty words. My body is still thrumming from it all, somehow aching for more.

After showering and dressing, I head downstairs. Luke and Rose are having breakfast. He's engrossed in whatever she's saying. It's been that way for four years. In fairness to Luke, Rose has blossomed into a stunning young lady. She's now a senior in high school and the two of them have the most adorable relationship. She's like a big sister to him.

I kiss Luke's head. "Hey, baby. Did you two have fun last night?"

He has a big, goofy grin. "Yes. Rose and I had a date and then she slept over. We had a slumber party."

Rose smiles at me. She gets a kick out of Luke's crush on her. "This little charmer insisted on having a candlelit pizza dinner last night. And he picked me flowers from the yard." She motions toward a vase with a few dandelions in it.

I turn to Luke. "I'd ask who told you that girls like candlelit dinners and flowers, but I'm pretty sure I know the answer."

"Uncle Trevor. He said you have to romance the ladies and treat them like princesses."

Rose blushes. "He does treat me like a princess. Some girl is going to be very lucky to have you as her boyfriend one day."

Luke puts his head down. "You don't want to be my girlfriend?"

She bites back her smile. "You're a little young right now, Luke, but maybe when you're older."

Rose and I smile at each other. They've had this same conversation a lot over the years.

"Did you hear that, Luke? Maybe one day when you're older. You're a lucky man. Rose is very pretty."

He nods. "She's the second prettiest girl I know."

"Who's first, Valentina?"

He looks up at me as if the answer is obvious. "You, Mommy."

My heart melts. I hug him. He really is the sweetest little boy. I'm so lucky. "Baby, go upstairs and grab your backpack. I'll walk Rose out and meet you in the car."

"Okay, Mommy." He wraps his arms around Rose. "Bye, Rose. Have a good day."

"You too, little charmer."

When he runs upstairs, I ask Rose, "How was he?"

She smiles as she blushes. "He asked me if I wanted to sleep in his room. He said I could have nightmares and might need him to protect me."

I shake my head. "I'm truly going to have my hands full in a few years."

She nods. "That's for sure. He's more romantic than my actual boyfriend. I might send him to Luke for lessons."

I laugh. "You didn't tell him that you have a boyfriend, did you?"

"Of course not." She looks at her watch. "I need to get going. Text me when you need me again."

"I will. Thanks for staying over on such short notice. I already sent you a Venmo."

"No problem. I hope it was because you had a hot date."

Now it's my turn to blush. I can't help myself.

She gives me a knowing look. "Good for you, Beth." She heads toward the front door. "I'll see you soon."

I drop Luke at school and head to my office. I can't wait to talk to Cassandra about last night. She'll be so proud of me. Unfortunately, I have a few morning meetings and calls, so it will have to wait.

I work for a few hours before finally making my way down to Cassandra's office. As soon as I walk in, her eyes widen. "Holy hell. You've finally been fucked properly."

I place my hands on my hips. "What makes you so sure?" Admittedly, my big grin is giving me away.

"Your shit-eating grin, your glow, the bite marks on your neck, and the limp you're sporting."

I'm busting with excitement to talk to her about it. I've heard countless sexcapade stories about her and Trevor for the past six years. Now it's finally my turn.

"Ooh. Who's she fucking?"

I turn my head and notice Darian for the first time. She's sitting on the couch and Melissa is right next to her.

I turn my attention back to my sister. "Cassandra, I didn't realize you have company. We can talk about this later?"

"I'll tell them anyway. You might as well spit it out."

My mouth opens in shock. "Is there no sister code?"

"Darian is like a sister to me. You know that."

Melissa scowls. "What about me?"

Cassandra shakes her head. "You're my mother-in-law. You won't even let me talk about my sex life with you."

Melissa nods. "That rule remains in effect. I don't need to hear about your crazy antics with my son."

Cassandra looks back at me. "Is the limp because you were fucked hard multiple times or because you finally opened up the back gates?"

"Cassandra!"

She shrugs. "What? Darian and Melissa both take it up the poop chute. It's not a big deal."

Darian and Melissa fall over each other laughing hysterically.

Through gritted teeth, I say, "There was no poop chute."

"So it was rough. Tell me about it."

"Cassandra, we'll discuss this another time."

Darian interrupts, "She doesn't want to talk about it in front of us. Leave her alone. Just tell us who. Anyone we know?"

I hesitate for a moment, but then proudly say, "Dominic Mazzello."

Darian's face lights up. "The hot guy that works for Reagan?"

I nod.

Melissa whistles. "I think I saw him once. He's smoking hot. Nicely done, Beth."

I can't help the dreamy smile on my face. "Thank you. I agree."

Cassandra says, "We're headed to lunch. Do you want to join us?"

"I have too much work. Stop by my office when you get back."

After lunch, she walks into my office and closes the door behind her.

"Spill the dirty, nasty details. Don't leave anything out. I want to relive your evening in real time."

I lean back in my leather chair and smile. "Oh, Cassandra, it was amazing. I didn't know it could be like that. I've been missing out. I came so many times. He's sexy and perfect, and the way he commanded my body...hmm." I bite my lip.

She has a huge smile on her face. "Finally. I'm so happy for you. Tell me how it all went down."

"I did as we discussed. I was in the sexy business dress. He had an immediate reaction when he saw me, but I played it cool. I was flirtatious and confident, like you told me. That was all on my way *into* the conference. When I walked *out* of the building, he grabbed me and threw me up against a wall. It was basically game on after that. It was like pouring gasoline on a fire. We did it in his car, against his car, on top of his car, in his kitchen, and then in his shower."

"And it was rough?"

I nod. "It was. *Really* rough. My body is marked, and my new dress is shredded."

"You liked it?"

I think about the way my body felt. The way it still feels. "Hmm. I loved everything about it."

She lets out a laugh. "It must run in the family. How did you leave things?"

"That's the kicker. We were in bed afterward and he was being so loving and sweet. I had to head home, so I stood up to get dressed. When he saw the marks and bruises on my body, he freaked out. He was chastising himself, repeating that he's no good for me. It was silent and awkward after that. I tried to reassure him, but I don't think it worked."

"What exactly did he say?"

"That he won't touch me again. I wasn't sure if he meant last night or ever again. I was afraid to ask."

She gives me her trademark Cassandra smirk. "But he didn't say anything about you touching him, did he?"

I narrow my eyes. "What do you have in mind?"

DOMINIC

Beckett Windsor walks into my office. He's an impressive figure. He's tall, like me, well built, with a full head of dirty blond hair. He must be a few years older than me.

I stand to shake his hand. It's not every day you get to chat with one of the most respected billionaires in the world. "Beckett, it's nice to finally meet you. I'm Dominic Mazzello. You can call me Dom."

He smiles though seems confused. "You as well, Dom, but I feel like we've met before. I never forget a face." He runs a finger along his lip as he thinks for a moment. "Were you at Reagan's birthday party a few years ago?"

"I was, briefly. I had to leave early to attend to a family matter."

"I think I remember seeing you that night. You were carrying an attractive brunette with the bluest eyes."

"You have a good memory. I was. She was injured and I was assisting her."

Those blue eyes have been playing in my head for the past two days. Watching them turn even bluer as she came over and over again on my cock and tongue.

She was completely unexpected. Her demeanor from the onset of the evening, toying with me, was incredibly hot. She seemed so receptive to the way I fuck but seeing her battered body afterward was upsetting. I was too rough. I lack control around her. I don't think I've ever wanted a woman as much as I want Beth O'Connell. I've picked up the phone ten times in the past two days to call her, but I haven't managed to see it through.

I'm brought back to the present by Beckett clearing his throat.

I motion toward one of the chairs in my office. "Please, have a seat."

He does as I do the same behind my desk.

I smile. "I know you've been here all day. Who have you met with so far?" Reagan told me that Beckett is considering working here. I was shocked. He sold his company to raise his young daughter a few years ago after his wife passed. He never has to work another day in his life, but he's considering coming here. It's hard to believe.

"I've met with Skylar Remington, Jade McGinley, and LeRond Bouvoir. After my time with you, I'll meet with Carter and Reagan."

"LeRond? Carter's assistant?"

He smiles and nods. "He's quite a character. I asked that I not only meet the high-level team, but an administrative level employee as well. Understanding the culture here is important. I believe you can best accomplish that by speaking with employees at all levels. LeRond has been here for fifteen years. That means something to me."

"LeRond is great. He's been with Carter that entire time."

"I know. I find that very telling. It's quite unusual for an executive like Carter to have the same assistant for so long. LeRond is obviously happy working here. He sang Carter and Reagan's praises. Literally, he sang."

I laugh. "That sounds like LeRond. Carter and Reagan are both beloved. They're firm but fair and practical. I was here under Carter's father's regime as well. They've completely changed things for the better."

"I remember him." He scrunches his nose. "He was rather...unappealing."

I let out another laugh. "That's a nice way of putting it. I would have left if it weren't for Carter and Reagan taking the helm."

"It seems you would agree with everyone else that Carter and Reagan are as genuine as they outwardly appear."

"Very much so. They're in this for all the right reasons. Finding smaller businesses that need our backing to grow. Identifying the right opportunities and building businesses from the ground up. Tell me, Beckett, why do *you* want to work here? You could just as easily start your own company."

"I don't know if you're aware of my personal circumstances, but my wife passed in childbirth a few years ago, and I'm going it alone with my daughter." I nod. It's well known. "She's just now starting school, freeing up some of my time. Enough time to work for someone, not enough time to run a business. They're two very different beasts."

"That's for sure. I'm a single father myself. Reagan and Carter are very supportive of my circumstances. They're product driven. They don't care if you get there in your pajamas in the middle of the night."

"That's how it should be. That's how I ran my business. How many children do you have, Dom?"

"Two. A boy and a girl. My daughter is seven, going on seventeen, and my son is three."

He gives me a knowing smile. "My daughter is five going on twenty-five. It's not easy."

I smile. "I suppose not." I divert the conversation back to business. "How did things go with Skylar and Jade?"

"Skylar was lovely. She's intelligent, in a bit of an understated way. There is nothing understated about Jade though."

I chuckle. "No, certainly not."

"She's got quite a mouth on her, and she's young to have the title she does."

"Jade is without a filter. Reagan is much the same, though ten years more refined. Jade is very young, but beyond her crazy demeanor, she's incredibly good at her job."

He nods. "She's certainly impressive. She doesn't lack for confidence. The artwork in her office was interesting to me. Very sophisticated. Not what I would expect from someone her age."

"Her mom's artwork?"

He looks shocked. "The artist is Jade's mother?"

"Yes, that's my understanding. She didn't mention it?"

He shakes his head. "No. Her mother is quite talented. I met her at Reagan's party. I have a few pieces of her artwork in my home."

I never thought about it. I suppose the paintings in Jade's office are nice. I personally don't know much about art, but Beckett is well known for being a patron of the arts.

"What a small world."

"Have you met Amanda?"

I shake my head. "No. Frankly, I didn't even know her name until you just said it. I try to remain professional in the office. I rarely get into discussions of anyone's private life, let alone Jade's. She's half my age and, frankly, I'm terrified of what goes on in that kid's personal life."

He lets out a laugh. "That's probably a good policy."

He looks around my office, likely noticing the minimal personal effects. I keep nothing personal in here. His wheels are clearly turning. "Mazzello. That's an Italian name, but you're not Italian. If I was a betting man, which I'm not, I'd place a wager that you're Cuban."

I nod. "I am." He's a smart man. He's done his homework.

"I've done some business in the past with the Amoroso family down in Cuba. Do you know them?"

I give him a small smile. "I'm guessing that you already know the answer, or you wouldn't have asked the question."

His eyes light up. "I do."

"My mother was an Amoroso. No one here knows that. I consider myself independently successful. I don't like to fly on the coattails of my family. I'm not involved in the family business at all."

"I respect that. Oddly enough, it was the fact that I couldn't find anything about you online that caused me to dig a bit deeper."

"I do my best for people not to have any understanding of the kind of money I have. As I'm sure you're aware, people treat you differently when they know."

He lets out a laugh. "Don't I know it. I wish I could hide it too, but that ship has sailed. Unfortunately, it's rare for me to meet anyone who doesn't know my background, though it's refreshing when it happens."

He looks like he's thinking of someone in particular. Before Beckett got married, his active personal life was splashed all over gossip magazines and websites. Since his wife's passing, I've seen nothing. He's maintained an extremely low profile.

"I imagine it is. For what it's worth, Carter is the same way. You'd never guess he's a billionaire. That's not how he conducts himself. He and Reagan are both down-to-earth and relatable."

"I'm gathering that."

"I assume you know that Reagan and Skylar's stepfather is Jackson Knight." Jackson is also one of the wealthiest men in Philadelphia. I have no doubt he's crossed paths with Beckett.

He nods. "Of course. Jackson and I go way back. We grew up in this business together. He's as solid as they come, and I consider him a friend. He's quite besotted with their mother. I've seen them out and about a few times."

"Honestly, I wouldn't know. I've only met her a small handful of times and all the encounters were brief."

We chat for a while, both about business and even a little personal. We hit it off, discussing the possibility of grabbing drinks sometime. I hope he ends up working here. It would be nice to have him around. I could learn a lot from a guy like Beckett. With the company getting younger and younger, I wouldn't mind someone a bit older as a co-worker. I'm one of the old guys now.

We shake hands again as he stands to leave to make his way down to Reagan's office for his meeting with her and Carter.

Seconds after he closes the door, there's a knock. I look around to see if Beckett left something behind. I don't see anything.

I shout, "You can come back in."

The door opens and, to my surprise, it's not

Beckett, it's Beth, looking stunning in a red business dress with gold buttons running down the front from top to bottom. She's such a stunning woman.

I can't help but smile as I stand. "Princesa, what a nice surprise. I've been thinking about you."

She gives me a seductive smile as our eyes meet. We move toward one another. I bend to kiss her cheek, but she grabs my face and turns it, running her tongue along my lips until I open my mouth for her.

This aggressive behavior from her is surprising in the best way possible. She's not who I thought she was.

I pull her body close to mine and run my tongue through her open mouth. The kiss quickly turns deep, but I'm wary of where I am. I pull away, though I keep her face close to mine and smile. "Lovely to see you too."

She runs her hands up my chest. "I thought I'd stop by for a quick hello. Maybe pick up where we left off the other night."

I pull out of her embrace. "No." I head back to my desk chair and sit. I need to put a barrier between us so I don't tear off her clothes and bend her over my desk. "You must be hurting. You need to heal. It's not happening."

She bites her lip for a moment before moving her hand to the top button of her dress. "I thought you might say that."

She begins unbuttoning her dress.

"Wh...what are you doing?"

"Taking what I want."

I watch on with rapt fascination as she unfastens every single button, all the way down, until the dress is completely open, revealing a red lace bra and tiny matching panties.

Oh. Shit. She's gorgeous. I'm trying to be strong for her sake but she's not making it easy. My cock certainly isn't getting the message that I'm not touching her again. It's pressing against my pants. I have to adjust myself to make a little room for its significant growth at the sight of her delectable body.

She removes the dress completely, throws it over a chair, and starts walking toward me. I hold up my hands. "Beth, I can't touch you. You need to heal."

"Yes, I heard you the first time," but she continues walking my way.

"Beth. Please. I don't want to hurt you."

"Yep. I understand." But she doesn't stop.

She reaches me and stands between my legs. My cock is now painfully hard at the sight of her like this. I move my hand up her soft, smooth leg. "I really shouldn't."

She breathes, "I know."

My eyes take her in, my hands on her bare hips. "Eres la mujer sexista que he visto." *You're the sexist woman I've ever seen.*

She smiles in triumph. As soon as I spoke Spanish, she knew she had me.

"But I don't want to hurt you. I'm trying so hard not to touch you."

She traces her fingertips through my beard. "No significa que no pueda tocarte." *It doesn't mean I can't touch you.*

At that, she drops down to her knees in front of me and slowly runs her hands up my thighs until she reaches my cock. After stroking it over my pants a few times, she leans over and softly kisses it. I'm a grown man with shit-ton of experience, and yet somehow, she's made it so I nearly blow my load from the feel of her warm breath on me. This woman makes me come undone.

She unbuttons and unzips my pants and then reaches in and pulls out my cock. This time, she gives me the same soft kiss on my bare cock. She lifts her head, looks me in the eyes, and licks her lips. I grip the sides of my chair to attempt to maintain control. I want to grab her hair and shove my cock far down her throat until she's gagging, but I can't do that with her.

After wrapping her silky fingers around me, she bends her head and, achingly slowly, runs her tongue up my length until she reaches the tip. She slides her tongue around my oozing tip, taking what I'm already giving her. "Hmm. You taste as good as I imagined. I've been dying to do this to you for a long time. I want you to come long and hard down my throat, Mr. Mazzello."

Who is she right now? She's definitely not the shy, delicate woman I thought she was. Whoever she is, I'm liking her. My cock is loving her.

Her tongue traces all the veins of my cock. She seems to be savoring this. What she's really doing is driving me nuts.

She continues teasing me for a bit before she eventually feeds my cock into that wet, warm mouth of hers. I watch it disappear as her tongue traces every engorged vein on the way in. I can already see red lipstick on my dick, the sight of which makes me groan in pleasure.

With her mouth wide open to accommodate my girth, she takes my cock all the way to the back of her throat. She's got one hand on the base and the other behind me grabbing the top of my ass to give her leverage.

She looks up at me with those spectacular blue eyes of hers, her dark, long eyelashes blinking a few times. This moment is every fantasy I've had over the past four years. Her with my cock in her mouth while those intense, gorgeous eyes stare up at me innocently.

I'm losing the battle of self-control. I run my fingers through her hair before I grip it tight and lift my hips to push myself deeper. "Ahora- chúpame la polla como una buena chica." *Now suck my cock like a good girl.*

She smiles just before she seals her lips around me and sucks so hard that I almost gasp in shock at the pressure.

Her suction snaps the last of my sanity and control.

I pull her hair as my hips take on a life of their own and thrust into her. Her cheeks hollow out, and my eyes roll around in my head at the extreme pleasure. She's like a vacuum cleaner with her suction. She could suck a golf ball through a garden hose.

In and out, harder and harder, she's going to town on me in the best way possible. The best part is that she's enjoying it. She's moaning. I can smell her arousal. I'm dying to sink some part of myself into it.

I'm so lost in pleasure that I barely notice my door opening. Fortunately, I have a large executive desk. Beth is hidden, as am I, below my waist.

Jade walks in and looks at me skeptically. "Dom, is

everything okay? You're sweating."

Beth freezes at the sound of Jade's voice. She pulls her mouth off me but continues pumping me with her hand.

I grit my teeth and feign a smile. "Yes, what's up?"

She looks around. Her eyes land on Beth's dress thrown across a chair. She smirks at me. "Actually, I need to grab something before we chat." She throws her thumb toward the door. "I'll be back in maybe thirty minutes or so."

She turns, clicks the lock on my door, walks out, and then closes the door behind her. She spared me on that one.

Beth gets right back to work with her magical suction technique. I push her head down until she gags on my cock, but she never stops or pulls away. She never breaks stride even though I can hear her gagging on me. Those blue eyes are watering and it's the hottest thing I've ever seen.

"Joder!- chupas una buena polla, princesa." *Fuck, you suck such a good cock, princess.*

She squeezes my balls as I feel them start to tighten. Her tongue moves all the way down my shaft until I can't take it anymore and explode into her mouth. It's a big load, but she takes nearly all of it.

When she pulls away, there's a little bit dripping down the corner of her mouth. I would do anything to get a picture of this moment. Her lipstick-smeared swollen lips. Her face flush from sucking my dick. My come leaking out of her mouth.

She takes her finger, scoops it up, and sucks it into her mouth, closing her eyes in utter bliss. I sit there with my mouth open in shock at the vixen before me.

I tilt her chin up to me. "Your turn, princesa."

She stands, straddles my lap, runs her fingers through my hair, and shakes her head. "No. Today was about you."

I run my hands up her curves, bearing the marks of our time together earlier this week. She places her hands over mine, encouraging my movements. She softly kisses me. "I don't want to play games, Dominic. We're too old for that nonsense. I want to be with you. I can't explain the intensity of my attraction to you, but I've never been this drawn to a man before in my life."

I kiss my way up her jaw. "I understand. I feel the same way."

"Then what's the problem?"

"I don't want to hurt you..."

"Stop saying that. The other night was the best sex of my life. *Nothing* physically hurt me. The only thing I want is more of it. More of you."

I rub her face. "It's not just the physical. I can't be in a monogamous relationship. I don't do monogamy. I would never want to hurt you in *any* way."

She immediately pulls away and stands. "Well that's a dealbreaker for me. My ex-husband cheated on me. It's monogamy or nothing for me. As much as I want you, I have too much self-respect to accept otherwise."

She turns and walks over to her dress, beginning to put it back on. When she's done refastening the buttons, she looks up at me. "You know what I want. The ball is in your court."

She unlocks the door and walks out, leaving me dumbfounded.

CHAPTER THIRTEEN

DOMINIC

It's early morning and we're on a Facetime call with Gabriela. Matteo is silent, as usual, but Valentina is going on and on about Beth. How much fun they had at her house, and how much Matteo adores her. I can see on Gabriela's face that she's not happy about it.

The kids run upstairs to get dressed, leaving Gabriela and me alone to talk. Her smile immediately turns sour. "Is she your girlfriend? I thought you didn't do girlfriends. Or is she just another one of your whores?"

I do my best to control my temper. The last thing I need is Gabriela knowing how much I care for Beth. I bite the inside of my cheek and calmly say, "Don't call her that. She's a friend, the mother of one of Valentina's classmates. I'm a single parent right now, Gabriela. She helped out with the kids. She's good to them. That's all you should care about."

"I'm their mother."

"No one is claiming otherwise."

"I don't like it. I knew I shouldn't have left them with you. They should be here with me in Cuba."

"It's not happening. You're not taking my kids from me."

She snaps, "They're *my* kids. Children should be with their mothers."

"They should be with their fathers too. Feel free to return home to them anytime, and we can go back to our shared custody. The kids live here in Philadelphia. This is their home. Does it matter to you that they're both flourishing at their new school? Valentina is more challenged. She's already made a ton of friends. I've seen several signs from Matteo of him coming out of his shell. This has been good for him. I was going to wait until you got back to talk to you about it, but I think they should stay at this school when you return. I'll buy you a house closer to me if you want."

I can see her steaming. She starts pacing. "I need to think. Maybe we need to go back to the courts on this. I want them with me, not a replacement mother that's your fuck of the week."

I grit my teeth and smack the table. "No es así con ella!" *That's not how it is with her!*

So much for controlling my temper.

She turns her head as if someone is calling for her. When her eyes meet mine again, she says, "We're not done with this conversation. Either my lawyer or I will be in touch."

Without another word, she cuts the feed.

BETH

I'm proud of myself for doing what I did in Dominic's office earlier this week. It was so out of character, but I feel like I'm changing. I'm taking charge of my life. I'm sick of being passive and not going after what I want in my personal life. I'm sick of settling. I want Dominic, but I meant what I said. I demand respect. I want him, and only him. If he doesn't want me in the same way, I will have to figure out a way to move on.

It looks like that's what I'm going to have to do. Until this morning, I didn't hear from him after my office visit. And he only texted me about the kids, not us. It's Friday. There's a bake sale on Monday, and Luke and Valentina were both assigned muffins. They want to bake them together, so we planned to do so tonight at my house since we're tied up all weekend with baseball games and his kids have soccer.

Nothing was mentioned of us. I guess he's not interested in me as much as I am him. Or perhaps he can't handle monogamy. His loss. At least, that's what I'm telling myself to try to move past the sting of rejection.

The good news is, I learned something about my needs in my short time with Dominic. I will no longer be a bystander in my own love life.

Dominic texted me again late this afternoon, asking if I could grab his kids when I pick up Luke from school today. He said he was hung up on a call and would be over as soon as he could. I happily acquiesced.

I bring all three kids to my house, feed them dinner, and then get everything ready to start baking. Valentina wants to wait for Dominic to make the muffins, but it's starting to get late, and we need to get them in the oven. She seems understanding. She's such a good kid.

I give Luke and Valentina measuring and mixing instructions. They're busy chatting away with each other while doing their respective jobs. It's cute. At some point, I hear him inviting her to an upcoming baseball game. I suspect Trevor is encouraging him to invite girls to games to watch him play.

I've got Matteo on my lap with a spoon, mixing some batter. He's so adorable, with dark hair and dark brown eyes. They're a different shade and shape than Dominic and Valentina's. His ex-wife must have these darker, rounder eyes.

I find myself wondering what she looks like. She's probably so different from me.

As I'm deep in thought, Matteo accidentally drops his mixing spoon on my lap. A huge blob sits on my pants. He turns around with his head down. He's got tears pooling in his eyes.

"Sweetie, what's wrong?"

He points down to the mixture that's now sitting on my pants. This isn't my first time baking with kids. I had changed into leggings and a T-shirt, but regardless, it was an accident. Even if I was in my work clothes, I wouldn't be upset with him. It makes me sad to see him almost scared about it.

"It's okay. It was an accident." I scoop up part of it with my finger and slide it into my mouth, bringing my finger back out with a pop. "Yummy. Thanks for dropping it, Matteo. I wouldn't have gotten to taste it if you didn't."

He smiles and it warms my heart.

I grab the last bit on my pants and offer it to him. He moves to take it into his mouth, but at the last minute, I smear it on his cheek instead. I then kiss it off him and he starts giggling uncontrollably. Big, deep belly laughs. I've never heard this much come out of his mouth.

I start laughing with him because his laugh is the cutest thing I've ever heard in my life.

All of a sudden, we hear, "Matteo?" We turn to see Dominic walking into the kitchen.

His hand is over his mouth in clear shock. I see tears stinging his eyes.

I turn to Valentina. "Honey, will you help your brother stir? I need to talk to your father for a moment."

She nods and walks over to us, taking Matteo's little hand. "Come on, Matteo. Help me and Luke mix the batter in our bowls." Matteo happily obliges.

I grab Dominic's hand and walk him out of sight around the corner. "What's wrong?"

"I've never heard him laugh like that. Maybe a giggle here and there, but nothing like that. My son is nearly four and I've never made him laugh like that. You've been with him twice and he's putty in your hands."

I rub his arm. "Maybe he's just starting to feel less anxious. You put him in the daycare to help him learn to socialize. Perhaps it's working."

He slowly nods. "Maybe. You're just so...so...good with him. He's comfortable with you. I've never seen him like that with anyone. Gabriela and I included."

Dominic still seems off. I don't think it's just Matteo. "Is something else bothering you? You don't seem right."

He rubs the back of his hand down my cheek. "Thanks for noticing. I tend to have a pretty good poker face, but you see right through it all."

"Tell me what's wrong."

"It's Gabriela. Valentina couldn't stop talking about

you this morning, and now Gabriela is jealous. She was carrying on about me trying to replace her while she's gone. She mentioned suing for full custody and moving the kids to Cuba."

I wrap my arms around his waist. "Oh, Dominic, I'm so sorry."

He holds me tight to him. "That's why I was late. I was talking to my attorney. He doesn't think she has any legal right to do so, but I'm still scared. I can't lose them."

I pull back and look up at him. "You won't. I don't know family law well, but I know enough to know that it's unlikely that it will happen. They don't actively pull kids away from their fathers for no good reason. They certainly don't send them to foreign countries, effectively stripping you of your parental rights."

He nods. "I hope so. I couldn't bear it."

"I know. Come on. Let's get back to the kids before they completely destroy my kitchen."

He smiles and we make our way back in. As soon as we do, we realize our mistake. They've already destroyed my kitchen. There's muffin batter everywhere. I don't know how it happened in the two minutes we were gone.

Dominic blows out a breath. "Oh boy."

The kids look guilty but all smile at each other like they've got a secret. I see that Trex is completely covered in flour.

We clean the kids and the cat, get most of the muffins in the oven, and then turn on a movie for them so we can clean in peace.

I ordered food for Dominic and me. He removes his shirt and tie, leaving him in a tight white undershirt. I can't help but stare at him. He's just so hot. Am I expected to concentrate when he looks like that? I bite my lip to stifle a comment about it.

He smiles. "You like what you see?"

"You know I do." I swallow, continuing to clean, unable to make eye contact. "But I know you don't. I get it. There's no need to make a big deal of it."

He lets out a breath as he turns to me. "Beth."

I'm trying to be strong and not feel the embarrassment of his rejection. I gather myself and turn toward him. "Wha..."

Before I finish my word, he takes a heaping handful of batter from the counter and flings it at my face. Half of my face is immediately covered in stickiness.

I wipe my batter-covered eye and look at him in shock. He simply smiles at me. It's softer and more playful than sexy, but everything he does is sexy.

I turn to the countertop next to me and grab a handful of batter sitting there. I hold my hand up.

His eyes widen. "Don't you dare." He points to his pants. "I'm in work clothes."

Without any further thought, I fling it at him. The gooey mixture spreads across his face and shirt, with a drop or two splattered onto his pants.

At the same time, we both reach for more batter. He grabs my wrist before I can throw anymore at him and spreads another handful across my face.

We're both laughing as he bends and licks it off.

I squirm in his arms, though he easily overtakes me. He holds my arms down as we continue to laugh, though as our eyes meet, the laughter subsides.

He runs his hands up my arms and shoulders until they reach my face. He grabs it with both hands and smashes his lips to mine.

The kiss goes from zero to sixty in less than two seconds. It's messy, sugary, and hot as hell. We're pawing at each other. His delicious tongue swirls around my mouth. Oh god, the way he kisses. I get so lost in it.

He moves his hands to my thighs, lifting me up so I can wrap my legs around him. I grip his shirt, attempting to bring him closer, as if that's possible.

An immediate ache develops between my legs. I squeeze my thighs around him, trying to gain some friction. This man drives me mad with desire.

My tongue is in his mouth, tasting every inch of him. Our lips move together perfectly. Sensually.

His hands are all over my body, lighting me on fire.

All of a sudden, I hear, "Mommy?"

Dominic and I freeze. I immediately unwrap my legs and slide down his body. Dominic and I stare at each other wide-eyed for a moment before turning to see all three kids standing there, all with huge, dopey smiles on their faces.

Valentina, with her sass, crosses her arms and asks, "Are you two boyfriend and girlfriend? You're not allowed to kiss unless you are."

Dominic grabs my hand and kisses it while staring at Luke. "Luke, I'd like to ask your permission to make your mom my girlfriend. I think she's the most special woman I've ever met."

I try to play it cool, as if my heart didn't just skip a beat. As if it's not the sweetest and most exciting thing I've ever heard in my life.

Luke thinks for a moment. "Does this mean I can't marry Valentina?"

I can't help but let out a laugh.

Valentina shakes her head. "You never had a chance with me anyway. You're not my type."

Luke looks like he's about to cry. I need to lighten things.

I scoop a heaping handful of batter and throw it at Valentina. It splatters all over her.

She gasps in shock before smiling and grabbing her own handful. It looks like she's going to throw it at me, but at the last second, she turns and throws it at Dominic. All. Over. Dominic.

And then all hell breaks loose. A full-fledged food fight is going on in my kitchen. We're all hysterically laughing, all covered in muffin batter. My kitchen is a mess, but I don't care. We're having a blast. Matteo is grinning from ear to ear as he's covered in batter, trying to protect himself.

The four of us gang up on Dominic, completely covering him in the batter. The kids all climb on top of him while I smother his face in the sticky mess. Matteo is now squealing with laughter. We all are.

Even little Trex has batter all over his fur as he rolls around in confusion.

We're in the midst of mayhem when I hear the doorbell ring. I assume it's the takeout I had ordered for Dominic and me. I dodge batter, walking out of the kitchen toward my front door. I yell back, "That must be our food."

As I make my way to the door, I feel Dominic's arms wrap around me from behind and lift me. He kisses up my neck. "Dinner is on me, princesa."

I screech. "You're getting me all messy."

He kisses my neck again. "Quiero ensuciarte más." *I want to get you messier.*

My breathing picks up. As soon as he talks in Spanish, I practically lose brain function. I'm putty in his hands.

He's licking batter off my face and neck as we're both laughing when I open the door. I look out and my face drops. It's not the takeout guy. It's Brittany and Mindy. They look at my batter-covered body and then they look at Dominic. Their chins legitimately drop when they see the sex god behind me, covered in batter with his muscular arms wrapped around me and his mouth on my neck.

I can't help but smile. Yep, I know I have the hottest man alive wrapped around me, licking me. I'm a lucky bitch. "Brittany. Mindy. Can I help you?"

Brittany studders, "W…w…we're patrolling tonight. We thought you might want to come. We brought you your shirt." She holds it up. It's literally a shirt with a big badge that reads M.O.M. Patrol. Both of their last names begin with the letter *M* while mine begins with an *O*. I notice they're both wearing the same one.

"I'm a little busy…umm…baking tonight. There's a bake sale at the school on Monday. We're making muffins."

Mindy mumbles, "Will he be on the menu?"

I press my lips together to stifle my smile. Not yours, but I hope he's on my menu.

"Sorry, I can't help tonight. Duty calls." I give them a wink before I start to close the door.

I hear Mindy say to Brittany, "He can butter my muffin. I'd lick that right off his face if I were her."

Brittany responds, "I just want to sit on his face."

I giggle as I close the door.

Dominic turns me around and gives me a quick, hard, batter-covered kiss. "That's not a bad idea. Why don't you sit on my face and then I'll butter your muffin?"

ONE HOUR LATER

DOMINIC

I'm tasting heaven as Beth rides my face. I mumble into her, "Sabes más dulce que la masa de molletes, princesa." *You taste sweeter than the muffin batter, princess.*

She moans my name as she arches her back and squeezes her tits in ecstasy.

After those women left, we cleaned the kids and cat and then put them to bed. We told the kids that there was going to be a sleepover because we needed time to clean the mess. Yes, we're shameless. We just wanted the time alone together.

We were planning to clean the kitchen and eat the dinner that had arrived, but we ended up tearing each other's clothes off and getting into the shower instead. I much prefer the meal I'm currently feasting on.

My tongue works her over as she grinds herself over me. I slide my fingers into her and suck her clit into my mouth. Her whole body starts to shake. I reach up and cover her mouth as her orgasm hits her. She bites my hand to keep her sounds at bay.

She's breathing loudly as I slide up so she's straddling my lap. My bare cock runs through her dripping, swollen, still trembling pussy.

I tuck her hair behind her ear and then run my fingers over her hardened nipples. "I've been thinking about this monogamy thing and what it entails. The perks." I smile. "Quiero estar dentro de ti sin nada entre nosotros." *I want to be inside you with nothing between us.*

She's still a bit out of it but gives a small nod.

I grab her face. "Did you understand me?"

"Yes. I have an IUD. I trust you to be clean." She moves her hips over me. "Just get inside me. Now. I need you."

Without waiting for me to answer, she lifts, brings my tip to her entrance, and begins to sink down onto me.

"Oh god, Dominic. That's so good. You're so big." She wiggles her hips as she slowly slides down and acclimates to my size, completely absorbed in the pleasure.

Feeling her around me with nothing between us is perfection. "Pienso que me va a gustar esto de la monogamia. Tienes el conno más húmedo, apretado, y suave, princesa." *I think I'm going to like this monogamy thing. You have the tightest, softest, wettest pussy, princess.*

She rocks her hips over me in a way I would never have thought imaginable. Something has awakened in her. She's not shy. She's wild and uninhibited, taking what she wants from me.

She rides me like a rodeo star. I let her go until she starts to lose control with her orgasm looming. She's getting louder and louder. She seems to have forgotten about the sleeping children in the house.

I sit up and bite her nipple. I see her eyes roll back in her head while her pussy clenches me. I love how much a little pain turns her on.

I move to kiss away her screams as I grip her hips and fuck her hard from below. She wraps her arms around my neck and meets me thrust for thrust as I piston into her.

The harder I go, the more she clenches around me, getting lost in the magic we make together.

Maybe I really can do this. I certainly have no interest in other women right now. I desperately want to try with her. I want it to work. I'm terrified that it won't.

CHAPTER FOURTEEN

BETH

I wake in the morning surrounded by Dominic's scent, with his arms cocooning me. His naked front is to my naked back.

I don't think I've ever woken up with such a feeling of contentment and bliss. I could stay like this forever. I never want to get up.

I can't believe I let him sleep here. In my bed. While Luke is home.

Was it a poor parenting decision? Probably. Do I care right now? Not in the least.

I didn't think twice about letting him sleep in my bed. It's the first time since my divorce that a man has been in my bed. The simple truth is, I want him here.

And we had sex without a condom. I put no thought into that either. I just wanted to feel every part of him moving inside me at that moment. This man fries my brain.

I turn in his arms, with only a thin sheet covering our bodies, and run my fingers and lips along his chest as I look up at the beautiful man in my bed. I'm sleeping with the sexiest man alive. I truly am the luckiest woman in the world.

His eyes are closed, but he smiles as he pulls my leg around him and nudges my opening with his hardened tip. In a voice that immediately awakens my arousal, he says, "Creo que necesito estar dentro de tu coño apretado otra vez." *I need to be inside your tight pussy again.*

"Este coño apretado está sufriendo por tu polla gigante." *This tight pussy is aching for your giant cock.*

A voice that isn't mine or Dominic's says, "Since when do you speak Spanish?"

Who was that? It couldn't be.

I lift my head and see Cassandra sitting in a chair in my bedroom. I plop my head back down and quickly remove my leg from where it's straddling Dominic. "Ugh, Cassandra, what are you doing here?"

"I thought I was coming over to cheer you up. Clearly you don't need it."

Dominic smiles as his eyes start to peel open. "Is her being here in the morning a normal thing for you?"

"Sadly, yes. Cassandra has no boundaries. In fact, I need to pull up the full blanket or she'll check you out."

Cassandra smirks. "I already did. You weren't kidding about him. Slow entry when she opens up the back door, Dominic. She's an anal virgin."

"Cassandra! Boundaries!"

I feel Dominic shaking in laughter.

I smack his chest. "Don't encourage her."

"I think she's hysterical. It doesn't bother me at all."

He begins kissing my neck. "Where were we?"

"My sister is in the room."

He continues kissing me. "It doesn't bother me at all."

"The kids will be up soon."

The kisses haven't stopped as he rolls on top of me. "It doesn't bother me at all."

Cassandra stands. "I'll leave you to it. Trevor is with all the kids downstairs. He's got them all cleaning that mess in your kitchen."

Dominic's lips are on mine before I can respond. I simply lift my hand and wave goodbye as she leaves and closes the door behind her.

AFTER ANOTHER INCREDIBLE round with Dominic, we quickly shower and make our way downstairs. I notice out of the corner of my eye that the kitchen is spotless.

Valentina and Luke are playing Trivial Pursuit. Brandon, Dylan, and Matteo are all doing a puzzle.

Brandon and Dylan are very chatty. I hope Matteo is managing. He seems to be. Trex is on his lap. The cat very clearly soothes him. I quietly point it out to Dominic, and he nods in understanding.

Cassandra and Trevor are sitting on the couch drinking coffee making googly eyes at each other. "Good morning."

Cassandra and Trevor turn and smirk at us. Luke looks up at me. "You slept late, Mommy."

Cassandra smiles. "She sure did. She must be well rested."

I jokingly scowl at her, and her smile only increases.

I make my way around to kiss all the kids good morning. When I get to Matteo, he holds on to my neck, so I lift him along with Trex. I rub his nose with mine. "Did you have a fun sleepover party?"

Of course I'm expecting a nod, but in a little, cute voice, he says, "Yes."

I snap my head toward Dominic. His eyes are wide and start to fill with tears.

He kisses Matteo on the cheek. "You have the most beautiful voice. I hope we get to hear it more often."

Matteo softly responds, "Okay."

Dominic visibly swallows.

Valentina harrumphs and crosses her arms. "Luke, you're wrong."

"No, I'm not. That's what it says on the card. *You're* wrong."

I run my fingers through Luke's hair. "What's wrong, baby?"

He looks up. "The question was *what's the capital of the state you live in?*"

Valentina nods. "And I said, *Harrisburg*. I know for a fact that I'm right."

Luke holds up the card. "See, Mommy, that's not what it says the answer is." He points to the answer. "It reads, *will vary,* is the answer."

Cassandra and Trevor start laughing. Dominic and I smirk at each other before I look back at Luke and Valentina. "Well, you're both right. The capital is *Harrisburg*, and the card does read *will vary*. Luke, honey, it means it will vary by state."

He puts his head down. "Oh."

Valentina has a huge, satisfied grin.

Trevor nods toward the kitchen. "There's coffee in there. We need to leave in a little bit for the game."

"Thanks."

Placing Matteo back in front of the puzzle, I see Trevor

silently tell Luke to fix his hair. I give him a disapproving look and he winks at me.

Dominic and I walk into my kitchen, where he pulls me into an embrace. He whispers, "Did you hear Matteo?"

"I did."

He smiles as he softly kisses my lips.

Trevor and Cassandra walk in. Dominic doesn't seem to care and continues to hold me close and softly kiss me.

We pull apart only when Cassandra hands us mugs of coffee.

I look around at my spotless kitchen. "Wow, Trevor, thank you for cleaning up."

He shrugs. "The kids did most of it."

I let out a laugh. "I doubt that."

Cassandra sips her coffee. "I guess you got over the whole sleeping naked thing."

I see Dominic and Trevor silently laughing.

Cassandra turns to Dominic. "You should be thanking me. You should have seen the granny gowns she used to wear to bed."

Dominic lifts my hand and kisses it. "She looks beautiful in everything." He smiles, "*And* nothing."

The three of them are grinning. I shake my head. "The three of you are a bunch of comedians."

Dominic kisses my cheek. "I have to run. They both have soccer games. I'll call you later." He wiggles his eyebrows. "Thanks for the muffins."

He calls for Valentina and Matteo and they leave.

Trevor wraps his arm around me. "You seem happy, Beth."

Cassandra scoffs. "She should be happy. She's finally been fucked properly. I was weeks away from loaning you to her."

He simply rolls his eyes and shakes his head at her antics.

She takes another sip. "Are you concerned about the kids knowing you're together? Do you think maybe it's a bit early for sleepovers that they know about?"

I sit in one of the kitchen chairs. "I suppose you're right. I didn't even think about it. I guess we're moving full steam ahead. I lose all rational thought around him."

She nods. "Just be careful. I saw Matteo's reaction to you. He's already attached. I didn't even know you were together and here you are playing one big, happy family."

"Dominic asked Luke for permission to date me. It was really sweet."

"How did he respond?"

"He asked if it meant that he couldn't marry Valentina."

Trevor lets out a laugh. "He's smitten with her. I'll have to divert him. Who's Rose? He talks about her too."

"Trevor, that's his eighteen-year-old babysitter. At your urging, he brought her flowers and made her sit through a candlelit dinner the other night."

He smiles. "Maybe he likes older women like me."

I cover my face. "Oh my god, Trevor. Cool it with the Casanova O'Connell stuff. He's seven."

"Just tell me if the babysitter liked it."

I blow out a breath. "She said Luke treats her better than her real boyfriend."

He lets out a laugh. "That's my boy."

I OFFERED to host Sunday night dinner this week. Darian and Jackson always host. I've been going there for six years and I want to reciprocate. The whole crew is coming. Jackson and Darian, her three girls and their spouses and children, and his three sons with their spouses and children. Melissa, Declan, and Jade are coming too. Jade texted me earlier to ask if her mother, Amanda, can come. Apparently, she's going through a divorce and is a bit down. I can certainly commiserate.

Luke is incredibly excited to have all the kids over to our house. Though Brandon and Dylan are the only ones that are technically his cousins, they all treat him like a cousin and Scotty is his best friend.

I contemplated inviting Dominic and the kids, but Cassandra was right about integrating the families. It's bad enough that we've done it with the kids. There's no reason to do it with the big crew just yet. Especially this crazy crew.

Cooking for thirty people isn't in my skillset, so I'm ordering takeout. Darian often orders Chinese food for everyone. I simply asked her for her standard order. I also don't have a table that fits everyone, so it will be buffet style.

Everyone filters in and I'm pouring drinks for all, except Reagan and Skylar who are pregnant. Jade brought a bottle of Snoop Dogg wine. The talking bottle seems to be amusing her and the kids.

Harley sits next to me with her glass of wine. "I hear you're dating Dominic. He's hot. Good pull."

I mumble, "Cassandra has a big mouth."

She shakes her head. "Scotty told me. Luke told him that Dominic asked his permission to make you his girlfriend." She touches her chest over her heart. "That's the cutest thing I've ever heard."

"It was sweet. Yes, I guess we're dating. It's new though. I'm not sure we should have involved the kids, but it just sort of happened that way."

She rubs my arm. "I think it's great. He seems like a nice guy. He's certainly good-looking. If you all ever need a getaway, feel free to use our shore house. You're welcome anytime."

Harley and Brody have a gorgeous shore house. It's huge and right on the beach. There's a deck overlooking the ocean and a rooftop hot tub. With it only being ninety minutes away, we've all spent a lot of time there since I've been included in family events.

"Thank you. I'll mention it to Dominic. It might be nice to get out of town for a weekend."

Skylar, Reagan, Jade, and her mother, Amanda, come sit with us. Jade is holding Trex. She lifts him up. "What's her name?"

"He's a boy. His name is Trex."

She looks under him. "I see no penis."

"Cat's penises are inverted unless they're aroused."

She shrugs. "I guess I don't do it for cats. Why is his name Trex?"

"I named him T-Rex because his front paws are so short and Luke loved dinosaurs at the time, but Luke couldn't pronounce it, so it evolved into Trex."

She nods in understanding. "Did you know that there are a lot of dinosaur romance novels?"

Harley and I look at each other in question. I turn back. "Like romance stories between dinosaurs?"

She shakes her head. "No, like a human woman and a dinosaur get it on."

Reagan and Skylar start laughing. I'm in shock. "Who wants to read about a woman getting it on with dinosaur? How would that even work physically?"

She shrugs. "I don't know, but it's definitely a thing. Some sort of fetish."

Amanda nods in agreement. "She's right. There are women into that. I saw one the other day titled *Jurassic Pork: The Lust World*."

Now we're all laughing. Reagan asks, "Is there one called Cock-A-Saurus Rex?"

Amanda smiles. "I don't know. To be clear, I don't read them, I've just seen them. I prefer to keep things in the human realm, though I did just read a genie romance novel by Jade Dollston and absolutely loved it."

Jade enthusiastically nods. "I read that one too. It was really good. I can handle a hot Cajun genie, but not a dinosaur."

I shake my head. "I certainly don't get the dino appeal, but to each their own."

Reagan turns to Skylar. "Maybe Lance could dress up as a dinosaur for you. A little *dino*play. Or a little *dino*lingus."

Skylar rolls her eyes while Harley and Reagan both laugh. I feel like I'm missing something here but don't bother to ask.

Jade ends the weird conversation by saying, "Mom, did I tell you that I was interviewing a man the other day and he was totally obsessed with your paintings in my office?"

Amanda smiles. "Oh, that's nice to hear."

"He seemed to know your real name."

I interrupt, "You don't sign Amanda Tremaine on your paintings?"

She shakes her head. "No. I've always signed everything *Enchanted*. At least after Jade was born. I thought it afforded some privacy if I ever hit it big and needed it. I love the word *Enchanted*. It's so whimsical."

Jade shakes her head. "Mom still believes in fairytales."

Amanda shrugs. "I do. That's why I'm getting divorced. I still haven't found my Prince Charming, but I believe he's out there." She turns back to Jade. "I wonder how the person knew me. What's his name?"

"Beckett Windsor. He's a famous billionaire entrepreneur."

Amanda's eyes widen. "Oh. I've...umm...met him before."

Jade lifts an eyebrow. "Since when do you rub elbows with the rich and famous?"

She visibly swallows. "I met him at Reagan's party a few years ago. He was very nice. We had a lovely conversation about art."

Amanda looks down, not making eye contact with anyone. Jade looks around at all of us and smirks. "Anything more to tell us, Mom? It seems like there may be more to the story."

Amanda shakes her head. "Nothing to tell. I was having a moment and he was very sweet."

I think we all know there's more to it than that, but no one says anything.

CHAPTER FIFTEEN

BETH

It's late afternoon at the office and my phone rings. I look at the caller ID and see that it's Dominic. I can't help but smile. I'm so smitten with him.

I click the accept button. "Hey, handsome."

"Hola, Aspiradora."

"Am I a vacuum cleaner?"

"The way you suck my cock is like a vacuum cleaner. I'm going to start calling you that instead of princesa."

I burst out laughing. "Is it a good thing or a bad thing?"

In a sexy voice he purrs, "Oh, it's a *very* good thing."

I smile. "I'll have to give you a refresher next time I see you."

"That's why I'm calling."

"Because you want a blow job?"

He chuckles. "No...well yes, I always want you to wrap your lips around my cock, but that's not why I called. I want to see you tonight."

I can't help but get excited at the prospect. "I'd like that."

"I think you were right about animal therapy. I looked into it and spoke with Matteo's doctor. I told her about his reaction to Trex. She thinks it would be a great idea for him. I called the local animal shelter, and they have a puppy that seems to be a good match for us. I'm going to pick her up after work. Can you grab the kids and meet at my house?"

"Absolutely. He's going to be so excited. All the kids will be." I'm excited too. While I was in Dominic's house the first night we were together, I was a bit out of it and don't remember much. I remember a huge kitchen and bedroom, but that's it. I can't wait to see it all in the light of day.

"Thank you. Why don't you stop at your house and grab clothes for you and Luke so you can stay over."

I hesitate for a brief moment, wondering if it's the right thing to do, but I can't seem to help myself. I want to be with him. "You want another sleepover party, Mr. Mazzello?"

"I want some time with my aspiradora."

I giggle. "That can be arranged. I'll see you tonight."

"See you tonight, Aspiradora."

After work, I run home to pack. I've never been more thankful that Cassandra bought me all that lingerie for my birthday. I put some on underneath my clothes, pack Luke's bag, and head to the school to pick up the kids. I tell them that Dominic has a big surprise. They're buzzing with excitement.

We pull into the driveway of the address Dominic gave me, but it's not what I imagined. I know it was dark and I was wrapped up in Dominic last time, but I feel like I'd remember the house before me.

I look back toward Valentina. "Sweetie, is this the right place?"

She nods. "Yes. This is our house."

What the hell? It's not a house. It's a giant mansion on a huge estate. I'm sure Dominic makes good money working at Daulton Holdings, but not this kind of money. Clearly, I'm missing a piece of the puzzle.

Dominic had texted me the code to get inside, and when we walk through the door, my chin just about drops to the floor. It's enormous. How do I not remember this? I guess I was in an orgasm coma at the time.

Everything inside is completely state of the art and modern. There's not a single thing out of place. The walls are covered in windows overlooking what can best be described as a palatial estate with huge grounds.

Dominic texted that he was ordering dinner, but the kids complain that they're hungry. I head to the kitchen to find them a snack. I walk in and am flooded by memories of the dirty things we did on the kitchen island.

I look around, truly taking it in for the first time. I think the kitchen is bigger than the entire house I grew up in. It's got everything you could imagine. Huge counterspace. Every high-end appliance. Several ovens, plus what appears to be a pizza oven. And a few devices I've never seen before.

Wow.

Just as the kids are finishing their snack, we hear a car pull up. They all run to the front door, knowing there's a surprise.

Dominic steps out of his car with a huge grin on his face. Oh my god, he's so damn good-looking.

Valentina shouts, "Papa, what's going on?"

Dominic walks to his back car door and reaches in.

When he lifts back up, he's holding the cutest little puppy in his big arms. It's got auburn curly hair and looks like a teddy bear.

Valentina screams when she sees it, sprinting to her father. Luke, Matteo, and I follow suit.

Dominic crouches down. The kids all pet the cute puppy, who buries his head in Dominic's chest in fear.

Valentina looks at him wide-eyed. "Do we get to keep the puppy?"

Dominic nods. "We sure do."

Luke asks, "What's his name?"

Dominic replies, "It's a girl, and she doesn't have a name yet. I think we'll let Matteo name her."

Matteo's face lights up. "Me?"

"Yes." Dominic carefully places the puppy in his little hands. He rubs his face in her fur. I know immediately that this was a good idea.

All the kids' hands are on the puppy. Dominic reaches back into his car and grabs a big shopping bag.

He places it in Valentina's arms and says, "There are a ton of new toys in here. Why don't you guys take her to the backyard to see which ones she likes? Let her run around and get some exercise."

The kids all happily oblige as they disappear around the back of the house. As soon as they do, Dominic is on me. He presses my body to his car and his lips take mine. His hands move all over my body. His quick-forming erection pushes into my stomach.

He mumbles into my mouth, "I've missed you. I've been thinking about touching you all day. It feels like forever."

I smile as his lips move down my neck. "It's only been two days."

"Two days too long, Aspiradora."

I move my head and suck his lower lip into my mouth. Hard. Our eyes meet as I squeeze his dick and release his lip. "That's what I'm going to do to your cock later."

He moans while moving his hand up the back of my thigh under my skirt. He applies pressure to my panty-covered pussy. "Voy a hacer que te corras tan fuerte esta noche. Una y otra vez hasta que no puedas ver bien." *I'm going to make you come so hard tonight. Over and over until you can't see straight.*

My arousal is sky-high. I can't get over what this man does to my body. The way he looks, the way he smells, the way he touches me, the way he speaks to me. All of it ignites me.

I breathe, "Yes."

He smiles into my mouth. "Don't worry, I brought you a bag of toys too."

I swallow hard. I have no idea what that means.

The sound of giggles causes us to pull apart. The kids are getting louder and must be coming back around to the front. Dominic mouths, "Later," as I nod.

I need a minute to collect myself. My panties are soaked. I have to fan myself with my hand to calm down.

Dominic is now a few feet away from me, but he inhales deeply. He turns around, looks down at the area now throbbing for him, gives me a sexy smile, and licks that lower lip of his. His ability to smell my arousal is not helping my current situation.

The kids come into sight. Valentina shouts, "I think she's hungry. She was trying to eat the grass. And she kept trying to hug our legs."

Hug our legs? I have to hide my smile. It figures

Dominic would have a horny dog. "She must be a hugger like your father."

Dominic winks at me before he pulls out a big bag of food from the trunk of his car. As soon as we walk in the door, the dog takes off for the kitchen table. The kids had dropped a few of their snacks on the ground, and she quickly gobbles it all up. I guess she was hungry.

We have dinner while the dog has hers. I turn to Dominic. "What kind of dog is she?"

"She's a Goldendoodle. Part Golden Retriever and part Poodle. They're supposed to be excellent with kids."

As the puppy finishes her dinner, she flops over to us and starts eating what the kids have dropped on the ground from their dinner.

Matteo watches her with glee. It's adorable.

Dominic smiles as he looks at Matteo. "Have you thought of any names?"

In his little voice, he says, "Aspiradora."

I snort my drink from my nose and start coughing. Dominic silently laughs as he looks at Matteo. "Why Aspiradora?"

Matteo points to the puppy continuing to clean the food off the ground. I get it. The dog is like a vacuum cleaner.

Dominic nods. "Well, Matteo, I *love* the name Aspiradora. It reminds me of someone I know." He smirks as he gives me a little side-eye. "Maybe we can call her Dora as a shorter nickname."

Matteo smiles and nods in agreement.

Luke looks up at me. "Mommy, Colton said that the little league is doing a father-son night at the Phillies baseball game next week." That's the local professional baseball team in Philadelphia. "Can you ask Uncle Trevor to take me?"

I had seen that email come through. I know Trevor will be out of town that day. I considered calling Gary, but we haven't seen him in six months. I was planning to ask the little league if I could go with Luke but didn't want to mention it until I had an answer.

I give him a small smile. "Honey, Uncle Trevor is out of town that day for work. I'll ask if I can take you."

Luke puts his head down. "No, that's okay. I don't want to be the only one there with a girl. Maybe next time Uncle Trevor will be in town."

My heart breaks for my baby. He got such a shit deal when it came to his father. Trevor said he'd cancel his trip, but I wouldn't let him. He does enough for Luke.

Dominic shrugs. "If you want, I'll go with you, Luke. I've been dying to take Matteo to his first game. Maybe the three of us can go together. You can teach him about the players."

Luke's face lights up. "Can he, Mommy?"

I turn to Dominic. "Are you sure?"

He smiles. "Absolutely. If you're good with it." I nod, trying not to let my emotions overtake me.

Valentina interrupts, "Excuse me, baseball isn't only for boys. Maybe I want to come too."

I can't contain my smile. Valentina is a girl after my own heart. "You're right, though I'm happy to spend that day with you doing whatever you want."

She thinks for a moment. "I'll think about it and get back to you."

I wink at her. "I was thinking of heading to Scotty's house that day to hang with his mom. You're welcome to come with me and spend time with Scotty."

Her eyes widen. "That sounds fun. I'll do that."

Neither Luke nor Dominic look happy. I laugh inwardly.

Dominic turns back to Luke. "You know, Luke, I was a pretty good ballplayer when I was younger. I played in college, but then I hurt my elbow after my first year and stopped playing."

I didn't know that. I'm realizing there's a lot I don't know about Dominic. So far, our relationship has been very physical. Perhaps we need to spend a little time talking and getting to know each other. Though the thought of Dominic in a baseball uniform runs through my mind. Holy shit, I would give anything to see that.

He continues, "My teammates are still my best friends. Maybe someday soon we can all throw around the ball."

Luke smiles and nods in excitement. "What position were you?"

"I was a pitcher."

Luke's eyes light up. "That's what I am."

"I can show you a few pitches if you want. I had a wicked curveball."

"That would be awesome. Thanks."

Dominic smiles. "Do you know how to score a game?"

"No."

"When we go to the game, we can buy a few scorecards. I can teach you and Matteo. It's a fun way to watch the game."

Luke is practically bouncing in his seat.

While the kids are chatting, I lean over to Dominic and squeeze his leg. I whisper, "You're going to get the full aspiradora treatment tonight, Mr. Mazzello."

He licks his lower lip as he squeezes my hand in return.

THE PUPPY IS in her cage for the night and Dominic is reading to the kids. It gives me time to get myself ready, both physically and mentally. I only have a vague understanding about his past sexual encounters, but it's obviously extensive. I want to give him what he needs.

I'm particularly happy with the wardrobe I packed for this evening. I think back to when Cassandra bought it for me. I was confident that I'd never wear it. Yet here I am, wearing crotchless panties and a bustier that lifts my boobs into my neck.

I hear him close the door to the kids' room, which is at the far end of the hallway from his giant master suite. I sit on the end of the bed and lift one foot onto the bed, spreading myself wide. I lean back on one elbow as I attempt to channel my inner sex goddess.

He walks in the room and stops short when he sees me. "Mierda." *Holy shit.*

His eyes darken and he licks his lower lip. I know what that means. My body is buzzing with anticipation.

He walks toward me, stopping between my legs. He silently runs his eyes up and down my body.

After a few moments, he runs his thumb over my now red-painted lips. "Me vas a chupar la polla?" *Are you going suck my cock?*

I nod as I wrap my lips around his thumb and suck it hard. His eyes flutter.

He runs his thumb from my lip, down my chin, through my breasts, and down through my pussy.

"You're wet, princesa. Does thinking about sucking my cock turn you on? La idea de estos labios rojos envolviéndome te hace mojada?" *Does the thought of these red lips wrapped around me make you wet?*

I nod again.

He slowly slides his thumb into me and then pulls it out, bringing it to his mouth. He gives it a long lick with that thick tongue I fantasize about. "Sabes lista."

You taste ready.

I've been planning a slow seduction, but what I really want is to jump on top of him and impale myself on him.

He begins to unbuckle his belt, but I stand and place my hands over his. "Let me do it."

He licks his lower lip again. My hands are shaking in anticipation. I'm throbbing between my legs.

I gather myself and lick across the seam of his lips as I slowly unbutton his shirt. After removing it, I rub my hands all over his chest in appreciation for the chiseled, perfect man before me.

I kiss my way down, taking in his scent along the way. It's so uniquely him and does amazing things to my body. I'm in so deep with this guy.

I kiss my way down until I'm on my knees. Pulling down his pants and boxer briefs, I take his massive length into my hand and look up at him. "I want you to take me how you need it tonight. No rules. No limits."

He nods as he grabs the giant head of his cock and smears it all over my lips. I can taste the saltiness leaking from his tip.

"Saca la lengua." *Stick out your tongue.*

I do and he squeezes his tip so a little more pre-ejaculate seeps onto my tongue. I suck his tip hard for a moment to make sure I get it all.

He moans in pleasure. "Mi aspiradora perfecto."

I run my hands up his massive thighs. They're so hard

and muscular. When perfection was imagined, it was Dominic Mazzello they had in mind.

"Desliza tus dedos en tu coño." *Slide your fingers into your pussy.*

I do. I'm excessively wet. It's practically pouring out of me. I can hear the sounds of my arousal as I push them in and out.

He grabs my hair and pulls it tight and growls, "Abre bien la boca." *Open your mouth wide.*

I do as he feeds his cock all the way in. I swirl my tongue around every inch I can manage along the way.

He pushes until he meets the back of my throat. "Abre tu garganta para mi polla."

Open your throat for my cock.

I take a few breaths and relax as my throat begins to accommodate him.

I seal my lips around him and suck hard. He rattles off a few Spanish expletives.

He slides back out and then slams it back in. My gag reflex triggers, but I will it away. I want to give him what he needs. Truth be told, I get off on him taking me as he needs it.

He pulls my hair and fucks my mouth like he fucks my pussy. Hard, wild, and deep. My eyes are watering and drool is coming out of my mouth, but I get the job done.

The way he's truly letting go is driving me crazy. I can't believe I'm about to come from giving a blow job, but that's exactly what's about to happen.

I moan into him. That seems to set him off. He pushes in deep one last time and comes down my throat. I feel his salty warmth sliding down.

My orgasm is cresting at the vision of a feral Dominic

standing over me coming into my mouth. My body starts shaking.

He pulls his cock out. "Are you about to come?"

I breathe, "Yes."

He lifts me onto the bed and practically dives headfirst into my pussy. That tongue of his plunges into my channel while his thumb pushes onto my clit.

My back arches. I grab for sheets and fist them like I'm going to tear them. Two long pumps of his magical tongue later and I start seeing stars as my orgasm rockets through me.

I somehow manage to grab a pillow to smother my screams, or it would wake the whole neighborhood, and the next closest neighbor is about a mile away.

I can't see yet, but I sense his body move away from me. Just a few seconds later, I feel his warm mouth surround my nipple, and then I feel a sharp squeeze.

I blink my eyes open. He's got some kind of contraption on my nipple. He tightens it a drop and a post-orgasmic tremor ripples through my body. Why does that feel so good?

He does the same thing with my other nipple. Holy shit. My orgasm hasn't totally receded. This is making it roll on. My legs are shaking.

Every time he tightens it, my orgasm rises back to the surface. I can't otherwise move. I feel almost paralyzed, paralyzed with pleasure.

He lifts me and sits at the end of the bed. I notice a giant mirror on the wall that we're now facing.

He moves me so that I'm straddling his body, with my back to his front. "Mira, princesa. Mira lo bien que nos vemos juntos." *Watch, princess. Watch how good we look together.*

He lifts me and brings his tip to my entrance. I slowly sink down onto him while my whole body shudders. I squeeze my eyes shut.

"That's it, princesa. Take me deep. Open your eyes and watch."

I open them in time to see his massive length slowly disappear inside me. It's hard to imagine how it fits, but it does. Perfectly.

I work my way down until I'm seated to the hilt. His hands rub my hips, but we don't otherwise move. We simply stare at each other in the mirror. I've never watched myself have sex. This is the most erotic image I've ever seen in my life.

I look at my breasts, currently covered in nipple clamps. I'm straddling the most sensual, attractive man in existence, with his body inside mine. The best part? He's looking at me like I'm everything. In this moment, I feel like I'm everything. This. Is. Heaven. I could stay here like this forever.

He peppers kisses up my back until he gets to the spot where my neck meets my shoulder. He sinks his teeth into me. The pain is a direct line to my clit, which hasn't really stopped pulsating from the last orgasm.

I reach back and run my fingers through his hair as I begin to roll my hips on top of him. His hands, mouth, and teeth move all over my body.

Somehow, the clamps are making my inner walls more sensitive than ever. I can feel every crevice and vein on his cock moving in and out of me.

"Dominic, I'm coming again. You feel too good."

"Espérame." *Wait for me.*

How am I expected to wait when this is my image. Even if we didn't move, I would come just from what's reflecting back at us in the mirror. If he starts speaking Spanish again, I'll never be able to hold off.

He grabs my hips in a way that I know will leave marks as he increases the pace and veracity of his thrusts into me.

"Oh god, you're deep." He's definitely reaching the very end of me.

I continue rolling my hips, keeping up with his thrusts. We work together so beautifully. I know we were made for each other. I'm mesmerized watching this all unfold in the mirror.

My eyes move up our joined bodies until they meet his gaze. As soon as our eyes meet, I feel my pussy squeeze him hard. That's my tipping point.

"Joder. Eso es bueno, princesa. Déjalo." *Oh fuck, that's good, princess. Let go.*

We both give in to the overwhelming sensations and come together. My come flows out of me, covering him as he pumps me full of his own ejaculate.

He gradually slows his thrusts. I don't want to move though. Collapsing my body back onto his, I turn my head and our lips instinctually find the other, as a long, lazy kiss consumes us.

When we pull away, he smiles into my mouth. "That was amazing. Your pussy is still fluttering around me."

"You're going to live inside me. You're not allowed to leave."

He smiles again as he holds me tight.

We eventually clean up and lay in bed after a marathon of the best sex I've ever had. I'm tracing circles on his chest. "Dominic, tell me about this house."

"What do you mean?"

"I mean I know you must do well at Daulton, but this

mansion is something extraordinary. I'm obviously missing something about your background."

His jaw tightens a bit. "I don't like to talk about it, but my mother came from a lot of money. Her family owns the biggest sugar cane farm in Cuba. They have for generations."

"Owns, as in currently?"

"Yes. My younger sister and cousins run it now. There were hopes that it would be me, but I had no interest in running a sugar cane farm, and even less interest in living in Cuba."

"Do you go there often?"

"Not since my mother's funeral over ten years ago."

"So you don't see your family?"

"My father lives here. I see him all the time. He and my mother lived here before she died. She only went to Cuba at the end because she wanted to be buried there. My sister and her family visit from time to time. My kids have never been to Cuba. When Gabriela's mother eventually passes, I suppose that will be their first time going."

"You told Luke earlier that you played baseball in college. I didn't know that. It must have been exciting."

"It was until I got hurt off the field. Then it was catastrophic. I had hopes of playing professional ball, but they were immediately dashed with my injury."

"Will you tell me what happened?"

"I'm tired. Not tonight. It's a long story. Another time."

It's obviously painful for him. I decide not to push.

I WAKE in the morning to a quiet house. I'm on my back. Dominic is sound asleep. His face is nuzzled in my neck and his hand is on my boob.

I can't help but study the outline of his handsome face. He really is the most attractive man I've ever seen. And the things he does to my body? I nearly let out a moan just thinking about our evening.

I reach over for my phone and order us some breakfast. I carefully get out of bed, throw on Dominic's work shirt from yesterday, and make my way downstairs to deal with the puppy.

She's excited to see me, though she immediately starts humping my leg. That's one horny dog.

I let her out back to pee and then feed her. While she's eating, I hear a car pull up. I don't want the delivery person to ring the doorbell, so I make my way toward the front door. Before I get there, the door opens, and an older man walks in.

He smiles as soon as he sees me. He has the same smile as Dominic. "You must be Beth. I'm Martino Mazzello. Dominic's father. You can call me Marty."

"It's nice to meet you." I hold out my hand, but he hugs me. I look down at my state of undress. "Excuse my wardrobe. I didn't know you were coming."

He smiles again. "Oh, please. It's been a long time since I've walked into a house and was greeted by a beautiful, half-naked woman. I more than welcome it."

I giggle. "I'm glad to indulge you."

He winks at me. "I'm just happy to finally meet you. I've heard so many wonderful things."

At that moment, Dora comes flopping into the foyer. His face lights up. "This must be the new puppy. How precious."

I pick her up so he can pet her. "This is Dora, as named by Matteo."

As soon as I set Dora down, she immediately starts humping Marty's leg. He and I both let out a laugh.

"She's a little…"

"Loving?"

I smile. "Yes. That's a good way to say it. She's loving. I should probably take her for a walk. I'm going to get dressed. I ordered some breakfast. Please join us. I got plenty for everyone."

"Wonderful. Why don't I walk with you? We can get to know each other."

"I'd like that. Give me two minutes."

I quickly run upstairs. I see Dominic still sound asleep. I think he got even sexier overnight. Is that possible?

He stirs a bit. I see him reach for my pillow and sniff it, which seems to lull him back to sleep.

Maybe I should crawl back into bed…Oh shit. His father.

I quickly dress and head back downstairs. The food has arrived, and he carried it into the kitchen.

We head out back with the dog. Marty loops his arm through mine. "Tell me about the woman that has my son so enamored."

"He talks about me to you?"

"Of course. Why wouldn't he? We're very close."

"Oh, well it hasn't been that long."

"My dear, my son has been enamored with you for over four years." Knowing that warms every inch of my body. "Tell me about your family."

"My father passed when I was a little girl. My mother, about six years ago. I have an older sister and a seven-year-old son, Luke."

"It must have been hard to lose your father so young, for both you and your mother."

I nod. "It was. I hate that I have so few memories of him, but my mother always told me stories."

"Did she remarry?"

"No. He was it for her."

He nods. "I certainly understand that. I lost my Valeria ten years ago. I miss her every day. She and Dominic were close."

I smile at that. "That's very sweet."

He squeezes my arm. "Tell me, are you enamored with my son the way he is with you?"

I love that he's protective of Dominic.

"Honestly, Marty, I've fallen very hard, very fast. It's a little scary. He's easy to love."

He stops our forward progress. "You love him?"

I blow out a breath. I didn't mean to say that out loud, but certainly can't deny it. Squeezing him, I say, "I think I might, but let's keep that between you and me for now."

He lets out a laugh. "I'm pleased to hear it. He had an unhappy marriage. There was never any love. I begged him not to marry her."

"Why did he?"

"That's a story for him to tell, but everyone should experience true love in their life. He thought he did when he was a young man and never moved on. Until now. I've never seen him this way about a woman. I've worried for so long, but perhaps now I can stop."

That's a lot to unpack.

We walk back into the house and Matteo is in the kitchen. He immediately reaches for me, and I lift him, kissing his cheek. He hugs my neck and kisses me back. "Are Luke and Valentina still asleep?"

He nods. Dora jumps up on me, clearly looking for Matteo.

"Dora has eaten. Do you want to play with her?"

His face lights up. "Yes."

I set him down and they start running around the house. I move to set out the breakfast when Marty grabs my wrist and pulls me into a hug. "Thank you. You're wonderful with him. I've never seen him so warm with anyone. He's obviously taken to you like my son has."

"Hands off my girl, old man."

We turn and see Dominic in the doorway with messy hair and a big smile. He's wearing a white T-shirt and gray sweatpants. Because my mind isn't dirty enough when it comes to Dominic, him in gray sweatpants will now move to the top of my dirty Dominic fantasies. It should be illegal for him to look like this first thing in the morning.

Marty doesn't let go. He says, "I don't know, son, you may have some competition. I think she's a little sweet on me."

Dominic jokingly shoves him aside, grabs my face, and kisses my lips. Right in front of his father.

"Ugh, they're kissing again, Luke."

I smile into Dominic's mouth as I hear Valentina's voice. Dominic pulls away and winks at me.

Marty says, "There's my beautiful girl."

Valentina turns and notices Marty for the first time. Her face lights up. "Papa Marty!" She runs and jumps into his waiting arms. It's clear they're close. It's so nice. I hate that Luke doesn't have my parents as grandparents in his life.

He offers his hand to Luke. "You must be Luke. You very much resemble your mother. Look at those gorgeous eyes you both share."

Luke shakes his hand in return. "You look like an older Dominic."

Marty smiles. "I know. Dominic is a lucky man. He'll get to look like me when he eventually grows up."

We all laugh. I love the fun, casual interaction Marty has with everyone.

We sit down and enjoy a nice, big family breakfast.

CHAPTER SIXTEEN

TWO MONTHS LATER

DOMINIC

I'm finishing up at the office on a Friday. I look at my calendar and see my monthly reminder to check in on Lindsay, Sebastian's ex-wife. I dial her number.

She answers right away. "Hey, Dom. Did you get your calendar reminder to do your monthly check in with me?"

I chuckle. "How did you know?"

She giggles. "It's clockwork every month. I appreciate the sentiment though."

"I just want to make sure you're doing okay."

"I know. You're so sweet. Honestly, it's still a struggle at times." Her voice cracks. "I miss him."

"I know you do. You can do so much better than Sebastian though. You deserve someone worthy of you."

"Yep, that's what everyone keeps telling me. Maybe one day soon my heart will get the message, but today is not that day. Anyway, I'm looking forward to seeing you tonight and meeting your girlfriend."

Beth and I are going to Claudia and Kevin's tonight for dinner. I didn't realize Lindsay was coming too. I play it cool though.

"That's right. We can catch up then. I'm excited for you to meet Beth."

"I'm excited that you're actually dating someone. She must be pretty special."

I smile. "She is. I guess I'll see you in a few hours."

"See you then, Dom. And thanks for always checking in. It means a lot to me."

"My pleasure."

As soon as I end the call, my cell phone rings, and I see that it's Sebastian. I accept the call. "To what do I owe the pleasure of a call from the one and only Sebastian Monroe?"

I hear him blow out a long breath. "I've had the week from hell. I need to blow off some steam. Want to go out tonight?"

"Why? What happened?"

"Work is stressful and just some other shit. Want to hit a club with me? I need to get laid."

"Seb, you know I'm seeing someone. I'm not going to a club with you. I rarely did that when I wasn't seeing someone, certainly not now. Plus, we're having dinner at Kevin and Claudia's tonight."

"Oh. Why wasn't I invited?"

"I imagine it's because Lindsay is coming."

"You guys are fucking taking her side? Inviting her to things and not me?"

"There are no sides. You're our friend. She's our friend. She most definitely did nothing wrong in your divorce. You were too dumb to realize how good you had it."

He blows out a breath and mumbles, "I know. Believe me, I know."

That's the first time he's admitted anything along those lines. I've suspected he has regrets, but I've never heard him outwardly articulate it.

"You okay, Seb?"

"I...I miss her. Maybe I'll come by."

"If you're going to fuck with her head, don't bother. It's not fair to her."

He blows out an audible breath. "I guess you're right. Have a good night. Maybe we can catch up another day."

"Sounds good."

I'm about to hang up when he says, "Dom, you're pretty into this woman you're seeing?"

"I am."

"I'm happy for you. I haven't seen you remotely date since..."

"I know. It's going well though. I don't want to fuck it up."

"Hey, make sure this one is good for you. The last one wasn't, and I don't mean Gabriela."

"I hear you. She's different. I'm the one that's not good enough for her."

"You're the best man I know, brother."

I smile. "Compared to you, anyone is good."

"Dick. Catch you later."

As soon as I hang up, my phone rings again. What the hell? I'm trying to get out of here.

I see that it's Gabriela and answer, "You've landed?"

"Yes. A while ago. I was able to catch an earlier flight. I just picked up the kids from school."

"Did you check it out? What do you think?"

"I did. It looks nice. Valentina hasn't stopped talking about school. And Matteo is different. He seems happy. Relaxed. Maybe you were right."

"He's getting better. I can see it."

"Valentina can't stop talking about your puppy. Matteo was beaming at the mention of her name. I might have to meet her...once she's housetrained."

I can't help but smile. Gabriela doesn't like anything messy. A puppy definitely isn't in her comfort zone.

"Yes, Dora has been wonderful for him. My friend suggested a pet to help with Matteo's anxiety. I think it's already working."

"Is that Beth?"

"It is."

"According to the kids, she's your girlfriend. Is that right?"

I was planning to talk to her about it while she's home. "Yes."

"I thought you don't do girlfriends."

"Maybe I'm changing."

Silence.

"Gab?"

Her voice is barely a whisper now. "I'm here. Why couldn't it be with me?"

I sigh. "I'm sorry, Gab. I really am. Listen, I know

you have to get back down to your mother in a few days. There's a school holiday show on Monday. You'll be able to come, right? I know the kids would love to have you there."

"I'll be there. Will...will she be there?"

"Her son goes to the same school. I imagine she will."

She's silent for a moment before saying, "Okay. I'll have the kids Facetime you in the morning."

"Have a good night. Enjoy your time with them."

BETH

I see Dominic's car pull into my driveway. I poke my head into my family room. "Luke, Rose, I'm leaving."

They both look up from the blocks they're building on the ground and smile. "Bye, Mommy."

"Bye, baby."

I open the door just as Dominic is about to knock. His hand is still in the air. "Oh, I was going to save you the trip..."

Before I finish, he pulls me into his arms and takes my mouth in a deep kiss. He's the most outwardly affectionate man I've ever been around. I thought Trevor and his whole family were full of affectionate men, but Dominic takes it to another level. He never cares who's around, the kids included. He will touch me and open mouth kiss me anywhere, anytime. I can't say I mind it at all.

I lean into him and thread my fingers through his curling hair. It's usually styled, but at the end of the day it often gets messier and curls a bit. It's so sexy. Everything about him is sexy.

"Beth, is it okay…"

Rose stops mid-sentence when she sees Dominic and me making out at the front door. I pull away from him and turn around, trying to gather my senses.

Rose's eyes are wide open. I see her mouth, "Holy shit."

"What's up, Rose?"

"I was just going to ask if he can stay up a little late. I'm introducing him to cheesy eighties movies tonight."

"That's fine."

Dominic tilts his head so he can see Rose. "Hey there. I'm Dominic."

She smiles, clearly affected by the gorgeous man before her. She says, "I'm available…I mean, I'm Rose."

Dominic smirks. This must happen to him all the time. "It's nice to meet you, Rose." He takes my hand. "We should get going, princesa. We're already late. I got held up."

He starts walking out. Rose mouths to me, "He's so hot."

I mouth back, "I know."

Dominic tells me a bit about his friends on the way. Kevin was one of his best friends and teammates in college. He met Claudia their senior year and they have been inseparable since. They have two kids much older than ours. The ex-wife of his other close college friend, Sebastian, will be there too. Her name is Lindsay. They've remained close with her despite the divorce. He told me she is still struggling with it, but that Claudia is a good friend to her.

We arrive at their house. It's a beautiful, large colonial home in a nice Philadelphia suburb. I'm a little nervous, but

Dominic takes my hand in his big, warm one which immediately settles my nerves.

Before we get to the door, it flies open with a teenage boy running out. He immediately stops when he sees us and smiles. "Hey, Uncle Dom. I haven't seen you in a while."

Dominic hugs him in a familiar way. "Benny, my boy. How are you?"

He fake punches Dominic in the stomach. "Stop calling me Benny. It's Ben now. I'm not five anymore."

Dominic smirks at me. Clearly he does it to get a rise out of him.

Ben turns and looks at me. "Who's the hottie?"

"*Benny*, this is my girlfriend, Beth." Is it weird that I get butterflies when he calls me his girlfriend?

I hold out my hand. "It's nice to meet you, *Ben*."

Ben laughs. "See, Uncle Dom, I've known her for three seconds and she gets my name."

Dominic smiles. "Where are you headed?"

"I'm going to hang with my girlfriend. I'll catch you later. Mom has the margarita mix out. I need to get out of dodge before she starts dancing on the table and making TikToks."

Dominic laughs as Ben heads to his car.

The door is open so we walk inside. The house is traditional and warm. It's neat but not too neat. It looks like a family lives here.

We hear voices in the kitchen and walk in. They look up and smile when they see us.

A man that I assume is Kevin gives Dominic a huge hug. He looks like an older version of Ben, being tall and skinny with light brown hair.

An extremely attractive woman with long, straight dark

hair and hazel eyes greets me. "I'm Claudia, you must be Beth."

"I am. Thank you for having us." I hand her a bottle of tequila that Dominic had in the car for her.

She smiles. "You know the way to my heart. We were just about to make margaritas. Are you in?"

I enthusiastically nod. "You bet I am."

She turns to a sexy blonde with tight curls. "This is Lindsay."

I hold out my hand, but Lindsay hugs me. "I'm so happy to meet you, Beth. Dominic hasn't introduced us to a girlfriend in...well...ever."

The two of them giggle and Dominic playfully scowls at them as he kisses them both on the cheek. He's warm to them. It's clear that they're all close.

The five of us chat for a few minutes while drinks are being made. Dominic's hands don't leave my body for a single second. My waist, my hand, my arm, my hip, my shoulder. Even my ass seems to be fair game in mixed company.

Kevin mentions wanting to show Dominic something, leaving us girls alone. As soon as they go, both women look at me.

Claudia sips her margarita. "Okay, what have you done to Dom?"

I pinch my eyebrows. "What do you mean?"

Lindsay looks at Claudia and then me. "We've never seen him like this. His hands were all over you. He doesn't stop staring at you. So like she asked, what have you done to him?"

I shrug. "He's a super warm guy. Has that not always been the case?"

Claudia shakes her head. "I've never seen him like this

with a woman. I don't think in five years of marriage to the wicked witch of the west I ever saw him touch her once. I *know* I didn't see him stare at her the way he stares at you."

I can't help but smile. "I have no idea. This is how he's been the entire few months we've been together."

Claudia nods. "And you got him to get a puppy? I never thought I'd see the day."

"I didn't force him. I simply suggested it. I thought it might be a good idea for Matteo. Why is it so strange for him to have a dog?"

"Have you noticed a museum-like quality to his house?"

I think for a moment. "I guess everything is very clean and organized."

"Yes. Gabriela was crazy about that. She likes everything in perfect order. Obsessively. Everything has to look impeccable for her. She wears designer clothes to soccer games and carpool lines."

Claudia twists her lips. "Obviously you're beautiful. You must also be really good in bed."

I nearly spit my drink.

Lindsay laughs. "Ugh. I don't even remember what sex feels like anymore. It's been nearly a year and a half. I swear I heard my vibrator speak last night. It said, *fuck, this bitch again?*"

The two of them start laughing. I like them. They're warm and funny.

I try to give her an understanding smile. "I went through a divorce too. It's not easy. Just know that it eventually gets easier."

She nods. "Thanks. I get that, in theory. It just hasn't been my reality yet. Maybe one day soon."

Claudia throws her arm around Lindsay. "The good news is that you're young." She looks at me. "Lindsay is only thirty-one." She turns back to Lindsay. "You're beautiful. Your body is still killer. And you're one of the best people I know. Sebastian wasn't ever good enough for you."

A deep voice says, "That's true."

We all look in the kitchen doorway and see a man smiling. He's got a full head of jet-black hair and blue eyes. He's not as tall as Dominic or Kevin, but he's extremely muscular and handsome.

Lindsay's eyes immediately water. "Seb, what are you doing here?"

He swallows and his brow furrows, obviously uncomfortable with her being upset. "The whole gang is here. I thought I'd come by. And I wanted to meet the famous Beth." He holds out his hand and smiles. "I'm Sebastian Monroe. It's nice to finally meet the woman who has my friend off the market."

I shake his hand in return. "Nice to meet you too."

It turns quiet. There's a lot of tension in the room.

He looks back to Lindsay. "Linds, can we talk for a minute?"

Claudia shakes her head. "Sebastian, Kevin and Dom are in the mancave. Go hang with them. Leave her alone. Stop fucking with her head."

"Butt out, Claudia, I want to talk to my wife."

Tears now stream down Lindsay's cheeks. Wow. She's still in love with him. She croaks out, "I'm not your wife anymore. Your decision, not mine. Just go with your friends."

He pauses for a moment before he eventually nods and leaves the room.

Lindsay starts sobbing into Claudia's waiting arms. I mouth to Claudia, "Where are the shot glasses?"

She points to a cupboard. I open it, grab three shot glasses, and then fill them with tequila.

Lindsay and Claudia pull apart, and I hand them each a glass. "Lindsay, I promise the pain eventually goes away and something much better comes along. When I see my ex-husband now, I find myself wondering what I ever saw in him. I feel absolutely nothing for him, and we have a child together."

I hold up my glass with theirs. "To moving on."

ONE HOUR LATER

The three of us are giggling hysterically. I shake my head. "No Claudia, you're Dorothy. I'm Rose and Lindsay is Blanche."

Claudia pouts. "Did you even watch *The Golden Girls*? You're Sophia. I'm Blanche."

I think for a moment. "Then who's Lindsay?"

Lindsay smiles. "All I know is that Seb is Stan, the douchebag ex-husband."

Now we're practically on the floor laughing.

The men walk into the kitchen. Dominic gives me a sexy smile. *Fuck, he's so hot.*

The men all start chuckling.

I cover my mouth. "Did I say that out loud?"

Dominic nods as he makes his way to me, grinning widely. He wraps his arms around me. I think he intends on giving me a quick kiss on the lips, but I grab his neck and deepen the kiss. I can taste the bourbon and cigars on his tongue. I love that taste. It's so Dominic.

I mumble into his mouth. "Take me home and fuck me senseless."

His eyes widen and he covers my mouth. Everyone else is laughing.

"How much have you had to drink, princesa?"

"Just a few shots. Seven or eighty."

He smiles and nuzzles his face into my neck.

Claudia says, "Aww, remember when we were like that, Kev?"

Kevin grabs her and dips her. "We still are." He kisses her long and hard.

They laugh into each other as he pulls her back up.

Sebastian smiles at Lindsay. "We had it pretty good for a while, didn't we Linds?"

She gives a small smile. "We did."

He obviously still cares for her too. Why did they get divorced?

We have a fun evening with them. Sebastian and Kevin tell me all kinds of fun Dominic stories from college, though oddly enough, there's no mention of their time playing baseball.

THE NEXT MONDAY afternoon at school is the big holiday assembly. Dominic told me that Gabriela will be attending. I'm a little nervous about it.

I walk in and see Dominic seated. He has empty seats on either side of him.

He stands when he sees me and kisses my cheek. "Hello,

princesa." His eyes move up and down my body. "You look stunning."

I did wear a particularly stylish suit to work today, knowing I was meeting Gabriela.

We sit and he laces his fingers through mine. He leans over and rubs his nose along my neck. "I love the way you smell."

An intruding female voice says, "Hello, Dominic."

We look up and I see a woman who must be a damn model. She looks like Sofía Vergara. She's gorgeous, with a perfect body, and is dressed right off a fashion week runway.

She sits on the other side of Dominic.

Keeping his fingers laced with mine, he leans over and kisses her cheek. "Gabriela, this Beth. Beth, this is Gabriela."

She gives me a nod and a fake smile. I'm pretty sure I do the same. "Nice to meet you, Gabriela."

Fortunately, the lights dim, and the show starts so we can temporarily end this awkward encounter. Dominic places my hand on his giant quad muscle and keeps his hand over it, aimlessly stroking my fingers with his. Gabriela must look over at it ten times per minute. I think back to what Claudia and Lindsay said about him not being affectionate with her.

I also notice her staring longingly at Dominic from time to time. She may still be in love with him. I can't blame her for that. I imagine a man like Dominic is nearly impossible to get over.

Luke and Valentina's class perform several holiday songs. It's adorable. We smile and laugh through it all.

Matteo's class then takes the stage. I didn't realize they'd be performing. They're singing *Silent Night*. Matteo's mouth is moving, but I doubt he's actually singing.

When they get to the final verse, he steps forward on his own. Dominic and I look at each other. There's no way.

But then he opens his mouth. Matteo not only sings a verse solo, but his voice is angelic. Gabriela has a look of pure shock on her face. Dominic and I both have tears streaming down our faces.

Dominic wraps his arm around me and pulls me close, kissing my head. Gabriela keeps looking at the interaction, but I don't care right now. Matteo is shining. I'd rather watch that.

When the show is over, all the kids run off the stage to find their parents. I hug Luke. "You were great, baby."

He smiles. "Did you hear Matteo? His voice is insane."

"I know. He was wonderful."

Matteo's class is being led off the stage by their teachers, understandable for that age group. Dominic immediately grabs him and swings him around. He giggles. "Matteo, you were amazing."

I fully believe that what happens next is the reason for everything going to hell with Dominic.

When he sets Matteo down, Matteo runs right past Gabriela and jumps into my shocked arms.

I'm not sure what to do. I don't want to disrespect Gabriela, but I certainly won't reject Matteo.

I squeeze him. "You were amazing, sweetie. You have a beautiful voice. You made your Mommy so proud. Give her a hug too."

We both look Gabriela's way. If looks could kill, I'd be dead.

CHAPTER SEVENTEEN

BETH

Christmas has come and gone. I was with my extended Knight/Lawrence family and Dominic was with his father and cousins. He had a joint Christmas with Gabriela until it was time for her to head back to Cuba. Being cognizant of how things went at the holiday show, I thought it best to keep my distance while she was around.

We haven't seen each other in a week. It's the longest we've gone since we started dating. I've truly missed him.

We decided to take Harley up on her offer to stay at their shore house for New Year's Eve. They have a firepit and a huge hot tub on their roof. The house is right on the beach, though it's certainly not *swim in the ocean* weather.

Nonetheless, the kids and Dora have been playing in the sand for hours. The dog is running around like crazy, humping anyone that passes by. She'll sleep well tonight.

Dominic and I are cuddled up with a blanket on the deck watching them. His hands have been all over my body since we got here. He's always affectionate, which I love, but he's taking it to another level right now. Pushing the envelope.

His hand is squeezing my inner thigh and his lips are on my neck. "I need you." His hand moves up my thigh.

I grab his wrist. "Dominic, the kids are twenty feet away. As soon as they go to bed, you can have your wicked way with me, but you need to be patient."

"Let's put them to bed now."

I let out a laugh. "It's three in the afternoon."

He tilts his head back and blows out a long breath. "This is the longest I've ever gone without having sex."

I look at him in shock. "One week? One week is the longest you've ever gone?"

He gives me a boyish smile. "Since I was about sixteen years old, yes."

I mumble, "Maybe you really are an addict."

He lifts me and places me on his lap. "Yes, now feed the beast."

I can feel his giant erection on my leg. He's hard as a rock. He wasn't kidding. I think he is an addict. "Tell me what a normal week would look like if I wasn't in the picture."

He shakes his head. "No. That's not a good idea."

"Tell me. I want to know more about the things you like to do." I live in fear of not keeping him sexually satisfied. How can I do that when he hasn't shared certain things with me?

"I'd have a lot of sex."

"We have a lot of sex."

"Not this week we didn't." He rubs his nose in my neck. "Te extrañé; tu olor, tu sabor. Necesito todo." *I missed you. I missed your smell. I missed your taste. I need all of it.*

As soon as he starts talking in Spanish, I lose all touch with reality and my train of thought. My lips immediately move to his. His tongue pushes into my mouth.

God, I missed him too. His scent. His taste. All of him. It's only been a week and he's turned me into an addict. But I'm not addicted to sex. I'm addicted to Dominic Mazzello.

The kiss escalates quickly. I whisper into his lips, "I need you too."

He slips his fingers into my leggings and panties and runs his fingers through me. Oh god, yes. I've missed this.

He pushes in deep. I feel my whole body relax while he moves his fingers in and out, knowing exactly where to curl them. I have to grab his shirt to stay upright.

I rub my face on his neck and close my eyes. "Ah, Dominic. I've missed your touch."

He continues pumping in and out of me as his thumb moves to my clit and begins to circle. My body is an instrument and he's the maestro.

I moan, "I need more of you." I rub his cock. "I need all of you inside me."

His other arm is squeezing me tight. He's about to lose control.

My orgasm is right there, quickly rising to the service at his long vacant touch. I can't help but let out a small moan.

"Correte para mi, princesa. Luego voy a darte lo que quieras." *Come for me, princess, and then I'll give you what you want.* He bends his head and bites my nipple through my shirt.

That's it, I squeeze my eyes shut as I try to remain quiet through my orgasm. I'm quickly losing the battle. He sucks my tongue into his mouth before I can scream too loudly.

He unexpectedly pulls his fingers and mouth away and

nods toward the beach. As my vision begins to return, I see Luke walking toward us.

"Mommy, I need to go to the bathroom. Can I go inside?"

I take a deep breath to gather myself. "Let me rinse off your feet. We don't want to bring sand into the house."

I slide off Dominic's lap and notice the giant bulge in his pants. I quickly cover him with the blanket.

He sticks the fingers that were in me into his mouth and winks at me. His eyes then flutter. "Hurry back, princesa. We're not done."

He's so fucking hot. I just...

"Mommy, I really have to go."

I break out of my Dominic trance and snap my head toward Luke. "Sorry. Let's get you cleaned up."

I hose off Luke's feet and then take him to the bathroom. When he's done, he asks to go back outside. I nod and he runs off.

I clean up the small amount of sand that fell from him in the bathroom and then start to head back outside. When I pass the pantry, one of the doors swings open, and Dominic pulls me inside and closes the door.

His lips immediately find mine. His tongue moving across mine as his hands move all over my body.

I feel his impossibly hard cock rubbing against me. He's so worked up.

"No puedo esperar hasta la noche, princesa." *I can't wait until tonight, princess.*

He pulls my pants and panties down to my knees and turns me around. "Ponte las manos en la pared. Saca tu culo para mí." *Put your hands on the wall. Stick your ass out for me.*

I do as I'm told. I came five minutes ago, but I'm already swollen and throbbing for the sex god I'm dating.

He moves his fingers through me. "Va a ser duro y rápido." *This is going to be hard and fast.*

Sounds good to me.

He then runs his tip through my wetness until he finds my opening. He slams his massive cock into me. All the way in. He's so damn big. It stings for a moment.

"Ah, Dominic. Relax. Give me a second."

He doesn't. He begins hammering into me at a relentless pace. "No me digas que me relaje. Este coño es mío." *Don't tell me to relax. This pussy is mine.*

His dirty words are all that my body needs to loosen up enough to take the pounding he's giving me.

He reaches under my shirt and violently pulls down my bra, grabbing onto my breasts and squeezing them hard. He's a bit out of control right now, but I don't mind. He lights up my body in a way I've never known. I love how much he needs me right now.

He bites and then licks up my neck until I turn my face. I suck his tongue into my mouth, and he groans.

He's fucking me so hard that my body is lifting off the ground each time he pushes deep into me.

Our mouths continue to move together. We're all lips, tongue, and teeth. This is dirty and wild sex. I love it.

I open my eyes and look at him. His hair is a bit disheveled. He's got a little sweat on his face. He's so into this. Into me. I've never seen anything more perfect.

He spanks my ass hard before moving one of his hands down to my clit, rubbing his fingers in fast circles. "Correte para mi, princesa." *Come for me, princess.*

Because Dominic Mazzello completely owns my body, I do. I come immediately. I come powerfully.

As soon as he feels me go, he pumps me three more hard times before he pushes in deep, stills, and grunts into my cheek.

He drops his mouth and breathes hard into my neck. "Thank you. I needed that."

I turn my head and smile into him. "The pleasure was all mine."

WE'VE EATEN a nice dinner and have the firepit roaring. The kids are making s'mores and having a great time. Luke looks so happy with Valentina and Matteo. This is what it would be like if I gave him siblings. I have a pang of guilt that I haven't done that for him. I can't deny that I've begun to hope that this can be our normal. Our everyday life.

Dominic fiddles with his phone and Spanish music starts playing. I look at him in question. "Dancing to the Cuban Rumba is a New Year's Eve tradition in our family."

I scrunch my face. "I'm not a very good dancer."

He winks as he takes Valentina's hand as they begin to move to the music. They both dance beautifully. They're next to each other as their hips and arms both move in unison. They both have big smiles on their faces. It's clearly something they've done together many times before.

I see Matteo shaking his hips too. Luke looks on in wonderment.

Valentina offers Luke her hand and starts to show him how to move. He's picking it up quickly as his little hips sway to the music. He and Valentina are both giggling. It's adorable.

Dominic starts to offer me his hand, but Matteo steps

in front of him and offers me his. Dominic and I smile at each other as I take Matteo's hand.

He's trying to show me the moves. He's a good dancer. I had no idea. We're both moving to the music now, and Matteo has a huge smile on his face.

Dominic looks on with pride. "Matteo, you may be the best dancer in the family. I had no idea."

If possible, Matteo's smile gets even wider. When the first song is over, he hugs my leg. I rub his back. "Thank you for helping me. You're an amazing teacher."

He nods as another song begins playing. We all dance for several songs, having a great time. I don't think I'm very good, but it doesn't matter. This is the fun, full family life I've always wished for.

Dominic disappears momentarily but then returns with a shopping bag. He pulls out five older looking dolls. Valentina and Matteo seem to understand what he's doing and immediately grab one each. Valentina takes an extra and hands it to Luke.

I see Luke bite his lip. "Umm, thanks, but I don't like playing with dolls."

Dominic, Valentina, and Matteo laugh. Dominic wraps his arm around Luke. "In Cuban culture, we burn dolls on New Year's Eve. We believe it gets rid of all the bad things that have happened in the past year. Any bad memories and regrets are left in the past and burned away. Only good things moving forward."

Luke scrunches his nose. "You throw them in the fire?"

Dominic nods. "Yes."

Luke's eyes light up. "How cool."

Dominic smiles at me as he hands me my doll. We all stand around the fire with our dolls. "Everyone, think of the bad moments for the last time. Once you throw it in the fire, you will never think of them again."

I close my eyes and think of the loneliness I've felt for so long. The void in my life. The void in Luke's. I pray they are nothing but forgotten memories. Dominic, Valentina, and Matteo have already filled our lives with so much joy.

Dominic wraps his arms around me and softly kisses my neck. "I know we're thinking the same thing. Throw it in. Our time apart is in the past."

The kids excitedly and happily throw their dolls in the fire. I do the same and Dominic kisses me again. Him openly giving me affection has already become our norm. The kids barely even notice it anymore. I can't remember a time in my life that I've been as happy as I am in this very moment. I want it to last forever.

He whispers in my ear, "It's time for them to go to bed and for you to make good on your promise to let me have my wicked way with you."

It's no small feat getting the kids to bed after the s'mores, but we eventually do. They're all sleeping in the bunkbed room. Dominic leaves while I read them one final story.

When I get back to our bedroom, I see my pink bikini laying on the bed with a note.

Mi amor,

Póntelo. Solo esto. Prometo mantenerte cómoda. Encuéntrame en el techo.

–D

My love,

Put this on. Only this. I promise to keep you warm.
Meet me on the roof.
-D

He called me his *love*. I smile at the notion.

I slip into the bikini and look at myself in the mirror. Am I perfect? No. Does Dominic always make me feel beautiful? Yes. He worships my body in a way I've never felt before. He makes me feel perfect.

My feelings for him are so strong. It's both exciting and terrifying.

I run my fingertips across my neck, down my chest and stomach, and then eventually around my hips. There's a small bite mark on my neck from our time in the pantry, but I know it will all be marked by the morning. I smile at the thought of what's to come. The way he ignites my body. The way I never know what's coming from him.

I head up to the roof. When I walk out into the frigid December air, I hear soft music playing and see that the hot tub cover has been removed. The jets are on. Dominic has his back to me fiddling with the hot tub controls. He's in a bathing suit too. His back muscles are perfection. He's so broad on top and trim in the waist. I want to run my tongue all over him. I plan to.

The music is Spanish, but it's much slower than what we listened to earlier.

I make a noise and he turns, breaking out into a huge smile. He looks my body up and down and licks his lower lip. "Eres tan hermosa. Dentro y fuera." *You're so beautiful. Both on the inside and outside.*

I stare at him in awe. Dominic Mazzello in a bathing suit exceeds every fantasy I've ever had. My mouth is physically watering at the sight of him.

I point to the speakers. "Are we dancing again? I

wouldn't mind seeing your hips move now that we're finally alone."

He smiles. "They're going to move, I promise. We listened to the faster Cuban Rumba music earlier." He holds out his hand. "Now it's time for the slow version."

I take his hand and he pulls my body to his. It's cold out here, but his body is warm and mine instantly heats at his touch.

He wraps his arms around me and starts moving to the beat. He pulls my ass tight, so my body is flush to his and I'm forced to move in the same rhythm.

This must be what heaven feels like. Dancing, skin to skin, in the big, strong, warm arms of Dominic.

He twirls me a few times, but always brings me back close to his body, moving to the beat. His lips move up and down my neck, and his hands move up and down my body, but he never stops dancing. This may be the most sensual thing I've ever done in my life.

We do this for a few songs. His hands have touched every inch of me except where I need him the most. His lips find mine but then move across my neck and shoulders. I expected him to attack me when I walked out here. Not this slow seduction. It's making me want him all the more.

I whisper, "Dominic." I'm reaching the point where I'm aching for him.

He pulls the strings on the back of my bikini, causing it to fall from my body. My breasts spill free.

He tosses the bikini top to the chair and dusts his fingertips over my hardened nipples. "Tan perfecto." *So perfect.*

He moves his hand along my face. "I don't want to avoid your questions, princesa. I want to answer them. I want to be honest with you."

I nod, knowing he's about to give me some part of him. Some part I've never heard before.

"The club I go to is called Hush Hush. It's a place for like-minded people to go and explore their sexuality. Their sexual fantasies. Their sexual needs."

"What do you do there?"

"Well, I haven't been there in months, not since we started dating, but I used to do a few different things. I sometimes had sex with women who enjoy it the harder way I do it."

I'm trying to remain stoic, knowing it's hard for him to share, but the thought of him with other women is making me sick to my stomach.

"What else?"

"I enjoy watching."

"You watch other people have sex?"

"Sometimes, but often I simply enjoy watching women's pleasure."

I look up at him. "What exactly does that mean?"

He swallows, clearly struggling to share this with me.

"When I go to the club, I don't always have sex with the women. I often watch them pleasure themselves."

Oh. I didn't expect that. "Is that what you want? You want to watch me touch myself?" Merely saying the words out loud has my face flushed. I've never had anyone watch me do that.

He tucks my hair behind my ear and licks his lower lip. "I would like that. Very much." He motions his head toward the wide ledge next to the hot tub.

I walk over toward the ledge and turn back to him. "I want you to talk me through it."

He nods. "Take off your bikini bottoms."

"In Spanish. Tell me what you want in Spanish."

He smiles. "Quita tu bikini." *Take off your bikini bottoms.*

I slowly slide them down my legs and kick them to the side. I'm standing there completely naked. My skin is covered in goosebumps, but it's not from the cold air. It's from the heated gaze of Dominic as his eyes move up and down my body. The promise of what's to come.

"Siéntate y abre las piernas ancha." *Sit down and spread your legs wide.*

I sit down on the ledge. There's enough room for me to rest my feet on it, which I do. My legs are spread wide open. I'm completely exposed to him.

He reaches into a bag and pulls out a vibrator, handing it to me.

Dominic's cock is poking through the top of his bathing suit. That thick, hard, angry, perfect cock of his.

I breathe, "I want to see you too. All of you."

He slides down his bathing suit, grabbing onto his heavy cock, giving it a few long pumps. He's just so... masculine. I can feel a thumping between my legs. Moisture is beginning to pool.

"Turn the vibrator on and run it through your pussy."

I do as I'm told, slowly running it through me. I'm sensitive to the touch, already swollen and ready for more. His mouth opens wide, and his breathing picks up. I see pre-ejaculate begin to ooze from his tip.

"Deslízalo dentro de ese coño apretado." *Slide it inside that tight pussy.*

I slip it inside myself and begin to move it in and out. I arch my back and moan. "Oh, Dominic, this feels good."

I do my best to put on a good show for him. Him watching me do this is incredibly erotic. I didn't realize how much I'd enjoy being watched while doing this to myself.

His hand wrapped around his cock is pumping harder and faster. I see him battling with control.

I'm only two minutes into this when he walks, no stomps, over to me and grabs my wrist, causing the vibrator to leave my body. He pulls my hand to his mouth and licks my juices off the vibrator. "Jesús, sabes deliciosa. Te necesito en mi lengua. No puedo esperar un minute más." *Jesus Christ, you taste good. I need you on my tongue. I can't wait a minute longer.*

He sinks to his knees and spreads me wide, licking through me and cooing, "El nectar de los dioses." *The nectar of the gods.*

I'm so sensitive. I buck my hips as he fully sinks his face into me.

He takes the vibrator from me and sticks it back into my channel, while his tongue makes its way to my clit. "Ah, Dominic. That's good."

He mumbles into me, "Este coño será mi muerte." *This pussy will be the death of me.*

His tongue is teasing me until his circular strokes become more consistent, all while he moves the vibrator in and out of me. My hands are on his head, encouraging him.

My hips move in rhythm with his actions, as we reach perfect harmony. The dual sensation of the vibrator and his tongue are quickly pushing me to the edge. My orgasm is barreling headfirst toward me.

I feel one of his fingers move around my back entrance. I've never done anything there before, but I'm willing to try with him. Frankly, I'd let him do anything he wants to my body.

Without stopping the movements of his tongue or vibrator, his finger breaches my back entrance. The feeling is so unexpected. I'm on stimulation overload with three things now going on at once. My entire world disappears as I experience a pleasure I've never known. I'm floating in the clouds right now.

The tingling is all over my body, spreading down my arms and legs. I can legitimately feel it in my toes. I hear Dominic growling something, but I can't make out the words. I'm too absorbed in what's happening to my body.

I begin shaking. With absolutely no control over my movements or screams, I yell out into an explosive orgasm. The most explosive I've ever had.

How have I lived over thirty-five years without this kind of bliss? Without this man?

Before I have the chance to regain my senses, Dominic's mouth takes mine and his cock slams into me. I scream into his mouth, but he swallows it down.

My vision hasn't returned, but his tongue is engulfing my mouth, covering it with my taste. His cock is deep inside me, deeper than I've ever felt anything or anyone.

I wrap my legs around him as he pistons into me. He's shouting Spanish expletives in between biting me all over, but I haven't regained consciousness enough to register anything else.

This man was made for fucking. When he gets like this, he's not gentile and he's not tender. He's an animal. It's raw, passionate fucking, and I love every minute of it.

Every time with him I don't think I can be fucked any harder, but then he shows me I can. It makes me forget about everything else going on around me. It's just me and him and the special music we make together.

I'm holding on for dear life as he takes what he needs from me. I peel my eyes open. He's covered in sweat and his slack jaw tells me he's right here with me. But when his smoldering eyes meet mine, another orgasm slams into me out of nowhere. I'm not sure the last one ended before this one hit, but those eyes bore into my soul and my body belongs to him.

I bite his shoulder as my entire body convulses.

He yells out, "Joder, princesa." *Oh fuck, princess.* As he pushes deep and comes hard inside me.

His movements begin to slow. We're both sweaty, breathing heavily, looking at where our bodies meet, as if finding it hard to believe that we've achieved another level of pleasure. Another level of intimacy.

The smell of sex is in the air. It's intoxicating.

My body is still jerking. His forehead meets mine. I smile into his lips. "I thought you like to watch."

He blinks a few times as he regains his breath. "I normally do. I just...I just needed you so badly. I couldn't control myself. Tu me consumes, princesa." *You consume me, princess.*

He kisses me. Hard. Long. Deep. This man is everything as he pours his heart into me through this kiss. I'm in love with him. I know I am. I'll never want another man for the rest of my life.

Still wrapped around him, our bodies practically stuck together, he picks me up and walks up the steps of the hot tub. He slowly enters, still holding on to me. We acclimate to the hot water, and he eventually sits, never letting go of me.

We sit in comfortable silence for a few minutes. Our bodies have just been through something rigorous, and we're both enjoying the soothing warm water and the tender closeness to each other.

I rub his beard with my thumb. "Tell me something about you that I don't know."

He smiles. "I was a mama's boy growing up."

I giggle. "It's hard for me to imagine you as a boy." I rub his sexy chest. "You're all man now."

"I was. In some ways, I'm a lot like her. She went against her parents' wishes when she fell for my father. They wanted her to marry a pure Cuban man and take over the family business."

"Sugar cane, right?"

"Yes, plus they've invested in many other successful Cuban businesses through the years. My grandparents had four girls, and she was the oldest. It was assumed she'd marry a Cuban man and the business would pass to them. But when she was in college, she met my father and they fell madly in love. Her family wasn't happy when she fell for a half Italian man. It took years for her to return to her family's good graces. They were equally upset when I refused to partake in the family business."

"Was your mother upset too or just your grandparents?"

"She understood. She lived in America and always knew I was never going to live in Cuba. It's why I honored her dying wish."

"Which was?"

"To marry Gabriela."

What? "That's why you married her? You *never* loved her?"

He shakes his head. "Never. I respect her as the mother of my children, but that's as far as it ever went. Her insides don't match her outsides. They never have."

He tucks my hair behind my ear and softly kisses my lips. "Not like you, who's beautiful inside and out." He sighs. "I've thought about it a lot through the years. I think her asking me to marry Gabriela was her way of trying to do good for her family. Uniting the two most powerful families in Cuba would have made my grandparents very happy."

"Wow. I have no words for that. I can't believe you felt compelled to marry out of obligation. It's like a movie. Not real life."

He nods. "Gabriela's mother was my mother's best friend since they were kids. Their fathers were best friends too. They hoped our union would merge the two businesses, but running either business in Cuba was never in the cards for me."

"Were you friends with Gabriela growing up?"

"We were often forced together, but I never cared for her. My father begged me not to marry her. He knew I didn't love her. But it was important to me to honor my mother's dying wish. I won't say it was a mistake. I have my children. I didn't think someone like me should ever get married. I assumed I wouldn't have children."

"Why wouldn't you get married?"

"I was jaded by love very early on and, as you know, I'm a lot to handle."

I tighten my hold on him. "I like handling you, Mr. Mazzello. And I *really* like when you handle me."

He squeezes me back. "I'm trying to be what you deserve."

"I know you are. If it ever feels like too much effort, and you want something else, I need you to tell me before you act. If you love someone, truly love them, it shouldn't be hard to remain faithful. Being with another person should be detestable to you."

My eyes widen at what I just said. "I didn't mean..."

He silences me with a kiss, mumbling, "I know what you meant."

I want to ask him about why he's jaded on love, but he's

revealed a lot tonight and I don't want to push or ruin our intimate moment. He'll tell me when he's ready.

He deepens the kiss. I can feel he's already hard again as he slides it through my wetness. He's like a damn machine.

"Te necesito de nuevo." *I need you again.*

I close my eyes and let out a small moan.

He smiles. "You like when I talk Spanish. It turns you on."

I bury my head in his neck in embarrassment. "It does. I should admit something to you too."

I pull my head up so I can look at him. He seems curious. "I've watched a lot of Spanish porn during the past few years since we met. *A lot.* That's how I learned Spanish. I have a photographic memory. I picked up the entire language watching porn with dirty-talking Latino men."

He starts laughing. Loudly. "That's the greatest thing I've ever heard."

I giggle. "I know. It's crazy. But that night at Reagan's party, you drove me wild with your talk. I couldn't get it out of my mind. I guess a fetish was born."

"We're a bit more alike than I thought. You like watching too."

I never thought about it that way. Maybe he's right. "Except I've never caught a live show."

His face lights up. "Is it something you'd like to do with me sometime?"

I hadn't considered it. "Maybe."

"Good. Now, siéntate en mi polla y ordéñalo seco." *Sit on my cock and milk it dry.*

CHAPTER EIGHTEEN

BETH

Cassandra pokes her head in my office. "I'm having lunch with Darian's girls today. Why don't you join us? I think Jade is coming too."

"It's nice that you do that. You're so involved in their lives."

She shrugs. "I didn't have my kids until I was fifty-one. Harley, Reagan, and Skylar have always felt like my own. I love them as if they are. I was always heavily involved in their lives, but when Scott passed and Darian wasn't functional, they really needed me. He's been gone for over a decade now. Sometimes it's hard to believe."

"It's great that they have you. I'd love to come."

We walk into a nice restaurant. Harley, Reagan, Skylar, and Jade are already there. Harley and Jade are drinking what appears to be lemon drop martinis. Reagan and Skylar are sticking with water.

They all smile as we sit. Reagan says, "Aunt Cass, we ordered you vodka. Beth, we got wine for you."

They're so thoughtful. I look between Jade and Reagan and shake my head. "I still marvel at your resemblance. You two look like sisters, not cousins."

Jade interrupts, "I have better legs." She must be six feet tall, so yes, her legs are long. Reagan isn't quite that tall, though significantly taller than me.

Reagan lets out a laugh. "It's cool. I have a better rack."

Jade jokingly narrows her eyes. "That's because you're pregnant and your tits are out of control. Normally, it's pretty close."

Reagan pats Jade's head. "If that makes you feel better about it, sure." She looks back at me but nods Jade's way. "This bitch uses my face to get VIP entry into clubs and restaurants."

Jade giggles. "Guilty as charged." Reagan is well known around town. They roll out the red carpet for her everywhere she goes. We all know that Jade sometimes pretends to be her to get all the perks of being the very well-known Reagan Lawrence Daulton.

Reagan shakes her head. "I don't think you've been out as much lately though. Do you have a secret boyfriend we don't know about?"

Jade's eyes briefly widen. She's hiding something. "I don't do boyfriends."

Reagan looks at her suspiciously, clearly not believing her. I don't believe her either, but I have no interest in pushing her on the issue.

Cassandra sips her vodka and then looks around the table. "Ladies, I brought Beth today for a reason." She did? "She's seeing someone with a few kinks."

Why do I continue to tell her *everything* about my sex life?

I elbow her. "Are we seriously discussing this at lunch with them?"

Jade lets out a laugh. "Did you find another man with a foot fetish? I hope he's *toe*tally hot."

I smile as I shake my head. None of them let me live that one down.

Cassandra continues, "Not so much a fetish but a few kinks. Beth has concerns about it."

I shake my head. "I don't have concerns. I just asked you if it's normal."

She nods. "I told her *lots* of people have kinks. Way more than she realizes. Would you all care to share? I don't know about Jade, but I know the rest of you keep things pretty spicy."

They're all silent. I turn to Cassandra. "They don't want to share. It's fine. Let's move on."

Reagan shrugs. "I don't care if you know. Carter and I like to have sex in front of people. We do it all the time."

My mouth drops in shock. "People you know?"

She shakes her head. "No, not normally. Though one time Mom and Jackson almost saw us have sex."

Harley spits her drink. "What? I didn't know that. Tell us about it."

"We went to a voyeur club where some people like to watch, and some people like to be watched. We're obviously the latter. We were in a room with a one-way mirror, so we couldn't see who was watching us. We started to get it on when Mom's fucking voice came on the intercom shouting for us to stop. They turned on the lights in their room. I guess Mom and Jackson go there to watch people have sex. I had no clue."

Harley, Skylar, Jade, and Cassandra are all hysterically

laughing. I have my hand over my mouth. "That's horrible. Was it awkward afterward?"

"Fuck yes. For months, Jackson couldn't even look me in the eyes. Fortunately, we hadn't undressed yet. That would have been worse. But we go there and some other similar clubs every few weeks. We've done a handful of other things along those lines. There's something about being watched that we both enjoy."

Jade mumbles, "Can I watch you two? That sounds hot." Jade unashamedly has a crush on Reagan's husband, Carter.

Reagan rolls her eyes.

Cassandra turns to Harley. "What about you and Brody? Care to share with the class?"

Harley scrunches her nose. "I'm not sure it's a kink, but Brody's *very* into the dirty talk and *very* into using toys on me."

My mouth drops again. He's a lot like Dominic. "Sweet, laid-back Brody is a dirty talker?"

Harley gives a sinister smile. "Filthy." She mock shivers. "And it's so hot."

The girls all start giggling again.

I certainly can't deny that. Dominic's dirty talk is such a turn on. It's not just the dirty talk, it's the Spanish dirty talk that does it for me. There's something about it that makes it even filthier.

Cassandra nods to Skylar but she's quiet. She's the shyest of the girls. I squeeze her hand. "You don't have to share if you don't want."

She shrugs. "It's fine. Everyone here but you knows anyway. I'm into role-play."

"What do you mean?"

"I mean we play various roles and act them out."

"Like what?"

Harley mocks, "I know she likes being a naughty nurse and treating her patient."

Jade adds, "And a fireman. We know Lance plays a very sexy fireman."

Skylar subtly nods. "Yep. Stuff like that."

"Wow. I had no idea about any of this."

Cassandra looks at Jade. "What about you? You seem like you could be a freak in the sheets."

I shake my head. "Cassandra, she's young, leave her alone." Jade is only twenty-two. Darian's girls are all close to my age, in their thirties.

Jade gives a mischievous smile. "I don't care about sharing. I like being tied up and choked."

Darian's girls burst out laughing again. Cassandra just smiles and shakes her head. I'm sitting there in complete and total shock. She's so young, yet she's so confident and uninhibited about it all.

Reagan asks, "Who is it that's tying you up and choking you?"

"Hmm, no one you know."

Reagan turns to me. "More importantly, who have you been sleeping with and what are his kinks that have you all twisted up?"

Harley turns to her. "You don't know who she's seeing?"

"Obviously not or I wouldn't have asked."

I give a self-satisfied smile. "I've been seeing Dominic for the past few months."

Reagan's big blue eyes widen. "*My* Dominic?"

I shrug. "I'd argue that he's mine, but yes."

Her eyes light up. "Holy shit. I had no idea. He's so damn secretive. I didn't even know he had kids until he had to change his work schedule with his ex-wife out of town indefinitely."

"Yes, he's very private."

I see Jade deep in thought. "Beth, do you own a red Prada dress with gold buttons?"

I know where she's going with this. "Maybe."

"Were you in Dominic's office a few months ago?"

I smile. I'm totally busted.

She returns my smile with a playful one of her own.

Reagan pinches her eyebrows. "What am I missing?"

Jade responds, "Let's just say you're not the only one getting a little in-office action, Reagan." That was about as discreet as Jade's capable of. "And Beth's knees probably have rug burns from Dominic's carpet."

So much for being discreet.

All the girls start laughing. There's something so endearing about this open, loving family.

Jade looks at her watch. "I have to run in two minutes. I need to get waxed for the gyno."

I look at her in question. "You groom yourself for a gynecology appointment?"

She stares at me like I've got three eyes. "Yes. Of course. Anytime a man is going to be in my vagina, I want her to look her best."

"It's a doctor. It's clinical for them." I turn to Harley. "Right?"

She nods. "Yes, Jade. Your gyno isn't checking out your vagina for its beauty."

Jade shrugs. "I'm not going in all wild. My vagina will put her best foot forward at all times for all men who dare enter."

These girls are a riot.

DOMINIC

I'm having lunch with Sebastian and Kevin today. I can't help the smile on my face. I'm really falling for Beth. I hadn't thought about Hush Hush until she brought it up when we were at the beach a few weeks ago. I'm surprised that it hasn't even crossed my mind.

Sebastian shakes his head. "You're so fucking pussy whipped. It's pathetic. I never thought it would be you."

I smile into my drink. "I suppose I am."

Kevin looks happier than anyone. I turn to him. "Why are you so damn happy?"

"Because I *finally* have someone on my side. It took twenty years."

Sebastian shakes his head. "I was happily married for five years."

Kevin looks at him. "If you were so happy, why did you divorce her and break her heart? You'll never find anyone better than Lindsay."

Sebastian tilts his head up and takes a huge breath before looking back at us. "What do you want me to say? I was a fucking idiot. I was selfish. I didn't realize how good I had it. I was immature. I hate myself for it. I wish I could do it over again."

Kevin and I look at each other in shock. Sebastian admitting all that is a big deal. I place my hand on his shoulder. "Have you told Lindsay any of this?"

He looks pained. "I want to. I mean, I've tried to get her alone a few times, but Claudia is like a watchdog." Kevin smirks. "Honestly, I don't want to give her false hope. I need to wrap my head around being truly faithful before I approach her."

I nod. "Don't even think about messing around with her until you get there. She doesn't deserve to be dicked around more than she already has. If you go there, plan on forever."

He slinks down into his chair. "I know."

Kevin scrunches his nose. "I wouldn't wait too long. I think she has her first date next week. Claudia set it up for her."

Sebastian's eyes look like they're going to pop out of his head. "What the fuck, Claudia?"

"It's not my wife's fault. In a few weeks it will be a year and a half since your divorce. It's not like you sit at home pining for her like she is for you. Claudia is just trying to help Lindsay finally move on. She's being a good friend."

I look at Sebastian. "He's right. She's not going to wait forever for you to grow up. Get your head on straight for her."

Sebastian nods. "I think I'd rather talk about you, Dom. How are things with you and Beth?"

I smile. "Amazing. I'm thinking of asking her and Luke to move in with us. I hate that we have to spend so many nights apart. I want them with us."

They both have shocked looks on their faces. Sebastian turns to Kevin. "It's like déjà vu. It's been over twenty years, but when he's in, he's all in. Full steam."

I snap, "It's nothing like that. You were right back then that she was no good for me, but it's different this time around. Beth is amazing. I thought I was too fucked up to give myself to one woman again. It turns out, I was just waiting for the right one. I have no desire for anyone else. You guys like her, right?"

They enthusiastically nod their heads. Kevin places his hand on my shoulder. "You found the right one this time. And I've never seen you this happy."

I turn to Sebastian. "What about you?"

"You're happy and I'm happy for you. Just take it from me, get rid of your past demons before you try to move on. I fucked things up with Lindsay because I wasn't in the right headspace. I couldn't let go of certain things."

I get back to my office and think about what Sebastian said regarding my past demons. I haven't let anyone in for over twenty years because of what happened. Maybe I need to confront it. Confront her. The woman who broke my heart. The woman who altered the course of my life.

I pull up the google search bar on my computer when there's a knock at my door. I look up and see Reagan. "Come in."

She walks into my office. "I'm really sorry to do this to you, but is there any chance you can fly to Chicago this afternoon to close the Jennings purchase? All of a sudden, they want us there in person. Skylar and I aren't allowed to fly at this point in our pregnancies. Carter is afraid to be that far from me. I know it's asking a lot with the kids, but you're the only other person I trust to close this. It's just one night."

I don't want to let her down. She's been so flexible with me these past few months. "I'll figure something out. I have someone who can probably stay with the kids for a night."

She smiles. "Is that someone named Beth O'Connell?"

I guess the news is out. I nod. "It is."

"I had lunch with her recently. She's quite smitten with you."

I can't help but smile. "I'm smitten with her as well. She's an amazing woman."

"She is. Well, thanks for doing this. I'll email everything you need."

"No problem."

She leaves and closes the door behind her. I look back at my computer to the google search bar. The cursor is blinking, taunting me. I haven't looked her up since the day she imploded my life. I have no idea what happened to her or where she lives. We never even had the chance to say goodbye. Maybe it's time to reach out.

I take a deep breath and start to type her full name.

Amanda Tremaine

Very little information pops up. I guess she never became a famous artist like she wanted to. She was extremely talented. I've always half expected to walk in somewhere and see her name on paintings, but I never have.

The only thing I'm able to gather from my search is that she still lives in Philadelphia and has a daughter. Do I really need a conversation with her at this point? Part of me thinks it's crazy, but then part of me knows that I haven't been in a real relationship until now because of her, so maybe I do. Maybe I need to know what I did wrong.

An email comes through from Reagan. I need to get caught up on the file before I leave.

I close the search window. I've got a lot going on right now. Perhaps I'll look into finding her another time.

CHAPTER NINETEEN

BETH

The kids all go to bed and I'm alone in Dominic's huge house. It's even bigger when no one else is awake. He must get lonely when he's home alone without his kids.

He asked me to stay here with them for the night while he had to go out of town. It's easier with the dog for us to stay here than my house. I don't mind.

I walk around until I get to his study. I'm hesitant to go inside, not wanting him to think I'm snooping, but I do.

I walk in and take in the impressive surroundings. I've seen the multitude of picture frames before, but I've never been able to truly study the photos.

I closely examine them now. There are several of Valentina and Matteo over the past seven years. Dominic is in some of them, but I don't see Gabriela in any of them.

I see a few photos of Marty and a woman I assume is Dominic's mother, including a few of a much younger Dominic. I run my fingers over one where he's clearly laughing. He's always been so handsome.

There's one that must be in college with Sebastian and Kevin, all in their baseball uniforms. They're smiling, with their arms around each other. It's sweet and, as expected, Dominic in a baseball uniform is orgasmic.

I'm suddenly very aware of the camera in the top corner between the wall and ceiling. He said he keeps valuables in his office and runs the camera as a security measure. I find myself wondering if Dominic is watching me. The thought that he might be excites me.

I smile as an idea occurs to me.

I go upstairs to his bedroom, strip off all my clothes, and slip into one of Dominic's work shirts. He loves when I wear them, and I love being surrounded by his scent. I throw on my high-heel shoes, grab my laptop, a toy, and head back to his study, closing and locking the door behind me.

I pour myself a glass of bourbon from one of the many bottles in here. I quickly down it, needing a little liquid courage for what I'm about to do.

I pour another glass and bring it over to his desk, setting up my laptop, and sitting in his big, leather chair. I pull up my favorite porn website and select a video. I turn the volume up so the cameras can potentially catch that I'm watching Spanish porn.

After I lean back into the chair and lift my heel-clad feet onto the desk, I spread my legs and slowly unbutton his shirt, letting it fall open to expose my entire body.

Dipping the toy into my glass of bourbon, I rub it around my nipples until they harden. I bring it to my lips and slowly coat them in bourbon too, sucking the tip at the end.

Still looking into the camera, I lick my lips in the most

seductive way I can. The thought of Dominic watching me, touching himself to me, is a huge turn on.

The dirty Spanish-speaking men on my laptop make my body flush. One of them says, "Abre estas piernas para mí. Quiero ver tu coño." *Spread those legs wide for me. I want to see your pussy.*

I imagine Dominic saying those words to me and spread my legs as far as they can go, exposing myself fully to his camera. I slowly run the vibrator down my body, through my breasts and past my stomach until it reaches the slickness of my center.

Closing my eyes, I moan as I run it through myself. I mouth to the camera, "So wet for you," as I slide it deep into my core and turn it on.

I throw my head back and breathe, "Oh, Dominic, you have no idea how much I wish it was your cock inside me right now. That big cock of yours pounding into my tight, wet pussy. Can you hear how wet I am?"

I pump it in and out several times. I bring the fingers of my other hand to my clit and begin to circle my swollen button. My hips begin to take on a life of their own as they gyrate and get absorbed in the pleasure.

I've spent so much of the past few years indulging in self-pleasure, but knowing he's possibly watching me and can watch this scene over and over has my arousal reaching new heights when I touch myself.

I move my hand up and grab my breast, tugging on my nipple. "Dominic, I wish your hands were on my body right now. Your big, sexy hands. And your tongue. That thick, magical tongue of yours. I'm imagining it in my pussy, licking through me, sinking into me, all over me. Can you taste me, baby?"

I moan as my orgasm begins to approach. "I'm about to come. Are you touching yourself too? Stroke hard, baby. Come with me. Imagine my lips around that magnificent cock of yours, sucking it hard the way you like it. That's it. All the way down my throat. I love when you're deep down my throat."

I lick my lips. "I can almost taste you. I want it. I want you. Come in my mouth, baby."

Seriously, I don't know who I am right now, but I like this uninhibited version of me. He's drawn it out of me.

I'm pumping the vibrator hard, fast, and deep. I bite my lip as my orgasm rises to the surface and I close my eyes, imaging Dominic, and finally go over the edge on a loud moan.

As the orgasm passes, I let out a few heavy breaths and regain my senses. I remove the vibrator from my center, bring it to my mouth, and look straight into the camera. I breathlessly moan, "Hurry home," as I suck it into my mouth.

I'm suddenly awakened in the middle of the night to Dominic's scent and his naked body covering my back as he enters me.

Somehow the shirt of his that I'm wearing is lifted, my panties are nowhere to be found, my legs are spread wide, and I'm completely exposed.

I turn my head to him and croak out, "What's going on? I thought you weren't coming home until tomorrow?"

He looks like a man possessed. "Te necesito. Necesito estar dentro de ti. No me detengas, princesa. Por favor." *I need you. I need to be inside you. Don't stop me, princess. Please.*

I spread my legs wider and tilt my ass up to give him better access as he pushes in deep. I moan, "I'll never stop you."

"Me vuelvas loco. Mi necesidad de ti me está consumiendo. No puedo controlarlo." *You drive me crazy. My need for you is consuming me. I can't control it.*

I smile into my pillow. I know the feeling.

"Lo necesito duro." *I need it hard.*

I breathe, "Yes. Take what you need. Give it to me." I push my ass back encouraging his movements.

He bends one of my knees, lifting it as high as it will go and immediately begins to pound into me like a wild beast. My knee is by my ear. I look back. He's lifted himself so his arms are straight, his hair is messy, and the look in his eyes is animalistic.

I'm not sure whether I'm more scared or turned on by his seemingly manic need for me right now, though I'm pretty sure it's the latter.

With each thrust into me, my body is lifted off the bed. That's how hard he's pummeling into me. The bed is smacking the wall. It feels like it could break.

He gives my ass hard smack and I suck in a breath at both the shock and joy of it.

He leans on one elbow, shoves his thumb into my mouth, and swirls it around before removing it and circling my back entrance. I close my eyes and brace for what I know is coming.

His thumb pushes into my ass. I grip the pillows and let out a loud moan.

He maintains his relentless pace while thrusting his thumb deep into me. Holy shit. That feels good.

The dual sensation is quickly pushing me to the edge. My whole body starts to shake.

"Oh god, Dominic. I'm coming."

"Córrete para mí. Corre por toda mi polla." *Come for me. Come all over my cock.*

I squeeze my eyes shut from the onslaught and everything goes dark as I explode into my orgasm.

As soon as I'm done, he pulls out, violently rolls me over, and shoves his cock directly into my mouth. He pushes it straight to my throat and comes long and hard.

I start to gag on the sheer volume, but he pushes harder and says, "Tómalo todo." *Take it all.*

And I do. I take every last ounce as I swallow it down. His thick cock lays in my mouth while he completely empties himself.

When he's done, he pulls out and straddles his legs over my body while breathing hard.

He's so dominating. I look up at him and breathe, "I guess you got my message."

He pinches his eyebrows together. "What message?"

"The camera in your study? The little thing I did for your benefit."

"Oh, I don't monitor those. I have a security company that watches them for me."

I gasp and cover my mouth. Oh my god.

My face must show my shock because he starts laughing. "I'm just kidding, princesa. No one but me will ever see that beautiful look on your face when you came in my office chair, with your legs spread across my desk. I hope your juices are on my chair so I can smell you every time I sit there."

So. Fucking. Hot.

He rubs his fingers over my face. "It was the sexiest thing I've ever seen. I went straight to the airport and demanded a flight home. I couldn't wait another day to be inside your body."

He slides himself down until he falls naturally between my legs. His lips take mine as he kisses me. His tongue moves through my mouth, undoubtedly tasting himself on me. I do love the way he kisses. It's just so perfect.

We kiss for several minutes until I feel him harden again. The man is a machine. His tip nudges at my entrance, but he doesn't push it in. He continues moving his big lips over mine.

I run my hands up his chest. His feel and smell overtake my senses. He's so perfect and he's mine.

His tip is sitting at my entrance, teasing me. Driving me crazy with need mere minutes after coming. I thrust my hips in an attempt to get him deeper.

He smiles into my mouth. "Paciencia, princesa." *Patience, princess.*

"I want you. Please."

He nods as he begins to enter me, one achingly slow inch at a time. Once he's all the way in, he stills, taking my face in his hands. Our eyes meet and something happens. Something passes between us.

"Has llenado mi corazón de una manera que nunca supe possible. Eres mi corazón." *You've filled my heart in a way I never knew possible. You are my heart.*

He begins to move gently inside me. He's never taken me gently. For the first time, we're not fucking, we're making love.

It's long, beautiful, and everything. No inch of my body is untouched. I've never had a more intimate, perfect moment in my life. I'm so madly in love with this man.

When we're done, I lay on his chest as the morning sun

peeks through the curtains. I look up at him, "I love you, Dominic. Te amo." *I love you.*

As he begins to open his mouth, his phone rings. He picks it up and looks at it but denies the call. He places it down. "Gabriela. Her timing is impeccable, as always."

"If she's calling this early, it must important."

His phone rings again. He looks and rolls his eyes. It's clear that Gabriela is calling again.

"Dominic, you should answer it."

He blows out a breath but does accept the call. In a deep, gravelly voice he snaps, "What?"

His face immediately drops. "Oh, Gab, I'm so sorry."

Her mother must have passed.

"No, they're not awake yet."

I can hear her speaking, but I can't make out what she says.

"Yes, I'll book us the first flight out. We'll be there as soon as we can. Que descanse en paz." *May she rest in peace.*

He hangs up. "Her mother died."

I nod. "I gathered. What can I do to help?"

He closes his eyes as his head sinks further into the pillow behind him. "Make it so I don't have to go down there."

"You have to. She was Valentina and Matteo's grandmother."

He sighs. "I know. It will be a long, drawn-out mourning process. We'll have to go for two weeks." He squeezes my naked body tight to his. "I can't go that long without you. I really don't want to go."

I give him a small smile. "But you will because it's the right thing to do."

He nods. "I hate to ask, but would you mind taking Dora? You can stay here if it's easier."

"We'd be happy to take Dora, but for two weeks, I want to be home. She'll be fine at our house."

VALENTINA AND MATTEO are understandably upset when they awaken to us telling them about their grandmother. I pack their bags for them. He said two weeks, so that's how I pack.

Luke and I drive them to the airport. Dominic looks pained on the ride there. He has my hand on his thigh and strokes it over and over. He seems panicked and nervous in a way I've never seen from him before.

I whisper, "You'll be back in two weeks. We can talk every day." I smile. "Maybe I can put on another video show for you to keep you going."

He brings my hand to his lips and kisses it. "I don't deserve you."

We arrive at the airport and help them remove all their luggage. I hug and kiss Valentina and Matteo, assuring them that I'll see them in two weeks.

I fall into Dominic's arms and take in his scent. I can't believe I have to go two weeks without this. I lift my head and kiss his cheek. "Call me when you get settled in."

He nods, still looking pained. He pulls away and starts to lift his luggage, but immediately places it back down, turns to me, grabs my face, and, uncaring that the kids are there, takes my lips in his.

I grab onto his shirt and kiss him right back. The kiss turns a bit passionate for our surroundings, but it happens. We keep going until we hear all three kids laughing.

We smile into each other's lips as the kiss ends.

They pick up their luggage and walk into the airport.

At the last second, Dominic turns around and mouths, "Te amo." *I love you.*

My heart just about explodes in fullness. Dominic Mazzello loves me. Holy shit.

Little did I know, it would be the last time I saw him.

CHAPTER TWENTY

DOMINIC

I'm sweating bullets the entire way to Cuba. I'm trying to put on a brave face for Valentina and Matteo, but I have an uneasy feeling about this trip. Gabriela's family is a powerful one.

I feel like I'm stuck between a rock and a hard place. How can I deny Gabriela having her children come to her mother's funeral? But I'm fearful of what waits for us when we land. My father didn't want me to go.

I hope I'm not making a mistake.

As soon as we land and I see the men in suits waiting for us at the airport, I know I did.

BETH

Dominic didn't call last night when he landed. I tried to call, but it wouldn't go through. It said the phone was no longer in service. Maybe in the rush of leaving he forgot to add an international plan to his cell phone service.

I'm at the office talking to someone when my cell rings and it reads out of area. Normally I wouldn't answer, but because Dominic is in fact out of the area, I do. "Hello."

"Beth."

His voice immediately soothes me. It's been one night, and I already need to hear it.

I smile. "Hey, handsome. I miss you. My bed was lonely without you last night."

He's silent for a moment. "We need to talk." I can hear that his breathing is labored.

"Is everything okay?"

"No. Gabriela is moving to Cuba permanently. Her father isn't well, and she wants to stay to care for him. I can't continue to deny my kids their mother. We're...we're going to stay down here...permanently."

I'm stunned into silence. It takes me a few moments before I can muster a reply.

"We?"

"Yes. I can't be away from the kids. I'm moving down here too."

"What about your job?"

"I spoke with Reagan. I'm taking a leave of absence."

"What about us?"

He doesn't answer right away. My heart is pounding hard in my chest.

I continue, "I guess we can talk on the phone, and I can come visit you. Will you be able to visit too?"

He blows out a breath. When he speaks, his voice is shaky. "You know I can't handle long separations. It's not who I am. I think we should both move on."

My body tightens. Tears sting my eyes. "What are you saying? Are you breaking up with me?"

He croaks out, "Yes. It's for the best."

Yesterday we exchanged I love yous. Today he's breaking up with me? This doesn't sound right.

"I don't understand. What changed in one day? I love you, Dominic. I'm *in love* with you."

He's silent for a moment. Maybe he'll change his mind. "I...I can't be with you anymore. It's not going to work for me. My children are my priority." I hear voices in the background. "I have to go. I wish you and Luke well. Give him my best. Goodbye."

He hangs up.

I'm in shock. I feel the world spinning. My chest starts to hurt. I lean back as tears stream down my face.

Just like that, without any real explanation, I'm alone. Again.

CHAPTER TWENTY-ONE

ONE YEAR LATER

BETH

Steven throws his arm around me. "Another win for you, Beth. Since you've become a partner, you've been on fire. If I knew it would have brought out this animal in you, we would have made you a partner earlier."

I fake a smile. "Thanks, Steven." I think it was a compliment. I'm not sure. I was pretty good at my job before too. That's why I was made a partner, dickhead.

I was voted a partner nearly a year ago. It coincided with a broken heart, so I've truly thrown myself into work in a way I never have before. I needed the distraction. I needed somewhere to channel my hurt and anger.

Cassandra smiles too, but I know her well enough to know it's not a real one. She nods in agreement. "It's not every day you make a grown man cry."

I shrug. "People don't like to lose money."

She mumbles, "Or everything they have in this world."

Steven's cell phone rings. He looks at it. "Excuse me, ladies. I need to take this. Again, great job, Beth. Keep up the good work."

He walks away to answer his phone and I look at Cassandra. "You don't seem very happy. I just crushed this. Our client practically had an orgasm when he heard the outcome."

"I'm happy for you. You know I'm not a fan of some of your tactics of late, but there's no denying the outcome."

"What's your fucking problem, Cassandra?"

The corners of her mouth turn down. "I'm not the one with a problem, Beth."

"I'm sorry that I'm not a pushover anymore."

"I never thought you were at work."

"Just in my personal life."

"I think you've proven in the past year that you're no longer that either."

"What's that supposed to mean?"

"Nothing. I'm sorry." She looks hopeful for a moment. "Do you want to come over for dinner to celebrate?"

I shake my head. "No, I have plans."

Her face drops again. "Are you going...there? I don't think it's healthy for you right now."

"No, I'm not, Ms. Nosy. Not that I'm interested in your opinion, but I'm having dinner with Shawn."

She mumbles, "Poor guy."

"Fuck you, Cassandra. I'm a grown woman. Get out of my personal business. I don't need your judgment."

She's about to say something else but thinks better of it. She turns and heads back toward her office.

I take a deep breath and head to the bathroom. I lock the door behind me and look in the mirror. I barely recognize my own reflection. I'm not physically different, but inside I'm unrecognizable. What is wrong with me? I hate what I've become, but I can't seem to help myself. The bitterness consumes me. I despise the fact that I've pulled away from Cassandra, but that's what has happened. I've pulled away from everyone I care about except Luke.

I couldn't tell you the last time I was with Cassandra outside of the office. It's been several months since I went to a Sunday night dinner. Sometimes I let Harley take Luke, but I don't go. I can't be around all that love and happiness when I know I'll never have it for myself. I had it for the briefest of times and had it torn away from me.

Why is that? What is it about me that makes me unlovable? Everyone I've ever loved has left me. I know I'm just beating Cassandra to the inevitable punch.

I teeter somewhere between embarrassed and sad when I'm around people who knew about Dominic. I have no doubt they're thinking that I don't have what it takes to hold onto a man. That I'm pathetic. They're right. I *am* pathetic.

I lay awake at night thinking of my last night with Dominic when I told him I was in love with him. He obviously never cared for me. I was all in. I can't believe I let myself get so swept up in him. What's worse is that I did it to Luke. I should never have involved him. He didn't understand why we couldn't talk to Dominic, Valentina, and Matteo after they left. One day we were playing happy family, and the next, they left our life without a trace.

I didn't know what to say to him. Dominic changed his number. I had no way of getting in touch. Those first few weeks I sent texts to his cell, but they bounced back. The same went for his email. I was tempted to ask Reagan if she knew how to get in touch with him, but that would have made me sound even more pathetic than I was. So I let go. I let go of everything and everyone. All that's left now is a shell of the woman I once was. I go through the motions of life with no joy. Luke is my only source of happiness. That's how it will be for me moving forward. I've come to accept it.

"BETH, did you hear what I said?"

I shake my head. "I'm sorry, Shawn, what did you say? I was distracted."

He grabs my hand from across the dinner table at the nice steakhouse where we're having dinner. He peppers it with soft kisses and lovingly rubs it with his thumb. "I've enjoyed our friendship and all our nights together over the past eight months, but I want to take things to the next level. I want us to date. For real. I'm extremely attracted to you. I want to explore a physical relationship with you. I want you to finally let me meet Luke. I want to be a part of your life."

"You are a part of my life. We're together at least three or four nights a month."

"You know what I mean."

I give him a small smile. "Shawn, you've been an amazing friend to me, but I told you from the beginning that I'm damaged. I can't offer you what you want. I don't see a situation where I'll ever let another man meet Luke. It took him a long time to get over my ex. I won't make that mistake again. As for me...I'm broken. Irreparably broken." I barely whisper, "I just can't. I'm so sorry. I thought I was clear on what we were."

His shoulders drop in disappointment. I hate that I'm

the cause of it. He's such a good man and has been such a kind, patient companion to me this year.

"You were clear. I've just held out hope that you'd eventually change your mind."

I squeeze his hand in return. "I won't. If you'd rather spend time with someone who can give you what you deserve, I more than understand it. In fact, it's probably for the best."

"Are you going to spend your life alone because some asshole broke your heart? You're too good for that. You're the one who deserves more. You deserve everything."

I look at him. He's so handsome and genuine.

Why? Why can't I be attracted to a normal, kind, loving man like Shawn? He might love me if I let him. He probably wouldn't dump me on a whim, though I'm hardly a good judge of character. But I'm certainly never putting myself out there only to be beat down and abandoned again. It's not worth the risk.

About eight months ago, we worked together on another file. Despite me having left our first date abruptly that night when Dominic cornered me, Shawn asked me out again. I told him I was nursing a broken heart and wasn't up for dating.

He suggested a friendship. A shoulder to cry on. I was still a mess and desperate for male companionship, so I took him up on his offer. I hadn't been out socially since before Dominic left.

Before Dominic left. That's what my life has turned into. Who I was before Dominic left, and who I've become since. B.D. and A.D.

Shawn and I hit it off as friends. We've spent so much time together this year. We're each other's constant dates at functions, he keeps me company on the nights that I'm alone, when the darkness falls over me, and is always good for a laugh or two when I need it the most.

"I'm sorry, Shawn. That's all I can say right now." I stand. "I think it's time for me to go."

He pinches his eyebrows together. "Why don't we have another drink? I don't want you to leave upset."

"I'm fine. I have some work to do tonight anyway." I don't, but I'm not interested in this conversation with him. It's clear we want different things.

"I'll drive you."

I give him an apologetic smile. "I drove myself, remember?" I try to do that as much as I can. It makes the end of the night much easier.

I walk over and kiss him on the cheek. "You're a wonderful man and an incredible friend. You'll find the right woman one day. It's not me though. I'm not good for anyone."

He kisses me back. "You're wrong. One day you'll realize that."

There's no sense in arguing. "Good night, Shawn."

"Good night, beautiful."

I aimlessly walk for a bit thinking about what he said. He's not wrong. I deserve to be happy. I've been anything but this past year, just going through the motions.

The weeks after Dominic left and cut off all communications were the worst of my life. Worse than when Gary and I first split. Worse than when my mother died. With her, at least I knew it was coming and prepared myself. With him, it came out of nowhere. I was blindsided. I was madly in love with him and then he vanished into thin air. He dismissed me from his life as though I meant nothing. Less than nothing.

Worst of all, Luke was heartbroken. He adored

Dominic. At the time, Trevor was the closest thing he had to a father figure, but Dominic was spending more and more time with him, and Luke fell for him too. He fell for the happy family life we both had been craving.

Luke kept blaming himself. I have no idea why. I told him it wasn't his fault, but I was barely holding my head above water at the time. If I'm being honest, I don't feel that much differently now. I've just learned how to mask my pain from the world.

I live in quicksand. The more I move, the further I sink.

The ride home feels quick because my mind is moving a mile a minute. I replay my last conversation with Dominic, as I've done thousands of times over the past year. He so easily dismissed me and has clearly forgotten me. I haven't heard from him since his goodbye call. He's probably fucked half of Cuba by now. Pain laces through me at the thought of him with another woman. Women.

I pull into my house and see the lights on inside. Huh, I don't remember leaving them on.

I walk in and see my ex-husband, Gary, sitting on my couch. "Gary? What are you doing here?"

He blows out a breath. "Luke didn't want to sleep over. He said he needed his own bed, so we came back here. He's asleep. I was just waiting for you to come home."

I nod in understanding. "I'm sorry. Maybe one day soon he'll feel comfortable staying at your place. I thought tonight was finally the night. He promised it was."

He looks defeated. "When do you think it will happen?"

I roll my eyes. "I don't know, Gary. You abandoned him for over seven years. You can't just waltz back in and expect him to act as if everything is perfect with you."

"I'm trying, Bethy."

Ugh. I hate when he calls me that. I always have.

"I know you are. But it won't happen overnight."

"It's been six months."

Six months ago, Gary came walking through our door after having not seen him in nearly a year. Literally, he just walked in my front door. He claimed to have seen the error of his ways and begged for a chance to truly be in Luke's life. In fairness to him, he's made more of an effort in the past six months than the entire rest of Luke's life combined. Luke isn't completely sold on the idea. He doesn't trust Gary. I don't blame him.

He even bought a small house a few blocks away so that Luke could walk between our houses. He comes to most things for Luke. I'm hopeful Luke lets him in at some point. I'm sure part of his fear is what he felt after Dominic left.

"Just keep trying. Little by little, things will get better. You can't force it. Trust is earned."

He nods. "You're right." He looks behind me as if ensuring that I'm alone. "You're not making a night of it with your date?"

"Not that it's any of your business, but it's not like that between Shawn and me. We're just friends."

He rubs my shoulder with his hand. "I'm glad to hear that. Do you ever think about me? About us?"

I shake my head and deadpan, "Not even a little bit."

Now he's rubbing both of my arms as he brings his body closer to mine. "You're so beautiful. We were good together. We could be like that again."

I think my chin legitimately drops in shock. "Do you have amnesia? We were not good together, and it will *never* happen again."

He smiles suggestively. "I bet you miss how good things were with us in bed."

"You mean the bed you brought someone else into?"

He cringes. "That was a long time ago, Bethy." He shuffles nervously. "I imagine it's been a while for you. If you need help in that department, I'm here." He playfully moves his eyebrows up and down. I feel bile rising to the surface of my mouth.

After my time with Dominic, I know that what Gary and I did can barely be considered sex. It was nothing compared to the passion and fire I shared with Dominic. My body burned for him. It still does. I know for a fact that I'll never have that again with another man.

I feel no need to tear Gary down though. I step away and say, "I think it's time for you to go. Don't bring this up again. It will never happen. I want you to have a good relationship with Luke, but it will only ever be Luke."

"Okay, but if you change your..."

"I won't. That's a guarantee."

Gary nods and leaves. I blow out a long breath. What a weird night. Propositioned by two men, neither of which I feel an ounce of passion for. At least Shawn is a good guy and I feel bad about it. Gary must be smoking crack if he thinks I would ever fall into bed with him again. That cheating bastard will never be more than Luke's father to me.

I walk into my kitchen and take out a bottle of wine. My wine refrigerator used to be full, but now it's nearly empty. I think I'm turning into a full-blown alcoholic, needing my nightly dose of *medicine*. Several glasses of medicine.

The only bottle left is Snoop Dogg wine. Jade turned me on to it and it's shockingly good.

I pour myself a large glass and down the whole thing in one go. I pour another before returning the cork to the bottle and placing it in the wine refrigerator, pretending that it will be my last glass of the night.

I should take a hot bath and try to relax. Who am I kidding? I'll do what I do most nights while Luke is asleep. Touch myself while watching Spanish porn. Maybe a day will come when I don't need dirty talking in Spanish to get off. That day certainly isn't here now.

I start to leave the kitchen when the doorbell rings. That's odd. Gary must have forgotten something.

I walk to the front door and begin to open it. "Since when do you bother to ring the doorbell, Gar..."

But it's not Gary.

It's Dominic.

I gasp as my hand shakes and I almost drop my glass of wine. Somehow, he grabs the glass to steady it and removes it from my hand.

I whisper, "Dominic," as my eyes immediately fill with tears. If possible, he's gotten even more attractive. The simple sight of him has a million emotions rising to the surface. I'm catapulted back to the day after he left, when the pain sliced through me like a knife.

"Princesa, eres más bonita que recuerdo. Me quitas el aliento. Dios, como te he extrañado." *Princess, you're even more beautiful than I remember you. You take my breath away. God, how I've missed you.*

Tears begin to stream down my cheeks.

He attempts to take a step into my house, but that snaps me back to reality. How dare he. I hold up my hand. "Stop. You're not welcome here."

I grab my wine glass from him and down the whole thing. I place it on the table next to my front door while wiping my tears and steeling my voice. "What do you want?"

"Can we talk?"

"I have absolutely nothing to say to you."

He attempts to grab my hand, but I pull it away. He looks at me in genuine shock. "You're acting very cold, princesa. This isn't like you."

"I'm cold? *Cold* is callously and abruptly cutting someone from your life who loves you. I'm not the one who did that and I'm not the same woman you once knew. Like I said, what do you want?"

"To talk to you. Can I come in?"

"No. Of course not. You didn't just leave me, Dominic. You left Luke too. He was devastated. I can't risk him seeing you. I don't ever want you around my son again."

His face drops as he nods. "I understand. Can we talk outside?"

I step onto my front porch and close the door behind me. "I've had a long day. Just spit it out and leave."

He moves to rub my arm, but I pull away again. He was always touchy-feely. It's second nature to him. I loved it so much, but I certainly don't want it now. I can't handle it now.

He runs his fingers through his beard. "Beth, this has been the worst year of my life. Things I couldn't share with you on the phone. It was dangerous. I needed to spare you what I knew was coming."

"Don't be so dramatic, Dominic. You dropped me like I was one of your hookers. That's probably all you ever saw me as."

"You know that's not true. I only did what I did for my children. You don't understand, Beth. I barely saw my kids this past year. There were legal battles and backroom deals being made. I had to do what was necessary to get my kids back. Cutting ties with you was part of that. It's not what I wanted."

"Did you get them back?"

He nods. "Yes, but it was a long, windy road."

"Are they okay?"

He shakes his head. "Not really. They're confused. Gabriela's father was feeding them lies about me. Valentina was too smart for them, but Matteo has returned to his quiet demeanor."

My heart breaks for those kids, especially Matteo. "I'm sorry for what they've been through."

"They'd like to see you and Luke. Dora too. We just got back today. It's the first thing they asked about."

I shake my head. "I'm sorry, but I don't think that's a good idea. I don't want them getting any false hope that we'll all be spending time together again. You know I adore them, but I can't do it to them or Luke and, honestly, I'm not sure my heart can take it. Dora lives with my sister. I couldn't handle the reminder of you."

His eyes fill with tears. "I've missed you. So much."

I momentarily close my eyes. "Don't."

"Please. I've missed talking to you. I've missed spending time with you. Touching you. I've thought of you every single day and night for the past year."

What an asshole. "Did you think of me when you fucked your way around Cuba for a year?"

"I..."

"Did you expect me to just fall straight into your bed after a year? We could have spoken. I would have visited. I would have waited for you. All you had to do was ask. You chose to completely cut me out of your life with only the courtesy of a few short lines. You changed your damn phone number."

"It wasn't my choice. You can't think that's what I wanted."

"It *was* your choice. It's clearly what you wanted."

"Please let me back in." He chokes on his emotions for a moment before he whispers, "I need you."

I can't help the tears now streaming down my cheeks. "What about what I needed?" I tap the left side of my chest. "There's nowhere to let you in anymore. I'm empty inside. You made sure of that."

"That's not true. You have the biggest heart of anyone I've ever met."

"*Had*. Like a fool, I *had* a big heart. It was yours and you shattered it into a million tiny pieces. It will *never* be whole again. I keep a small part of it pumping for Luke and my sister. That's it. The rest of it is dead."

He looks pained. He has no right to feel that way. He did this to us, not me.

I feel rage pushing to the surface. I clench my fists at my side. "Do you hear me, Dominic? You. Fucking. Broke. Me. I have nothing left to give you or any other man. I never will. Now get the fuck off my property before I call the police. Don't ever contact me again. Don't go near my son. We don't want to see you. You can go straight to hell."

I turn around, walk back inside my house, and quickly close the door. I slide down to the ground and cry myself into oblivion.

DOMINIC

She walks inside her house and slams the door in my face. I was expecting trepidation. I was expecting tears. Hell, I even considered the fact that she might be with another man. What I wasn't expecting was her being cold and nasty. That's not her. That's not the Beth I know. Knew.

I make my way home and pull into my long driveway. It's hard to believe it's been over a year since I've slept here. The last time I slept in my bed, it was with Beth. We made love for hours. She told me she loved me. She looked at me with trust. She trusted me with her heart, and I did what she said. I broke it.

I walk in and see my father sitting there with a bourbon for himself and another he holds out for me. "How did it go?"

I take the glass as I shake my head.

He nods in understanding. "I thought it might go that way, all things considered. Give her a little time."

"I don't think so, Dad. She hates me. *Really* hates me." Tears sting my eyes. "I've lost her."

"Did you explain everything?"

"She wouldn't listen. She didn't want to hear it. I can't blame her." I look down. "A man walked out of her house when I arrived." Seeing that drove a dagger through my heart.

"It's been a year, Dominic. What did you expect? She's a beautiful, smart, young woman."

I run my fingers through my hair as I sip my bourbon. "I don't know. I didn't expect the cold woman I saw tonight. I didn't expect to see a man at her house. I'm not sure who he was. She said she has nothing left to give me or any man. That she's empty inside. I fear the pained look on her face will never leave me, knowing I caused it."

"If she's pained, she still cares. Even though you asked me not to, I tried to reach out to her a few times while you were gone. She said it was too hard to talk to me. That's because she loves you."

"Maybe you're right. She was different though. She was so callous. I've never seen anything but kindness and warmth from her until tonight."

"That comes only from heartache. You and I both know that's not who she is. If you love her, and I think we both know you do, keep chipping away. Her reaction tells me she's not over you. It tells me you have a chance."

I nod. "I'll try. How were the kids?"

"Not a peep since you left. They're happy to be home and sleeping peacefully for the first time in a year."

"Thanks for coming. I couldn't go a night back here without seeing her."

He places his hand on my shoulder. "Anytime. I'm just happy you're home. I've missed you so much. All of you."

CHAPTER TWENTY-TWO

DOMINIC

I was up all night. I need to figure things out. I need to understand what's going on with Beth. She's not the same woman I left a year ago.

There's only one person to talk to right now. I quietly make my way into Beth's law firm and knock on Cassandra's door. No one else is here. I know she's usually in early before anyone else.

"Come in."

I open the door and she looks up. The smile on her face quickly fades. She breathes, "Oh fuck."

I smile. "Good to see you too, Cassandra."

"Don't let her see you. She'll kick you in the balls."

"I saw her last night."

"Well, you're alive, so that's promising."

"Barely. She's different."

"Pft. That's the understatement of the year."

"What happened to her?"

"You, Dominic. She snapped when you dumped

her so abruptly. I've never seen anything like it in my life. Darian was deeply depressed for a long time after her husband passed, but Beth has been something different. She's cold and bitter in her personal life, and nasty and calculating at work."

"Tell me what's going on with her."

"She clammed up. I mostly only see her in the office. I barely have a relationship with her anymore. She'll drop Luke to hang with my kids now and then, but that's it. I don't know what to do for her. I'm at a loss."

"I don't understand."

"She was in love with you. It's not like you gave her the slow let down or she saw it coming. You just called her and ended things without any real explanation, and you completely cut off communication. You canceled your fucking cell phone. She barely left her bed for the first month. She was a zombie for two or three more. Then one day, she just put up a steel curtain and she's been that way ever since. She said her days of being a pushover are done. She's been cruel and distant ever since. With everyone. *Everyone.*"

I sit down, unable to stand a moment longer. "What can I do to help?"

"Honestly, I don't know. Why don't you start by explaining yourself. I'm pretty sure you loved her too. Something doesn't add up to me. It never has."

I nod. "My ex-wife's maiden name is Navarro. Does that mean anything to you?"

"One of the most wealthy and powerful families in Cuba. Our paths have crossed on a few deals."

"Not *one* of the most powerful. *The* most

powerful. I don't know what Beth has shared with you, but I married Gabriela out of family obligation. My mother's maiden name is Amoroso."

She nods in understanding.

"As I'm sure you know, the Amorosos have one of the most successful sugar cane businesses in Cuba. It's been around for generations. My mother and Gabriela's were childhood friends. My mother's dying wish was for our families to finally unite. I did it for her."

"What fucking century do we live in?"

"I know it's hard for you to understand. Regardless, it happened."

"Go on."

"Gabriela's father was agitated that the kids were with me instead of with her in Cuba. When we landed in Cuba for the funeral, I saw her father's men waiting to escort us. I knew that was trouble. In Cuba, the mother has most of the rights. A Navarro has *all* the rights. Every judge and politician are in their back pockets. I don't think Gabriela wanted to stay in Cuba, but her father pulls all the strings, especially her purse strings."

I take a deep breath. "I called a lawyer down there right away. He told me I had rights but was looking at a two-to-three-year process to see it through. In the meantime, the kids would have to stay with Gabriela and her family. If I left Cuban soil, it would basically mean I was giving up my rights to my children."

"Wow, Dominic. I'm so sorry. It sounds terrible."

"They take everything into account, including intimate relationships. My lawyer told me I needed to end things with Beth. I did it so abruptly and without explanation because if I told her what was really going on, we both know she would have waited for me. I couldn't do it to her."

"You're right. She would have."

"How could I ask her to wait three years for me? I couldn't come home. She definitely couldn't come there. I told her what I did hoping to give her a clean break. The chance to move on."

"She didn't. She's wrecked."

"What can I do?"

She leans back in her chair and steeples her fingers. "Did you tell her any of this?"

"I tried. She wouldn't listen. She kicked me out and threatened to call the police. She told me she never wanted to see me again."

She takes a deep breath and rubs her temples. "I can't say I'm surprised. I want to help you. I hate what's become of her. We miss her. We want the real Beth back. The cold bitch routine is just that, a routine. We both know it's not who she is inside."

"I know it's not her. I want the real Beth back too. I...I saw a man leave her house last night."

"What did he look like?"

"Fair-skinned, light brown hair, tall."

"Oh, that was probably her ex-husband."

"He's back in the picture?"

"He's back in the picture for Luke. Beth definitely has no interest in him. I'm not on the inside anymore, but from what I gathered, he's making a real attempt at a relationship with Luke."

I smile. "I'm happy for Luke."

"But Beth has some other weird shit going on."

"Like what?"

"There's an attorney named Shawn who's madly in love with her."

"I remember him."

"She spends time with him, but I don't think it's physical. I think it's companionship for her. For him, he's dying to get in her pants. Honestly, I think she keeps him around to have some amount of control over a man. I truly feel bad for him. I think he has real feelings for her."

"I guess I understand her need for control. It's not like I love her spending time with another man, but it's understandable. That doesn't sound so weird to me."

"That wasn't what I was referring to. She goes to some underground club to get her kicks."

"What club?"

"Hush Hush. I believe she learned about it from you."

I give a short nod, unable to form words.

"I've looked into it. It has some high-end prostitution, and they cater to a variety of kinks. Mostly it's just a regular sex club. I don't know what she does, but I know she spends too much time there. She won't discuss it with me."

I place my hand over my mouth and close my eyes. "My sweet Beth goes to that place?" I say it more to myself than her, having a hard time believing it.

She nods. "Look, Dominic, I'm not one to judge. I'm not squeaky clean. To each their own. All I know is that my sister is a mess. She was the happiest I've ever seen her when you two were together. Your break-up destroyed her. We need to fix her."

I have no words.

"Do you love her?"

Without any hesitation, I say, "Yes."

"Do you want her back?"

"More than anything."

"If I help you and you break her heart again, the Navarro family will look like a walk in the park."

I smile. I love how much Cassandra loves Beth. "I want forever with her. I've never been more certain of anything."

"No more skeletons."

"None."

"Okay, let's get your girl and get the real Beth back."

"Thank you."

"By the way, I have your dog."

"I heard. How is she?"

"Good. She's keeping Dick company, though Dick is old and is having a hard time keeping up with her."

"Who's Dick?"

"*My* dog."

"You have a dog named Dick?"

She smirks. "I do. I had him long before Trevor and I got together. I like having Dick around, Dom."

"I bet you do."

BETH

"I think I see two kids on the back porch of three one four Berkshire. I repeat, three one four Berkshire. Over and out."

Mindy and I look down at the walkie talkie she's holding and hear Brittany's voice coming through.

The light on the device turns green again. "You two go around the left side of the house. I'll come in from the right. Over and out."

I can admit that I've grown to like Brittany and Mindy. I patrol with them once or twice a month. They didn't truly know me before. I feel like I can let my guard down and just be silly with them. There's no judgment. Just looking for teens getting it on. I don't really engage in busting them, but I have fun walking around the neighborhood with these two whackos.

Mindy holds down the button and responds. "We're on our way to the den of sin. Over and out."

I roll my eyes. Three one four? That's Giselle's house. I don't really want to bust Hazel, but I follow Mindy.

She pushes my head down and whispers, "Stay down. We don't want them to see us. The element of surprise is important."

"Is this really necessary? They're not bothering anyone. I'm sure they're just kissing. Hazel is barely fourteen."

"Kissing is a gateway drug, Beth."

We approach. There are definitely two people getting it on. I can make out that the female is between the male's legs. I'm not sure I want to see Hazel like this.

I hear Brittany on the walkie talkie. "Three, two, one, pounce! Over and out!"

She shines the flashlight at the couple.

Oh my god. It's not Hazel. It's Giselle and some guy. Giselle is on her knees on the deck, sucking his dick. She looks up into the light. "What the fuck?"

Even though we're standing five feet from each other, Brittany yells into the walkie talkie, "Abort mission! Abort mission! Over and out!"

I can't help but laugh at her absurdity and the absurdity

of the whole situation. And then I keep laughing...and laughing...and laughing. Everyone else, including the poor guy who just had his dick sucking session interrupted, starts laughing too.

I have to sit down because my sides hurt from the laughter. That might be the best laugh I've had in a year. I needed it.

Giselle stands and then sits next to me and wraps her arm around me. "It's been a long time since I've heard that."

It has. Just as I've distanced myself from my sister, I've distanced myself from Giselle too. She's tried hard to be a good friend, but I've completely shut her out.

The guy tucks himself in. Giselle looks over at him. "Go inside. I'll be there in a few minutes. I'll take care of you." She turns to Brittany and Mindy. "You two cockblockers go home. I need a minute with my best friend."

They turn to me, and I nod that they should go.

When they disappear into the night, Giselle squeezes my hand. I see tears in her eyes. "I've missed you."

I sigh. "I've missed you too. I'm sorry. I'm going through something and I'm just having trouble managing."

"I know, but that's when you're supposed to lean on your friends. And your family. I miss you. Your sister misses you terribly. She's a mess over the state of your relationship. It took you two so long to find each other. Why are you sabotaging it?"

I put my head down. "I don't know. I think I've been ashamed. I fell so hard for him. I'm such a fool."

"He's the fool. Not you."

I swallow. "He's back."

Her eyes widen. "What?"

"He's back. He came over last night. I think he

legitimately thought we were going to pick up where we left off."

"What did he say?"

"He was droning on and on that he needed to explain things to me. I just can't be around him. It hurts too much."

"What did you do?"

"I kicked him out and told him never to contact me again."

"Good for you. Fuck him."

"What about you? What are you up to? Who's the blow job guy?"

She snickers. "Half a blow job. His name is Jordan. I've been seeing him for about two months. We honestly were just sitting back here to enjoy the nice night, but one thing led to another."

"Two months? That's a lot for you. You must really like him."

"I think I do. He's divorced too. He's not into the twenty-something anal train, so that's promising. I know he's not as gorgeous as Tom, but I'm not going for looks this time around."

"Aww. That's so sweet. You deserve a good..."

"I'm going for dick size. Jordan has a nine-inch hammer and knows how to use it."

I burst out laughing. That's not what I was expecting her to say. She simply winks at me.

I squeeze her hand. "You're happy?"

She nods and I lean my head on her shoulder. "God I've missed you. I've missed laughing with you."

"Can we consider your coldness thawed?"

I let out a breath. "I hope so."

"Good. Do you want to go out with us this weekend?

I'd like you to meet him when his cock isn't stuffed down my throat. Maybe we'll all have a little fun. Jordan told me about a new bar geared toward an over-thirty crowd. Let's check it out."

I'm not sure I'm up for that, but the truth is that I miss Giselle. I want to spend time with her, and I should get to know her new man.

Smiling at her, I say, "I'd like that."

CHAPTER TWENTY-THREE

DOMINIC

We're mostly unpacked, and I'm heading into the office today to beg for my job back. I miss being at Daulton Holdings. I miss helping small companies become big ones.

I'm wearing my best suit. It's a blue pinstripe. I look down at myself. I haven't worn a suit in so long. I feel more like myself when I wear one.

I get off the elevator and run into LeRond, Carter's assistant. He screams. "Oh my god, Dominic!" He practically leaps into my arms for a hug. "We've missed your sexy ass around here."

He does a little celebratory dance.

I chuckle. "I've missed being here. How are you?"

"Oh, you know, kicking ass and taking numbers. Being Carter's bitch has its privileges. Are you looking for him?"

"I'm looking for both of them."

He pinches his lips together. "They're no doubt

together somewhere. They've been like dogs in heat lately. They're not in his office. I'd check in with Sheila before you walk in hers."

"I always do."

"Smart man. Good to see you back here, Dom."

"Thank you."

I head straight for Reagan's office. When her assistant Sheila sees me, she breaks out in a huge smile. "Dominic Mazzello? How wonderful to see you."

I return her smile with one of my own. "It's good to be seen. I'm excited to be back. Is she in?"

Sheila nods. "Yes, but Carter is in there. Give it about fifteen more minutes before you go in. It's been an...active month for them."

I let out a laugh. Some things never change. "I heard Beckett Windsor eventually started. Where is his office?"

Though Beckett was offered the job after I met with him, his daughter had a few issues and he temporarily declined. I had heard he started shortly after I left.

Sheila scrunches her nose. "He's in...well...he's in your office."

I wince. I suppose that makes sense. "Thank you. I'll be back in a bit."

I head down to my old office and knock on the door. A deep voice says, "Come in."

I walk in and he looks up. He gives me a genuine smile as he stands. "Dominic. How fantastic to see you."

I immediately notice that he has a split lip and a bruised eye. He waves his hand. "Oh, it's nothing. Tell me, are you back with us?"

"I'm not sure. I haven't spoken to Reagan yet."

"I have no doubt she'll bring you back on."

He motions around the office. "I hoped this was only a loaner, so I didn't change anything. I'll happily move to another space." I look around. It's the exact same as when I left. Even my bourbon and box of cigars are sitting in the corner. The only additions are two pictures on his desk. One of a little girl I assume is his daughter, and one of a woman I assume was his late wife.

"That was very kind of you. We'll see what Reagan says."

"I don't know much about your circumstances. Reagan and Carter were tight-lipped. I hope your family emergency has resolved itself."

"It was a battle for a long time, but it has. How are things going for you here?"

"Very well. I like it here. Reagan and Carter are as billed. I'm happy being back in the fold, but I'm equally happy to go home in the evening to my daughter without the headaches of running my own company. There have been a few international deals, so I've gotten to travel abroad a bit."

His phone buzzes and he answers, "Yes, Sheila?"

"Sorry to disturb you, Beckett, but Reagan and Carter are...done. She wants to see Dominic."

I yell out, "I'll be right down."

Beckett playfully smiles at me. "You could have better prepared me for how...frisky they are."

I let out a laugh. "Sorry about that."

He chuckles in return.

I head back toward Reagan's office. Sheila nods for me to go in. Reagan, Carter, and Skylar are all in there. All three embrace me when I walk in. It's a nice feeling.

Skylar grabs my arm and squeezes it as she leads me to the sofa. "I missed you."

"I missed you guys too. I assume congratulations are in order for all of you."

She smiles. "Yes, I had a little girl, Rylee. Reagan had a son, George. Both look like their daddies."

I turn to Carter. "After your grandfather?"

He nods as I shake his hand in congratulations. Carter's grandfather, George Daulton, founded this company. He was known to be a great man. He died in a plane crash when Carter was a kid, but apparently they had been very close.

We all sit in the more casual area of her big office. Reagan settles into Carter's body as if it's the most natural thing in the world. I miss that type of unforced intimacy. I miss it with Beth.

Reagan looks at me. "Are you back for good or in for a visit?"

"I'm back for good."

"Did your family situation get sorted out?"

I blow out a breath. "It was a long battle, but it's all resolved. My kids are home where they belong. They're a little battle scarred, but we'll get through it."

"I'm glad to hear it. Have you seen Beth?"

I nod. "I have."

"How did that go?"

I shrug. "Not so great."

She bites her lip. "Yeah, you did a number on her. She's been a mess. We barely see her anymore. She's disengaged from the family."

As if I wasn't feeling guilty already for what I've put her through, and how it's affected her. I can't believe she's abandoned her family, especially when she needed them the most. I'm going to fix it.

"I spoke with Cassandra yesterday. She brought me up to speed. It sounds like I have my work cut out for me."

She nods. "You do. Good luck. So are you hoping to come back to work?"

"If you'll have me."

"You're sure you're back? Your timing was rough last year. Skylar and I had our babies right after you left. Thank god Beckett started then. I'm not sure what we would have done without him."

"I understand. I'm back for good though. I promise. It's gone well with him?"

"It has."

"How's everyone else? How's Jade?"

She smiles. "She's out on maternity leave. She should be back in another week or two."

"Jade has a baby? She's a mother?"

The three of them laugh. Reagan stands. "We'll save that crazy story for another day. You and Beckett figure out the office situations. He and Skylar will get you updated on all the current projects."

"That's it? I'm back?"

She looks surprised. "I told you your job was safe, Dom. I'm a woman of my word. And our company is better with you in it. All three of us wholeheartedly believe that." She looks around to Carter and Skylar and they smile in agreement.

I spent the rest of the day having everyone bring me back up to speed on things. Beckett insisted I take my office back. He wouldn't consider anything else. He's a good guy.

WHEN I SPOKE with Cassandra the other day, she said she'd investigate a few things and get back to me. She just texted me that Luke has a sleepover tonight and she's pretty sure that means Beth will be at Hush Hush.

We have dinner with my father. It's nice to be back with him. He visited a few times, but it's not the same as having him around all the time. He's my best friend. My most trusted confidant.

After the kids go to bed, he offers to stick around to give me time to go out. I didn't give him details. I simply told him that I was doing what was necessary to get my girl back. He didn't ask any questions. He wished me luck.

I walk into Hush Hush wearing dark jeans and a jacket with no tie. I look around and don't see her at first. It's dimly lit in here, giving almost a jazz club type vibe, but I'd know the shape of her body if I saw her standing in the crowd, and I don't see her. Maybe she didn't come. I'll wait around for a bit to see if she shows up. Cassandra was confident she would.

I head to the bar and order a bourbon on the rocks. I look around and see a few familiar faces from my time here, but it's been a while, and most are unfamiliar now.

When I accept my drink, I lean on the bar scanning the room when a blue dress catches my eye. A familiar blue dress. I turn and see Beth wearing the same dress as the night we met. I catch her profile as she turns to him. She's so damn beautiful.

She's sitting on a couch talking to a Latino man. They both have drinks. Their backs are to me, but I see him leaning her way, about to make his move.

I do my best to remain calm. That's until I see him touch her. Then I see red.

I quietly walk over. His hand is on her exposed thigh and working its way up higher. I reach from behind them and grab his wrist. "Quite sus manos de mi propiedad." *Get your hands off my property.*

Beth turns to me, and her blue eyes widen. "Dominic? What are you doing here? How did you..." Her eyes narrow. "Oh, I know what you're doing here. It's what you've always done here. I guess old habits die hard."

"I'm here for you. We need to talk. Let's go. We're leaving. You don't belong here."

The man snarls at me. "Fuck off, man. She's with me."

I get up in his face. "This woman is mine. She belongs to *me*, not you. You have no chance of being with her tonight or any night. If you know what's good for you, you'll walk away."

Beth touches his hand. "Marco, give us a few minutes. I'll come find you when we're done so we can pick up where we left off."

The asshole nods and then stands and leaves. When he's out of earshot, she looks up at me. "What do you want? I told you to leave me alone."

"I want you to hear me out. I want you back in my arms. Back in my life."

Her eyes fill with tears. For the briefest of

moments, her new hard exterior is softened and she's vulnerable. Her shoulders slump. "Why are you doing this to me? Haven't you hurt me enough? Just let me live my life."

"From what I hear, you haven't been doing that."

She mumbles, "Cassandra."

"She loves you and is worried about you. So am I."

She pulls her head away from my gaze and I see a tear trickle down her cheek. As quickly as it came, that's how quickly she wipes it away. I rub my hand down her cheek. "Princesa."

BETH

"Princesa."

I push his hand away. "Don't call me that. Don't call me anything."

My chest feels tight. I can't breathe in his presence. The pain feels as fresh as the day he cruelly cut me out of his life.

Just then, Crystal, the owner of this place, comes over to us. "Dominic Mazzello? Is that you?" Dominic turns his head toward her. "It *is* you. We haven't seen you in ages."

He nods. "Hello, Crystal." He kisses her cheek. "It's good to see you. You look well."

She looks at me before turning back to him. "I see you found the latest and greatest dark-haired, blue-eyed beauty. She's very popular." She smiles at me. "He only likes them with dark hair and blue eyes. At least for the past five years or so. I'll leave you to it."

She walks away.

I stand. "I guess you have a type, and I was just one of many."

I turn and run away with the tears breaking free. I start to move faster toward the hallway. I don't want him to see me cry.

"Beth, come back." He chases after me. Damn these high heels slowing me down.

He grabs my arm and pins me to the wall. I shake my head as the tears flow. "Go find another woman with dark hair and blue eyes. I'm sure any of them will do."

He tilts his head to the side. "Why do you think I asked for women with dark hair and blue eyes?"

"Because that's your type."

"Did you hear her say *five years*?"

I nod.

"Because that's when I met you. Since meeting you, I've only been able to be with women that resemble you because you've been all I've wanted since the second I laid eyes on you."

What?

He rubs his hand up my arm. My goosebumps betray me. He smiles. "Why were you with a Latino man?" he asks accusatorily.

I whisper, "You know why."

He presses his hips into me. I can feel his erection. I can smell him. Oh god I've missed his scent. It's pure Dominic. My body involuntarily reacts to it.

I look around. It's one of the dark hallways with sex viewing rooms. No one is here. We're in the shadows. No one could see us even if they were.

His lips are near mine. "Tell me, Beth. Tell me what you do here. Do you have sex with strangers?"

I shake my head.

He pushes his body hard on mine. "I didn't think so. Tell me what you do."

I look up at him and shamefully admit, "I find men and ask them to talk dirty to me in Spanish while I touch myself. I let them watch."

"Why can't you do that at home with your computer?"

I look down as more shame washes over me. Tears are falling down my cheeks. I whisper, "Because I feel closer to you here."

He runs his hand up my inner thigh. I start to tremble at his long-absent touch.

His fingers brush over my panty-covered pussy. "Nadie más ha tocado ese coño mío, ¿verdad?" *No one else has touched this pussy of mine, have they?*

Oh fuck, I'm screwed.

I shake my head again. I can't bear to have another man's hands on my body.

He pulls my panties to the side and swipes his finger through my sex.

"Tu coño sabe a quien pertenece. Sólo se moja para mí. Solo me quiere. Soy el único hombre que lo tocará." *Your pussy knows who it belongs to. It only gets wet for me. It only wants me. I'm the only man that will touch it.*

I thrust my hips at him but say, "We can't. We shouldn't. I don't want you." My words and my body's reaction couldn't possibly be more opposite.

He sinks two fingers into me, and I can't contain the moan. I grab his shirt as he starts to move his fingers in and out of my body. I think my eyes roll around in my head.

"Puedo sentirlo, princesa. Estás goteando sobre mi mano. Tu cuerpo traiciona tus palabras." *I can feel it, princess. You're dripping down on to my hand. Your body betrays your words.*

My thoughts exactly.

I breathe, "Kiss me. Please." I'm so starved for him.

He smiles as his lips take mine. His thick tongue moves directly into my mouth. His kiss. His taste. Oh. My. God. I've missed this. Our kiss at the airport was my last kiss. I've replayed it in my head thousands of times. None of those dreams did it justice.

His fingers pump in and out of my body while his tongue does the same in my mouth. I can already feel the tremors. This is going to be the quickest orgasm of my life.

I know the moment he realizes it because he smiles into my mouth before pulling his lips and fingers away. No!

He turns me around and opens a curtain. It's a window. Two people are naked and having sex on a couch. We're now watching them. The woman is on top. She's totally absorbed in the pleasure.

Dominic's back is pressed to mine. "Tell me, do you also watch couples have sex when you come here?"

I nod.

"I know you do. You like to watch, just like me. Do you touch yourself when you watch them?"

I nod again.

"Show me."

I do nothing.

He lifts my dress and takes my hand in his. With his fingers over mine, he slips them down the front of my panties. Our intertwined fingers run through me. I'm soaked.

"Estás tan mojada, princesa. Verlos te excita." *You're very wet, princess. Watching them turns you on.*

Maybe to some extent, but he's the one who really turns me on.

He moves his fingers over mine in circles over my clit. "Keep moving them."

I do while he slides his fingers back into me.

My temporarily abandoned orgasm builds right back up in seconds. I can barely stand. I'm leaning all my weight on him. I reach back with my other hand and grab onto his shirt.

The woman in the room is screaming. They both look like they're about to come.

"Correte para mi, princesa. Muéstrame como yo lo que le hago a tu coño. Mu'strame cómo controlo tu placer. Solo yo. Solo seré yo." *Come for me, princess. Show me what I do to your pussy. Show me how I control your pleasure. Only me. It will only ever be me.*

I squeeze my eyes shut and nearly collapse as a monster orgasm works its way through my body. The best one I've had in a year. Dominic has to completely hold me up as I lose all control of my limbs.

I'm breathing heavily as his fingers slow.

He pulls his fingers out and grabs my hand that's still in my panties. He immediately slips his fingers and mine into his mouth. "Tu sabor es mi postre favorito. Dios, como lo he echado de menos. Te he extrañado." *Your taste is my favorite dessert. God how I've missed it. I've missed you.*

I regain my senses as remorse and humiliation suddenly wash over me. He's been back for two seconds, and I already let him finger-fuck me in the hallway of a sex club. What's the matter with me?

I straighten my dress and attempt to gather myself. He rubs his nose along my neck. "I'm taking you home and making love to you all night."

I turn around, rear my hand back, and slap him hard

across the face. He jumps back in shock. His hand touches the newly reddening spot on his face.

"I told you to stay away from me. Thanks for the goodbye orgasm you owed me. For the last time, don't come near me. We're done."

CHAPTER TWENTY-FOUR

BETH

The Uber drops me at the front of the house. I frantically knock at the door. It opens and Trevor answers. He's got a towel around his waist. His hair is messy. I've clearly interrupted them, but I don't care. I need my sister.

He takes one look at my tear-soaked face and holds out his arms. I collapse into them. He squeezes me tight and kisses my head. "It's going to be okay. We'll help you. Beth, she misses you. She misses her sister. It took you two so long to find each other. Don't push her away. She's heartbroken over it."

I nod as I sob into his arms. I miss her too. What have I done?

Suddenly we hear, "Secretariat, where are you? My ass won't fuck itself."

I feel Trevor shaking in laughter. He shouts back, "We have company, Sexy. Throw something on and come downstairs. But I'll consider that invitation wide open for later."

I can't help but giggle into him. I lift my head when I hear footsteps coming down the stairs. I look up and see my beautiful sister. I've treated her like shit for the past several months. I owe her an apology.

I nod at her and smile. "Nice robe." She's in the same white silk robe she bought me.

She smiles in return. "All my granny gowns must be in the wash."

We both smile at the ongoing joke, picking up right where we left off.

Trevor starts up the stairs but turns back. "It's good to have you here again, Beth."

I nod in gratitude. "It's good to be back."

Cassandra wraps her arm around me. "I'm guessing you saw Dominic tonight?"

I sigh as I lay my head on her shoulder. "I let him finger-fuck me to orgasm in the dark hallway of a brothel while we watched people have sex and then slapped him across the face and told him to stay away from me."

She's silent for a moment taking in the whole ridiculous yet true statement. "Does that mean we're drinking wine or vodka?"

At the same time, we both say, "Vodka," and then giggle.

We walk into her home office, arm in arm. It's a cozy room with a small bar, fireplace, and sofas. She pours us both two big glasses of vodka.

Trevor appears with a sweatshirt and sweatpants and hands them to me. "I thought you might want to change out of your dress."

"Thank you."

He disappears again.

I look at Cassandra. "He's legitimately the best man I know."

She nods. "He is. I'm the luckiest woman on the planet. And not just because he's hung like a horse and fucks like a stallion."

I smile. I've missed her mouth.

She hands me my glass and I take a huge gulp. Her eyes widen. "Slow down, killer."

I place the glass on the table, stand, and turn my back. "Can you unzip me? I need to get out of this dress."

She does and I let it fall to the floor.

She whistles. "You've got a hot bod. I can't believe you hid it with those granny gowns. That should be a crime."

I roll my eyes as I put on the clothes Trevor brought and sit back down.

She nods at me. "Tell me what happened before the finger-fucking."

"He came to Hush Hush. I'm not sure if he was there for me or anyone with a pulse."

"He was there for you. I spoke with him. I knew Luke was sleeping out tonight. I told him you'd likely be there."

I guess that makes me feel a little better.

"You spoke with him?"

She nods.

"What did you guys talk about?"

"We'll get to that in a minute. Tell me what happened tonight."

"I was talking to a man. He had his hand on my leg. Dominic came over to us and grabbed the guy's wrist. He told him that I was his property and to fuck off."

She bites her lip. "That's kind of hot."

I close my eyes. "It was insanely hot. Everything about him is hot. I'm powerless to his words and his touch. He's my kryptonite."

She takes another sip of her drink. "Keep going."

"They were about to get into it. I didn't want a fight, so I asked the other guy to wait for me elsewhere. Then the madame came over to us and was fawning all over Dominic. She made some mention of the fact that I'm his type since for the past five years he's only wanted women with darker hair and blue eyes."

"So basically, since he originally met you, he's only been with women that look like you."

"You figured that out faster than I did. I assumed I was just one of many and got up to leave. He chased me down the hallway and pinned me to a wall. He told me about being with women that look like me because he's wanted me that whole time. He asked me about the men I see there."

"There's no way you have sex with them. It's not in your grain to have casual sex like that."

I nod. "I know. Dominic is not only the last man I had sex with, but he's the last man to touch me."

"Then what do you do at that club?"

"Do you promise not to make fun of me?"

"No."

I let out a breath. "Mostly, it makes me feel alive. It makes me feel wanted."

"I get that after what he did to you."

"There's more to it. You know what the Spanish dirty talk does to me. Sometimes I watch people have sex, but primarily I find men who can talk dirty to me in Spanish and then I touch myself to it. I let them watch me." The tears form again. "I want to allow another man to touch me, but I'm never able to see it through. I fear I never will be."

"How did things become physical with Dominic?"

"Once he realized what I do there, he saw it as his opening. He started talking dirty to me in Spanish. I'm a goner when he does that. Once he began touching me, it was game over. Do you know what it's like to go a year without a man touching your body?"

She shakes her head. "No, I don't."

"I had no control over anything. I think I came in under a minute. At least that's what it felt like. When I returned to planet earth, he made mention of taking me home for sex. That's when I slapped him and told him to fuck off."

"I really think you should talk to him and hear him out."

I whisper, "I can't. He heartlessly cut me off. I can't get past it. I never will."

"He had legitimate reasons."

"Tell me. Tell me what they are."

"I think it should be him."

"Please. I need this."

I see her internally struggling before she eventually gives in. "Beth, his kids were basically kidnapped by his ex-wife's family. Did you know that she's a Navarro?"

I shake my head. "No, I didn't." The Navarro family is a well-known Cuban family. They're very wealthy and have a huge property portfolio. They own half of Cuba and now half of Miami too. I imagine they have a lot of influence in Cuba.

"The laws down there are different. They favor the

mother. If he wanted to see his kids again, he had to play their game."

"And cut me off in such a cold-blooded way?"

"He thought he was doing it for you. He didn't want you to sit around and wait for him."

"That's such bullshit. He's a fucking sex addict. He did it so he could fuck around down there."

She shakes her head. "I'm a pretty good judge of character. I don't think that was his reasoning. He loves you. He desperately wants to be with you. He's worried about you. Honestly? I am too."

I blow out a breath. "I'm sorry for how I've been. My heart is completely broken. I can't explain the feeling adequately. I feel like I was shown true love and happiness and then had it ripped away. It hurts so bad that I feel like I can't breathe at times. I'm broken. Something died in me when he treated me the way he did. I erected a barrier so no one could hurt me again, but I foolishly cut you out in the process. Can you forgive me?"

I put my head down in shame.

"Of course I can. And I get that, but being cold and unkind isn't you. Luke is picking up on it. He's such a sweet, thoughtful kid. He gets that from you. He gets everything from you. You being emotionless is going to rub off on him."

She's right. I need to set a better example for my son. And it's not like being cold has been fun for me. I'm more miserable than ever.

"I'll try to be better. Dominic coming home isn't going to help."

"Please hear him out."

"I don't know if I can." I take a few more sips of my vodka. "Do you know how he got the kids back?"

She shakes her head. "No, we didn't get into that. We really just talked about you."

I nod and take her hand. "I'm truly sorry for how I've been. I miss you. I love you."

She squeezes my hand in return. "I love you too."

CHAPTER TWENTY-FIVE

DOMINIC

I'm spending the evening with Sebastian, Kevin, and Claudia. I've missed my friends so much. We haven't ever been separated this long in our entire twenty-five years of friendship.

We head to a famous steakhouse in the city for a nice meal. It's very old school in its ambiance. We're sitting in big, leather chairs as we enjoy our gourmet meal.

I'm brought up to date on Kevin and Claudia's kids. Benny is now in college and their daughter is about to graduate high school. I can't believe I missed his graduation. It pains me. I need to make it up to him the next time I see him.

Sebastian seems miserable. He's unusually quiet. No sexcapade stories. None of his normal swagger. It's bad.

Kevin and Claudia are currently arguing the merits of voluntary and involuntary farts.

Claudia shakes her head. "Your farts are worse because you do it on purpose. I at least attempt to hold mine in and take care of business discreetly."

Kevin gives her an incredulous look. "I so love it when I'm spooning you in the middle of the night and you rip one right onto me."

"I don't do it on purpose. I'm asleep. You birth two children and then let me know if all your systems are in perfect working order. Mine are involuntary. Yours are voluntary. It's so much worse. You don't care that I'm lying right next to you."

"That's marriage."

"Is it also marriage to go to the bathroom without bothering to close the door? I don't need to hear the nightmare going on in there. Why would you want me to hear it? Don't you want me to be attracted to you? I would never subject you to that."

"That's what guys do." He looks at me. "Right?"

I chuckle at their interaction. I've missed this. I haven't smiled this much in a year. It feels good.

"I'm staying out of your marital farting and bathroom habits conversation."

Claudia giggles. "I suppose we can shelve this for another time."

Kevin leans over. "I'm telling you, her *involuntary* farts are deadly. Worse than Sebastian's one-hour stints in locker room bathrooms before each game."

I smile and look at Sebastian, who has been in outer space all night. He's not even listening to the conversation. His face is void of expression.

He excuses himself to the bathroom. I ask Kevin and Claudia about it. "What's wrong with him?"

Kevin just shakes his head. "He's been a wreck for a while now."

Claudia smirks. "He had it coming. About six months ago, he went to Lindsay and begged her to take him back. She told him he was too late. I'm so proud of her for that. She dated a man for a few months, but that fizzled. She's finally going on dates though. I'm happy she's moved on. In all honesty, I'm happy she stuck it to him. He deserved the rejection."

Sebastian is my best friend, but I can't disagree with Claudia. "Do you still see her?"

Claudia nods. "Yes. All the time. She's one of my best friends. That didn't change just because Sebastian is an asshole."

I can't help but smile. I love Claudia's fierce loyalty.

Kevin shakes his head. "I don't think he's sleeping around anymore."

"Wow. That's shocking."

Kevin nods. "It is. I think he sees all his friends with families and realizes he may have missed the boat. Speaking of families, how are your kids managing?"

I shrug. "Confused. I don't blame them. I'm confused too. I'm just happy Gabriela did the right thing in the end. It cost me a fortune to get her off daddy's payroll, but I don't care. We're back where we belong. I bought her a house near mine so the kids can go back to their school starting next week."

"And Beth?"

I shake my head. "Not good. She told me we're done and to stay out of her life." I stare off for a moment before turning back to them. "She's changed.

She's bitter about everything. She's bitter toward me. I thought we had a breakthrough the other day, but then she turned cold and slapped me."

Claudia scoffs. "Can you blame her?"

"No, I suppose not. I'm not sure what I was expecting, but her coldness wasn't it. It's out of character. I spoke with her sister. She's said Beth has been in a bad place since I left. I thought I was doing right by her handling things as I did. Perhaps I was wrong."

She nods. "You should have told her the truth. I offered to do it for you."

"I know, and I appreciate it, but I couldn't ask her to put her life on hold. I didn't know when or if I'd be back."

She gives me a compassionate look.

Sebastian rejoins us. "Let's get out of this stodgy place. I can't take it. Let's have some fun, like the old days."

Claudia looks up at him. "What do you have in mind?"

"Let's go to a bar. Let's go dancing. Anything but sitting around and stuffing our faces talking about flatulence."

I shake my head. "I told you I'm not into the twenty-something scene. We've outgrown it. Not to sound like an old man, but it's loud and the music sucks. I'll pass."

Claudia smiles. "Actually, a new club opened, geared toward an over-thirty crowd. Maybe we can check it out. If it's too young, we can leave." She looks out the window. "If we're going, let's do it before the rain comes. It's supposed to storm tonight."

I'm not in the mood for this, but I've missed my friends and want to spend time with them. It won't hurt to go for a little bit. I'll stay for one drink.

We head to the club. Well, I wouldn't call it a club. It's a bar with music that isn't crazy loud and isn't all rap. It's a lot of older rock-n-roll.

Sebastian and I offer to go to the bar to order drinks. Claudia is anxious to get Kevin on the dance floor. With his hands on her hips, she leads him that way.

As we wait for drinks, I watch them dancing. She's in his arms and they're both grinning. They're moving to the beat of the music, completely in sync with one another. Every few seconds he kisses somewhere on her body. Her neck, her shoulders, her face, her lips. It's sweet how much they still love each other after all these years.

At some point, I notice her eyes widen. I follow her line of sight and see Lindsay dirty dancing with some guy. Shit. This evening isn't going to end well.

She's in a tight, short, purple dress. Lindsay is a very attractive woman, with killer curves and wild blonde curls. The dress leaves little to the imagination.

Claudia grabs Kevin's hand and they make their way to us. "I don't love this place. Let's go."

Sebastian scrunches his nose, "What? We just got here. Relax. Let's have some..."

And then his eyes find Lindsay. He breathes, "What the fuck?"

I look over and the guy is whispering in Lindsay's ear while she smiles. His hands are on her waist.

Sebastian stands but I grab his arm. "Don't make a scene."

He turns his head to me. "What do you want me to do, Dom? Watch her with some other guy? I can't do that. That's my wife out there."

Claudia interrupts, "Your *ex*-wife. It's been well over two years. Let her go. She's finally happy."

He starts pulling his hair, clearly tormented. I hate seeing my friend like this. Why was he such an ass in the first place? He loves her. I know he does. It didn't have to be this way.

He takes a few deep breaths. I think he's calming down, but then he says, "Fuck this."

He marches over to Lindsay. I see it in her eyes the second she notices him stalking her way. She breaks out of the man's embrace.

I move to stand behind my friend, both to support him and contain him if needed.

He grabs her arm. "What are you doing with this loser?"

The guy puts his hand on Sebastian's chest. "What's your problem, dude? Back off."

Sebastian swats his hand away. "My problem is that you've got your hands all over my wife. *My* wife."

The guy holds his hands up. "Sorry, I didn't know she was married." He mumbles, "She didn't act like it."

Lindsay places her hands on her hips. "I'm not married. This is my *ex*-husband. *Ex*, Sebastian. We're no longer married. Get that through your thick skull."

Sebastian is seething. I don't think I've ever seen him like this.

He looks her up and down. "What the hell are you wearing?"

"A dress."

"It's too small."

"You didn't used to mind it. You didn't mind the access it afforded you. Regardless, how I dress isn't your business anymore. You made sure of that."

He looks back at me and I place my hand on his shoulder. "Let her go. It's time."

He toggles his eyes between all of us until they return to Lindsay. His gaze slowly moves up and down her body. The air suddenly shifts. She was previously looking at him with contempt. Now she's licking her lips looking like she wants him to devour her.

He takes two strides toward her and smashes his mouth with hers.

She initially starts pounding his chest to fight him, but it quickly turns into her grabbing his shirt, keeping him close, kissing him just as much as he's kissing her.

He roughly pulls her flush to his body. The kiss is turning heated. *Very* heated. Way too heated for this setting. His hands move up the backs of her legs until they disappear under her dress.

Kevin and I look at each other and smile. Claudia sighs in resignation. I suppose we all knew on some level that this was inevitable.

Without breaking the kiss, Sebastian lifts her, and she wraps her legs around him, neither caring that her dress rides up. He walks off the dance floor toward a dark corner.

When they were dating, and even their first few years of marriage, them getting carried away and having sex in public places was the norm. I guess old habits die hard.

I'm watching them walk away when a certain ass on the far side of the dance floor catches my eye. I'd know that plump, perfect ass anywhere. Beth is here. She's in a short, white dress that's flowing as she swings her hips. My cock takes immediate notice.

Without giving it a second thought, I instinctually walk that way. I see she's dancing with Giselle and some guy. That guy better not be with her.

As I get closer, I notice his hand on Giselle's lower back and sigh in relief. Beth's back is to me, but Giselle's eyes meet mine as I make my way to my girl. I see a small smile creep up on her lips.

BETH

I'm dancing up a storm, having a great time with Giselle and Jordan. He's such a sweet guy and he dotes on her. I'm happy she's found someone like him. It gives me a dash of hope that maybe one day I'll move past Dominic and find someone.

I love this place. It's so fun and not overcrowded with young people. It's nice to let loose and be with my best friend again.

My eyes are closed, and my arms are in the air. I must be crazy because I think I smell Dominic. I inhale deeply. My body always reacts to his scent, and it's most definitely reacting now.

I dream of his hands on my hips as we dance to the fast beat. It seems so real. I feel his body pressed to my back. His enormous erection on my ass.

Our hips move together, just as they did the night we met and the night we danced on Harley's roof.

He's whispering dirty things in Spanish in my ear before his lips move across my neck.

My panties are soaked from a damn dream. I keep my eyes closed. I don't want to wake up from this feeling. I miss him so much.

I turn around and his scent becomes stronger. His arms are around me. I reach up and can feel his soft beard. That sexy beard I love running my fingers through. I make my way to those soft lips. I have memories of those lips on my body, making me feel things no man has ever made me feel.

As if it's the most natural thing in the world, our lips come together. His taste is everything. It's familiar. It's comfortable. It's the man I love so deep to my core that I seem to imagine him when I can't have him.

His big hands grab my ass and pull me tight to his hard body. This is the best dream ever. I'm afraid to open my eyes and return to loneliness.

The song ends and I blink my eyes open. I expect to see open space. Hell, I half expect to see some other man that I was mistaking for Dominic. What I didn't expect to see was Dominic standing in front of me. Did I just make out with him on the dance floor?

My lipstick on his mouth gives me my answer.

My jaw drops. I turn my head and look at Giselle. She's smiling and winks at me.

I turn back to Dominic. He cups my cheek. "Come home with me. Please."

I pull away. "No. Never again. I won't let you or any man ever hurt me ever again."

I turn and rush toward the front door as the tears break free. I open it to see that it's pouring outside. I don't care. I step into the rain. It soaks me in seconds. Honestly, it feels good on my overheated body.

He rushes out after me, also not caring that it's raining. "Please, princesa. Let this anger go. Let me explain things. We belong together."

I hold my hand up for a taxi and one stops. I open the door and turn back to Dominic with my shoulders down. "It's over. Just let me go. For the last time, we're done."

I get in the cab and watch him disappear behind me.

CHAPTER TWENTY-SIX

BETH

I arrive home, immediately undress, and get into the shower. My bones are chilled from being in the rain. I was shivering the whole cab ride home, both from the cold and my encounter with Dominic. I turn the water as hot as I can stand it until I eventually feel the shiver work its way out of my body.

When I step out, I hear thunder crackling and the rain pounding my house. For some reason it soothes me. I think of my father when it rains like this. I used to get scared during thunderstorms, but he would make a fort in the family room and tell me that nothing could get to us in the fort. It's one of my only memories of him and I hold onto it for dear life.

I throw on my white silk robe, looking at myself in the mirror and giggling. I guess it really is better than the granny stuff I used to wear.

I walk downstairs and pour myself a glass of wine,

thinking about the evening. I was totally lost in him tonight. Why can't I shake this man?

Perhaps it's because I'm in love with him.

Maybe I should do as Cassandra and Giselle want and hear him out. But I'm so afraid of the hurt and pain.

Apparently, Cassandra got to Giselle, because all night she was in my ear about talking to Dominic. That's a complete shift in her advice from a few days ago.

I turn the lights off, preparing to head up to bed. As I do, thunder cracks and lightning momentarily brightens the sky. I see a figure standing on my front lawn. A familiar figure.

I run to the front door and open it. Dominic is standing there in the rain. He's in a white undershirt and the pants he was wearing tonight.

Besides a clenching jaw, he's unmoving and completely drenched. His clothes stick to his muscular body. My eyes unashamedly take him in. He's complete and total perfection.

I shout, "Dominic! What are you doing here? It's storming. Are you crazy?"

He runs his fingers through his soaked hair. It's dripping down onto his equally wet face. He says nothing, only staring at me from about twenty feet away with the gaze that has so often been my undoing. It still is.

I stare back from the dry confines of my doorway. He looks edible. I look down at what I'm wearing. My nipples are currently betraying my otherwise cool demeanor. He undoubtedly can see them through this flimsy, white silk robe.

He shouts, "We're not done. We'll never be done. Me perteneces. Siempre lo harás." *You belong to me. You always will.*

My body takes on a life of its own as I step out into the rain. The downpour immediately soaks me again. My hair is drenched. My white robe clings to my body like a second skin. It's completely see-through now.

I slowly walk until I'm halfway between my door and Dominic. The rain pours down on both of us as his eyes move up and down my body.

He licks across his lower lip, and then repeats, "Me perteneces." *You belong to me.*

The simple fact is, he's right. My heart, body, and soul all belong to him. There will never be anyone else for me but Dominic.

As if completely in sync, we both take two steps toward each other at the same time. His mouth collides with mine. His hands grip the backs of my legs and lift them until they're wrapped around him. I grab onto his hair with both hands as our tongues perfectly intertwine like no time has passed.

I've missed being in his arms, his taste, the way my body reacts to his touch.

The cold rain continues to pelt our bodies, but neither of us cares. We're back in each other's warm arms where we belong.

His soft, demanding lips move over mine, taking the ownership I know only he possesses. He tastes like bourbon and cigars, and it's perfect. It's Dominic.

His hands move all over my body as my bare pussy is rubbing on his covered hardened length. It's been so long. I need to feel him moving inside me again. I'm crazed for it.

I swivel my hips over him, and he moans into my mouth. "Te necesito." *I need you.*

I pant, "Yes."

He pulls the top of my robe down over my shoulder,

exposing my breast. Grazing his teeth down my neck, he bites me hard enough that I know I'll have a mark. I nearly orgasm from it. That's how much I've missed him marking my body.

He kisses his way down until he takes my nipple into his warm mouth, biting it and then sucking it hard.

I pull his hair as I arch my back. "Oh god, Dominic. I need you too."

I move my hands down and unbuckle his belt, suddenly desperate to get him inside me, uncaring that we're on my front lawn. I'm about to reach into his pants when a bright light shines in my face.

I hear a voice, "We've got a live one. Over and out."

Dominic and I both freeze. He pulls my body flush to his so my breasts aren't as exposed, though there's not really much he can do with what I'm wearing.

The lights are on our faces, so we can't see anything, though they eventually drop the flashlights down as we hear their footsteps approach.

My fucking luck, Brittany and Mindy are standing there in their *M.O.M. Patrol* shirts with golf umbrellas and police-worthy, giant flashlights. Both have huge grins on their faces.

Mindy giggles as she nonchalantly says, "How's it going, Beth?"

"It was going great until about ten seconds ago. Why are you two lunatics out in the rain?"

Brittany smiles. "We could ask you the same, though I'd go out in the rain naked for him too."

I feel Dominic laughing into my neck, refusing to even look at them.

Mindy shakes her head. "Sorry, Beth, but according to our patrol guidelines, we have to take photos of all offenders for the neighborhood watch social media. It's in the homeowner's association rules."

I roll my eyes and wave at them. "Goodbye, ladies," I say as they both turn to leave in a fit of giggles.

I'm still wrapped around Dominic. He grabs my face, bringing me back to us. "Are you alone? Can we go inside?"

I appreciate that he's considering Luke right now.

I kiss up his neck and breathe, "He's not home. Take me inside. I need your body on mine. In mine."

He marches us right into the house and closes the door, pinning me to it. The water drips off our bodies, pooling on the floor.

I immediately peel off his shirt as he removes my robe, leaving me completely naked.

His eyes roam my body as mine roam his. I run my hands over his broad chest. God I missed him.

He runs his nose up and down my neck, applying small bites along the way. "I've missed your smell. Your taste. It's all so uniquely you."

I shiver at his touch and words as I begin to unbutton and unzip his pants, pulling him out.

I nearly forgot how thick he is. It's large and engorged. I'm dying for him to be inside me, but god knows what he's been up to in our time apart.

I look him in the eyes. "I need you to wear a condom. I don't want to know what's gone on in the past year, but I do know I need you to wear one. Let's go upstairs. I have some in my drawer."

He nods in understanding, as he pulls us off the wall and walks up my stairs to my bedroom, still holding me.

He gently lays me down on my bed with my legs spread and simply stares at my body. His eyes take in every inch of me.

Dominic Mazzello's gaze has been my Achilles heel for over five years. There's always an intensity to the way he looks at me. It affects every inch of my body, the body currently on display for him. Ready for him. He simply needs to take it.

He slowly runs his fingertips over me, starting at one set of lips and ending at the other. When he reaches my center, his eyes flutter. "He extrañado este coño bonito rosado." *I've missed this pretty pink pussy.*

Fuck. His words do me in as he pushes two fingers into my body. I can feel myself clench around them. He releases a string of Spanish expletives at the sensation before pulling his fingers out and sucking them into his mouth.

As soon as he does, his engorged cock starts leaking. It's incredibly satisfying to physically watch the effect my taste has on him.

I reach over and run my fingertips over his tip, gathering his juices. I bring them to my mouth and suck my fingers. His taste is so uniquely Dominic and I'm desperate for it.

I whisper, "Dominic. Don't make me wait any longer."

He discards his remaining clothes and stands over me naked, giving himself three long tugs. He's the most dominating, masculine man I've ever remotely imagined. It oozes from his pores.

I reach into the drawer in my night table and pull out a condom.

He grabs my wrist and says, "There's been no one."

My brows burrow in confusion. It can't be what it sounds like. "What? What do you mean?"

"There's been no one, Beth. I haven't touched a woman since the last time I touched you over a year ago. A wise woman once told me that if you love someone, truly love them, it shouldn't be hard to remain faithful. Being with another person should be detestable to you. The mere thought of touching another woman is detestable to me."

I'm in shock right now. My mouth moves, but no words come out.

He lays down and moves to position himself between my legs. "I did what I needed to do for my kids, and we'll talk about it soon, but my heart never left you. Not for a minute. I couldn't betray you. I didn't want to. I always knew I'd eventually come back to you. I didn't know if you'd still be available, but I had to try. I was faithful. If you'll have me, I always will be."

A single tear trickles down my cheek as some of the tiny broken pieces of my shattered heart start to fuse back together. I need his closeness to me right now. I need our two bodies to become one.

I dig my heels into his ass and push my hips up, forcing him to enter me. He follows suit and thrusts himself hard until every inch of him fills me.

He closes his eyes as utter bliss consumes him as much as it consumes me. It's been so damn long. It's like I was missing a part of me that's finally returned, making my body whole again.

His hand cups my cheek. He begins moving slowly in and out of me, kissing me all over, whispering words of adoration in Spanish.

But this isn't what I want right now.

I grab his face and stare into his eyes. "Dominic, neither of us have had sex in a year. I've been starved for your inner animal. I crave him." I thrust my hips up. "Mark me. Make me yours. Fuck me like you missed me. Fuck me like you need me. Fuck me hard. I need it."

His eyes darken and he licks his lower lip, the fucking sexiest image on the planet.

He throws my legs over his shoulders, opening me to his mercy. His mouth takes my nipple and bites it, hard.

I moan. Yes. I need the pain with the pleasure. I breathe, "Give it to me, Mazzello."

He lifts up on his arms and rears his hips back and slams into me. Deep.

I scream out.

"Te gusta?" *You like that?*

I nod, unable to form words at the depth of him inside me.

He does it again and again and again. Our bodies smack loudly as they meet over and over.

I throw my head back. "Yes! Like that! Harder!"

I scrape my nails down his chest, and he yells out as I break through his skin.

He grabs onto my hair while pounding into me. My eyes flutter.

"Mi princesa quiere el dolor." *My princess loves the pain.*

Fuck yes, I do. "I need more. More of it."

He pulls out and rolls me over, smacking my ass the hardest he's ever smacked it. That sets me off and my body starts convulsing. I grip the sheets with my fists. My pussy completely floods and I come. He's not even inside me, he simply spanked me as hard as he could and I freaking came. I didn't know that was possible.

"Mierda." *Holy shit.*

I imagine he's shocked. I'm shocked too.

He sinks his head between my legs, lifts my hips, and spears me with that Herculean tongue of his. I can hear him slurping my come, which is still dripping down my thighs.

His tongue pushes in and out of me, dragging my orgasm out. "Ah, Dominic."

It begins to wane, but he smacks my ass again and

another orgasm hits me out of nowhere. My body is shaking again, and I scream out into my pillow.

Dominic lifts up. "Necesito sentirlo en mi polla." *I need to feel that on my cock.*

He slams back into me and then really lets me have it. My bed is smacking against my wall. I'm afraid it might actually break this time. Well, I don't give a shit if it breaks as long as he keeps doing this to my body.

He growls, "Te gusta duro?" *You like it hard?*

"Yes. Harder. More. I want more. Give it all to me."

I'm not sure he can go any harder, but I want everything he has.

I feel his teeth before I feel his lips as he bites my shoulder, breaking skin. And I come again.

My body is clenching and trembling.

He groans, "Oh fuck," as he swells inside me, emptying himself and filling me with his warm seed.

He collapses on top of me, completely out of breath and covered in sweat.

He immediately starts to kiss my shoulder where he bit me. I smile knowing I'll be marked all over. I haven't been marked by him in over a year. I've missed it.

He rolls and sinks down in the bed next to me, pulling me on top of him, so my front is to his. I have no use of my limbs at this point. He has to manipulate my body into place.

"I think we broke your wall."

I look up and realize he's right. We put a giant hole in my drywall.

I smile. "I guess we can call that a glory hole."

He laughs. "I suppose it is." He rubs my ass, which is undoubtedly red and likely will bruise. "Did I hurt you? Are you in pain?"

"I came when you spanked me. Twice. And then I came again when you bit me. Does that sound like I wasn't enjoying it?"

"I just don't want to hurt you."

I lift my head so our eyes meet. "You've never *physically* hurt me."

He nods in understanding. "Are you ready to hear me out?"

I kiss his chest, knowing that he must have suffered this past year and not sure if I can stand to hear about it. I mumble into him, "How about I draw a bath and pour us some bourbon. Then we can talk."

He nods. "I'll go pour the bourbon and you draw the bath."

"Okay."

He rolls me off him, stands, and walks out of my bedroom naked. I can't help but watch his yummy ass as he goes.

He yells from the hallway, "I know you're checking out my ass."

I grin and yell back, "It's a good ass."

"A great ass!"

I lean back and smile to myself. It feels so good having him back. I feel whole again. I feel like I can breathe for the first time in over a year.

***

DOMINIC

I'm at her bar pouring our drinks when I hear the front door open. A man's voice says, "Bethy, where are you?"

I walk out to the foyer, not caring that I'm completely naked. It's the same guy I saw leaving this house a few days ago. It must be her ex-husband. I know he has a habit of walking in. She mentioned it once before.

His eyes widen when he sees me. "Who the hell are you?"

I puff out my chest. "It doesn't matter. Don't just walk into her house anymore. You don't live here. You're barely a man, not supporting your ex-wife or your child. She's done it all on her own. Show her some fucking respect in her home."

I've rendered him speechless. Beth comes flying down the stairs. She's wearing one of my work shirts. It's the one she wore home the first night we were together. She must have kept it, which makes me happy.

I love that her hair is messy, and she looks fully satisfied and freshly fucked. Though I suppose my state of undress gave it away already.

"Gary, what are you doing here?"

"I know Luke is sleeping out. I saw a light on. I thought we could hang."

I interrupt. "I'm hanging with her."

Beth's eyes move down to my cock hanging heavy, and she smirks. "You're certainly hanging."

I smile back at her and wink. "He wasn't *hanging* a few minutes ago. He was standing tall." I lick my lip. "Inside you."

Her eyes widen. "Would you like to go upstairs and put something on?"

"No." I cross my arms defiantly. I'm not leaving her here, half-dressed, with this douchebag.

She walks over and stands in front of me, with her back to me. I wrap my arms around her and pull her to my body. She's mine, asshole.

I feel her gulp. "Gary, I'm obviously busy and, as I told you last week, I don't have any interest in *hanging* with you. You have no reason to be here when Luke isn't."

I bark out, "And fucking knock."

He looks at me. "Who *is* this guy?"

"This is Dominic."

"Her boyfriend."

She snaps her head to me and gives me a disapproving look.

"I don't want you bringing home random guys and having them around Luke."

Beth places her hands on her hips. My princesa is mad. I love when she gets feisty. "First of all, Dominic isn't a random guy. I've known him for five years. Second, you have no actual legal rights to Luke. You have access because I grant it to you. You have no say in who is and isn't around him, or who is and isn't in *my* home. If I want to fuck Dominic on every surface of this house, I can and I will." She points to the door. "Luke has a game tomorrow. I'll see you there. Good night."

Gary shakes his head. "Who are you right now, Bethy? This isn't you."

"I'm a woman who's sick of being jerked around by every man in my life. And don't call me Bethy. I hate it."

I harden at the way she's talking right now. I hear her suck in a breath the moment she feels it on her back.

She leans back, keeping her body tight to mine, obviously not wanting him to see it.

Gary nods and mumbles, "I'll see you tomorrow," as he walks out the door.

When the door closes, she turns around and lifts an eyebrow. "What was that?"

"You know I don't like that he walks in here unannounced. And since when do you guys *hang*?"

"I don't *hang* with him." She looks down at my cock, which is hard as rock right now. "Did you have to emasculate him with your chorizo grande?" *Large sausage.*

I let out a laugh. "Chorizo grande?"

She smiles and nods toward my erection. "At least he didn't see it in that state. He would have peed his pants."

"I can't help that I like when you get feisty." I run my fingers over her shirt. My shirt. "I love that you kept this."

She looks down at it as her face softens. "It smelled like you for a few months. I needed it."

I tilt her chin up. "I love seeing you in it. It's sexy as hell. Everything about you is sexy." I nod toward her bar. "I saw the Cuban cigars over there."

She keeps her head up. "I don't smoke them, but the smell reminds me of you. Clearly I've missed you."

Like with my shirt, she says it without any shame. I love this confident Beth. I *really* love how much she needed reminders of me all year. My cock gets even harder and starts oozing for her.

Her eyes take notice, and her breathing picks up. She grabs my cock, licks her lips, and says, "Suddenly

I'm very hungry for breakfast foods," as she drops to her knees.

AFTER A MINOR YET WONDERFUL DETOUR, we're finally soaking in her tub with our glasses of bourbon. Her hair is up in a messy bun and her legs are draped over mine. Her cheeks are flushed from what we just did. Her neck, shoulders, and breasts are covered in my marks. I've never seen anything more perfect.

She leans back, looking content with her eyes closed. Icy Beth seems to be gone. At least for now.

"You're breathtakingly beautiful, princesa."

She smiles as she opens her eyes. "Thank you." She lets out a giggle.

"What's so funny?"

"Gary is at his house right now looking at his dick in the mirror realizing he's not half the man you are. Not even a quarter."

"Un chorizo pequeño?" *A small sausage?*

She smiles. "They're all small next to yours." She takes a slow sip of her bourbon as her face turns serious. "Tell me what happened over the past year. Tell me why you ended things with me. Help me understand."

I nod, knowing it's finally time to talk to her about everything. "I assume you now know that Gabriela is a Navarro?"

She nods. "Cassandra told me. I know they're powerful, but are they corrupt?"

"Yes and no. I don't know of anything illegal, but they still use old-world tactics to get what they want.

Their influence in Cuba is unmatched. When I landed in Cuba, her father had guys waiting for us and took us to her family's compound. I didn't even get a chance to express my condolences before I was informed that my kids were staying with Gabriela in Cuba. I could leave or stay, they didn't care. I tried to plead with Gabriela. She doesn't even like living in Cuba or dealing with her overbearing father. But I think she thought...she thought..."

"That she could get you back this way."

"Yes. How did you know?"

"It was clear to me when I met her that she's still in love with you."

I nod as I take a sip from my glass. "I don't know if it's love, but it's clearly what she wanted. I immediately went to a family lawyer down there. He told me it was going to be a long process, as the laws there heavily favor the mother and *very* heavily favor Navarros."

"Where did you stay?"

"With my sister. That was the only silver lining in any of this. Spending time with her and her boys. Anyway, the lawyer told me I was looking at a two-to-three-year process, but if I left Cuban soil, I would effectively be throwing in the towel and giving up all rights."

Her eyes fill with tears. "You should have told me. I would have come to you and helped. I would have visited as much as possible."

I look down. "I know. But me having a girlfriend would have also worked against me in the case. You don't understand how it is down there. The laws are different. They track your cell phones, your emails, everything. I turned it all off. That's why I didn't attempt to work remotely for Daulton. I'd be putting them at risk too."

She whispers, "I would have waited for you."

I set our glasses on the ledge, pull her into my arms, and kiss her head. "I know, mi amor, but I couldn't do that to you. What if it took three years? What if I lost and had to stay down there just to see my kids? It wouldn't have been fair to ask you to put everything on hold and wait for me. I set you free so you could live your life. I did it the way I did so you could move on. I thought I was doing what was best for you."

She lets out a sob into my chest and I kiss her head again over and over.

She lifts her head and looks at me with those shining blue eyes. "But *you* didn't move on?"

I shake my head. "No. I knew I'd come back for you one day. I prayed you'd still be available and would want me, but I had to let you go at the time. I believed it was the right thing for you, albeit painful for me."

She opens her mouth to speak, but then closes it, laying her head back on my chest.

We're silent for a few minutes until she asks, "How did you win? How did you get them back in only a year?"

"Gabriela realized she and I were never going to happen, and she was miserable living in Cuba under her father's thumb again. He told her she would be cut off if she left. I basically offered her full financial support. It's just money. I don't care. I have plenty. We reached a deal. I bought her a new house near mine so the kids can stay at the school, she has a more than generous monthly stipend, and I have all the passports in my possession."

She sighs. "I'm sorry for what you've been through."

"I'm sorry too. For what you and Luke both went through with us leaving. Can I see him?"

She shakes her head. "I don't think so. I swore I'd never let him meet another man I'm dating."

I wince. That stings. Am I just a random man she's dating?

She holds my face in her hands and looks me in the eyes. "I think we did it wrong the first time around."

"What do you mean?"

"We involved our kids so early on. Too early. You're not supposed to do that until you know each other. Until you're all in and sure about where things are headed. It's not fair to them otherwise. We played one big, happy blended family, when we should have been getting to know one another in private, away from the kids. We had this immediate physical connection. Don't get me wrong, I loved our sex life, but did we really get to know each other? Did we really talk? You don't know about my life growing up. I know little about yours. I know you loved someone once, but I don't know what happened. I know you planned to play professional baseball, but I don't know why you didn't."

I nod. She's not wrong.

"Honestly, Dominic, I was so worried about keeping you sexually satisfied, that I lost a little of myself. That's on me, not you. I think I've done it in all my relationships, not just with you. I did a lot of soul searching this past year. I realized that I've always been a pushover in my personal life, valuing others' needs above my own. I don't want to do that anymore."

I smile. "I like this new you. You should always have what you want. Your needs should be met. I liked what I saw downstairs with your ex."

"Good, because that's the new me."

"It turned me on."

"I noticed."

"And you more than sexually satisfy me, princesa. Don't ever doubt that."

"You require a lot of sex, Dominic Mazzello." She smiles. "You're an addict."

I nibble at her lips. "Maybe I'm just addicted to you."

She bites her lip and then sighs. "I wish there was something we could share that you've never shared with anyone else."

I apply a little pressure to her back entrance.

She giggles. "Not something *I* haven't done, something *you* haven't done."

"How about truly falling in love? I haven't done that with anyone else. I do love you, princesa. I hope you know that."

She runs her fingers through my hair and softly kisses my jaw. "I love you too. I know you're the man for me. Me slowing things down has nothing to do with that. I just want to date you before we jump in full steam like we did the first time around. I want to do it right this time. You and me, alone, spending time together."

"Are you asking me to be your boyfriend?"

She smiles again. "Yes, I am. I want to go to

dinners with you and learn about you. I want you to learn about me. If, after everything, we want to make this more permanent, then the kids can come back into the fold. Does that make sense?"

"I accept your terms. Why don't we get some sleep, and in the morning, we'll go for a long walk, and I'll fill you in on some things that have shaped me. You're not the only one who did a bit of soul searching this year."

She wraps her arms around my neck, kisses up my jaw, and grinds herself onto me. "I just got you back. I don't think I'm ready to go to sleep quite yet."

I run my hands up her soft body. "I don't think I'm the one who's the addict."

CHAPTER TWENTY-SEVEN

BETH

I wake up feeling the best I have in...well...a year. I'm back in Dominic's arms where I know I belong.

I can feel his morning wood pushing up against my ass. I wiggle a bit.

He moans. "Don't even think about it. We're talking this morning before we have to get our kids. *Talking*."

I smile. As much as I want him right now, I know him turning down sex means he heard what I said to him last night.

I reach over and grab my phone to check the time. "I've got about two hours until I need to be at Luke's game."

"Valentina has a soccer game. I need to go by then as well. Fortunately, they let her back on the team."

"I miss her. How is she?"

"Happy to be home. I think that was another reason Gabriela gave in. The kids were miserable."

"And Matteo?"

"Quiet again."

"Cassandra has Dora. You should get her back for Matteo."

"I know. I'm not sure what to do. I imagine Dylan and Brandon have gotten attached to her, but Matteo keeps asking."

"Cassandra told them from day one that she was only going to be with them for a little while. She's prepared them. They have another dog. They'll be fine. He needs Dora more than they do."

"Yes, I heard about Dick. Who names their dog Dick?"

I giggle. "My sister. She had him way before she was with Trevor. She said it was her way of ensuring she always had dick in her bed."

I feel him shaking in laughter. "That sounds like Cassandra."

"It does."

"How's Luke?"

I blow out a breath. "Honestly, he struggled when you left. I think he was starting to see you as a father figure. It was another disappointment on that level for him. He's had so much of it in his short life."

He squeezes me. "I'm so sorry. One day, when you're ready, I promise to make it up to him."

"We'll see." I reluctantly get out of bed. "I'll start the coffee. You get dressed."

I start to walk out of the room naked. As I'm walking, I say, "I know you're checking out my ass."

He yells, "It's a good ass."

Giggling to myself, I yell back, "A *great* ass!"

After I switch on the coffeemaker and get dressed, we place our coffee in to-go cups and head out for our walk. I look up at him. "Tell me about your first love."

He gives me a small smile. "Her name was Mandy, and

she was an artist. I met her my freshman year of college. She was a year older. A bit of a free spirit."

"Most artists are."

He nods. "Yes. I fell quickly. She was sweet and kind and beautiful. I thought she was my forever. A few months in, she started falling in with the wrong crowd, doing drugs. She began to change. I was an athlete. I had no interest in that lifestyle. I honestly thought it was just a little marijuana. I didn't realize it was more than that for a while. Sebastian wasn't a fan of hers because of it. He thought she would drag me down. He didn't think she was as into me as I was her. It turns out, he was right."

He then tells me the story of how he found her on ecstasy one night. He tried to take away the drugs and get her out of a bad situation, but the police came and arrested him for possession.

"I was suspended from the team pending a drug test. When that eventually came back clear, I was reinstated to the team. I was excited to tell Mandy. She was beside herself with guilt over the fact that she may have cost me my dream. I couldn't wait to go and tell her I was back on the team and she didn't need to feel guilty anymore."

He looks down as if it still pains him all these years later. "I walked into her room, and she was in bed naked with two men. I don't know what she was on, but it was extreme. She was completely out of it. I lost my temper and grabbed one of the men. He reached for something sharp and started swinging aimlessly. He ended up stabbing me in the elbow."

"That big scar? I've seen it."

He nods. "Yes. It sliced through every tendon and muscle. My career ended in that moment."

I stop and wrap my arms around him. "Oh, Dominic, I'm so sorry. That must have been terrible for you."

"I was completely devastated and heartbroken at the time, both because of my baseball career ending and losing Mandy. But it's been twenty-five years. I've moved past it."

"What happened to her?"

He shrugs. "I don't know. I never saw or spoke to her again after I left her bedroom for the hospital. She dropped out of school and disappeared. I was angry. I didn't consider chasing after her. I had never met any of her family. She said she had none. She vanished, and I was too messed up to do anything about it."

"You never looked her up?"

"Before I left for Cuba, Sebastian suggested looking her up for some closure. Obviously, my experience with her shaped my relationships with women for the past twenty-five years. In thinking about it over the past year, I realized that going to the sex club enabled me to keep women at arm's length. No feelings, no pain. I had confided in him that I was planning to ask you and Luke to move in with us, and he encouraged me to reach out to Mandy to finally get some closure before doing so."

What? That's news to me. "I didn't know that you wanted us to move in."

"I never got the chance to discuss it with you before I left." He's quiet for a brief moment. "I did search her name. Nothing much came up. She lives in Philly and has a daughter. There was nothing else."

"Do you want to speak with her?"

"I'm indifferent to it. It doesn't take a shrink for me to know that I kept an emotional distance from women because of how much she hurt and betrayed me. I would have liked a proper goodbye, and perhaps to know what I did wrong, but that was a long time ago." He takes me in his arms. "Maybe I was just waiting for you my whole life, princesa."

I want that to be true, but I think I agree with Sebastian. He has no closure on his first love. It impacted him so deeply that he never dated anyone until me. That can't be healthy.

I momentarily forget about the troubles of his past when his lips brush across mine and he gifts me with the sweetest kiss. It's not intended to lead anywhere. He's simply loving me.

It's taken all of twelve hours for me to completely fall back in love with him. If I'm being honest with myself, I know in my heart that I never stopped.

I do want things to work out, but we have to take it slow. We're both damaged.

"Luke, hurry up. I need to get to work."

"I'm coming, Mommy."

He walks down with his hair combed perfectly. It's always messy, so I know something is up. He's also wearing his favorite blue shirt, the one he only wears for special occasions.

I give him a skeptical look.

"Valentina is back at school. I want to look good."

I play innocent. "Oh, that's wonderful. How is she?"

"A little different. A little quieter."

"Make sure you're a good friend. I'm sure it was hard to be away from her friends and school for a year in a foreign country."

"I know." He's quiet for a moment as he looks down. "Are we going to see Dominic?"

I hate how much he hurt when Dominic left. I'm sure

it didn't help that I was a mess. I hadn't realized how much he'd come to rely on our pseudo-blended family. That's exactly why I need to keep my time with Dominic separate from Luke. If things go south, I can't let him go through that again.

"I'm sure we'll see him at school events."

"So we won't spend time all together, like we did before?"

"No, honey, not right now. I don't think it's a great idea. But we have that overnight camping trip toward the end of the school year. You'll probably see him then."

He mumbles, "I guess."

He looks sad, but I know this is best. Maybe a day will come when it's time for us all to be together again, but I'm not doing it until we're one hundred percent certain about our future. When we truly know each other and have no more obstacles.

CHAPTER TWENTY-EIGHT

DOMINIC

The past few weeks have been great for me and Beth. We're not together as much as we were before, or as much as I'd like, but we're genuinely dating.

We go out for dinner, we go out with friends, both mine and hers, and we do a lot of talking. She was right about needing to get to know each other. I do feel like I know her so much better now, and I know she feels the same about me.

I learned more about her father and her ex-husband. How she's a bit damaged over losing them both. I realize how much my actions exacerbated her issues. I hate myself for doing that to her.

I finally worked up the nerve to call Cassandra about Dora. She was understanding. When I pick the kids up from Gabriela's house tomorrow, we're heading over to Cassandra's to get Dora back.

But tonight, my kids are with Gabriela and Luke is

with his father. After not seeing Beth for six days, I finally get some time alone with my girl. We've both had a long week at work and just want to stay in and watch a movie.

She opens the door when I arrive and I immediately take her in my arms, burying my nose in her neck and taking in her sweet scent. "I've missed you, princesa."

She pulls back and I notice for the first time that she looks sad. "What's wrong, mi amor?"

"I got my period. I legitimately burst into tears. Our first night together in a week. I'm sorry."

I let out a laugh and kiss her hand. "It's not your fault. We'll cuddle and watch the movie. I just need to be close to you. To hold you. I've missed you all week." And for the past year.

She buries her head in my chest. "Okay. I'll still take care of you."

I smile into her head. "It's not necessary. We're in it together."

We're now almost done with the movie. Her head is on my chest with my arm around her and we have a blanket across us. I can feel her breath. I can smell her shampoo. She's been aimlessly running her nails softly over my legs. It's driving me crazy. I'm hard as a rock. I can't even focus. I have no idea what's going on in the movie. I hope she doesn't notice.

I may have discreetly googled *sex on your period* at some point during the movie. I learned a few interesting facts.

When it's over, she stands and stretches. Her T-shirt lifts just enough so that I can see her belly. I desperately want to lick her creamy, soft skin.

"I'll be right back. I need to run upstairs to change my tampon."

I quietly walk upstairs behind her. As soon as she goes in the bathroom, I quickly remove all my clothes and then follow her in.

Her eyes widen. "What are you doing?"

I bring my body flush to hers, running my thumb across her lip. "You want to do something I've never done before?"

She looks up at me through her long lashes. "Like what?"

"I've never had sex with a woman while she's been on her period."

She scrunches her nose. "I don't know, Dominic. I've never done that either."

"I've heard that you're more sensitive during your period. You may enjoy it."

I see a small smile break out on her face. "And that's knowledge you just happen to have?"

I give a guilty smirk. "I may have looked it up during the movie."

She giggles and mouths, "Addict."

"Just for you. We can do it in the shower. Quiero esta intimidad contigo. Necesito sentir tu hermoso coño que me rodea." *I want this intimacy with you. I need to feel your beautiful pussy around me.*

Her breathing picks up as she narrows her eyes. "You don't fight fair. You know what that does to me."

I nod as I slowly lift her shirt over her head. She grants me access.

I toss it to the side and then remove her bra, looking at her beautiful breasts and dusting my thumbs over her nipples until they harden. "Que perfecta." *So perfect.*

I bend to remove her leggings and panties, leaving her completely naked. I have to grab my cock for some relief. It's already weeping for her.

I run my fingers up her inner thigh. Just as I'm about to reach her pussy, she grabs my wrist. "That's too much."

"I want to experience everything with you, princesa. I want all of you."

She bites her lip, but eventually removes her hand from my wrist. While staring at her eyes, I grab her tampon string and pull it out. Without breaking eye contact, I toss it in the toilet.

I turn on the shower. As we wait for it to warm, I pull her into my arms, loving the feel of her naked body on mine. As if neither of us can wait another second, our lips naturally come together like old lovers.

Her tongue moves softly over mine as I savor her taste. My hands move all over her body, and hers on mine. She's smooth and feminine. Utter perfection.

I feel the steam coming from the shower and know it's time. Reluctantly breaking the kiss, we step in.

The water pours over us. I lift her body so she can wrap her legs around me.

I push her back to the tile. My severely engorged cock is resting on her warm pussy as the hot water rains down on us.

Perhaps it's the fact that I've never done this. Perhaps it's the intimacy of the situation. Perhaps it's the fact that I'm madly in love with her. But I don't think I've ever wanted her more than I do at this moment.

I look down and spit into her pussy. She sucks in a breath, but as I rub it through her folds, she moans.

Grabbing fistfuls of my hair, she breathes, "I can't believe how much I want you right now. Get inside me."

She lifts herself enough for my tip to find her entrance. We both look down as I push forward and slowly disappear into heaven.

She's soft and warm. I've missed being inside her all week. I crave this feeling with her. The closeness. The love we share.

I pull out and slam back into her. Her head gently falls back onto the tile wall. "Oh my god, I *am* more sensitive." I can already feel her pussy clenching around me, and it's been one stroke.

I begin thrusting in and out of her, establishing a rhythm. She's going out of her mind pulling my hair, yelling my name, and writhing in my arms.

I tease her nipple with my tongue before giving it a small bite. Her pussy tightens. She loves a little pain with her pleasure. She was made for me. I'm sure of that.

"Mi princesa tiene un coño avaro." *My princess has a greedy pussy.*

The warm water is hitting our bodies as we both work toward our orgasms. Her hands move all over my body. It's like she can't get close enough.

Our mouths come together again. With the water hitting us, the kiss is sloppy, passionate, needy, and sexy as hell.

I lick my way down to her breasts again, showering them with the attention they deserve.

I bite her nipple one more time and she yells, "Ah, Dominic." She scrapes her nails down my neck as her pussy begins convulsing into her orgasm. She's screaming as if there's no one around for miles. It's a good thing we're alone.

She's gripping me so tightly, I have no chance at holding off as I come long and hard deep inside her.

My movements slow and then still. I pull her close. She's still wrapped around me with all the trust in the world. We're both breathing heavily, but I gave her a short, hard kiss in appreciation.

When I eventually peel my chest from hers, she starts laughing.

"What's so funny?"

"I can't believe how sensitive I was. I've been missing out."

I smile. "Now we can do this for a week every month."

She mouths, "Addict."

I set her legs down, but when I do, I see my come dripping down the insides of her thighs. There are a few red streaks in it.

For some reason, it's incredibly erotic to so clearly see the mixture of our fluids. I reach down and scoop it up in my hand. I don't know what comes over me, but I rub some of it across her chest and some across mine.

She swallows and breathes, "Dominic," as we stare at each other.

I lift her hand and place it over my rapidly beating

heart. "Te amo con todo mi corazón." *I love you with all my heart.*

Her eyes turn glassy as she looks up at me. "I love you too."

The next thirty minutes are spent in the shower kissing and slowly washing each other. It's a level of intimacy I've never before experienced.

I ARRIVE at Cassandra's house the next day with Valentina and Matteo. When she opens the door, Dora comes sprinting toward Matteo and leaps into his arms as if no time has passed. She licks every inch of Matteo's face. He's laughing in a way I haven't heard for a long time.

Cassandra smiles at the interaction. Brandon and Dylan run toward us. I look at them. "Wow, you two have gotten so big," I marvel. "Brandon, you look so much like your daddy. Dylan, you look like your mommy."

Cassandra fist bumps her. "Lucky kid. Why don't you guys help Matteo and Valentina gather all of Dora's toys."

The kids all happily run off. I turn to Cassandra. "Thank you for this. I hope Brandon and Dylan are okay with losing her."

"They have Dick, and maybe we'll consider a puppy for Christmas this year. One that doesn't hump everything in sight. That's the horniest dog I've ever met."

I let out a laugh. "I guess she hasn't outgrown that. Thank you for putting up with her."

"I'm fifty-six and I haven't outgrown it yet." She smiles. "And I owe you for fucking some happiness back into my sister. She's like a different woman since you came back into her life."

I can't help the big grin on my face. I feel the same. "I'm happy to hear that. I think we're finally in a good place."

"And you talked her into period sex last night. That couldn't have been easy."

I can only shake my head. "Do you two have any secrets?"

"No, and by looking at the scratch marks on your neck, I'm thinking it went pretty well."

I narrow my eyes at her. "If you need details, you'll have to get them from her."

"I already did. I'm just fucking with you." She looks back, and when she sees no kids, she turns to me and asks, "Have you gotten the kids together yet?"

I shake my head. "No. She doesn't want to. She wants to keep our dating life separate from the kids. I didn't completely get it at first, but I do now. We've gotten to know each other on a much deeper level this time around. There are no distractions when we're together."

"I know, but you guys seem like you're all in. I understood right after you got back, but I'm wondering what the holdup is now."

"I suppose I can broach the subject with her again. The hardest part is only seeing her once or twice a week. That and I'd like to see Luke. I know I hurt him when I left. I want to make things right. And my kids adore Beth. They keep asking why we haven't seen her."

She thinks for a moment. "Darian and Jackson are having a pool party in two weeks when they open their pool for the season. That might be a good time to get them together. It's a bigger group. Less pressure."

I shrug. "The ball is in her court. I'm following her lead. I'm grateful for the time we have."

CHAPTER TWENTY-NINE

BETH

There's a knock at my office door before I look up and Cassandra appears. "Hey. What's up?"

She walks in and closes the door. "I saw Dominic yesterday."

"Yes, I know. Thank you for taking care of Dora. I heard she was excited to see Matteo."

"She was. It was adorable." She sits down in one of my chairs and smirks.

"What are you smiling about, crazy lady?"

"I saw his neck."

I scrunch my nose. "I may have gotten a little carried away the other night."

Her eyes twinkle. "More than a little."

I lean back in my chair. "I lose my mind with him. He's so hot."

"Where do you guys stand?"

"What do you mean? We're together and we're happy. It's pretty simple."

"What about the kids?"

"I told you, I want to keep things separate this time."

"I understood that at first, but you guys are in a good place now. What's the holdup?"

"I don't want to ever put Luke in a position to be hurt by a man again. Hasn't he suffered enough with men coming in and out of his life? Trevor is the only man there for him. As much as I appreciate everything he does, I'm sad for Luke that his uncle is the only consistent man he can count on."

She nods, though I sense her wheels turning. They usually are. "How are things with Gary?"

"He's making an effort. I certainly don't think Luke completely trusts him yet. And that's why I can't bring Dominic back into the fold. What if Gary disappears and then Dominic does the same? That would devastate Luke."

"How did things end with Gary?"

"You know he cheated on me."

"Was that all there was to it?"

"Where are you going with this?"

"Honestly, I find it weird that you don't want to move forward with Dominic when he seems all in this time around. What's holding you back?"

"Things are good. Why rock the boat? Luke's heart is safe."

"You don't want any more from Dominic than one night a week?"

"Of course I do, I love him, but I value my son above myself." I have no idea where this is coming from. "Did Dominic say something to you? We haven't remotely discussed it in weeks."

"He'd gladly progress things. He wants to spend more time with you than he is, and he misses Luke."

"He said that?"

She nods.

I blow out a breath. "Luke has asked for him too." I shrug my shoulders. "I'm not sure what the right answer is. I want to trust in us but look at my track record in the trust department."

"You don't trust him?"

My eyes start to fill with tears. "I don't trust me. I've misjudged every man I've ever been with. Not just Gary. Think of the string of losers I've dated through the years."

"You didn't misjudge Dominic. And we all make mistakes until we find the one that isn't. The one that's our forever. Do you realize how many frogs I kissed before I met my prince?"

"You think Dominic is that for me?"

"I do. He seems pretty sure about your future. That you have one."

I can barely whisper, "I'm scared, Cassandra. If he spends time with Luke, and I spend time with his kids, we're all so vulnerable."

"I understand." She's quiet for a moment. "You're going to Darian and Jackson's pool party next weekend, right?"

I nod. "This weekend is Luke's class camping trip. It's the following weekend, right?"

"Yes. Maybe bring him and his kids to that. It's a bigger group where he knows almost everyone. It might be a casual way to all spend time together."

"I'm not sure. That crew is out of control at times."

"That's what makes it easier."

"Hmm. Maybe. I just don't want to rush this. He told me about his first love recently. I don't think he has closure with her. I'm not sure I'm ready to pull the trigger until every potential obstacle is removed."

"That's why I think the bigger group setting would be best. So much less pressure. Dipping your toes in the water. It's like in middle school when you don't go on one-on-one dates, you go with a group to make it less pressure filled."

I let out a laugh. "That's kind of true."

She smiles. "What's the camping trip you mentioned?"

"They call it parent-child bonding in the wilderness, but it's mostly fathers. Luke refused to allow Gary to go, so I'm going. It's not my idea of fun, but at least Dominic will be there, though he doesn't keep his hands off me when we're together. Not for a second. The kids will probably pick up on it there."

"He's not an animal. He can control himself."

I mumble, "He's a little bit of an animal."

She laughs.

"I think Brody is going with Scotty. Giselle's ex is going with Colton."

"Oh, right. I heard Brody mention it the other day. He was trying to talk Harley into going. She was having no part of it."

I nod. "I don't blame her."

"Was Gary upset that Luke didn't want him to go?"

I shrug. "Honestly, I'm not sure if he knows about it."

Smiling, I say, "I forgot to tell you something a few weeks ago. Per normal, Gary just walked into my house. Dominic was downstairs buck naked, dick hanging. And he didn't give a shit about being naked in front of Gary. Poor Gary probably had a heart attack after seeing that monster."

She starts laughing. "That's hysterical. What Happened?"

"Dominic was getting all alpha, puffing his chest, but I

stepped in. I very clearly told Gary he's not welcome when Luke isn't home. I finally let him have it a little bit, saying a few things I haven't had the balls to say all these years. The good news is he now knocks before entering."

"That's progress. The past year wasn't easy, but you're coming out on the other side of the tunnel as the best version of yourself. I'm proud of you."

I'm a bit choked up with emotion and don't respond.

She stands and looks at her watch. "I have a few calls to make. I'll see you at the game tonight, right?"

"Of course."

WE'RE SITTING in the stands as Luke's baseball game is about to start. Cassandra and Giselle are on either side of me.

Gary approaches and nods at me. "Hey, Beth."

I inwardly pat myself on the back at the fact that he no longer calls me *Bethy*.

"Hi, Gary."

He shakes Tom's hand and sits next to him. They begin chatting.

Giselle whispers, "Oh shit."

"What?"

She motions her head toward an approaching figure. "George is here. He's walking over."

Cassandra looks at me in question.

I smile. "Her father-in-law is a character. He's got one arm and the biggest mouth you've ever heard."

Cassandra looks at me in question. "He's a loud-mouthed, one-armed man?" I nod. "I don't think I've ever met one of those. Bring him on."

We hear George shout at Trevor, "Why the hell is my grandson batting eighth? He hit better than everyone in the last game."

Tom practically jumps out of his seat. He whisper-yells, "Dad, I told you you're not allowed to yell at coaches. Who told you there was a game?"

"I joined the Gram thing so I can keep track of the schedule."

I turn to Giselle and mouth, "Gram thing?"

She rolls her eyes. "Instagram. The team has an account." She shakes her head. "This is why Tom's sister's kids give him fake schedules. No one can handle his mouth."

He looks up at Giselle. "Well, well, look what the cat dragged in. How are you, red?"

Giselle gives an amused smile. "Hi, George. Lovely to see you as always."

He barks, "Go tell the stupid coach that Colton should be batting higher in the order. That coach doesn't know his ass from a hole in the ground."

Tom places his hand on George's shoulder. "Dad, keep your voice down. And don't curse. There are kids around."

Cassandra looks at us. "Wait. His name is George?"

Giselle reluctantly nods, knowing where she's going with this. "Yes. Don't start."

Cassandra and I start laughing. Giselle's last name is Washington. "His name is George Washington?"

Giselle again simply nods her head in exasperation.

George starts to climb the bleachers. Cassandra holds out her hand for him. "George, can I offer you a *hand*?" She smiles and winks at him.

Giselle and I look at each other and try to hold in our laughs.

George looks at her with a small smile creeping on his face. "I could use an arm, not just a hand."

The three of us burst out laughing. Giselle helps him sit. "Good one, George. Now sit down, stay quiet, and don't embarrass Colton."

He squeezes her arm. "I miss you, red. None of my kids will cut my food for me or tie my shoelaces. You're the only one."

She squeezes his arm in return. "You just call me when you need help. I'll be there." Giselle's rough exterior is only on the exterior. She's a marshmallow inside.

Cassandra asks George, "How did you lose your arm? Chopping down a cherry tree?"

George looks her up and down. "I like that you don't tip-toe around me. Most people do."

She shrugs. "It's not really my style, George. Speaking of which, that coach who you claim doesn't know his ass from a hole in the ground is my husband, so watch it before you *accidentally* lose another arm."

"I didn't know any cougars like you when I was younger. I wish I had."

She pats him on the head in a condescending manner. "George, I don't think you could have *hand*led me. I'm a lot for a man with two hands, let alone one."

George bursts out laughing. He turns to Giselle. "I like your friends better than Tom's. It's probably because you have a bigger dick than him."

Giselle practically falls on the ground laughing. Poor Tom's face turns bright red.

We watch the game and, for the first time since I've known him, George doesn't yell at the coaches. It took my sister to finally put him in his place.

When the game is over, I see Luke walk over to the

opposing bleachers. There's a little girl around his age sitting there that he approaches.

I'm standing with Cassandra when Trevor walks over to us. "Check out Luke. He's been working on this girl for over a month."

We watch as Luke talks to her. He says something that makes her laugh. He then hands her a baseball. She looks around, checking to see if the coast is clear, and then leans in and gives him a peck on the lips.

I gasp.

Trevor pumps his fist. "Yes! I told him it would work."

"You told him giving her the ball would get him a kiss?"

"I told him to tell her it was from his big hit. The one he just let her know was specifically done in her honor."

The girl leaves. Luke has a huge, goofy smile. He starts sprinting toward us and leaps into Trevor's waiting arms.

"Did you see, Uncle Trevor? She kissed me, just like you said she would. And she's a year older. I've never kissed an older woman. I think that was the best kiss I've ever had. You're right. Older women are much better kissers."

Cassandra covers her smile with her hand. I feel like my head is going to explode. I'm going to kill Trevor for this.

Trevor smiles at Luke. "I told you so. You played it perfectly."

He wraps his arms around Trevor's neck and squeezes him tight. "You're my best friend, Uncle Trevor."

Trevor has tears in his eyes when he says, "You're mine too, buddy."

Shit, now I can't be mad at Trevor. He's legitimately the only man Luke has ever been able to rely on. He's the only man *I've* ever been able to rely on.

CHAPTER THIRTY

DOMINIC

Valentina's class has an overnight campout in the woods this weekend. It's up in the Pocono Mountains on a lake. They're doing a few land activities and a few water activities. She's been excitedly talking about it since we got back from Cuba. Matteo is home with Gabriela.

I'm looking forward to seeing both Beth and Luke. I haven't seen Luke since I've been back. I have a special gift for him, but I didn't bring it for fear of ruining it. I want to tell him about it though.

There's a caravan of drivers. Beth thought it best for us not to go together, so she's with Tom and Colton. I'm riding with Scotty and Brody.

Brody is super laid-back, and we have an easy conversation on the way up. I learn that he grew up in California. He came to Philly to run the neurosurgery department at Pennsylvania Hospital. He taught a few medical school classes and that's where he met Harley when she was a student. He didn't go into details, but it sounds like it was a little scandalous at the time. Harley's now a heart surgeon at the same hospital.

He smiles. "How is it working with Reagan and Skylar? They must be a handful."

I let out a laugh. "Skylar is easy. A little stubborn at times, but otherwise she's easy to work with. Reagan is a ball of fire though."

"Believe it or not, she's tamer now than before she met Carter. She was even crazier then."

"It's hard to imagine."

"It's true." He sighs. "But they have a great family. They're very close. The three girls share everything. *Everything.*"

"Yes, apparently sisters do that."

"You mean Cassandra?"

I nod. "I didn't realize people knew about Beth and I."

"Cassandra is as much in the fold as Darian and the girls. There are zero limits to what they discuss. Poor Beth reluctantly gets sucked in at times. Just wait until you attend a big family meal. They get out of control."

I hope we get to the point where Beth invites me to a family meal. What Cassandra said has my head spinning. I feel like I've shown her I'm committed. Why aren't we spending time together as families? It's time.

I look at him. "Don't mention it while we're here. She's not ready for the kids or anyone to know about us yet, and I'm trying to respect her wishes."

"No problem. I understand more than most. Harley insisted on keeping our relationship a secret for a very long time. She thought it would hurt her career if people knew we were together. I hated loving her in secret, but they're smarter than us and know what they're doing. We have to respect their wishes."

Maybe he's right. I just despise how much it limits my time with her.

We arrive at the campground. It's quite beautiful, overlooking the lake.

I see Beth and Luke setting up their tent with the only other mother and son duo. I want to go to her but know she wouldn't want that. How am I going to keep my hands off her all night?

Luke looks up and notices me. A smile breaks out on his face, and he starts running over for a hug. He squeezes me tight. "I was hoping you were coming."

We pull away and I look at him. "I missed you. You've gotten so big. You look like a man now." I whisper into his ear. "I have a special present for you. I'll give it to you the next time I see you."

He has a huge grin on his face. Beth watches our interaction and smiles. I swear my heart skips a beat. She's in jeans, an oversized sweatshirt, and no makeup, with her hair in a ponytail. I've never seen anything more beautiful.

Brody mumbles, "If you look at her like that, everyone will know."

I nod as I turn my head away. I can't help myself.

Valentina notices Beth and sprints into her arms. Beth peppers her face with kisses, and Valentina giggles. I can't hear what they're saying, but they're both grinning from ear to ear. I love the affection they have for each other.

Luke pulls my hand toward Beth and Valentina.

"Come see my mom. I know she missed you. She was really sad when you left."

"I missed her too." He thinks it's been over a year when it's only been four days, but it feels like a year.

"Mommy, look who I found. Dominic."

I bend to kiss her cheek. "Good to see you, Beth." I linger a few seconds too long and take in her delicious scent. I whisper, "Eres comestible." *You're edible.*

As I pull away, I see her bite her lip. All I ever have to do is speak Spanish to her and her arousal skyrockets. I love it.

I give a long sniff and then wink at her. She mouths, "Addict," and I smile.

After everyone sets up the tents, half the class is assigned a hiking trail, and half is assigned watersports. We'll flipflop activities in the afternoon.

Beth and Luke are in our group, as are Brody and Scotty. The kids all run ahead, leaving the three of us chatting.

Brody says, "I'm not sure I should tell you this, but the kids are planning something. A special covert operation."

Beth and I look at each other in confusion.

He nods. "Yep, it's called *Operation Alone Time.* They're convinced that if they get you two to spend time alone tonight, you'll get back together. Luke and Valentina seem to want it." He smiles. "They asked me to lock you two in the port-a-potty. I had to tell them that it's not a romantic place."

The three of us laugh about it.

Beth shakes her head. "That's kind of cute, but a port-a-potty? Hell no."

I grab her hand and kiss it. "Don't knock 'til you try it, princesa."

Brody smiles at our interaction. "I remember what it was like to sneak around." He lets out a laugh. "Be careful, though. Scotty was conceived during our sneaking around."

Beth squeezes my hand in silent innuendo. Yep, my girl is game for some sneaking around.

BETH

This has officially been the day from hell. Not that the activities are bad. They're fine, and Luke is blissfully happy. It's hell to be around Dominic but not to be able to have him close. I've grown accustomed to how touchy-feely he can be. I need his hands on my body.

We're now on the lake doing various activities. Frankly. I'm having a hard time focusing. Dominic in a bathing suit is slowly killing me. He's the sexiest man in existence.

And then he makes it worse by being so great with the kids, especially Luke. Luke's reaction to seeing him today has me thinking. Maybe it's time for us to involve the kids. If we did, I'd be sleeping in that tent tonight with him instead of with Rachel, the talker. She doesn't shut up. I get that we're the only moms here, but give it a rest, woman.

As if I willed her to come to me, she sits down next to me on the dock. "Are you looking at Dominic or Brody, because holy hell! Eye candy explosion and vagina butterflies. Am I right?"

Did she just say *vagina butterflies*?

I narrow my eyes at her. "Brody is like family to me. *Married* family."

In fairness to her, Brody is gorgeous. He's got blond hair, blue eyes, and a body that looks like he works out all day, not spends his time in surgery all day. But that's not who I'm looking at. I'm looking at the man that's causing me to get in the water every few minutes just to cool down.

She smiles. "So it's Dom. I've always wanted a Latin lover. I hear it's amazing. And he's so big. I bet everything is big." She's got no idea just how right she is. About all of it.

She keeps rambling on, but I'm not listening. I'm looking at my man, who's suddenly become the forbidden fruit. I'm dying to take a bite.

He turns and looks at me, taking in my bikini-clad body. He licks that lower lip of his, which drives me wild. Who am I kidding? Everything he does drives me wild.

My nipples harden. I think he has nipple-radar because his eyes immediately drop to my breasts.

He turns around and discreetly adjusts himself.

Knowing he's hard right now has my whole body on high alert. We're definitely not making it through the night.

"What about you, Beth?"

I turn to Rachel. "Sorry, what was that?"

"I asked if you're a sound sleeper."

"Oh, I guess."

"Well, I'm out like the dead, so just shove me hard if I'm needed during the night tonight."

"Sure thing." Not a chance.

WE COOK hotdogs and roast marshmallows by the campfire. Besides having to mostly keep my distance from Dominic, it's been a fun day and night. As disappointed as I was for Gary that Luke didn't want him coming, I'm glad I got to come here to watch him in his element. He's very popular. Everyone seems to like him. It looks like he and Valentina picked up right where they left off, being close friends. That makes me happy. I can't help but imagine them as siblings one day. It's hard for me to stop my mind from going there.

Luke taps my arm. "Mommy, now it's time for hide and seek. I need you to go to our tent while we hide."

"Okay, baby."

I make my way to our tent and climb inside. As soon as I do, I see Dominic in there. The tent is then zipped closed from the outside.

Luke yells, "Count to seven-thousand four-hundred and twenty-eight." I hear him and Valentina giggling as their voices get further away.

Dominic smiles. "I think I like *Operation Alone Time*. By my math, we've got just over two hours to do anything we want."

Without any further conversation, we move toward each other until our lips meet. He immediately lifts me up so I can wrap my legs around him. His tongue moves into my mouth as he works his hands up the back of my sweatshirt. His hands on my bare skin are like gasoline to the flames for me.

I run my fingers through his hair. "Fuck, Dominic. I need you."

"Sabes a malvaviscos. Quiero frotarlos por todo tu cuerpo y luego lamerlos." *You taste like marshmallows. I want to rub them all over your body and then lick them off.*

Completely uncaring where I am, I lift my sweatshirt over my head and toss it to the side. He pulls down my bra and sucks my nipple into his mouth.

Like an out-of-control savage beast, I'm grinding myself against his hardness.

As he moves his mouth to the other nipple, he breathes, "Necesito follar estas tetas." *I need to fuck these tits.*

At this moment, he can fuck any part of me he wants, as long as he fucks me.

My leggings are still on, and I think I'm thirty seconds away from an orgasm, when we hear, "Okay, Mommy, come find us."

Shit. What happened to our seven-thousand seconds?

We break apart as I slide down his body until my feet hit the ground. We're both a bit out of breath. I pick up my sweatshirt and slide back into it.

He grabs my chin. Hard. "Tonight. After the kids go to bed. You're mine."

I nod. Doesn't he realize that I'm forever his?

WE AGREED to meet one hour after the kids go to their tents. Several of the adults will remain awake, so we'll need to slip far enough away from camp where we won't be seen or heard. We decided to meet by the dock.

It's been the longest hour of my life. The first half was spent getting Luke off his marshmallow sugar high. The second half has been spent trying to get away from Rachel, who I can't seem to shake.

I'm texting Cassandra, looking for advice on how to get away from this damn woman.

> Me: I've got a stage five clinger. Help me shake her.

> Cassandra: What's she doing?

Me: She follows me everywhere and tells me random stories. I just spent fifteen minutes hearing about her hemorrhoid flareup last week.

Cassandra: LOL

Me: I've never had a hemorrhoid, but I'm now well-versed on the fact that you have to sleep with your thumb up your ass to get any relief. I hope I never need to find out firsthand.

Cassandra: Is it firsthand or first-thumb?

I snort a laugh.

Me: I laughed out loud at that one. Now the crazy lady is looking at me like I'm the crazy one.

Cassandra: Have Dominic save you. Don't you guys have an SOS signal?

Me: No. I'm supposed to be meeting him now for a little...fun.

Cassandra: Ooh, sex in the woods is hot but be careful. Trevor and I did it once and both got poison ivy from it.

Me: Thanks for the advice. Just tell me how to get rid of her.

Cassandra: Tell her that dinner is bothering your stomach. No one wants to be around a person with gastrointestinal issues.

Me: Good idea. Thanks.

Cassandra: Text me later and tell me about the sex.

I roll my eyes. She's like a teenager, not a grown woman in her fifties, though I wouldn't have her any other way.

I grab my stomach. "Rachel, dinner isn't sitting so great with me. I'm going to find somewhere private. I won't be back for a while."

"Oh no, I have lots of medicines for that."

Of course she does. She's one of those super prepared moms who always walks around with a pharmacy in her purse.

"No, I think I just need to go to the bathroom." I start walking away. "See you later. Don't wait up."

She's finally out of sight. I make my way to the dock and Dominic is already there. When he comes into view, the moonlight illuminates his face. He looks like a Greek god. How is it my life that I get to spend time with this wonderful, beautiful man who loves me?

He turns around and smiles like we've got a secret, which we do. Like an impatient child, I run the last ten feet and leap into his waiting arms.

I wrap myself around him and sink my face into his neck, taking in his delicious scent. I feel tears stinging my eyes. He pulls my head up. "What's wrong?"

I sigh. "I can't do this anymore."

His eyes widen. "What do you mean? What can't you do?"

I run my fingers through his beard. "Be apart. I can't do it. I miss you when we're not together. Let's tell them. Let's tell everyone."

He breaks out into the biggest grin I've ever seen. "I'd like that." He squeezes my ass. "But for tonight, it's just you and me, princesa." He pulls me tight so I can feel him. Every long inch. "I've been hard since I saw you in that bikini today. "Necesito estar dentro de ti." *I need to be inside you.*

I smile into his mouth and reach my hand down to further confirm the truth of his statement. "Why don't I get on my knees and take care of this? Aspiradora is feeling mighty inspired tonight."

He runs his tongue across my top lip. "I've got plans for us, princesa."

He carries me to the end of the dock and sets me on my feet. There's a small wooden paddleboat tethered. The bottom of it is covered in several blankets.

I practically jump up and down in excitement. "Is this for us?"

He nods. "Get in. I'll paddle us out away from the shoreline. Out of sight."

He helps me onto the boat, and I sit on one of the two small benches. He steps in and sits across from me on the other. As he paddles us out toward the middle of the lake, I can't help but be captivated by his arm muscles, currently bulging through his T-shirt.

This feels like a scene from a movie with the full moon and clear sky full of stars. It's all reflecting off the water. With the trees in the background, it's so beautiful.

I smile. "This is very sweet and romantic, Mr. Mazzello."

"I have to admit, I'm having very unsweet and very unromantic thoughts about you right now."

"Tell me what you have in mind."

He licks his lower lip. "Estoy pensando en cómo se sienten tus tetas perfectas en mis manos. Estoy pensando en probar tu bonito coño rosado. Estoy pensando en ti corriéndote en mi lengua y luego otra vez en mi polla." *I'm thinking of how your perfect tits feel in my hands. I'm thinking of tasting your pretty, pink pussy. I'm thinking of you coming on my tongue and then again on my cock.*

I squeeze my legs together to tame the deep throb. I feel like I'll die if he doesn't touch me in the next ten seconds. "Stop rowing." He does. "Touch me. I need you to touch me."

He slides down to his knees in front of me, between my legs, as he runs his hands up my thighs.

He moves his nose to my leggings-covered center and inhales deeply. "The scent of your arousal drives me nuts."

Sexiest. Man. Ever.

At his urging, I lift my hips so he can pull down my leggings and panties all at once. While he does that, I take off my sweatshirt and bra.

He removes his T-shirt in that sexy, one-handed way that you rarely see in real life, but somehow this man is my reality. Before Dominic, I had only had sex in a bed. Mediocre sex. My current reality is that we're getting naked on a small rowboat in the middle of a lake where I know he's about to give my body unimaginable levels of pleasure.

He bends his body and runs his nose and tongue through me, much as he did over my clothes a few moments ago, but this time with full access. He looks up at me with an expression of pure ecstasy on his face and licks his lips like he's got dessert spread all over them.

I run my hand down his chest. "I need to taste you too."

He turns around and lays back, so his head is under my legs. His long legs are bent and draped over the other bench, but his entire torso fits on the floor of the boat.

I drop down to my knees, which are now on either side of his head. My pussy is right in his face.

I run my hands appreciatively over his body until I reach his sweatpants. I pull them down until his cock springs free. I've never thought about a penis as being attractive or unattractive. I guess that was until I met Dominic. His is just like the rest of him. Big, thick, sexually charged, sexy, and calls to me on a level I never could have imagined.

I bend my head down and lick him from his oozing tip to his heavy, full balls.

He mumbles, "Mierda." *Holy shit.*

As I take hold of the bottom of his shaft, he grabs my ass and pulls me down, sinking his tongue inside me. Deep inside me.

I run my tongue all over every vein and crevice as I marvel at his raw masculinity. I lift him and take his massive cock into my mouth, wrapping my lips tight and sucking hard. He loves when I do that to him.

He moans, causing his tongue to vibrate in my pussy. The way his tongue moves inside me makes my whole body shudder.

My hips begin to gyrate. He's so good at this. He always makes me come quickly.

I continue sucking him, taking him deep down my throat. I've got one hand on his balls and the other on the base of his shaft.

His hips begin to move too. We're both making noises, completely consumed in the pleasure.

He moves his thumb to my clit and applies pressure. As soon as he does, my eyes roll to the back of my head and my orgasm crests powerfully. I have to lift my head a bit off his dick but continue sucking his tip as the waves of my orgasm rush through me.

He licks through my sensitive flesh a few times before saying, "Turn around and ride me, princesa. Toma mi polla en tu dulce coño." *Take my dick into your sweet pussy.*

I place one foot on the floor of the boat, readying to stand. I don't realize how unsteady the boat is or how dazed I still am from my orgasm, and before I know it, I'm ass over head, stumbling into the dark water. I let out a screech on the way down before the cold lake water envelops my body.

When I get my bearings and break back through the surface, I do so in time to see Dominic mid-dive into the water. When his head lifts above the surface, he frantically searches for me.

I reach for him, and he immediately pulls me into his arms, treading us both in the deep water. "Are you okay?"

I smile. "My pride is damaged, but I'm physically okay."

He starts laughing and I join in. "I can't believe I just fell in. I can't believe you dove in after me." I wrap my legs around him. "But what I really can't believe is that you're still hard."

"I don't think he had time to go down, and now that you're in my arms, he's not going anywhere except into your warmth."

At that, he swivels his hips until his tip meets my entrance and he pushes into me. Straight to the hilt. My laughter quickly turns into a moan. I squeeze my eyes shut at the surprise intrusion. As always, it takes a few seconds for me to get used to his massive size.

He grabs my lower back with one hand, and with the other, he grips the side of the boat for leverage. I link my ankles behind his back and pull his face to mine for a kiss.

He begins to thrust in and out of my body as our wet kiss becomes needy. I can taste myself on his tongue and it's driving me crazy.

I tilt and swivel my hips to help his movements. It takes

both of us to make it work in the deep water, but it's more than working.

His hand on my body slips down to my ass, his finger teasing my back entrance. I mumble, "Get it in me."

He immediately slips it all the way in. I think my eyes cross from the pleasure of it.

I pull his hair and breathe, "More. I need more."

He adds a second finger. "Te gusta cuando estoy en tu culo. ¿Verdad, princesa?" *You like when I'm in your ass, don't you princess?*

"Yes. I want it. Deeper."

He pushes them in deeper. I'm so full of him. I love when I'm aware of nothing else in the world except Dominic filling me, both physically and metaphorically.

We're in cold water, but I'm saturated with warmth. His warmth.

His teeth gently tug my earlobe and then graze down my neck until he bites my shoulder.

"Oh god, Dominic. I'm coming again. Come with me."

His fingers remain knuckle-deep, pushing as far as they can go. He thrusts his cock into me faster.

"Mierda. Me estás apretando." *Oh shit. You're squeezing me.*

I can feel my walls tighten around him as his cock swells. That sets me off and we both grunt loudly into our mutual release.

As his strokes begin to slow, I collapse my head onto his shoulder, completely breathless. "I love you. So much."

He rubs his cheek against mine. "I love you too, but let's get out of here. We don't know what lurks in these waters."

I giggle as he pulls his fingers and cock out of me. I hate when he exits my body. I don't usually know the next time he'll be inside me again, and it gives me a sense of loss and longing.

He lifts me into the boat before instructing me to distribute my weight on the far side so he can pull himself in.

I start to pick up my sweatshirt, but he stops me. "Not yet. I don't want tonight to end. I hate when we're done. I never know when I'll be inside you again. Let me hold you for a bit. I want you close to me."

I love this man so much. I love that he feels the same way I do. He truly owns my heart, body, and soul.

He somehow maneuvers his big body on the floor and encourages me to nuzzle my back into him. He pulls me close and peppers my back with kisses.

He drags his lips closer to my ear. "How do you want to tell the kids?"

I think about what Cassandra said about easing into it with the bigger group setting. It's not a terrible thought.

"Why don't you come to Darian and Jackson's pool party next weekend? I like the idea of spending time together in a bigger group. It's a little less formal. We don't need to just blurt it out. We can gradually spend more time together and eventually let them know."

"Okay. Once they know, will you, Luke, and Trex move in with us? I hate spending nights away from you."

"That's because you're a sex addict, Mazzello."

He tickles me and I giggle. "I'm not a sex addict. I'm a Beth addict."

I smile at him having the same thoughts I've always had. I'm addicted to him. I have been since the moment I saw him again last year. Maybe since I met him over five years ago.

"Let's see how things go with the kids being back in the picture and we'll circle back to this."

I sense a little disappointment in his tone when he says, "Whatever you want."

I need to change the topic. "Tell me something I don't know. Tell me about your father. I only met him that one time." I adored him. He was so sweet.

"He's dying to see you again. To get to know you better. He's my best friend, always in my corner. He begged me not to take the kids to Cuba last year."

"He did?"

"Yes. He had a feeling the Navarros would cause trouble. I should have listened to him. It could have spared us all so much pain."

"Hmm."

"What I love the most about him is the way he loved my mother. He was madly in love with her. He treated her like a queen."

"I guess I know where you get your sweetness from."

He aimlessly runs his fingertips along my hip. "Only with you, princesa. Only with you."

I turn my head and kiss his arm that's under my head.

He nuzzles his nose into my neck. "What about your parents? Tell me something I don't know."

"I don't remember much about my father. I just remember him always making me feel safe. Cassandra won't talk about him. I wish she would, but she didn't have a relationship with him after the age of ten or eleven. She considers him a terrible, cold father. That's not my memory of him or how my mother described him. My mother loved him, and he loved her. I know he went through a tough time emotionally before he met my mother. I think Cassandra got all the bad, and my mother and I got all the good. That's why she stayed out of our lives for so long. She resented it."

"I love your relationship with her. She's almost like a mother to you. An immature, crazy, foul-mouthed, over-sexualized mother."

I giggle. "That's true, but if there's one thing I know for sure, it's that she loves me. When you have no parents left, it means the world to have that from your sister. I'm so thankful we found each other. I mistreated her this year, but she never stopped trying to get through to me. She never gave up on me. I know I can count on her."

"She wants what's best for you. She's always looking out for you."

He's right. In her special way, she looks out for me like a parent. I never thought of it that way.

We're silent for a bit as his hands and lips continue to explore my body. I feel him harden again against my ass. I wiggle it and he groans.

"Dominic, why don't you ever try to take me there. It's always only your fingers."

"I don't want to scare you away."

"But I want to give you everything you need."

"You're what I need. You said the last time around you felt like you stressed about keeping me sexually satisfied. I don't want you to do anything because of that. We'll do things as they come naturally. We have all the time in the world. There's no rush."

"I want you to take me there. And I want to go back to Hush Hush with you."

"What? No. I'm not taking you there ever again."

"I want to experience it with you. How much would you enjoy watching a woman touch herself while you're inside me? Or watching another couple have sex while we do the same?"

He lifts his head, undoubtedly in shock. "You would be into that?"

"I would be into watching any sexual act with you touching me. I can't imagine anything hotter."

He sighs. "I'll think about it."

"And my ass?"

He smiles into my neck. "That I'll do."

"When?"

"What's the rush?"

I reach between my legs and pull his hard cock, so it runs through my lips. "I'm wet. Your semen is still dripping out of me. Use it." I swivel my hips so he can feel it.

"Not here. You're not ready."

"You just had your fingers in me. Try it. If it doesn't work, we'll wait."

I don't know why, but I need everything from him in this moment. I need to give him every part of my body, connecting myself to him on every level.

He runs his cock through me a few more times, covering it in our mixed fluids. He then reaches his hands between my legs and gathers a handful of those fluids, spreading it across and into my ass.

I feel his tip at my back entrance. "If it hurts too much, tell me."

I nod.

He pushes the tip in an inch or two. I feel a burn, but it's bearable. I reach back and encourage him. "Keep going. I'm okay. I want it."

He lifts my top leg and brings it over his, widening me.

He runs his fingertips up my leg until he reaches my clit, which he begins massaging with his fingers.

"Hmm. That feels good."

It must loosen me, because he's then able to push in a few more inches. I let out a loud moan, feeling incredibly full.

"You're doing so good, princesa. Tu culo perfecto está estrangulando mi polla." *Your perfect ass is strangling my cock.*

That emboldens me to push back onto him those last few inches. I close my eyes, breathing heavily at the mix of pain and pleasure. He remains still inside me, simply kissing up my back, arms, and neck. He continues circling my clit, helping me loosen into this overwhelming, yet welcome, intrusion.

I take deep breaths until the sting gradually slips away and the pleasure takes over. He's in me. It no longer hurts. I'm giving him something I've never given another man. Another first that belongs to him. I've never felt closer to another person than I do him right now.

"You can start moving."

"Are you sure?"

"Yes. I want it. You feel amazing."

He begins his movements in and out of me. He never stops peppering my body with kisses, making me feel cherished and loved.

This isn't dirty, as I always assumed. It's tender, intimate, and beautiful. He whispers words of love and devotion the whole time as he owns every inch of my body.

Dominic gives me a different kind of orgasm to any I've ever had. It depletes us both of energy in an unexpected and overpowering way.

When it's over, I feel more content than I ever have in

my life. So much so that my eyelids are heavy. Feeling the warmth of his love is the last thing I remember before sleep finds me.

CHAPTER THIRTY-ONE

DOMINIC

I wake hearing a familiar man's voice. I feel Beth in my arms. Last night was incredible. I smile into her back, momentarily forgetting the other voice. I love waking up with her.

"Dom, did you hear me? The kids are, like, three minutes behind me."

My eyes snap open and I look up and around. It seems the boat drifted ashore while we slept, and Brody is standing over us with his hand covering his eyes.

"Shit. Beth, wake up."

She mumbles, "No. I'm happy right here." She wiggles her ass onto me. "I'm never moving."

"The kids are coming."

She starts to sit up, but I hold her down. I turn to Brody. "Go delay them. Tell them you saw a bear. Buy us time."

"Yep. I will." He jogs back toward the trees.

Beth turns her head to me and smiles. "Whoops. I guess we fell asleep."

"Whoops? That's all you have to say right now? You're very unaffected by the current situation and the possibility of many people seeing us naked in a boat."

She sits up and starts to dress, as if in no rush. "I'm learning not to sweat the small stuff. When you experience the pain I went through last year, it gives you a certain amount of perspective. We're in love. This is what people in love do."

"I guess you're right. Nothing says love like a little sodomy in the middle of a lake."

She giggles. "Maybe I'll have that embroidered onto a pillow."

I smile.

We quickly dress, me much quicker than her. I start to get out of the boat when she grabs me around the waist and squeezes me as she looks up and into my eyes. "Last night was the best night of my life." She buries her head in my chest. "I don't want it to end."

I kiss her head. "Soon, my love. Now let me take care of the boat."

She nods and removes her arms. I drag the boat to tether it back to the dock just as the kids come within view.

Luke runs to Beth, and I hear him say, "Mommy, where were you? You weren't there when I woke up."

She hugs him. "Sorry. I didn't want to wake you. Dominic and I went for a morning walk."

He gives her a giant grin. "Does that mean he's your boyfriend again?"

She smiles and tickles his stomach. "I don't know. We'll talk about it."

He turns his head to Valentina and shouts, "I think our plan worked!"

Valentina's face lights up.

Beth looks at me and winks.

***

BETH

"Yes, Rachel, I slept in the tent. You were asleep when I got back and asleep when I woke up early. You're a very sound sleeper."

"And where did you go?"

"For a walk."

"With who?"

This fucking woman.

I look for Dominic across the camping area. He's talking to Brody, but he sees me. I widen my eyes and motion my head toward chatty Cathy.

I see him smile before he shouts, "Beth, can you come help me with something?"

I look at Rachel. "Sorry, Dominic needs me."

I quickly walk over to them. "Thank you. She's interrogating me about last night."

Brody nods. "She asked me this morning if I had seen you. I told her you got up early."

"Thanks, Brody."

I feel my phone buzz in my pocket and pull it out.

Cassandra: Did you get your field plowed in the forest?

I let out a laugh.

Me: Maybe.

Cassandra: Did you get your hole filled on the hill?

I smile.

Me: I had all my holes filled. ALL of them.

My phone immediately rings. I step out of earshot of anyone, knowing what's coming.

I accept the call and nonchalantly say, "Hey, sis. Anything new with you?" I can't help but grin.

"The poop chute is open for business?"

I giggle. "I suppose it is."

"How was it?"

I sigh. "Amazing. The whole night was amazing. We ended up on a rowboat in the middle of the lake under the moon and stars. It was the best night. I'm so in love with him."

"I'm happy for you. Does this mean you're going to tell everyone?"

"Yes, we talked about it. I like your idea about Darian and Jackson's party. We'll take it from there. He asked us to move in with them. I told him I wanted to wait on that."

"I understand. Have a safe trip back. I'll see you in the office tomorrow."

CHAPTER THIRTY-TWO

DOMINIC

Today is the day we're letting the kids and everyone else know that we're together. I'm not sure I love doing it at Darian and Jackson's, but Beth has it in her head that easing them in like this is best, and I'm letting her steer the ship.

It's been a long week. I've had a lot on my mind. I've felt a little off kilter with a few things weighing on me, but a relaxing afternoon with my girl is just what I need.

I head to Gabriela's to pick up the kids. I knock on the door, and she answers dressed like she's about to hit The Met Gala.

I smile. "You look nice. Do you have plans today?"

"Actually, I have a date."

"That's wonderful." I haven't heard of her dating anyone since our divorce. I know it was a struggle for her. "Anyone I know?"

She shakes her head. "No, he's new to the area. I need a fresh start."

"Have a great time. I hope it goes well."

"Thank you."

I look inside. "The house is starting to look good. You're happy here?" Once I got Gabriela to agree to move back, I called my realtor and told her to find Gabriela a nice house near mine. I didn't care what it cost, I just wanted it done.

"I am. I'm happy to be back, away from my father. Honestly, I don't mind being a little closer to the city. It's been nice. I hadn't considered it before. I suppose I was a little secluded at the old house. The kids are blossoming at school. You were right about that place, Dom. It's good for them."

Something is different about her today. She rarely gives me the satisfaction of telling me I'm right about anything.

"Is everything okay?"

"Yes, just a little introspection of late. I'm not happy with the bitter woman I became." She looks down. "I loved you my whole life, and you never returning those feelings made me into something I'm not proud of." She looks back up. "I'm sorry for what I put you through. Truly. I hate myself for what it did to the kids. I understand that you and I will never happen. I need to move on. I need to try to find my own version of happy."

I nod. "I'm glad. I hope you find it. You deserve it." I shift on my feet a bit nervously. "I should tell you that Beth and I are back together."

She gives me a small smile. "I suppose I knew it was coming."

"She's wanted to keep it private as we figured things out, but we're going to tell the kids today. I feel like you should know that as their mother."

"Thank you. I imagine they'll be excited. They adore her and her son."

"I think they will be too. Gab, she's good to our kids. From your perspective, that's the most important thing."

She nods. "I know." She takes a breath. "Can I ask you something?"

"Of course."

"Are you...are you...faithful to her?"

"I am."

Tears fill her eyes. "Just not to me."

I place my hand on her shoulder. "Gab, don't do this. You knew what our marriage was. I never hid anything from you."

She wipes her eyes. "I know. I'm sorry. You're right." She straightens her spine. "I hope you two are happy together. I really do."

I hear the kids making their way to the door, fortunately putting an end to this conversation. Dora is with them, glued to Matteo's side. Gabriela acknowledged how important Dora is to Matteo's mental health and agreed that she'll stay with Matteo, regardless of which house he's staying at. That's a big step for Gabriela, being a bit of a clean freak.

She whispers, "Your dog is the horniest dog I've ever seen. Do the kids understand what she's doing?"

I have to cover my smile as I whisper back, "I know. They think it's hugging."

She giggles. "Let's hope it stays that way."

Both kids embrace me. I look at them. "I missed your faces. Do you guys have your bathing suits on?"

Valentina nods. "Yes, I'm so excited. Scotty said his grandma has a huge pool and the biggest playroom he's ever seen."

"I heard the same. Let's drop Dora at our house, and then we have one more errand to run before we go over there."

An hour later, we pull into Darian and Jackson's property. It's enormous. The house is nearly all glass, looking like it belongs in Malibu more than Philadelphia.

Beth had texted to walk in and head straight back to the pool, so that's what we do. The house is immaculate. Incredibly modern. We can see everyone by the pool through the big glass wall, so we head that way.

As soon as I walk out, I see Beth in her pink bikini, heading my way with a big smile. Luke practically jumps out of the pool and shouts, "Valentina," as he runs past Beth and hugs Valentina.

I'm not sure how Beth wants me to act with her, though every part of me wants to touch her. She answers my question right away by leaning her entire body into me and softly kissing my lips.

I pull her close and say, "You look beautiful," and then whisper, "y deliciosa."

She smiles as she bends to hug Matteo. He squeezes her so damn tight. She kisses his cheek. "I've missed you. You've gotten big and handsome like your papa."

Matteo grins. His eyes then toggle between me and Beth. I notice that Valentina and Luke are doing the same. So much for slowly spending time together. The kids are too smart for that.

Valentina crosses her arms. "You two kissed on the lips. That must mean you're boyfriend and girlfriend again." She turns to me with her sass. "Right, Papa?"

Beth stands and I tuck her under my arm. I look down at her and she nods. I turn back to the kids. "I guess you're right. That's exactly what it means."

Luke's eyes widen. "Is it because we locked you in the tent?"

Beth lets out a laugh. "Yep, it was all you guys. You made it happen."

Luke and Valentina high-five.

I reach into my bag and pull out something. Luke looks at it in question. "Why is that baseball in a plastic cube?"

"It's signed by my all-time favorite Cuban-born baseball player, Rafael Palmeiro. He was a superstar when I was a kid. He signed this ball for me. I found it in some of my belongings in Cuba, and I thought you might like to have it."

Luke looks shocked. "For me? To keep?"

I nod.

He gives me just about the biggest hug his body is capable of. "Thanks, Dominic. I'm going to put it right next to my bed, so I see it every morning when I wake up."

He turns to Beth. "I don't want to get it wet. Will you hold it for me?"

"Sure, baby."

He grabs Valentina's hand. "Let's go swimming." He takes one step and then stops. He reaches his other hand for Matteo. "Come on,

Matteo. Come meet the rest of my cousins." Matteo takes his other hand, and they happily head to the pool area where it looks like there's eight other kids already having fun, including Scotty, Dylan, and Brandon.

I look down at Beth. "That went well."

She leans her head into me. "It did. They seem happy. Thanks for the thoughtful gift." She pinches her eyebrows. "Is everything okay? You seem off."

This woman misses nothing. "Just a few things on my mind. I'm fine. Happy to be here with you."

"Okay. Come say hi to everyone. I'll introduce you to the people you don't know."

Before we can move, Jackson and Darian walk over. I shake his hand and kiss her cheek. Darian smiles. "Dominic, it's so good to see you again."

"Thanks for having us."

She looks between me and Beth. "I hope you'll become a permanent fixture here."

I squeeze Beth. "Thanks, Darian. I hope so too."

I make my way around and say hello to those I know, Reagan, Skylar, Harley, Cassandra, and their families. I meet Jackson's two other sons, Payton and Hayden, as well as their wives, Kylie and Jess. Their children are in the pool with the rest of the kids.

Jade is there with her baby daddy, Collin. He looks familiar to me. I think I've seen him at the office a few times.

She introduces me to her son, Tyson. I smile. "He looks just like you, Jade." He's got blond hair and blue eyes.

Collin nods. "I'm starting to wonder if I'm the father."

Jade turns to him. "I told you, you're one of five or six guys it could be."

The two of them smile in a way that I know they're kidding.

Collin peeks into the diaper. "Have you seen that sucker? The lucky kid is definitely mine."

Jade starts laughing and he smiles with her.

I whisper to Beth, "He's kind of perfect for her crazy ass."

Beth giggles. "You don't know the half of it. They're absolutely a perfect match."

Just then, a familiar-looking attractive blonde woman and man walk out. Jade says, "This is my father, Declan, and my stepmother, Melissa."

I mumble to Jade, "You look exactly like your stepmom."

She laughs. "I know. Totally. I look nothing like my actual mom. She'll be here soon though if you want to meet her. Darian bought one of her paintings. She's delivering it. She should be here after lunch."

"I'd love that. The woman who birthed crazy Jade. I can only imagine."

Jade simply gives me her mischievous smile.

We have a fun day in the sun and pool. Valentina and Matteo have been happily playing with the others. This is nice for them.

I keep checking my phone and Beth notices. "Are you sure everything is okay?"

I nod and lie, "Yes." I don't want to put a damper on today.

Jackson fires up the grill and starts cooking for this army. The kids eat burgers and dogs by the pool. Without me saying anything, Beth goes out of her way to ensure there's no cheese on Matteo's burger. Despite the fact that she hasn't been with him in over fourteen months, she remembers. My heart warms at the notion.

The adults all sit at a big outdoor table. As soon as we're seated, Reagan's phone starts ringing. She looks at it in confusion. "Dominic, you're calling me."

I grab my phone from my back pocket. "Whoops. Sorry. It must have accidentally dialed you." I place it on the table so it doesn't happen again.

Reagan and Trevor start laughing. Jackson just shakes his head. Clearly I'm missing something.

Trevor winks at me. "We have a very strict butt dial rule in this family, Dom. If you butt dial someone, you have to tell your most embarrassing sex story and then pick someone else to tell one as well. That person picks another, and then the next picks one more."

I see a bunch of other smiles at the table. This is clearly a fun family.

Jackson closes his eyes for a moment. "Sorry, Dom. These two are relentless. Just get it over with or they'll hound you. Don't worry, there's nothing you can say that hasn't already been said at this table before. No one here has any boundaries."

It's kind of ironic that he's talking about boundaries. His hands have been all over Darian all day. I think he applied suntan lotion to her body for an hour, and definitely in some places that aren't exposed to the sun.

Skylar too. I'm used to seeing her in business mode. Watching her husband, Lance, grope her all day is a little bizarre for me. He completely dotes on her, even calling her sweets all the time.

Trevor is staring at me and I'm not sure what to say. I look at Beth and she shrugs. "House rules. You've got to follow them. Out with it, Mazzello."

I lean over and whisper, "Can I tell them about Saturday night?"

"I think that's *my* most embarrassing story but go for it. This crew has certainly seen me at my worst."

I straighten my back. "Well, the other night, Beth and I were on a small boat in the middle of a lake and things were...happening, and she was a little dazed."

Cassandra interrupts, "Why were you dazed, Beth?" She has a huge grin.

Beth doesn't miss a beat. "Because I had just had the first of three orgasms he gave me that night. I couldn't even see straight." She smiles innocently and a few people chuckle.

I continue, "Anyway, we were switching positions and she was out of it. She tripped, naked, and flipped over the side of the boat into the water."

Everyone starts laughing, including Beth and me. Trevor asks, "What did you do, Dom?"

"I dove in after her. I wasn't sure if she hit her head. She did a complete flip. It wasn't graceful."

Beth jokingly elbows me, and I just smile at her.

Reagan says, "Okay. Pick your next victim."

I look around. Cassandra and Trevor are too easy. I think I know too much about Reagan and Carter. Hayden's wife, Jess, has been fairly quiet. I nod at her. "Jess?"

She scrunches her nose. "Hmm. Let me think." She looks over at Hayden. "Should I tell them about the shower the other day?"

He nods. "That was funny. Yes, tell them that one."

"Hayden and I were in the shower the other day. He was on his knees with his head between my legs. All of a sudden, Kai walks into our bathroom." Kai is their son who's the same age as Matteo. "He asked what Daddy was doing on his knees."

Hayden laughs. "Jess panicked."

She nods. "I did. I said something about me helping Daddy pray because I was pretending to be a priest and that playing priest is a really fun game."

Everyone starts laughing again and she places her hands over her face in embarrassment. "I don't know where I came up with that, but now Kai wants to *play priest* with all his friends. *All* the time."

Trevor smiles at her. "Father Knight, who do you select next?"

She looks around the table. "Hmm. I feel like Darian has never shared."

Reagan scoffs. "That's because she and Jackson practically have sex at the table. I don't think she gets embarrassed."

Darian narrows her eyes at Reagan. "We do not. Not today, anyway." She smiles. "I'll tell an old one. Your father and I made a sex tape in a rather compromising location, and it was subpoenaed in a court case."

Skylar's jaw drops. "What? You and Dad made a sex tape?"

Darian nods. "We did. When we were dating. It was when there were still camcorders and eight-millimeter tapes. We recorded ourselves and then Dad used the same tape to record some property he was looking at. The deal went south, and everything was subpoenaed, including the tape. I was frantic about it. You're not supposed to tamper with evidence after it's been subpoenaed, but I told him he better erase that part first. Honestly, I have no idea if he did. When I'm gone and you three go through all our tapes in the boxes in the basement, beware." She giggles.

Reagan shakes her head. "Ugh, I'm officially not ever going through those tapes."

Darian looks around the table. Her eyes land on Declan. "I'm in the mood to mess with you today." She turns to Jade. "Let's hear what you've got."

Declan practically growls. "Don't even think about it, Jade."

Jade rolls her eyes. "I just had a kid, and he thinks I'm still a virgin. I'm giving a dirty one, Dad, so cover your ears or walk away if you can't handle it."

I see Collin shaking in laughter. Declan stands. "I'm running to the restroom. Be done when I get back."

When he walks inside, she and Collin smirk at each other. She turns back to the table. "I was deep throating Collin several months ago. His dick is pierced. The piercing got stuck on my tonsils and I couldn't pull away."

The table is now rolling in laughter.

"I had a mouthful of his cock for like thirty minutes and, trust me, it's a lot of cock."

I'm sitting there wide-eyed. Beth leans over and whispers, "Every damn meal with this crew. This is what happens."

"It legit took thirty minutes for him to stop being hard so I could wiggle free."

Collin shrugs. "My dick was all the way down your throat. I couldn't control it."

"Apparently he gets off on my pain." She smiles at him. "Anyway, it definitely tore my tonsils. I had a sore throat and a scratchy voice for two weeks."

Reagan is practically on the floor hyperventilating in laughter. Cassandra and Trevor aren't far behind.

Jade looks at her phone. "Oh, Mom's here with your painting, Aunt Darian. I'm going to open the door for her. Where do you want her to leave it?"

Darian thinks for a moment. "Put it in Jackson's study for now so it's out of the way. Tell your mom to come join us when you're done. I saved her some food."

"Will do."

She stands and walks inside.

About five minutes later, she walks back out. Jade is roughly six feet tall, so I can't make out her mother behind her at first. She's much shorter than Jade. But when she does come into view, all the wind is knocked out of my lungs. I blurt, "Mandy?"

CHAPTER THIRTY-THREE

BETH

"Mandy?"

Amanda looks at him in complete and total shock. Her hand covers her mouth. Tears immediately spill over her eyes and drip down her cheeks.

Dominic looks at me before turning back to her. He's white as a ghost. He barely blinks, completely frozen.

Jade's eyes move between the two of them. "Mom, how do you know Dominic?"

"He...he...he was a friend from college. Just before I dropped out."

Jade nods, apparently understanding the significance of that.

Dominic finally blinks. "Jade, your mother is Amanda Tremaine? But your last name is McGinley."

"My parents were never married. I use Tremaine as my middle name and McGinley as my last."

Amanda looks at Jade. "How do *you* know Dominic?"

"I work with him."

Dominic stares at Jade. "How old are you?"

Jade answers, "Twenty-three."

I see Dominic doing the math in his head.

Amanda shakes her head. "She's not yours, Dom. She was born nearly two years later."

Because Jade is, well, Jade, she says, "Wow. I've always had a crush on him. We could have had a major Greek tragedy on our hands. Are you sure I'm not his?"

I'm pretty sure Jade is simply trying to break the obvious tension, but she's not helping. I don't think anything can help the awkwardness of it all.

Amanda rolls her eyes. "Look at you and look at Dom and me. Does it look like the two of us would have produced you? I haven't seen Dominic in twenty-five years."

Cassandra, never one to mix words, asks, "What the fuck is going on here? I feel like I'm in the Twilight Zone."

I answer, "Dominic and Amanda dated when they were in college." And she's the only other woman he ever loved. And her actions ended his career. And she ruined him for all other women. And, judging by his reaction, he might still love her.

Darian clears her throat. "Dominic, if you and Amanda would like some privacy to talk, feel free to use Jackson's study."

He looks at Amanda and she nods. He stands. I desperately need him to acknowledge me in this moment. A kiss. A touch. A look. Anything.

But none of that happens. He forgets I exist. Just like those who came before him.

He walks toward her, and they embrace in such a familiar way. I can't hear what they're saying, but their arms are around each other.

I thought my heart was put back together. That I was truly whole for the first time in my life. That we were unbreakable this time around. I thought I did everything right.

I was wrong. My heart is breaking all over again. I can't help the tears spilling from my eyes as they disappear into the house. All without him looking back at me. Not once.

I need to get out of here before I have a full meltdown. I stand, but before I can move there's a hand on my shoulder. "Don't even think about running right now."

I whisper to Cassandra, "I need to leave."

"No, you need to stay. Let's go for a walk and cool down." She turns to Trevor. "You'll keep an eye on the kids?"

I assume he nods. My head is down, avoiding the sympathetic looks likely being thrown my way. The same looks I've received many times in the past from this group. I can't bear to make eye contact with anyone.

She pulls me into her body, and we walk away. They have a large property so we can easily head out of sight. As soon as we are, she turns to me. "What's the story?"

"He told me about his first love, Mandy, the artist. Obviously I had no idea it was Amanda. It's a common name. He was completely in love with her in college. He thought she was the one. At some point, things headed south when she fell in with a rough crowd and started doing drugs."

She nods. "We know she was an addict. She got clean when she became pregnant with Jade."

"Right. Well, Dominic was on his way to becoming a professional baseball player. Because of her antics, he got injured and it ended his career. After the incident, she disappeared without a trace, and he never saw her again. He admitted to me that he never felt closure with her. He also never dated anyone after her because of how she broke his heart. That's why he went to Hush Hush. He didn't want to risk his heart again." I turn to Cassandra. "She's the one that got away."

"That was a long time ago. He loves you now."

I shake my head. "Did you hear me? She's the one that got away. And he's been acting weird all week. I think he's been having second thoughts about us."

I sit down in the grass, unable to stand anymore. "What have I done, Cassandra? What have I done to deserve so much pain and loss in my life? I lost my father when I was a little girl. You wanted nothing to do with me for most of my life. My husband couldn't be faithful to me. I lost my mother by the time I turned thirty. I dated a series of mediocre men, who would rather jerk off on a hooker's feet than be with me. Dominic left me last year, and he's about to leave me again. Am I such a bad person that I deserve all this heart break? Am I unlovable? Am I simply destined to be alone?" I wipe the tears. "I wish he never came into my life. Now that I know what true love feels like, having it taken away makes the pain so much worse."

I have to take another moment. I whisper, "I feel like I'm hurting more often than I'm not. Besides my mother, no one in my life has ever prioritized me."

She sits next to me and wraps her arm around me. "I don't think Dominic is leaving you. You're jumping to conclusions."

"Even if he doesn't, I can't stand in the way of his love for her."

"I think you're wrong. And I'm sorry I was a shitty sister. You know it had nothing to do with you. You were an extension of him, and I hated him. I know you didn't, but I did. I know what it's like to feel abandoned and unloved. Remember, I was the one Dad left. Do you know my last conversation with him?"

I shake my head.

"It was the morning of my college graduation. He was calling to tell me he was missing the graduation ceremony because you had a dance recital. You were three and had your mother. I was fucking graduating from college and had no other family. Darian's family and Scott were the only people there to support me. He never was."

"I'm sorry."

"I know it's not your fault. But I need you to know why I couldn't be around you. You were the daughter he wanted. I was the daughter he didn't want. At least that's how I saw it at the time. I regret my actions, but I can't change the past. I'm here now, Beth. I always will be. I love you. I hope you know that." She has tears in her eyes. "When you pulled away this past year, it was devastating for me. Regardless of what happens with Dominic, please don't pull away again."

"I know. It was bad for me too. I won't. I promise."

I lean my head into her, and she holds me tight. For thirty years I wanted my absentee sister to love me. At least I have that.

We sit in silence for a while. She lets me cry.

After what feels like an eternity, I look up at her. "I don't want them all to see me like this. I think I should go home."

She steels her face. "No. I won't let you leave. You've changed in this past year and a half. You're different. You've learned to fight for what you want, and we both know you want him. You love him. I know for a fact that he loves you."

I'm silent.

"Reverse this situation. Gary was your first love. Let's say Gary left you without a word and showed up here today. Would you leave Dominic for him?"

"No. Of course not."

"Right. You said Dominic never had closure. That's what they're doing. Every single thing he says and does shows me that he loves you. Don't let your past ghosts haunt the bright future you have. Don't let past insecurities consume you. You're badass Beth now, the fighter. Don't fucking forget it."

I nod as my phone rings. I look down at it and then back up at Cassandra. "It's Dominic's father. Go back to everyone. I need a few minutes to collect myself."

"Don't you dare leave."

"I won't. I promise."

She walks away and I answer the phone. "Hey, Marty. Is everything okay?"

"Hello, my beautiful girl. I was looking for Dominic. He's not answering his phone. He said he was going to be with you today."

I try to get out words, but a sob breaks through.

"Beth, what's wrong?"

I whisper, "I'm afraid I'm losing him."

"Never. Tell me what's happening."

"He's in a room right now with his college girlfriend. His first love."

"Mandy? How did he find her?"

"It's a long story, but I know her. I obviously didn't realize the connection. She walked into the party we're attending and it's like the world stopped."

"Well, good."

"Why is this good?"

"He can have his proper goodbye. She disappeared on him after she hurt him. It shaped his relationships with women moving forward, and not in a positive way."

"Marty, do you think he should be with her? Do you think she's the one that got away?"

He lets out a laugh. "No. Don't be silly. He loves you. She was young, puppy love. You're forever love. You cured my son. I will be forever grateful to you."

My voice cracks again. "I can't lose him, Marty. I don't think my heart can take it."

"I know you had a father, and I'm not looking to step on any toes, but can I give you some fatherly advice?"

Here come the tears again. I barely manage, "Please."

"Beth, hear me. My son loves you. You've been his every thought for five years. You have no idea what he went through in Cuba to find his way back to you. He sacrificed a lot to come home. You two have a once in a lifetime love. Trust me, I would know. I had it too."

I smile, knowing he's right. I need to trust the strength of our love.

"Don't let your past troubles dictate your actions or feelings now." That's what Cassandra said. "And if he needs some sense smacked into him, you just call me."

I let out a laugh.

"Thank you. I needed to hear that." It occurs to me that he wouldn't have called me unless it was important. "I'm sorry, Marty, you obviously called for a reason. Is everything okay?"

"Yes. I had some testing done earlier this week. I know Dominic was worried. He's been beside himself for the past few days. I'm sure you've noticed that he's been distracted. I wanted to tell him right away that everything came back clear."

"I'm sorry you went through that, but I'm happy you're well. I'll have him call you as soon as I see him."

"Thank you. Beth, he loves you. Don't think otherwise."

"Thanks, Marty."

DOMINIC

Mandy closes the door to the study, and I can't help but take her in my arms. She feels familiar. It almost seems as if no time has passed.

She looks the same. Of course a little older, but still a stunning woman.

She cries into my chest. "I'm so sorry, Dominic."

"What are you sorry for?"

"I know I ruined your life."

I rub her hair. "You didn't ruin my life. I'm responsible for what happened to me. I lost my temper. I caused it. Regardless, I've had a good life. I have no regrets. My only regret was never getting to say goodbye to you."

She's still sniffling.

I pull back and look at her. "Why don't you have a seat so we can talk. I think we both have questions. I know I do."

She nods as she sits. I grab a few tissues from Jackson's desk, hand them to her, and then sit across from her.

"Mandy, tell me why you left."

She swallows. "Because of the guilt."

"What did you do? Where did you go? I know you had no family."

"Honestly, I was pretty fucked up for the next year or so. I floated around. The drug use became extreme. I was out of control. I became addicted." She looks down. "A lot of sex and a lot of drugs. It was bad."

"Why did you run and turn to all that?"

"I couldn't handle what I did to you. I numbed the pain."

I hate what she went through. I hate that I'm the cause of it.

She continues, "The next year, I met Jade's father, Declan. I assume you know him?"

"I just met him today."

"He's ten years older than me. He was a user too. Even worse than me. Together, we were toxic. We were on and off for a few months when I found out I was pregnant with Jade. That's the last day I ever used. He wasn't so lucky. It took him another eight years to shake it. Jade and I were very much on our own the first seven years of her life, struggling to make ends meet."

I had no idea Jade had it so rough, though I know Beth once referenced it. "I'm sorry for what you went through."

"It was tough, but we made it work for us. When Declan got clean, he began to help financially."

"That explains Jade's toughness. She's tough like you."

"I'm weak."

"You're strong. I can't imagine it was easy to go cold turkey when you found out you were pregnant, but you did. I can't imagine it was easy being alone with a baby, but you did it. You raised a superstar. Look at all Jade's accomplished at such a young age. She's the toughest young woman I know. It's clear where she got it from. You should be very proud of her."

She smiles. "Thank you. I am."

I return her smile. I look at the new painting sitting in the office. "It appears you're still a very talented artist."

"I never stopped painting, even at my worst. Though I had limited success until about five years ago. Things have sort of taken off since then."

She has a weird look on her face, but I don't push.

"I've seen your work in Jade's office. I didn't know it was yours, but I do now. The paintings are beautiful."

She nods in gratitude. "Thank you. What about you? What have you been up to?"

"I suppose you now know that I work at Daulton Holdings. I have two children. Valentina is eight and Matteo is four. They're in the pool if you want to meet them."

She smiles. "I'd like that."

"I'm divorced, and I've been seeing Beth for a while."

"I adore Beth. She's so sweet."

I nod. "She is. It's funny, I've thought about you some in the past year. I considered reaching out to you. Just to get a little closure. We never really had that."

"I suppose we didn't."

"Sebastian thought I should call you."

She frowns. I have no idea why. "You're still friends with him?"

"I am. Kevin too." I swallow for a moment. I know I'm not getting the full picture. "Can you tell me what happened at the end? I know you were on drugs, but I thought we were in love. Finding you in bed with two men impacted me on a deep level. I'd like to try to understand it. I've always just assumed you didn't love me the same way I loved you."

"I did love you, Dominic." She bites her lip. "I'm not sure I should tell you."

"It's been twenty-five years. I'd like to know and then move on. Please. Whatever it is, I can handle it."

She lets out a deep breath. "After your arrest and team suspension, Sebastian came to me. He told me I was pulling you down. That I was ruining your shot at making it to the big leagues. He said you were madly in love with me, and that if I loved you, I should do something drastic to change your mind and set you free." She momentarily looks down, as if the memory pains her as much as it pains me. "I staged the whole thing. Being in bed with those guys. I knew you were coming over to tell me about the suspension being lifted. I made it look like I was being intimate with them, so you'd break up with me. I never expected the fight, and I certainly never expected you to get injured." Her voice cracks. "I'm...I'm so sorry, Dominic."

All these years I thought something was wrong with me to make her seek comfort in two other men. I'm seething right now, but it's not at Mandy, it's at Sebastian for putting her in that position.

I reach over and take her hand in mine. "I don't

think you have anything to apologize for, but to the extent it helps you, I forgive you."

She whispers, "Thank you. It *does* help."

"Did you ever get married? Do you have other children?" I've never heard Jade mention siblings, but I rarely get into personal life discussions with her.

"Unfortunately, I never had any more kids. I wish I had, but the right opportunity never came along. Jade was my sole focus for a very long time. I was briefly married a few years ago, but it wasn't right. I'm dating someone now. We're *very* different, but I like him and I'm seeing where it goes."

I smile. "He's a lucky man." I stand. "Speaking of lucky men, I need to go find Beth. I was a little shocked to see you and didn't consider how it would impact her."

She stands. "Well, it was good to see you. You look great."

"And you haven't aged a day."

She smiles. "Still a sweet talker."

We walk back out to the pool area and Jade immediately comes to Mandy and wraps her arms around her. "Are you okay, Mom?"

Mandy leans into her. "Yes, baby, I'm fine."

Jade winks at me. "Did we settle my paternity? I've always wanted to call you daddy, Dom."

I smile and shake my head at Jade's antics. I look at Mandy, who's trying to hold back her laughter. "I can only imagine what a handful she was as a kid."

Mandy giggles. "You have no idea."

I look around but don't see Beth. Luke is still in the pool, but no Beth.

I turn to Cassandra. "Where is she?"

"She freaked out. She was upset, thinking that you were going back to Amanda and that she's your true love."

"What? Is she crazy? I love her."

"That's what I told her, but she wouldn't listen."

"Did she leave?"

"She was going to, but I talked her off the ledge. She asked for a little time to herself."

Cassandra motions her head around the corner.

I smile as an idea occurs to me.

CHAPTER THIRTY-FOUR

BETH

I'm lying in the grass with the sun beating down on my face. My hands are behind my head and my eyes are closed.

I can feel Dominic's presence before I hear him approach. That's how in sync my body is with his. I blink my eyes open just as he lays down next to me and we turn toward each other.

I stare at him. I never want to wake up another day in my life without this view. I lick my dry lips. "You're mine, Dominic. No one else can have you."

A small smile finds his lips as he nods in agreement.

"I'm worth loving."

He takes my hand and kisses the inside of my palm. "I think I knew that the first second I laid eyes on you at Reagan's party. You've had me since that night. I'll never want another woman. Of that, I'm sure. I've made peace with my past. You're my future, princesa."

I sigh in relief. Tears sting my eyes. "I almost ran."

"I know. I'm glad you stayed. Don't ever doubt our love. You're mine. No one else can have you."

I smile at him repeating my words.

He pulls my body flush to his and gives me the sweetest, softest kiss. I'm so madly in love with this man, and I know he loves me too.

I hear a little voice. "Ugh. They're going to start doing that all the time again, aren't they?"

I lift my head and look over Dominic's body to see Valentina standing there.

Luke steps next to her. "Yep, they are."

Matteo wiggles in between them with a big smile on his adorable face.

Dominic starts to stand but stills when he's on one knee. The kids then all get on one knee too, right next to him. Luke is on his left, Matteo and Valentina are on his right.

Matteo holds out a ring box and opens it. The biggest diamond ring I've ever seen sits inside. In his sweet little voice, he says, "Marry me."

Dominic gives him a soft elbow to the side and mumbles, "That's my line."

I laugh as I sit up and lean back on my hands, staring at all four of them on one knee, all with grins on their faces.

I bite my lip. "Do I have to choose? Cause if I do, I think Matteo is my man. He's awfully cute."

The kids all giggle.

Dominic takes my hand in his. "Princesa, look around. Look at these faces. This is our family now." He turns to Valentina and Matteo. "We want Beth and Luke as our family, right?"

Valentina and Matteo both nod.

He turns to Luke. "Luke, is it okay if I ask your mom

to marry me? She's the kindest, smartest, most beautiful woman I've ever met. I love her so much. I promise to love her every day for the rest of my life." He holds out his hand for Luke to shake. "You have my word as a man."

Luke thinks for a moment. "That would mean I *definitely* can't marry Valentina, right?"

Valentina rolls her eyes. Dominic and I both smile. Dominic nods. "I'm afraid so."

Luke looks deep in thought. "But she'd be my sister and Matteo would be my brother?"

Dominic nods. "Yes."

"And we'd all live together?"

"Yes."

Luke's face lights up like it's Christmas morning as he shakes Dominic's hand. I can't help the tears in my eyes at seeing how happy he is at the prospect of gaining a brother and sister. A family.

"Okay, she'll marry you."

I clear my throat. "Excuse me. He didn't ask you if I would marry him. He asked your permission to ask me. I get to decide."

Luke gives a sheepish look. "Oh, that too."

Dominic turns to me. I look at his gorgeous face with a huge smile. "This isn't how I planned to do it, or when I planned to do it, but inspiration struck, and I think it's kind of perfect. I love you, princesa. I always will. Marry me."

I smirk. "And you just happened to have a massive diamond ring on hand?"

"The kids and I may have done a little shopping before we arrived. Are you going to answer me?"

I get on my knees and wrap my arms around his neck.

"I've waited my whole life for you, Dominic. I love you. Of course I'll marry you."

As soon as I kiss him, the kids start whining about it. We both laugh into each other's mouths.

Out of the corner of my eye, I catch my sister looking on with tears in her eyes. She mouths, "I love you."

EPILOGUE

ONE YEAR LATER

DOMINIC

"Mr. and Mrs. Mazzello, it's always good to see you."

I wrap my arm around Beth's waist and pull her back to my front. She nods. "You as well, Crystal."

"Enjoy your evening." She walks away.

Beth is in a tight green dress that shows her luscious curves. I kiss her neck while I pull her close. I whisper in her ear, "What do you want to do tonight, Mrs. Mazzello?"

She leans her head back and grinds her ass onto me. "I want to dance with my husband."

Even though music is always playing, people don't usually dance here, but that never stops us. If my wife wants to dance, we dance.

I turn her around, grab her hips, and pull her front tight to mine as she threads her fingers through my hair. She closes her eyes as our hips move together to the beat of the music.

"This reminds me of the night we met, princesa."

She opens her eyes and smiles, playing with the curls in my hair, pressing her chest to mine. "You have no idea how much you affected me that night."

"Creo que lo hago." *I think I do.* I thrust my hips so she can feel just how much dancing with her affects me.

Her eyes flutter. She breathes, "Kiss me."

I lick across her lips until her mouth opens for me and fuses with mine. Her tongue deliciously moves through my mouth, completely absorbed in our kiss, uncaring that people can see us. She's so hot.

She reaches down and rubs my painfully hardened cock. "I can't wait. I need you inside me."

"Paciencia, princesa." *Patience, princess.*

"If you want me to have patience, don't talk to me in Spanish."

I let out a laugh, and when I do, familiar faces catch my eye. I point so Beth sees what I'm looking at.

She turns her head and bursts out laughing. Darian and Jackson are in the corner on a couch completely making out. She's straddling his lap and his hands are on her enormous breasts. They're practically swallowing each other whole.

I've learned in the past year that Darian and Jackson are very affectionate and not at all shy about it.

Beth turns back to me. "I hope we're still doing that at their age."

"You realize your sister is that age and her husband is younger than you."

"You mean your new best friend?"

I smile. Trevor and I now coach Luke's baseball team together. He and I have struck up a friendship. It's been nice, given how close Beth and Cassandra are. Brandon and Matteo are going to start baseball this fall, and we'll also coach their team together.

Matteo has blossomed in the past year. I think our blissfully happy family life is just what he needed. That, and an outgoing big brother he idolizes. He, Valentina, and Luke are all close, and my kids treat Luke like a sibling now.

Beth laces her fingers through mine. "Let's go to our room. I reserved your favorite."

It took a little coaxing, but I eventually agreed to bring her here. It was right after we got married, which was a month after I proposed. Jackson flew us all to Hawaii on his private jet, my family and closest friends included. We were married in a small, intimate ceremony overlooking the ocean, surrounded by everyone we love.

Lindsay and Sebastian were so swept up in the romance of the weekend that they tied the knot too. Again. In fairness to Sebastian, he's completely different with Lindsay this time around. He's all in. Perhaps he needed that time apart to grow and realize that she's all he'll ever want. She's now pregnant with their first child.

I never confronted him about what he did with Mandy all those years ago. Beth helped me understand that he was trying to be a good friend and was looking out for me. I hate the pain and trouble it caused

Mandy, but he couldn't have known what would happen to her.

When we returned from our honeymoon, we came here, and we've been coming twice a month ever since. There's no sexual act she's unwilling to watch, and she loves when I fuck her while we watch together. She was made for me. I was always destined to find her.

As we make our way down the hallway, we hear a familiar laugh. I turn and see Reagan and Carter walking out of one of the rooms, looking like they just very much enjoyed themselves.

As our eyes meet, the four of us freeze in shock. We stare in awkward silence for a few beats until Beth says, "Don't go in the main area. Your mother is in there with Jackson."

Carter holds in laughter, but Reagan shakes her head and rolls her eyes. "How many sex clubs do I have to go to so I can get away from the two of them? We need a damn family sex club calendar." She sighs. "I guess we're heading out. Have fun."

As always, Beth and I enjoy our time there. I love how uninhibited she is. There's nothing she won't let me do to her body.

We pull into our driveway at the end of the evening. We moved into my house, and she transformed it into a warm, family home. It's completely different from before, and I love it. I love the warmth and happiness that Beth, Luke, and Trex have brought to us.

I open the car door for her. She steps out and runs her hands up my chest. "Are you ready for another round, Mazzello?"

I mouth, "Addict," and she smiles. "I'll pay Rose." She stayed with Matteo and Luke tonight. Valentina is at a sleepover. I lean over and whisper in her ear, "Sube las escaleras y desnúdate." *Go upstairs and get naked.*

Her face flushes and she nods.

We walk inside and are shocked by what we see. Luke and Matteo are both in suits. Full jacket and tie. Their hair is styled to perfection The dining room lights are off, but they're sitting at a table with Rose. A table set nicely with lit candles and flowers.

Beth lets out a long breath. "What's going on here, boys?"

Luke answers, "I'm teaching Matteo how to romance Rose."

Matteo nods with a big grin as he waves his hand in a dismissive fashion. "We're about to dance. Leave us."

Beth looks at Rose and she nods that it's okay. "I can stay a little longer. It's hard to resist these two charmers."

Beth says, "Thanks, Rose. I'm tired. I'm heading up to bed. I'll see the rest of you in the morning."

Beth goes upstairs and I pay Rose. I give her a little extra for indulging these two knuckleheads.

I look around. "Where's Dora?"

Rose answers, "She was in a *hugging* mood tonight, so we put her to bed early."

I nod at Luke and Matteo. "Make sure you walk Rose to her car when you're done. A gentleman should always walk a lady to her car at the end of the evening."

Luke rolls his eyes. "Duh. We know."

I feel my phone buzz in my pocket and pull it out. It's a text from Beth.

> Beth: Aspiradora is on her knees waiting. Over and out.

ACKNOWLEDGMENTS

To Beth and Dominic: I didn't think I would ever break out of my Jade and Collin hangover. Thanks to you two for making me believe I can continue to find my voice when I'm not sure I have any left. In the process, I fell in love with both of you and am obsessed with your story. I already miss you and am now enduring a Beth and Dominic hangover.

To the Queen, TL Swan: This amazing journey would never have begun if not for you and your selfless decision to help hundreds of women. You are a shining example of the girl power quotes I place in each dedication. This crazy and unexpected (see what I did there?) new path in my life has brought me so much happiness. I owe it all to you. Please know that I try every single day to pay it forward.

To Brittany Mckeel: You are one of the most selfless people I've ever met. I'm so fortunate to have you in my life. Thank you for your unwavering support. I hope you enjoyed the character written in your honor. *M.O.M. Patrol* for life!

To My Beta Readers: Stacey F. and **Fun Sherry**, you are my OGs and have supported me since day one. I wouldn't have kept writing if not for your encouragement. **Lakshmi** and **Thorunn**, I dedicated the damn book to you. What more could you want? On a daily basis, you two push me to be better and to always stay the path. **Amanda M.** and **Abby F.**, thanks to you both for making Dominic's Spanish dirty talk so damn hot. I can't tell you how much I appreciate you both. **Jade Dollston**, put simply, you make all of my books better. Don't worry, you can still have a dirty detention.

To My Bookish Besties - Jade Dollston, Carolina Jax, and L.A. Ferro: I love and respect each of you as individuals and as our badass girl army. The adoration and support we have for each other fills my heart. Our daily texts are my lifeline (and the only socializing I do at this point). The best part of this writing journey is my friendship with the three of you.

To My Amazing Street Team: You bitches are the best. I'm amazed every single day by your support and love for my books. I appreciate your posts, words of encouragement, and love for one another.

To My Incredible ARC Team: Thank you for avoiding your families the moment the ARC dropped in your mailboxes. I appreciate your time and thoughtful reviews. I read each and every one of them. I couldn't do this without all of you.

To Chrisandra and K.B. Designs: **Chrisandra**, thank you for making me feel illiterate. That's what makes you such a great editor. **Kristin**, thank you for helping this artistically challenged woman. You have breathed life into all of my books. I'm so proud of them thanks to you.

To My Family: I truly feel bad for you. An immature mother and wife can't be easy. To my daughters, thank you for tolerating me (ish). Thank you for telling everyone you know that your mom writes sex books. I appreciate that by the time you were each six, you were more mature than me. To my handsome husband, thank you for your blind support. You never question my sanity, which can't be easy. But let's face it, you do reap the benefits of the fact that I write sex scenes all day long.

ABOUT THE AUTHOR

AK Landow lives in the USA with her husband, three daughters, one dog, and one cat (who was chosen because his name is Trevor). She enjoys reading, now writing, drinking copious amounts of vodka, and laughing. She's thrilled to have this new avenue to channel her perverted sense of humor. She is also of the belief that Beth Dutton is the greatest fictional character ever created.

AKLandowAuthor.com

ALSO BY AK LANDOW

<u>City of Sisterly Love Series</u>

Knight: Book 1 Darian and Jackson

Dr. Harley: Book 2 Harley and Brody

Cass: Book 3 Cassandra and Trevor

Daulton: Book 4 Reagan and Carter

About Last Knight: Book 5 Melissa and Declan

Love Always, Scott: Prequel Novella Darian and Scott

Quiet Knight: Novella Jess and Hayden

<u>Belles of Broad Street Series</u>

Conflicting Ventures: Book 1 Skylar and Lance

Indecent Ventures: Book 2 Jade and Collin

Unexpected Ventures: Book 3 Beth and Dominic

Enchanted Ventures: Book 4 Amanda and Beckett

Signed Paperbacks: www.aklandowauthor.com/books

www.ingramcontent.com/pod-product-compliance
Lightning Source LLC
Chambersburg PA
CBHW062111290726
48975CB00001B/182